THE

"Who are you, *Englis*?" Zardalu asked, as he and the other vampires of Constantinople crowded about their captive.

The little one, stick-thin with her strange, disheveled wildness, moved close, considering James Asher with enormous demon eyes. Half her hair was braided or curled, the rest hung in a malt-colored tangle to her thighs. A necklace of rat bones and diamonds circled her throat.

"The Bey said we weren't to question him."

"Did he say I was not to question *you*?" Asher asked.

Zardalu's fangs gleamed. "Clever *Englis*! Of course you may. We are fellow servants of the Deathless Lord."

"Silence," hissed a one-eyed Janissary. "Would we have this infidel cry out to be saved?"

"Our friend knows better than that." Zardalu's cold knuckle brushed Asher's ear, then red nails clinched suddenly hard. Asher gasped, then gritted his teeth, forcing his mind from the pain. Just when he thought the claws must tear away flesh, Zardalu released him, smiling. "And he knows he will not escape."

There was blood on Zardalu's nails. The vampire held Asher's gaze as he licked them slowly clean . . .

Books published by The Ballantine Publishing Group
are available at quantity discounts on bulk purchases
for premium, educational, fund-raising, and special
sales use. For details, please call 1-800-733-3000.

TRAVELING WITH THE DEAD

Barbara Hambly

A Del Rey® Book
BALLANTINE BOOKS • NEW YORK

A Del Rey® Book
Published by Ballantine Books
Copyright © 1995 by Barbara Hambly
Excerpt from *Mother of Winter* copyright © 1996 by Barbara Hambly

http://www.randomhouse.com

Library of Congress Catalog Card Number : 96-96524

ISBN 0-345-40740-7

Manufactured in the United States of America

First Hardcover Edition: September 1995
First Mass Market Edition: November 1996

10 9 8 7 6 5 4 3 2 1

For George

With a prayer in the shadow
of the Aya Sofia

PROLOGUE

THE house was an old one, inconspicuous for its size. Curiously so, thought Lydia Asher, when she stood at last on the front steps, craning her neck to look up at five stories of shut-faced dark façade. More curious still, given the obvious age of the place, was the plain half timbering discernible under centuries of discoloration and soot, the bull's-eye glass of the unshuttered windows, the depth to which the centers of the stone steps had been worn.

Lydia shivered and pulled closer about her the coat she'd borrowed from her cook—even the plainest from her own collection would have been hopelessly fashionable for these narrow, nameless courts and alleys that clustered behind the waterfront between Blackfriars Bridge and Southwark. *He can't hurt me,* she thought, and brought up her hand to her throat. Under the high neck of her plain wool waist she could feel the thick links of half a dozen silver chains against her skin.

Can he?

It had taken her nearly an hour to find the court, which by some trick of chance had been left off all four modern maps of this part of London. The whole yard was adrift in fog the color of ashes, and at this hour—Lydia heard three o'clock strike in the black steeple of the crumbling pre-Wren church that backed the old house—even the little remaining light was bleeding away. She had passed the house three times before truly seeing it, and sensed that had the air been clear, it would somehow still have been difficult to look at the place. She had the absurd impression that by night, lanterns or no lanterns, streetlamps or no streetlamps, it would not be visible at all.

There was a smell about it, too, distinct and terrifying, but impossible to place.

She stood for a long time at the foot of its steps.

He can't hurt me, she told herself again, and wondered if that were true.

Her heart was beating hard, and she noted clinically the cold in her extremities, in spite of fur-lined leather gloves and two pairs of silk stockings under her dainty, high-heeled boots. Stouter shoes would have somewhat alleviated the situation, always supposing stout shoes existed that did not make their wearer look like a washerwoman—if they did, Lydia had never seen them—but the panicky scald of adrenaline in her bloodstream informed her that the cold she felt was probably shock.

It was one thing to speculate about the physiology of the house's owner in the safety of her own study at Oxford, or with James close by and armed.

It was evidently quite another to go up and knock on Don Simon Ysidro's front door.

Muffled by the fog, she heard the *tock* of hooves, the jingle of harness from Upper Thames Street, and the groaning hoot of the motorbuses. Another hoot, deeper, came from some ship on the river. The click of her heels on the dirty steps was the strike of a hammer, and her petticoat's rustle the rasp of a saw.

For all the house's age, the lock on the door was relatively new, a heavy American pin lock oddly masked behind what must have been the original lock plate of Elizabeth's time. It yielded readily enough to the skeleton keys she'd found at the back of her husband's handkerchief drawer. Her hands shook a little as she then operated the picklocks in the fashion he'd taught her, partly from the sheer fear of what she was doing, and partly because, law-abiding and essentially orderly, she expected a member of the Metropolitan Police to appear behind her crying, '*Ere, now, wotcher at?*

Absurd on the face of it, she thought. It was patently obvious that no representative of the law had set foot in this square in years.

She pushed her thick-lensed spectacles more firmly up onto the bridge of her nose—*Not only breakin' the law,* roared the imaginary policeman, *but ugly and four-eyed to boot!*—slipped the picklocks and skeleton keys back into her handbag, and stepped through the door.

It wouldn't be full dark until five. She was perfectly safe.

The hall itself was much darker than she had expected, with the wide oak doors on either side closed. Trimmed with a carved balustrade, generous steps ascended carpetless to blindness above. The passage beside them to the rear of the house was an open grave.

There was, of course, no lamp.

Mildly berating herself for not having foreseen that contingency—*of course there wouldn't be a lamp!*—Lydia pushed open one of the side doors to admit a rinsed and cindery light. It showed her a key on the hall table, and turning, she closed the front door. For a time she stood undecided, debating whether to lock herself in and observing the deleterious effects of massive amounts of adrenaline on her ability to concentrate . . .

How would I go about charting degree of panic with inability to make a decision? The workhouse wouldn't really let me put my subjects into life-threatening situations.

In the end she turned the key but left it in the lock, and stepped cautiously through the door she had opened, into what had probably been a dining room but was as large as the ballroom of her aunt's house in Mayfair. It was lined floor to ceiling with books: goods boxes had been stacked on top of the original ten-foot bookshelves, and planks stretched over windows and doors so that not one square foot of the original paneling showed and the tops of the highest ranks brushed the coffered ceiling. Yellow-backed adventure novels by Conan Doyle and Clifford Ashdown shouldered worn calf saints' lives, antiquated chemistry texts, Carlyle, Gibbon, de Sade,

Balzac, cheap modern reprints of Aeschylus and Plato, Galsworthy, Wilde, Shaw. In front of the bone-clean fireplace, a massive oak chest, strapped with leather and the only furniture in the room, held a cheap American oil lamp of clear glass and steel, the trimmed wick in about half a reservoir of oil. Lydia produced a match from her pocket, lit the lamp, and by its uncertain light read the titles of the several new volumes, half unwrapped from their parcel paper, which lay beside it.

A French mathematics text. A German physics book by a man named Einstein. *The Wind in the Willows.*

How much time left?

With a certain amount of difficulty Lydia produced from beneath her coat a curious device—a simple brass bug sprayer of the pump variety, its nozzle carefully capped with a pinch of sticking plaster—and a shoulder sling manufactured from a couple of scarves in last year's colors. She removed the cap, reslung the sprayer on the outside of her coat and, picking up the lamp, moved off through the house.

The first-floor room contained more books. The rear chamber, book-lined also, held furniture as well. A heavy table, strewn with mathematics texts, abaci, astrolabes, armillary spheres, a German Brunsviga tabulation machine, and what Lydia recognized dimly as an old set of ivory calculating bones. At the far end of the room loomed a machine the size of an upright piano, sinister with glass, metal, and ranks of what looked like clock faces, whose use Lydia could not begin to guess. Near it stood a blackwood cabinet desk, German and ruinously old, carved thick with gods and trees, among which peeped the tarnished brass locks to concealed recesses and drawers.

A wing chair of purple velvet, very worn and rubbed, stood before a fireplace whose blue and yellow tiles were smoked almost to obscurity, its arms covered with cat hair, an American newspaper lying on its seat. Movement caught her eye and made her gasp, but it was only her own reflection in a yellowed mirror, the glass nearly covered by a great shawl of eighteenth-century black point lace that hung over its divided pane.

Lydia set the lamp down and lifted the shawl aside. Thin and rather fragile-looking, her reflection gazed back at her: flat-chested and schoolgirlish, she thought despairingly, despite her twenty-six years. And despite everything she could do with rice powder, kohl, and the tiny amount of rouge that were all a properly brought-up lady could wear, her face was still all nose and spectacles. *Four-eyes*, they'd called her, all her childhood and adolescence—when it wasn't *skinnybones* or *bookworm*—and if her life didn't, quite literally, depend on how quickly she could see danger in this place, she'd never have worn her eyeglasses outside her rented Bloomsbury rooms.

Her life, and James' as well.

She let the lace fall, touched again the silver around her neck and the fat, doubled and trebled links of it that circled her wrists under cuffs and gloves.

Why a mirror? Something one wouldn't expect to find here. Did that mean the stories were wrong?

She picked up the lamp again, hoping the information she'd learned on the subject was even partially correct. It was a disgrace, really, that over the years more scientific data had not been collected. She would definitely have to write an article for the *Journal of Medical Pathology*—or perhaps for one of James' folkloric publications.

If she lived, she thought, and panic heated in her veins again. If she lived.

What if she were doing this wrong?

She found another floor of high-ceilinged rooms, plus attics, all of them filled with either books or journals. Her own experience with the proliferative propensities of back issues of *Lancet* and its competitors—British, European, and American—gave her a lively sense of sympathy, and an envious appreciation for so much shelf space almost, for the moment, eased her fear. *Lancet* went back to 1823, and she had little doubt the first issue could be found here somewhere. One small chamber upstairs contained clothing, expensive and relatively new.

From the first, all her instincts told her she must look down, not up, for what she sought.

The kitchen and scullery were on the ground floor, at the

back of the house, down that caliginous throat of passageway. Stairs corkscrewed farther down. The scullery contained a modern icebox. Lydia opened it and found a cake of ice about two days old, a bottle of cream, and a small quantity of knacker's meat done up in paper. Four or five dishes— including a Louis XV Sèvres saucer—lay on the floor in a corner. For the first time, Lydia smiled.

Boothole, wine cellar, vegetable pantry belowstairs, and many smaller rooms, low-ceilinged and smelling of earth and great age. The lamp flung her shadow waveringly over cruck-work beams, discolored plaster, stonework that spoke of some older building on this site. As in searching for the house itself—which had fallen out of all mention in the Public Records Office after the Fire of 1666—Lydia passed three or four times through the room that contained the trap to the sub-cellar. It was only when, failing to see any such ingress as she knew must exist, she studied the composition of the walls themselves that she narrowed the possibilities to the little store-room whose damp stone wall bore signs of having once supported a stairway.

Outside, the day must be slowly losing its grip on life. Trying to keep her hands from shaking, with cold now as well as fear, she pulled off her gloves and ran her fingers under the chair rail and around the heavy molding of the room's two doors. Near the base of the door into the wine cellar she felt a lever click unwillingly under her fingers and saw, in the dirty brazen light, the wider gap between two panels.

There was a latch on the inside of the movable panel so it could be opened from below, and a worn ladder going down.

As Lydia had guessed, the low room beneath looked as if it had been the subcrypt of a church, either the one that backed the house—in a square named, oddly enough, Spaniard's Court—or some forgotten predecessor. Barely visible in black paint on the ceiling groins were the words *Salvum me fac, Deus, quoniam intraverunt aquae usque ad animam meam.*

Lydia had not been raised a Catholic—her aunts considered even the inclusion of candles on the parish altar grounds for complaint to the bishop—but recognized, from her residency at St. Bartholomew's, the words from the Mass for Deliverance from Death.

A granite sarcophagus filled the far end of the chamber like a somber altar, all but concealing a low, locked door. Lydia stood before it for some time, holding the lamp high and gauging the probable weight of the stone lid. Then she knelt and studied the floor.

Dustless.

A laborious investigation of the cracks in the gray stone floor showed her the trapdoor, an eye-straining business by the amber glow of the lamp; she gave up early trying to do the business tidily and without griming and wrinkling her skirt, and it was equally impossible to keep her corset bones from jabbing her ribs and the pump sprayer from knocking her repeatedly on the elbow. Another squinting, painful half hour revealed the trigger to the trapdoor's catch behind the projecting stone frame of the chamber's inner door.

As she had deduced, the sarcophagus had nothing to do with anything. It was simply too obvious.

The steps leading downward were shallow, so deeply worn in the centers that she had to press her shoulder to one wall and brace herself against the other to maintain her footing. She guessed it was well past dark outside, and beneath her growing fear—the panicky conviction that she was completely unqualified to deal with the encounter that lay ahead—she wondered precisely how dark was dark enough. She suppressed the urge to check her watch and make notes.

The lamplight could not penetrate the night below her, and from that darkness rose the smells of wet earth, cold stone, and rust. Interestingly, there was no smell of rats.

The light slithered wetly over a grille of metal bars. Lydia pressed herself to it, maneuvered the lamp through and held it up to illuminate what lay within. The bars were old, the lock on them new and expensive and beyond the capacity of either the skeleton key or the picklocks. The lamplight reached only partway into the catacomb beyond the bars, but far enough to show her wall niches, empty for the most part, or occupied with the suggestion of ghastly *natures mortes*: skulls, dust, and shreds of fallen hair.

On the right-hand wall the shadows all but hid a niche whose interior no amount of angling the lamp would reveal.

But hanging over the edge, like ivory against the dingy stone, was a man's hand: long-fingered, thin, ringed with gold. Darkness hid the rest, and though the white hand itself looked as perfect as if painted by Rubens or Holbein, Lydia knew that its owner had been dead for a long time.

It's true, she thought, her heartbeat fast and heavy with fright. *Silly,* she added, for she had known already that it was true . . . it was all true. She had met this man and seen others like him from a distance.

But knowing, she had learned this afternoon, was different from seeing, and she felt very naked, uncertain, and alone in the dark.

I'm doing this wrong.

Her breath made a little apricot smoke in the lamplight as she sat down on the steps. Laying her weapon across her knees and pushing up her spectacles with one forefinger, she settled herself to wait.

ONE

ALL Souls and black rain, and cold that passed like needles through flesh and clothing to scrape the bones inside. Sunday night in Charing Cross Station, voices racketing in the vaults of glass and ironwork overhead like ball bearings in a steel drum. All James Asher wanted was to go home.

A day and a night spent burying his cousin—and dealing with the squabbling of his cousin's widow, mother, and two sons over the estate to which he'd been named executor—had reminded him vividly why, once he'd gone up to Oxford twenty-three years ago, he'd never had anything further to do with the aunt who raised him from the age of thirteen. It had just turned full dark, and Asher drew his greatcoat closer around him as he strode down the long brick walkway of the platform, jostling shoulders with his erstwhile fellow passengers in a vast frowst of wet wool and steam and reflecting upon the lethal adeptness of familial guilt. Outside, the streets would be slick and deadly with ice.

Asher's mind was on that—and on the hour and a half between the arrival of the express from Tunbridge Wells at Charing Cross and the departure of the Oxford local from Paddington—when he saw the men whom he would later have given anything he possessed not to have seen.

They stood under the central clock in the echoing cavern of the station. Asher happened to be looking in their direction as the taller of the two removed his hat and shook the drops from it, gestured with a gloved hand toward the iron frame into which boards bearing departure times had been slotted. Asher's eye, still accustomed to cataloging details after half a lifetime in secret service to his country, had already been caught by the man's greatcoat: the flaring skirts, the collar and cuffs of karakul lamb, the soft camel color and the braiding on the sleeves all shouting at him, *Vienna*. More specifically, one of the Magyar nobility of that city rather than a German Viennese, who tended to less flamboyance in their dress. A Parisian would have worn that smooth, well-fitted line, but probably not that color and certainly without braiding; the average Berliner's coat generally bore a striking resemblance to a horse blanket no matter how rich the man might be.

Vienna, Asher thought, with the tiniest pinch of nostalgia. Then he saw the man's face.

Dear God.

He stopped at the head of the steps down from the platform, and the blood seemed to halt in his veins. But even before his mind could form the words *Ignace Karolyi in England*, he saw the face of the other man.

Dear God! No.

It was all he could think.

Not that.

Later he thought he would not have seen the smaller man at all had his eye not been arrested, first by Karolyi's greatcoat, then by the Hungarian's face. That was one of the most frightening things about what he now saw. In the few seconds that the two men spoke—and it was not more than a few seconds, though they exchanged newspapers, an old trick Asher had used hundreds of times himself during his years with Intelligence—Asher's mind registered details that he should have seen before: the fiddleback cut of the small man's shabby black greatcoat, and the way the creaseless buff-colored trousers tapered to straps under the insteps. Under a shallow-crowned beaver hat his hair was short-cropped, and he did not gesture at all as they spoke: no movement, no change of stance, not even the shift of the gloved fingers wrapped about one another on the head of his stick.

That would have told him, if nothing else did.

Three women in enormous hats, feathers drooping with wet, intervened, and when Asher looked again, Karolyi was striding briskly in the direction of the Paris boat-train.

There was no sign of the other man.

Karolyi's going to Paris.

They're both going to Paris.

How Asher knew, he couldn't have said. Only his instinct, honed in years with the Department, had not waned in the eight peaceful years of Oxford lecturing that had passed since he quit. Heart pounding hard enough to almost sicken him, he made his way without appearance of hurry to the ticket windows, the small bag of a weekend's worth of clean linen and shaving tackle swinging almost unnoticed in his hand. By the station clock it was half past five. The departures board announced the Dover boat-train at quarter of six. The fare to Paris was one pound, fourteen and eight, second class—Asher had just over five pounds in his pocket and paid unhesitatingly. Third class would have saved him twelve shillings—the cost of several nights' lodging in Paris, if one knew where to look—but his respectable brown ulster and stiff-crowned hat would have stood out among the rough-clothed workmen and shabby women in the third-class carriages.

He told himself, as he bought the ticket, that the urgency of not calling attention to himself was the only reason to stay out of third class tonight. But he knew it was a lie.

He walked along the platform among women in cheap poplin skirts loading tired children onto the cars, screaming at one another in the clipped, sloppy French of Paris or the trilled *r*'s of the Midi; among men huddled, coatless, in jackets and scarves against the cold, and tried not to listen to his heart telling him that someone in third class was going to die tonight.

He touched a passing porter on the arm. "Would you be so kind as to check the baggage car and tell me if there's a box or trunk, five feet long or over? Could be a coffin, but it's probably a trunk."

The man squinted at the half-crown in Asher's hand, then sharp brown eyes went to Asher's face. "C'n tell you that right now, sir." Asher automatically identified the cropped *ou* and glottal stop *i* of the Liverpool Irish, and wondered at his own capacity for pursuing philological points when his life was in danger. The man touched his cap. "Near killed old Joe 'eavin' the thing in, awkward an' all."

"Heavy?" If it was heavy, it was the wrong trunk.

" 'Eavy enough, I say, but not loaded like some. No more'n seventy pound all told."

"Could you get me the address from the label? A matter of information," he added as the brown eyes narrowed suspiciously, "to the man's wife."

"Runnin' out on 'er, is 'e? Bleedin' sod."

Asher made a business of checking his watch against the station clock at the end of the platform, conscious all the while of the men and women getting on the train, of the thinning of the crowd that made him every second more visible, every second closer to a knife-blade death. Steam chuffed from the engine and a fat man in countrified tweeds, coat flapping like a cloak in his wake, hared along the platform and scrambled into first class, pursued by a thin and harried valet heavily laden with hatboxes and train cases.

He'd have to telegraph Lydia from Paris, thought Asher. It brought a stab of regret—she'd sit up tonight waiting for him until she fell asleep surrounded by tea things, lace, and medical journals, in front of the bedroom fire, beautiful as a scholarly sylph. For two nights he had looked forward to lying again at her side. Foul as the weather had been, she'd probably simply assume that the train had been held up. Not a worrier, Lydia.

Still the porter hadn't come back.

He tried to remember who the head of the Paris section was these days.

And, dear God, what was he going to tell them about Charles Farren, onetime Earl of Ernchester?

His hand moved, almost unconsciously, to his collar, to feel the reassuring thickness of the silver chain he wore beneath. It was not a usual ornament, for a man and a Protestant. He hadn't thought about it much, except that for a year now he had not dared remove it. It had slipped into place like those other habits he'd acquired "abroad," as they said in the Department; habits like memorizing the layout of any place he stayed so that he could move through it in the dark, or noting faces in case he saw them again in another context, or carrying a knife in his right boot. The other dons at New College, immersed in their specialties and their academic bunfights, never noticed that the self-effacing Lecturer in Etymology, Philology, and Folklore could identify even their servants and knew every back way out of every college in that green and misty town.

These were matters upon which his life had depended at one time—and might now still depend.

In the summer his students had commented, when they'd gone punting up the Cherwell, on the double chain of heavy silver links he wore on either wrist; he'd said they were a present from a superstitious aunt. No one had commented on or seemed to connect the chains with the trail of ragged red scars that tracked his throat from ear to collarbone and followed the veins up his arms.

The porter returned and casually slipped a piece of paper into his hand. Asher gave him another half-crown, which he could ill spare with his fare back from Paris to be thought of, but there were proprieties. He didn't glance at the paper, only pocketed it as he strolled along the platform to the final shouts of "All aboard!"

Nor did he look for the smaller man, though he knew that Ernchester, like himself, would be getting on at the last moment.

He knew it would not be possible to see him.

Eight years ago, toward the end of the South African war, James Asher had stayed with a Boer family on the outskirts of Pretoria. Though they were, like many Boers, sending information to the Germans, they were good people at heart, believing that what they did helped their country's cause— they had welcomed him into their home under the impression he was a harmless professor of linguistics at Heidelberg, in

Africa to study Bantu pidgins. "We are not savages," Mrs. van der Platz had said. "Just because a man cannot produce documents for this thing and that thing does not mean he is a spy."

Of course, Asher *had* been a spy. And when Jan van der Platz—sixteen and Asher's loyal shadow for weeks—had learned that Asher was not German but English and had confronted him in tears, Asher had shot him to protect his contacts in the town, the Kaffirs who slipped him information and would be horribly killed in retaliation, and the British troops in the field who would have been massacred by the commandos had he been forced to talk. Asher had returned to London, resigned his position with the Foreign Office, and married, to her family's utter horror, the eighteen-year-old girl whose heart he never thought he had the smallest hope of winning.

At the time, he thought he would never exert himself for King and Country again.

And here he was, bound for Paris with the rain pounding hollowly on the roof of the second-class carriage and only a few pounds in his pocket, because he had seen Ignace Karolyi, of the Austrian Kundschafts Stelle, talking to a man who *could not* be permitted to take Austrian pay.

It was a possibility Asher had lived with, and feared, for a year, since first he had learned who and what Charles Farren and those like him were.

Making his way down the corridor from car to car, Asher glimpsed Karolyi through a window in first class, reading a newspaper in an otherwise empty compartment.

The Dorian Gray beauty of his features hadn't changed in the thirteen years since Asher had last seen him. Though Karolyi must be nearly forty now, not a trace of silver showed in the smooth black hair or the pen trace of mustache on the short upper lip; not a line marred the corners of those childishly wide-set dark eyes.

"My blood leaps at the thought of obeying whatever command the Emperor may give me." Asher remembered him springing to his feet in the soft bright haze of the gaslit Café Versailles on the Graben, the bullion glittering on the scarlet of his Guards uniform; remembered the shine of idealistic idiocy in his upturned face. "I will fight upon whatever battlefield He may direct." One could hear the capital letter in *he*—the Emperor—and around him, his fellow *beau sabreurs* of the Imperial Life Guards had roared and applauded, though they'd roared louder when another of their number had joked, "Yes, of course, Igni . . . but who's going to point you in the direction of the enemy?"

Even when Karolyi had hunted Asher with dogs through the Dinaric Alps after torturing to death his local contact and guide—when it was blindingly obvious that his pose as a brainless young nobleman who spent most of his time waltzing at society balls rather than drilling with his regiment was a sham—that was still the Karolyi Asher remembered.

They'd never met face-to-face in that hellish week of hide-and-seek among the streams and gorges, and Asher didn't know if Karolyi was aware who his quarry had been. But passing along the corridor now with barely a glance through the window, he remembered the body of the guide, and was disinclined to take chances.

In any case, it was not Karolyi whom he feared most.

The third-class carriage was noisier than second, crowded and smelling of unwashed wool and dirty linen. A child cried on and on like the shriek of a factory whistle. Unshaven men looked up from *Le Figaro* or the *Illustrated London News* as Asher walked between the hard, high-backed benches. Yellow electric light jittered over cheap felt hats, wet paper flowers, plain steel pins; a woman said, "Hush now, Beatrice, hush," in a voice that held no hope of Beatrice hushing this side of the Gare du Nord.

Asher kept his collar turned up, knowing Farren would recognize him. It unnerved him to realize that the man might be in this carriage and he would never so much as catch a glimpse of him. He didn't like to think about what would happen to him in that case.

At the far end of the third-class car was a baggage compartment, given over to bicycles and crated dogs and an enormous canework bath chair. It was unlighted, and through its windows Asher could see the rain flashing like diamonds in the dirty light shining from third class. As Asher stepped through and closed the door, the cold struck him—all the windows had been opened, rattling noisily in their frames, wet flecks of water spattering through.

At his feet a dog in a cage whined with fear.

The smell of the rainy night could neither cover nor disperse the stink of death.

Asher looked around him quickly, kneeling so as to be out of the line of the window. Dim light came through the little judas on the door, but not enough; he fumbled a lucifer match from the box in his greatcoat pocket, scratched it with his nail.

The man's body had been folded small, knees mashed into chest, arms bent close to sides, the whole skinny tangle of him shoved tight into a corner behind a double bass in a case.

Asher blew out the match, lit another, and crouched to worm close. The dead man was young, dark, unshaven, with a laborer's callused hands and a roughly knotted kerchief around his neck instead of a cravat. His clothing smelled of cheap gin and cheaper tobacco. One of his shoes was worn through. Only a little blood had soaked into the neckerchief, though when Asher moved it down with one finger, he saw that the jugular vein had been cut clear through, a rough, ripping tear, the edges white and puffy, mangled as if they had been chewed and sucked. Asher had a scar that size where his collar pressed the silver links of the necklace against his skin.

A third match showed the dead man's face utterly white, blue-lipped, eyebrows and beard stubble glaring, though by the appearance of the eyelids he'd been dead for less than thirty minutes. Moving a frayed pants cuff, Asher saw the bare ankle had not yet begun to turn livid. Probably, Asher thought with a queer, angry coldness, it never would, much.

He blew out the match, stowed the stub—with the stubs of the first two—in his pocket, and slithered from between the bath chair and bass fiddle case. He'd passed the conductor in the second-class carriage, on his way down the train. The official's nearness had probably interrupted the murderer before he could dump the body out into the night, or perhaps Ernchester was waiting till they were farther from London. Asher left the compartment quickly, dusting his hands on his coat skirts and muttering to himself like a man who has not found what he sought. Nobody in third class gave him a glance.

By the time the train reached Dover, he suspected, the body would be gone. To call attention now to what he had found would only, inevitably, call attention to himself. He wasn't such a fool as to think he would then ever reach Paris alive.

In the dingy second-class compartment where he had left his satchel, a lively family of homebound Parisians had made themselves very much at home. They were passing bread and cheese among themselves; the *bonne femme* offered him some and a blood orange, while her *mari* laboriously scanned a battered copy of *l'Aurore*. Asher thanked her and fished out his own copy of the *Times*, most of which he had already read on the journey up from Tunbridge Wells, and wondered academically what he was going to tell whoever was in charge of the Paris section these days.

It was going to be a long night, he knew. He dared not sleep, lest Farren sense him through his dreams.

2/11/1908–0600   PARIS/GARE DU NORD
ERNCHESTER GONE TO PARIS WITH IGNACE KAROLYI AUS-
TRIAN SIDE STOP FOLLOWED STOP WILL HAND OFF COME
BACK TONIGHT JAMES

Ernchester. Lydia Asher laid the thin sheet of yellow paper down on the gilt-inlaid desk before her, heart beating quickly as she identified the name. *Gone to Paris with someone from the "Austrian side."*

It took a moment for the meaning to sink in, mostly because Lydia, although she could have distinguished a parathyroid from a parathymus at sight, couldn't immediately remember whether the Austrians were allied with the Germans or with England. But when it did, the implications made her shiver.

"Is it from the master, ma'am?"

She looked up. Ellen, who had brought the telegram to her with her tea, lingered in the study door, big red hands tucked under her apron. Last night's inky downpour had dwindled this morning to a slow, steady drench from a sky like steel; beyond the tall windows, Holywell Street was a shining pebblework of cobble and wet, softened by Lydia's myopia to a gentle sepia and silver Manet. The tall brown wall of New College across the road was nearly black with damp. Now and then a student would pass, or a don, faceless ghosts nevertheless identifiable—even as Ellen was identifiable—by their bodies and the way they moved: there was no question, to Lydia, of mistaking the little banty-cock Dean of Brasenose, with his self-important strut, for the equally diminutive but self-effacing Dr. Vyrdon of Christ Church.

Lydia drew a deep breath, blinking huge brown eyes in the direction of the dark square of the hall door, and realized for the first time that morning that she was starving. "Yes," she said. "He was called away unexpectedly to Paris."

"Tcha!" Ellen shook her head disapprovingly. "And in all that rain! What's in Paris that's more important than him coming home last night, and you so worried?"

Since Lydia couldn't very well reply, *Probably a partnership that will begin with Germany conquering England and end God knows where,* she said nothing.

Ellen went on cheerily, "I told you not to worry about Mr. James, didn't I, ma'am? With all that rain it'd stand to reason he'd be delayed, though I never did think of Paris, myself. Something to do with investments, like as not." Ellen had worked for some years for Lydia's father and was used to the fact that if the master of the house departed suddenly, it had to do with investments. "Though I didn't know," she added, with one of her occasional bursts of sapience, "as he had any."

"A few small ones," Lydia said truthfully, folding the telegram and unlocking a drawer of the gilt secretary at which she worked. Its contents exploded into a puffy mountain of household accounts and pathology notes. Lydia regarded the mess blankly, as if the entire desk were not awash with dissection diagrams, notes on the endocrine system, correspondence from other researchers on the subject of ductless glands, milliners' bills, menus, silk samples, copies of *Lancet*, and the first draft of her article on pancreatic secretions for the January issue of *British Medical Journal*, on which she'd been working when Ellen had made her entrance. She shook back the cloud of lace from around her hand and determinedly stuffed the contents back into the drawer, which she then forced shut. She opened two more drawers with similar results, finally poking the telegram down into the side among a sheaf of notes concerning electrostimulation's effect on the production of adrenaline.

Her friend Josetta Beyerly was forever joking her about not reading the newspapers even enough to know who the Prime Minister was, as if prime ministers—and in fact Balkan kings—didn't come and go at the drop of a constituency. Reading newspapers only caused Lydia to wonder whether people like Lord Balfour and the Kaiser suffered from hyperthyroidism or vitamin deficiency and how she could find out, and she'd found that the speculation distracted her from her work.

"He says he'll be back today." It was unreasonable of her, she knew, to feel relief. Jamie was perfectly able to look after himself, as she had known last night, lying awake and fingering the heavy links of the silver chain around her neck. When she had dreamed, it had been of a corpse-white face upturned in the distant gaslights of a London alleyway, strangely reflective eyes, and a mouth snarling to show the glint of outsize fangs. She'd awakened then and lain listening to the rain on the ivy until morning.

There had been no reason for her to be afraid.

Handing off, the telegram said.

There was no reason to be afraid now.

What was it in the telegram, she wondered, that snagged at the back of her mind like a hangnail on silk?

"Though it would be a shame," she went on thoughtfully, "if he didn't spend at least a little time in Paris, long enough anyway to buy himself a clean shirt and a box of bon-bons. He'd only his overnight things with him, you know, for his cousin's funeral."

Handing off.

Why did she think she'd heard the name Ignace Karolyi before?

And how on earth was he going to explain the Earl of Ern-chester to the Foreign Office men in Paris?

"I wonder if you could get me some of the toast I didn't eat at breakfast?" Lydia asked after a moment.

"Right away, ma'am." She heard the beaming smile in the housemaid's voice, saw it in the way her shoulders relaxed as she turned from the door. Ellen and Mrs. Grimes both consid-ered her too thin, though she had confounded their earlier threats—when she was in school, a gawky and bespectacled fledgling bluestocking—that no girl who went around with her nose in a book and not eating enough to keep a canary alive was ever going to catch a husband. In spite of daily reminders of her undesirableness, Lydia had always been aware that as the sole heiress to the Willoughby fortune, she would be inundated with proposals of marriage the moment she put up her hair.

Jamie told her she was beautiful, the only man she had ever truly believed.

Had Jamie ever mentioned Ignace Karolyi to her?

She didn't think so. She cast her mind back to the tall, self-effacing don who sat on the sidelines of her father's garden parties with her, talking of cabbages and kings—telling her about medicine in China and how best to go about studying for responsions without letting her father know. The gentle, com-petent man who never made demands on her, who guessed that a completely different person hid beneath her careful façade and accepted her exactly as she was. He'd always been close-mouthed, though even as a schoolgirl she'd suspected there was more to him than that almost invisible "brown" mien of his. Reticence was still his habit; after seven years of marriage his stories, like Mark Twain's, usually concerned men and women all named Fergusson.

That was what troubled her now. She'd heard, or read, Karolyi's name in some other context. *Read,* she thought . . . She couldn't put a pronunciation to the closing *yi.* Which meant she'd never heard Jamie say it.

She slipped her eyeglasses out from behind a pile of papers—concealing them when anyone entered the room was

a lifelong habit—and rose in a rustle of lace, crossing to her
side of the bookshelves, where she settled on the floor, her long
red hair hanging down her back, her plans to work at the Radcliffe Infirmary's dissection rooms that afternoon laid aside.
By the time Ellen reappeared with a tray of sandwiches and
onion soup—for it was well past noon—Lydia had remembered when and in what context she'd come across Karolyi's
name, and the recollection made her more uneasy still. She left
the tray untouched and ascended to the bedroom two hours
later to continue her researches in the back issues of *Lancet* and
Medical Findings stored under the bed.

She might not remember whether Germany had a Parliament these days or be able to tell a Bolshevik from a Men-
shevik, but she could remember to within a few months when
secretin had been discovered or the address of Marie Curie's
laboratory in Paris.

She was still reading at teatime when Ellen came up with
another tray and bullied her into eating half an egg and part of
a scone while Ellen built up the bedroom fire and turned up the
gas. Lydia had tracked down the reference, which had given
her, in turn, another name; she was dimly aware that she had
begun to count the hours between now and midnight, when, at
her best guess, James was due home.

If he didn't elect to remain in Paris overnight.

If something didn't go wrong.

If Ernchester hadn't seen him . . .

If he's staying in Paris, she thought, dabbing jam and
Devonshire cream on a scone and then setting it on the plate
to gaze at the darkening windows, *he'll wire me. He'll let
me know.*

And if he didn't?

She wondered if she could reach him by wiring the con-
sulate or the Foreign Office—or was it the War Office that
operated the Secret Service? Where *was* the Foreign Office in
Paris, anyway? Like most girls of wealthy family, her experience of the City of Lights had been stringently limited by her
preceptors to the Champs Elysées and the Rue de la Paix. If she
telephoned the Foreign Office in London—would that be in

Whitehall? Parliament? Scotland Yard?—they would only tell her lies.

She felt helpless, frightened, uncertain of what to do, because, unlike medical research, this was something for which she had never prepared.

And in any case, she realized, only now seeing the darkness beyond the curtain, they'd all have gone home by this time. As if to echo an affirmative, the Louis XV clock on the parlor mantel downstairs sang its five clear notes.

So all she could do was wait.

She fell asleep sometime after midnight across the foot of the bed, still wearing her fluffy rose-point tea gown, the eye of a maelstrom of medical journals that spread to the bedroom's door, and dreamed of crumbling houses in ancient cities, their stones mortared with dark blood and cobweb; of half-seen forms whispering in shadows centuries deep.

By morning James had not returned. But it wasn't until his second telegram that she decided to go up to London and seek out such a house herself.

TWO

"THE Earl of Ernchester is a vampire."

Streatham—a fussy, chinless man whom Asher had never liked—regarded him for a moment with narrow surprise in his light blue eyes, as if asking himself why Asher would perpetrate such a tale and if it constituted a threat to his position as head of the Paris branch of the Department. Asher had spent a good part of the previous night, sleepless aboard the Dover ferry and the train from Boulogne, trying to phrase an argument that would convince those in charge to either have Karolyi arrested in Paris—scarcely likely, since Karolyi never went anywhere without diplomatic credentials—or to assign a man to follow him, to at least see what his next step would be.

Lack of sleep, hunger, and sheer exasperation when the green-painted door of the town house on the Rue de la Ville de l'Eveque hadn't opened to his knock at five minutes after nine had had their effect. Sitting on a bench under the bare trees before the Madeleine, watching the town house for signs of life, with the chilling threat of rain blowing over him for twenty freezing minutes, he had finally thought, *To hell with it. I'll tell them the truth.*

Streatham ventured a small chuckle, like an agent offering a read newspaper on the Underground to the minor clerk of some foreign legation: a feeler to see how the land lies. "You aren't serious."

"Ernchester—or Farren, as he sometimes calls himself—Wanthope is another one of his names—is perfectly serious about it," Asher said grimly, remembering the dead laborer on the train. "Whether or not he's correct in his claims that drinking human blood has enabled him to live two hundred years, I know from my own experience that the man has abilities for which a foreign power would pay well. He can get past guards unseen. I don't know how he does this, but he can. He has an almost fakirlike ability to get in and out of places. And he can influence people's minds to an almost unbelievable extent. I've seen him do it."

In fact, Asher reflected, watching the thoughts pass almost visibly across the back of the Paris chief's shallow blue eyes, he hadn't seen Ernchester do any of the things he described. Of all the vampires who had ringed him like ghosts in last fall's misty London darkness, Charles Farren, quondam Earl of Ernchester, was one of the few who had not, to one degree or another, used the eerie abilities of the vampire mind to trap or hunt or influence him.

And as he'd watched the yellow pinpricks of the Dover lights vanish into the blackness of fog beyond the *Lord Warden*'s stern rail, Asher had reflected that that was one of the strangest aspects of the entire matter: that Ernchester had been the Hungarian's choice.

There were far more dangerous vampires in London. Why not one of them?

Streatham's mouth grimaced into what was probably supposed to be a smile. "Really, Dr. Asher. The Department genuinely appreciates your concern, particularly in view of the circumstances of your leave-taking . . ."

It was a gratuitous jab, and Asher felt a sting of annoyance.

"What I said and felt about the Department when I left still holds." He set down his teacup. At least they'd offered him tea, he thought, something he was unlikely to get elsewhere in Paris. "If the Department were about to be dynamited, I don't think I'd cross the street to pinch out the fuse.

"But this isn't the Department I'm talking about." His voice was level, but cold with an old rage burned now to clinkers and ash. "This is the country. *You cannot let the Hofburg hire the Earl of Ernchester.*"

"Don't you think you're exaggerating a little? Just because the Austrians are courting some hypnotist—"

"It's more than hypnosis," said Asher, knowing that if he lost his patience with this man, he'd lose all hope of getting his help. "I don't know what it is. I only know that it works." He drew a deep breath, realizing how little of the actual vampire power could be described. Even to someone who was willing to believe, he wasn't sure he *could* describe that curious blanking of the mind that vampires imposed on their victims, allowing them to move utterly unseen; the ability to stand outside a building or on the next street, or half a mile away, silently reading the dreams of whosoever they chose.

They were born spies.

Of course Karolyi, raised in the hotbed of Carpathian legends, would believe, or be ready to believe.

I am ready to do whatever my Emperor requires . . . He'd imitated the glowing-eyed gallantry of all those other young fools in the officers' corps, but even then Asher had known that Karolyi had been speaking the absolute truth. It was just that some people had a different view of that word, *whatever.*

Nothing really changed, he thought. He didn't know how many times he'd sat in this discreet town house within walking distance of the embassy during the years in which he'd ranged all over Europe, going out ostensibly in quest of moribund verb forms and variant traditions about fairies and heroes and coming back with German battleship plans or lists of firms selling rifles to the Greeks.

Those years seemed hideously distant to him, as if it had been someone else who risked his life and traded his soul for matters that had been obsolete in a year.

Streatham folded his hands, white as a woman's and as soft. With a kind of perverse relish, he said, "Of course, having been out of the Department, you wouldn't know about the reorganization since the end of the war and the old Queen's death. After South Africa, the budget was drastically cut, you know. We have to share this house with Passports and the attaché for

Financial Affairs now. We certainly can't ask the French authorities to order the arrest of an Austrian citizen just on your say-so—certainly not a member of one of that country's noble houses, not to speak of the diplomatic corps. And we can't spare a man to follow Karolyi around Paris, much less trail him to Vienna or Buda-Pesth or wherever else he'll be going on to."

"Karolyi's only a means to an end," Asher said quietly. "He's the only way you can track Ernchester . . ."

"And don't keep calling him 'Ernchester.' " Streatham peevishly aligned the edge of a report with the edge of his desk and centered the ink stand above it. "The Earl of Ernchester happens to be a good friend of mine—the *real* Earl of Ernchester. Lucius Wanthope. We were up at the House together," he added smugly.

By "the House" Asher knew he meant Christ Church College, Oxford, and wondered if that was the same Lucius Wanthope who'd been one of Lydia's suitors, eight or nine years ago. Streatham pronounced it *Want'p*, swallowing the middle of the word after the fashion of Oxford. "If this impostor is going about calling himself by that title, the least you can do is not subscribe to the hoax."

"It doesn't matter," Asher said tiredly, "if he's calling himself Albert of Saxe-Coburg-Gotha. And I know all about the reorganization and the budget. Have him followed. This was the address on his luggage. It's just a transit point, but your man can trace him through the local carting company. He'll be hauling a large trunk somewhere today, possibly to the Gare de l'Est to go on to Vienna, more probably to some house here in the city where they can set up operations. Find out who his connections are . . ."

"And what?" Streatham chuckled juicily. "Drive a stake through his heart?"

"If necessary."

Streatham's eyes—too close together in flaccid pouches the color of fish belly—narrowed again, studying him. Asher had washed and shaved in one of the public washrooms at the Gare du Nord after dispatching a telegram to Lydia, but he was well aware that at the moment he looked less like an Oxford don than he did some down-on-his-luck clerk at the end of the night on the tiles.

The Paris chief opened his mouth to speak again, but Asher cut him off. "If necessary I'll telegraph Colonel Gleichen at Whitehall. This is a matter on which we can't afford to take chances. I spent my last few shillings to follow them here, to warn you of a threat greater, in my years of experience, than anything currently facing our department. Believe me, I wouldn't have done it if I'd thought that Ernchester was just a stage hypnotist with a good act, and I wouldn't have done it if I'd thought there was any alternative to the danger we'll face if he does start working for the Kundschafts Stelle. Anything Vienna learns is going to end up in Berlin. You know that. Gleichen knows it, too."

At the mention of the head of MO-2's D Section, Streatham's face had slowly begun to redden; now he fetched an exaggerated sigh. "It'll put the entire Records Section days behind, but I'll pull Cramer off Information and assign him. Will that satisfy you?"

Asher fished his memory and came up empty.

"After your time," said Streatham, with a kind of breezy viciousness. "A good man at his work."

"Which is?"

"Information."

"You mean cutting articles out of newspapers?" Asher stood and picked up his hat. Outside the tall windows it had begun to rain again. The thought of the three-quarter-mile walk to Barclay's Bank on the Boulevard Haussmann gave him a sensation akin to the grinding of unoiled gears deep in his chest.

"Everyone in the Department has had to cover several areas of work these days." The enmity in Streatham's voice was plain now. "I'm very sorry about the inconvenience to you, and about the fact that the budget doesn't permit us to stand you your train fare home. Of course, you're welcome to a bed in one of the duty rooms . . ."

"Thank you," Asher said. "I'm just on my way to my bank." *This Cramer* is *cutting articles out of newspapers,* he thought.

"Don't let me keep you."

There had been a time, thought Asher as he descended the shallow sandstone steps, when he loved Paris.

And indeed, he loved it still. Against the cinder-colored street, the gravid sky, the white and yellow shapes of the bare sycamores, and the pale gold stone of the buildings seemed queerly bright. Windows were shuttered behind iron balconies; red and blue shop awnings seemed to blossom like flowers. Traffic was thick on the boulevard: cabs with their roofs shining with moisture; bright-colored electric tramways, hooting for right-of-way; stylish landaus, the horses puffing steam from their nostrils like dragons in the damp cold; men and women in daytime clothing the color of eggplant and wet stone.

A magic city, thought Asher. Even in his days with the Department, when he had made himself familiar with its thugs-for-hire, its safe breakers, forgers, and fences, he had still found it a magic place.

But he knew that he was hastening to accomplish his errands because he wanted very badly not to be in this city when the sun went down.

There was an ancient *hôtel particulier* somewhere in the Marais district, owned by a woman named Elysée. Since the night he had been taken there, blindfolded, and seen the white-faced, strange-eyed, beautiful creatures who played cards in its brilliantly lit salon, he had not felt safe in this city. He was not sure he would ever willingly spend a night here again.

At Barclay's Bank he established his credentials and withdrew twenty pounds—five hundred francs, far more than he'd need for a *prix-fixe* lunch in the Palais Royale and his return journey, but the discomforts of last night had rendered him unwilling to trust Fate again. It was well after noon, but the Vefory was still serving luncheon. He settled in a corner with an omelette, fresh spinach, bread and butter that had nothing in common with the English travesty of the same name, coffee, and a copy of *Le Petit Journal*. The next boat-train left at four. He had not quite time to visit the Louvre—only the booksellers on the quais, he thought, and a little while spent in the restful silence of Notre Dame.

It would be just getting dark as the train pulled out of the Gare du Nord, but that would be sufficient.

As he turned over the pages of the *Journal*, the top of his mind sifted and sorted the mishmash of Serbian demands for independence from Austria, Russian demands for justice in the Serbian cause, another massacre of Armenians by the new Turkish government, plots by the Sultan to regain his power, and the Kaiser's pursuit of ever faster battleships and ever more powerful artillery, while some other part of his thoughts seemed to see through those reports to the uses the Austrian Emperor—or the Czar or the Kaiser, for that matter—would have for a vampire.

In any direction he looked, the possibilities were terrifying.

Europe skated the rim of cataclysm, that much he knew. The German Kaiser was praying, literally and publicly, for an excuse to use his armies; the French were burning with pride, rage, and the old wounds of the Alsace. The Empire of Austria was trying to hold on to its Slavic minorities, while the Russians trumpeted their intention of backing up those minorities' "pan-Slav" rights. Asher had seen firsthand the weapons everyone was rushing to buy, the railway lines being constructed to carry men to battles, and in Africa he'd already seen what those weapons could do.

Would men who contemplated sending other men into machine-gun fire—or contemplated turning machine guns on soldiers with only rifles in their hands—shrink from handing over a political prisoner or two per week to someone who could slip into consulates, workshops, departments of navy and army utterly unseen?

He turned the page and, for a moment, saw their faces again in the dark of his mind. The coarse and powerful Grippen. Ysidro's enigmatic disdain. Bully Joe Davies. The beautiful Celeste.

The Earl of Ernchester.

Why Ernchester? he wondered again.

The weakest of them, strangely fragile, Grippen's fledgling and slave to the domination of the master vampire's mind. Did Grippen know the little nobleman had left London? Had made a pact with a foreign power? Had Grippen been approached first and refused?

No vampire, Elysée de Montadour had said, the gaslight gleaming queerly in her green eyes, *will do that which endangers other vampires by giving away their haunts, their habits, or the very fact of their existence to humankind.* A handsome woman, with nodding ostrich plumes in her hair, her green-black silk gown as stylish as if she had not been born in an era of panniers and three-foot coiffures. He remembered the cold strength of her hands, clawlike nails ripping open the veins in his arm to drink.

Why didn't Karolyi contact Elysée? he wondered. Or the Vienna vampires? Surely in that city, as in all cities where there were poor upon which to feed, one could find the hunters of the night.

He turned over the leaves of the newspaper, searching for mention of an insignificant laborer's body, found drained of blood on the boat-train. There was none.

"Dr. Asher?"

He'd been aware of the tall young man entering the restaurant, heading in the direction of his table; he'd identified his tailoring and his smooth, heavy-jawed face as English. The young man held out his hand, regarded Asher with frank brown eyes under an overhanging forelock of wheat-colored hair.

"I'm Edmund Cramer."

"Ah." Asher took the boy's hand, gloved in sturdy York tan, in his own. "He whose absence from Records will imperil the defense of the realm against the French."

Cramer laughed and took the chair Asher pushed slightly toward him with his foot. The waiter appeared with another cup of café noir and a bottle of cognac; Asher waved the latter away. "Well, it's true the whole outfit is rather cumberish these days, but Streats could jolly well have upped for a train ticket, not to mention lunch. You did get to your bank all right and all that?"

"You behold the spoils of my endeavor." Asher gestured grandly to the empty plates and handed the waiter two francs upon the man's reappearance with more café noir. "You have me followed?"

"Thought I'd find you in one of the cafés in the Palais," explained the young man. "Streats said you banked at Barclay's, and it's right round the corner. I'm on my way to the Hotel Terminus; thought I'd get a little more information on this Ernchester bird and his Hungarian friend." He flipped from his breast pocket the notepaper onto which Asher had copied the address of the Hotel Terminus, by the Gare St. Lazare. "The chief seems to think Karolyi's hot stuff."

Hot stuff. Asher looked into those luminous eyes and his heart sank. The boy was barely older than the students he was supposed to be lecturing today back at New College—and he breathed a peripheral prayer that Pargeter was taking his lecture as agreed if he were delayed in Wells. He couldn't let this beardless novice go up against a man like Karolyi, let alone Ernchester.

"He is deadly," Asher said. "Don't let him see you, don't let him get within arm's reach of you if you can help it. Don't let him know you're on his trail. I know he looks like he's never done anything but try on uniforms and trim his mustache, but that's not the case."

Cramer nodded, sobered by Asher's words. Asher wondered what Streatham had said about him.

"And Ernchester?"

"You won't see Ernchester."

The young man looked puzzled.

"That's his skill." Asher got to his feet, left a five-franc silver piece on the table for the waiter, and led the way to the door. "So we'll have to concentrate on keeping track of Karolyi. What money have you?"

Cramer's eyes twinkled. "Enough to get a train ticket at the last minute and not have to starve through the night."

"Something like that." It began to rain again as they emerged from the long doors of Vefory's into the arcade around the Palais Royale. The arcade was becoming crowded, the rain notwithstanding; gentlemen in top hats and expensive greatcoats from the Bourse and the nearby banks, and ladies in tulip skirts like brilliant flowers against the dripping gray monochrome of the hedges, trees, and winter earth of the central gardens. Halfway around the arcade Asher found the place he sought: DuBraque et Fils, Jeweler. Cramer watched in a certain amount of puzzlement as Asher purchased three chains, each about eighteen inches long, of what the jeweler assured him was sterling silver.

"Put this around your neck." He handed one to Cramer as they emerged into the arcade again. In many of the shops the gas had already been lit, and the light from the wide glass window winked on the bright links as Cramer tried to open the catch without taking off his gloves. "Ernchester really believes himself to be a vampire," Asher went on, winding another of the chains double around Cramer's wrist. "Wearing silver may just save your life."

"That far round the twist, eh?"

Asher looked up from affixing the second chain, met the young man's eyes for a moment, then returned his attention to the clasp.

"Don't underestimate him." The fit was close; Cramer was a well-fleshed young man. "Don't relax your guard for a minute once it gets dark. He's a lunatic, but that doesn't mean he can't kill you in seconds."

"Shouldn't we stop by Notre Dame for a crucifix, then?" A smile struggled on his face.

Asher remembered a lieutenant he'd known on the Veldt—Pynchon? Prudhomme? He'd had an East Anglian glottal stop, anyway—standing, hands on hips, staring out at the hot, dense silence of lion-colored land. *Well, they're just a lot of farmers, when all's said, aren't they?* "It's the silver that keeps them away," Asher said.

Cramer did not seem to know what to reply.

Even at the Palais Royale it was difficult to find an empty cab in the rain. They ended by taking the Underground to the Gare St. Lazare and crossing the square to the Hotel Terminus. "Should we ask at the cab rank?" Cramer indicated the line of light, two-wheeled fiacres along the railings of the *place*, the horses head down, rugged against the rain, the men grouped beneath the trees, wrapped in whatever they could find to keep warm.

Asher shook his head. "He'll have used a cartage company. It's a big trunk. A London four-wheeler could barely take it; a Paris fiacre's too lightly sprung. We'll just check here . . ." He ascended the gray granite steps of the Terminus, crossed the dark Turkey carpets to the lobby desk, Cramer at his heels like a well-bred but very large dog.

"Pardon," Asher said to the clerk, in the Strasbourg French of a German. He stood as the Germans stood, the set of his shoulders like that he had seen in South German officers, but without the Prussian stiffness which might have gotten him little help in this city of long memories. "I am trying my sister Agnes to locate; she was on the Dieppe train this morning to have come, and nothing of her I have heard. The matter is I do not know whether she travels under her own name, or that of her first husband, who was killed in Kenya, or of her second . . ."

As he and Cramer crossed the square again, Asher said, "Karolyi's checked in, all right." He ducked between a bright red electric tram and the shined and chauffeured automobile of one of the old *gratin*, turned up the Rue de Rome and again on the Rue d'Isly. "Name's on the register, or at least the name of one of his lesser titles. Now we get to do the boring and soul-destroying part . . ."

"I refuse," Cramer said cheerily, turning up his collar against the cold, "to believe there's anything more boring and soul-destroying than combing through a hundred fifty French newspapers per day—and that's just the political ones, mind, *and* just the Parisian ones—in search of 'items of interest' to the War Department. Do your worst."

Asher grinned and led the way up the steps of the modest Hotel d'Isly, no more than a door between a state-run tobacconist's and a workingman's *estaminet*. "There speaks a brave soul and true agent." He had almost forgotten, he thought, the light camaraderie of the King's secret servants. The boy had promise. Pity he had no better teacher for the time being than Streatham.

Resuming the stance and speech of the Strasbourg German, he presented the clerk on duty in the narrow upstairs lobby with a tale, not of a vanished sister, but of a vanished trunk: a meter and a half long, leather-covered oak with iron strapping. A confusion in the Gare, misplaced labels . . . No? No. Perhaps the *gnädige* Herr could give some advice on the local cartage companies, such as a man might have summoned to the Gare? The city directory, to be sure, could be purchased, but it gave little idea . . .

"The Bottin, pff!" The clerk gestured. "Here is the list we use, m'sieu, when we have a client with such a trunk. Not all are on the telephone, you understand, but for such as are, there is the cabinet . . ."

"Wunderschoen! The Herr is entirely too kind. Certainly all the calls will be compensated for. Please accept this token . . ."

"It's up to you now," Asher said softly as the clerk returned to his counter and Asher and Cramer were alone by the wooden confessional of the telephone cabinet. "You'll have to go along on foot and check the companies that aren't on the phone, but those are near enough to send a page with a note. I'll go back to the Terminus and keep an eye out for Karolyi. There's a café on the Rue d'Amsterdam corner of the Place du Havre, and another on the other side of the Rue du Rome; both of them command a view of the cab stand. I'll be in one or the other, or under the arcade of the Gare itself. If I'm not there— if Karolyi comes back and leaves again and I follow him myself—you wait for me there. The last train for London tonight leaves St. Lazare at nine. I'll look for you before half past eight. All right?"

Cramer nodded. "All right. Jolly good of you to point me out the way . . ."

Asher shook his head dismissively, rising to his feet and digging his gloves from his pocket. "Don't let either of them know you're on their trail. But don't lose them. It's more important than you know."

His smile was boyish. "I can only do my best."

Asher picked up the battered brown leather valise that had accompanied him throughout the day and nodded. "It's all any of us can do."

At the head of the stairs he paused, turned back to see the tall, stout form perched in the telephone cabinet, the desk clerk's list spread out on his knee. *No money to get anything more than that,* he thought, with a kind of despair. Paris wasn't a trouble spot. What experienced men the Department had were in Ireland or on the Indian frontier.

He almost went back.

And then what? he asked himself. *Volunteer to pursue Karolyi myself? Let the Department have me again, to do their bidding as I did before?*

But this was different.

It was always different, he thought bitterly, turning away. The only thing ever the same was that they wanted you to do it—and what it did to you inside.

Something hurt within him, like old wounds at the onset of storm.

At the café on the corner of the Rue d'Amsterdam, Asher ordered a café noir and settled himself to wait. Being unable to read the newspaper, he asked the waiter for pen and paper, and amused himself, between watching the cab rank, by observing the passengers going to and from the Gare, making a game of deducing financial circumstances, occupation, and family ties from details of clothing and manner and speech, less systematically than Conan Doyle's Mr. Holmes but with an agent's habit-sharpened skill. This was a good place for it; he heard three kinds of German, five Italian dialects, Hungarian, Dutch, and a half-dozen varieties of French. Once a couple walked by speaking Greek—brother and sister, he guessed from the familiar form of speech as much as the resemblance between them. Later a small family of Japanese passed, and he thought, *One day I'll have to study that tongue.*

If he survived.

The clock on the Trinité struck four, and he knew he had missed the afternoon boat-train.

There was still no sign of Cramer or Karolyi.

Periodically the waiters brought him coffee, but seemed content to let him remain. Asher knew there were men who sat in cafés throughout afternoon and evening, writing letters, reading, drinking coffee and liqueurs, playing quiet games of cribbage, dominoes, chess. Passengers came in for a coffee, or to wait for friends. The sky darkened to the color of soot, and bright white electric lights blossomed all around him in the square. The cab men changed their day horses for the beat-up screws they drove after sundown—why subject your good beast to the rigors of night work?—and lit the yellow lamps that marked their origin in the Montmartre quarter.

It was almost six when he saw Karolyi. The man had a lithe deadliness to him, like a cheetah masked as a house cat; his wide-skirted Hungarian greatcoat billowed around his boot calves in his haste, and he looked here and there quickly as he sprang up the steps of the Hotel Terminus, smooth strong chin and beautiful lips touched by the arc lights that left his eyes in his hat brim's shadow. It was the way he moved when he thought himself unobserved that had first made Asher wonder about him, back in Vienna. That, and the fact that he was clearly too intelligent to be content to do what he was doing.

Asher paid his bill and cursed the Department, gathered his valise and strolled casually across the square so as to be loitering in the dense shadows of the trees near the cab stand when the Hungarian reemerged from the Terminus' doors. He heard him speak to a driver, giving an address on the Rue du Bac. Because there was the possibility that Karolyi might change cabs, Asher simply told his own jehu, "Follow that cab—don't let him see us," and the man, a waspish little sparrow of a Parisian in a faded army coat and muffler, gave him a knowing wink and whipped up his disreputable old nag in pursuit.

They crossed at the Pont Royal, the lights of the Louvre shining on black water. Near the Quai d'Orsay, Karolyi dismissed his cab, and Asher followed him afoot along the crowded streets of the Left Bank. Beneath the trees of the Boulevard St. Germain, Karolyi picked up one of those bright-dressed, frowsy-haired women whom Asher had seen emerge, a little like vampires themselves, from the darkness as soon as the lamps were lit. He felt a pang of disgust, both with his quarry and with himself, but he continued to loiter just far enough behind to keep the man and his new companion in sight. They turned from the lighted boulevard into the dark blocks of old houses that had made up the quarter long before the Citizen King's improvements, stopped at a workman's café for a drink. Standing in the raw gloom of an alleyway, Asher heard the half hour strike from St. Clothilde; the whine of fiddles and concertinas reached him, and in the glare of the colored lights he saw gaudy petticoats swirl and striped stockings, and mouths opened in laughter behind the blue haze of cigarette smoke.

The night train was at nine. He wondered if he had time to leave word for Cramer and still catch it, or if he'd have to spend a night in Paris after all. The thought wasn't pleasant. At a sound behind him, he whirled, his heart in his mouth, seeing in his mind's eye the cold white faces, the strangely glittering eyes of the Master of Paris and her fledglings . . .

But it was only a cat.

If it had been Elysée de Montadour, he realized, he would have heard nothing.

When Karolyi and the woman emerged from the café, she was clinging to his arm, her great brassy fleece of hair hanging loose from its pins and her head lolling. Karolyi, Asher remembered, had always been very circumspect with the girls of his own class or the daughters of the wealthy Vienna *nouveaux riches*, instead preying incognito on suburban shop girls or driving out to the country inns to seduce the young girls who worked in the vineyards.

Their footfalls dripped on the moist pavement. As they approached Asher's unseen post in the alley, a man in a striped jersey and sailor's jacket stepped out of a doorway. "Got a couple sous for an honest man out of luck?"

When Karolyi said, in his icily perfect accent, "Go and have yourself stuffed," the man grew belligerent, blocking his way; though not as tall as the Hungarian, he was beefier, standing too close, threatening with the aggressive curve of his shoulder, the readiness of his hands.

"That ain't no way to—"

In one move Karolyi shucked the woman from his arm, leaving her to fall back against the soot-black wall, and lightly reversed the walking stick in his hand. Before the beggar could utter a sound, Karolyi brought the stick around sideways, hitting the skull with a crack Asher could hear where he stood. When the man slumped, Karolyi struck him again, heavy, deliberately, full-force blows, as if beating a carpet. Unhurried. It was not a neighborhood much frequented by the *guardiens de la paix*.

The woman stood, swaying, her fist in her mouth, blinking at the scene in stupefied horror. She made no move to flee, and Asher wondered if she were capable of it. When Karolyi had finished, he turned, taking her by the front of her jacket and pulling her to him again, and she sagged on his shoulder like one drunk or drugged. A little light from the café showed Asher the beggar's blood, inky on the uneven pavement; the man's breath was a wheezing, stertorous gasp.

Asher thought, *He needs help.* And then, *If I go to the café for it, I'll lose Karolyi.*

Silent as a lean brown cat in the shadows as he moved after the retreating pair, Asher remembered why he'd left the Department. Once you accepted the necessity of what you did—*whatever my country requires*—you might hate yourself, but you followed.

The house was one of those anonymous stucco-fronted Parisian dwellings in a narrow lane whose character hadn't changed since the days of the Sun King. Doors and windows were shuttered fast. As Karolyi unlocked the door of a downstairs shop, Asher ghosted through an alley a few houses farther up, counted chimneys, watched roof lines, and slipped into a clotted, weed-grown yard. Light shone behind shutters on the second floor, casting enough of a glow to let him see the broken-down shed that had once housed a kitchen amid a foul litter of rain barrels, old planks, broken boxes. All around him other shuttered windows made glowing chinks and slits of brass. The muck underfoot dragged his boots, the air nearly as thick, smothering with the stench of privies and of something newly dead.

He left his valise beside a rain barrel, scrambled with infinite care to the shed's roof. Through a broken louver he watched Karolyi tie the woman to a rickety chair. She was laughing, her head lolling back. "You like it like this, eh, *copain*? You want me to fight you a little?"

"*Igen.*" Karolyi had pulled off his gloves for the task, tossed his hat on the stained and sagging mattress of the bed. His face was as calmly pleasant as the face of a statue, his shoulders relaxed, as if he shed everything from him with the knowledge that whatever he did in the name of his country was acceptable and forgiven. There was genuine banter in his voice. "You fight, my little bird. See if it helps."

Beyond them Asher could see an enormous trunk that occupied all of one side of the room: leather, strapped and cornered with brass. It stood open, and the dim light of the oil lamp glinted on the metalwork, filled it with shadow, but Asher could see that there was a second, only slightly smaller trunk inside. The inner trunk could still easily have held a man.

A noise in the yard nearly stopped his heart; a hissing and a scuffle; rats fighting, he realized, leaning against the freezing brick wall. He remembered the smell of some dead thing near the shed.

When he looked back, Ernchester was in the room.

"You're late." By his voice Karolyi could have been speaking of a rendezvous for tea. "The train leaves the Gare de l'Est at seven-thirty. We've barely time to dispose of this little éclair before the carters arrive."

He stepped to the giggling woman, took the soiled lace of her collar and ripped her dress open to the waist. She wore a corset underneath but no chemise; breasts like loaves of fallen dough balanced precariously on top of the ridge of whalebone and canvas, nipples like big copper pennies. A cheap gilt chain glinted around her neck. She winked up at Ernchester, and with a flip of one knee tossed her skirts up over her lap. She wasn't wearing drawers, either.

"You got time before your train, *chéri*." She leaned her head back and made kisses at him with her painted mouth, then dissolved into giggles.

Ernchester looked down at her with no expression whatever. He seemed smaller than Asher remembered him, thin and nondescript in his old-fashioned clothing. Though no vampire Asher had ever met appeared physically older than the midthirties, Ernchester seemed somehow to have aged, even in the past year. It was nothing in his stance or his face; there was no gray in the close-cropped fair hair. But looking at him, Asher felt that he was seeing an empty glass, dry and coated with bitter dust.

"I've dined." He turned away.

"Oh, come on, *p'tit*," laughed the woman. "Ain't you got no taste for dessert?"

Karolyi muttered disgustedly, *"Sacrée couilles"*—not at the woman, but at the delay and the needless risks—and pulled a thin silk scarf from his coat pocket. With deadly delicacy he crossed it into a loop and dropped it around the woman's neck. She gasped, squeaked as her breath was cut off. Her body heaved and flopped, stockinged legs threshing; she kicked off one of her shoes in the death struggle, and it struck the wall with a smack.

Asher turned his face away, pressed his cheek to the cold brick, sickened and knowing that he was a dead man if he tried to do a single thing to stop what was going on. He was aware that from the moment Karolyi had picked her up, he—Asher— had known that she was going to die.

He was aware, too, that the noises in the room—the scraping and bumping of the chair, the obscene sounds the woman made as life blubbed and spurted and popped from her body—would cover the sounds of his departure, so that he could reach the Gare de l'Est before they did and see what train was leaving at seven-thirty.

He had been in the Department too long, he thought, slipping silently down the rain gutter. He knew there was nothing he could do to save that woman. The attempt would cost him his life, and cost England, perhaps, untold lives if the Kaiser got the war he wanted . . .

Coward, he cursed himself. *Coward, coward . . .* They had always said that the most important thing was to get home with the information, whatever the cost to yourself or others. Honor was another luxury the Department couldn't afford.

The clock struck seven, a reminder that time was short. Asher struck a pile of planking by the kitchen wall. Rats streamed in all directions in a hideous scurry of flying shadow, and there was the renewed stink of death.

He picked up his valise, but something made him turn and go back. Where the planks had fallen aside he could see a man's hand, palm upturned in a thin slat of light from the window far above.

I've dined, Ernchester had said.

Asher bent and moved the plank aside.

The face of the man pushed under the boards had already been gnawed; in any case, in the dense shadows it would have been impossible to tell who he was. But there was a silver chain around the plump wrist.

THREE

"I HAVE long deplored the manners of what fondly believes itself to be society these days."

Lydia gasped as if she had been wakened by a freezing drench of water. The pale man took the sprayer weapon from her grasp with one hand and with the other pulled her to her feet, the strength of his fingers on her elbow such that she felt instinctively he could, had he so wished, have snapped the bone within the flesh. Past his shoulder she saw that the grille stood open, though she had been aware of no movement on the part of the dead man within the niche.

For some moments, she realized, in a rush of frightened shock, she had been aware of nothing at all.

He stood beside her now, thin and cold and utterly correct in his long white robe. His eyes, level with hers—for he was not a tall man—were a light, clear yellow, flecked with the brown-gray that wood turns when desiccated with age.

He shoved her against the stone of the wall, and when he spoke, she could see the gleam of his fangs in the strangely reversed lamp glow.

"Not that proper manners, or genuine society, have existed in this country since the departure of the last of her true kings for France and the advent of that rabble of sausage-devouring German heretics and their hangers-on." There was no anger in his voice, nor wore his face any expression whatsoever, but his grip on her arm kept her pinned where she was. His hands were like marble—a dead man's hands.

He went on, "It has always been considered that a woman who sought a man out in his chamber while he slept did so at her peril."

James was in danger. Later on Lydia realized that only that fact gave her courage to speak. Her single encounter with Ysidro had been part and parcel of a greater jeopardy, and in that instance, she had known where she stood. This was different.

"I had to speak to you. I came in the daylight so the others wouldn't know."

He released her arm, but standing in the confines of the narrow stair, it was as if they embraced. She noted that no heat came from his body, and save for the very faint reek of old blood in the folds of his shroud, no smell. Except when he spoke, his body made no sound whatsoever, neither of breath nor of movement. All these data she observed, while aware that no analysis of them came anywhere near describing what he was like.

She pushed up her spectacles. "Lord Ysidro—Don Simon— I think my husband is in trouble. I need your advice."

"Your husband, mistress, has had all the boon and gift I could make him, and more, in the breath of life that still passes his lips." The sulfur eyes regarded her, remote and chill. Not catlike, nor snakelike, nor like any beast's, but neither were they a man's eyes. Even his lashes were white, like his hair. "And a second time will I fill his hands with undeservéd treasure, when I let you walk from this house."

"The Earl of Ernchester is selling his services to a foreign government."

Don Simon Ysidro's expression did not alter. Indeed, his face, still as the peeled ivory statue of some forgotten god, had shown neither anger nor scorn, as if over the years the flesh had settled to a final resting place on the delicate substructure of skull. Nor had his voice risen over the soft level that was almost, but not quite, a monotone, and all the more terrifying for that. Don Simon Xavier Christian Morado de la Cadena-

Ysidro was the only vampire Lydia had met. She wondered if others were like him.

"Come upstairs."

He handed her back her weapon and led the way, lamp upraised to shed light on the damp stone stairs. His feet beneath the hem of his shroudlike woolen robe were bare. Though Lydia's breath clouded gold in the lamplight, the owner of the nameless house seemed to feel nothing of the cold.

Four cats somehow materialized in the scullery, miawing to be fed, though Lydia observed that none came within arm's reach of the vampire. Ysidro set the lamp on the table and touched a spill to the flame. Though he was extremely difficult to see when he moved, Lydia had impressions, like frozen images from a dream, of white hands cupping light above the curved glass chimney and carrying it to the fishtail burners above the stove; of dense gold outlining the slight hook of the nose, the long chin and trace of shadow at the corner of his mouth. He opened the icebox, addressed the cats in Spanish and put meat and milk down for them. Then he stepped away from their dishes. Only then did they come close to eat.

"Where did you hear this?" He held a chair while she sat, then perched a flank on the corner of the table. His English was flawless, save for the faintest touch of a Castilian lisp, and the occasional oddly bent inflection that Lydia knew would have conveyed volumes to James. In the set of Ysidro's shoulders, the way he held his head, she saw the echo of a long-vanished doublet and stiffened ruff.

She held out to him the telegram she had received Monday morning from the Gare du Nord. "Ignace Karolyi is—"

"I know who Ignace Karolyi is." His voice still held no very great interest, as if all emotion had long been worn away by the sheer abrasion of passing time. Indeed, in stillness, Lydia had the odd impression that he had been sitting so on the corner of the table for years, perhaps centuries.

The vampire turned the paper in ivory fingers, raised it to his nostrils, then touched it, very gently, first to his cheekbone, then to his lower lip. "A Hungarian boyar and, like your husband at one time, a man who cherishes the honor of service to his empire above personal honor, though perhaps Hungarians as a rule do not consider truth and loyalty as the English do. A diplomat, and a spy."

"I didn't know then about Karolyi," Lydia said. Some of her panic was passing—at least he appeared willing to listen to what she said. "I mean, only what James says in his wire. But I recognized his name. I found it in one of the lists I made a year ago, when I was trying to track down medical doctors I suspected of contacts with vampires. I was making notes of every name I found in any article. This one was in an article about Dr. Bedford Fairport."

He tilted his head a little, like an albinistic bird. "The man who seeks to have men live forever."

"You've heard of him, then." Reading over the long series of articles last night, she hadn't thought of Fairport's work on the changes wrought in brain and blood and glandular chemistry over time in exactly that light—she doubted that Fairport himself would see it that way. But suddenly she knew that Ysidro was right.

"This was one of his early articles," she went on slowly. "Back in 'eighty-six or 'eighty-seven, when he first went to Austria to study those Styrian peasants who live to be a hundred and ten. He mentions that the private sanitarium he was given charge of is owned by the Karolyi family, and that it was Ignace Karolyi who made the arrangements. He mentions Karolyi in the next article as a financial contributor who made research possible. And then Karolyi vanishes. In fact, all reference to Fairport's funding vanishes. It's never mentioned again. I checked."

"It astounds me that I did not read that myself." Ysidro sounded not the slightest astounded. "But I subscribe to a good many journals, as I daresay you saw."

Lydia blushed. What had seemed, at the time, to be the necessary investigation of a vampire's lair became trespass in a gentleman's house. "I'm sorry," she stammered, but he vouchsafed no reply.

Instead his finger moved in the direction of the sprayer. "And what is this?"

"Oh." Lydia took the sticking plaster from her pocket and recapped the nozzle. "It's full of silver nitrate solution. One can buy it in any chandlery. I—well, James once mentioned that vampires sometimes slept several to a house. I didn't know what I might meet, you see."

She was afraid he would mock her, since, upon consideration, the weapon would certainly have been difficult to deploy quickly enough to do her any good. She had learned to deal with mockery from an early age over her medical studies, but this was a matter from which she could not simply walk away.

But the vampire only said, "Ingenious," and touched the side of the pump's reservoir with the backs of his fingers, then took them quickly away. In the pale gaslight, Lydia could see that his ears had been long ago pierced for earrings, like a Gypsy's. "Then this Fairport is in truth Karolyi's pensioner."

"I think so." Lydia held out to him another telegram, the telegram which, reaching her that morning from Munich, had caused her to pack her trunks, manufacture a moderately plausible tale for her servants, and take the train down to London in search of the man in whose kitchen she now sat, with the smallest of his cats—a sinuous shadow-gray tom—winding itself around her ankles.

Ysidro took the second paper from her hand.

LEAVING PARIS STOP STAYING EPPLER ADDRESS BOOK JAMES

"He's waxed cautious since his first wire." The vampire touched the paper to his lower lip again. "You conned this book of his?"

"After I decoded the message, yes." She reached down half unconsciously to stroke the cat, looking up at Ysidro where he sat above her, hands folded over his knee. His nails projected some half inch beyond the tips of his fingers and had a strange glassy appearance, far thicker than human nails. Some kind of chitin? It would be rude to ask for a cutting.

"The words 'address book' were the tip, you see," she explained. "It's a simple code; last for first, counting inward, and A means B, B means C, et cetera. He keeps duplicate books. Eppler is two from the end of the E's—Mrs. Eppler is the mother of an old pupil of his. She lives in Botley, about ten miles from Oxford, and it's ridiculous that he'd be going there from Paris. Two from the beginning of the F's was Fairport, in Vienna. As you see, the telegram was sent from Munich, at one-forty Tuesday afternoon."

"And I was that easy to find?"

Lydia hesitated, wondering if she should lie. Although her initial fears had subsided, she realized she was still in a great deal of danger. She supposed that if Ysidro didn't have the ability to make people stop fearing him, he would have starved to death centuries ago.

The greater fears still lay ahead of her, a vast uncharted territory of deeds she had no concept how to perform.

At last she said, "I knew about this house a year ago. In theory. I hadn't sought it out. But I looked up all the possibilities of vampire lairs for James while he was . . . working for you."

A small line printed itself briefly near the fanged mouth, and the smallest flare of annoyance moved Ysidro's nostrils. But he only said, "Then this Fairport is thought by the Department in Vienna to be their man—they, too, having missed the articles which speak of Karolyi's contributions to Fairport's research. No matter of surprise, given the fewness of agents and the troubles in the Balkans in that year, and in France. Afterward, one presumes Fairport would have known not to publish his patron's name."

"What it means," Lydia said quietly, "is that James is walking into a trap."

Ysidro remained still for some time, the telegram unmoving in his fingers, but Lydia could see thought and memory like swift-shuffled cards in the back of the jeweled yellow eyes. Remembering, she guessed, Fairport's articles on Hungarian and Romanian centenarians, his preoccupation with extending life, his work in a part of the world that James had described as a hotbed of vampire lore. Then he raised his head and said, "Await me."

And without seeing him leave, Lydia found herself alone.

She checked her watch, wondering how long "Await me" meant. If she herself were in a tremendous hurry, she could wash, dress, curl, frizz and put up her hair, and apply a judiciously minuscule quantity of rice powder, kohl, rouge, and cologne in just under two hours and a half, which her husband, manlike, seemed to consider an unreasonable length of time. At least, Lydia thought, she *knew* how long it took her to make herself presentable and allowed for it, unlike dandies of her acquaintance who lived in the fond delusion that they could assemble the component parts of their façade in "only a moment, my dearest Mrs. Asher." She remembered the clothing in the dressing room upstairs, by the finest tailors in Saville Row. James had warned her, and now she knew from terrifying experience, how fast vampires could move, but she also knew that males as a species tended to potter, fidgeting endlessly with cravats and shifting coins, notebooks, and theater tickets from pocket to pocket as if fearing they would capsize if not properly trimmed. She wondered if death altered this.

Twenty-five minutes, she made a mental wager with herself, and was within three of it when she turned her head to find Ysidro at her side again. In his cinder-gray suit, his flesh white as the linen of his shirt, he seemed more ghostlike than he had in the white robe, as if the clothing were a barrier, a shadow of distance.

"Come."

The alleys and back streets through which he led her were unlit and stinking, full of furtive movement. She guessed their route was not a direct one, but could not be sure, for as soon as they descended the front steps of his house, he took her spectacles from her. Moreover, she was aware that three or four times in the fifteen minutes of their walk, he touched her mind with the blankness, the empty reverie, that vampires apparently could extend. She had the sensation of waking repeatedly from dreams to find herself each time in a new street or court, blinking at ten shades of blurred darkness all spangled with the colored embers of reflected pub lights, with Yiddish or German or Russian yammering on all sides from the little knots of seedy, bearded men clustered in doorways or around chestnut vendors' braziers. The men would step aside unconsciously to let Ysidro pass, not looking at him, as if they, too, partook of his dream of invisibility; their clothes smelled of hard work and poor diet and not enough hot water for washing.

Every other week Lydia took the train down to London to work in the dissecting rooms of St. Luke's. Men like these, with their brown, broken teeth and their flea bites and their dirty, callused hands would be delivered by the workhouse vans, smelling of carbolic and formalin, dead of tumors that had burst untreated, of pneumonia, of consumption, or the other ills of poverty, so that she and others like her could study the intricate beauty of muscle and nerve beneath the knife.

It was the first time in her scholarly life that Lydia had been among them living, and her mind swarmed with questions she wished to ask them about the food and working conditions that had contributed to their pathologies. On the other hand, she felt very glad of Ysidro's protection.

They crossed a plank bridge over water nearly invisible beneath low-lying fog, passed the wry, dark roofline of some very ancient church. In time they traversed a sordid alley behind a pub near the river and descended an areaway thick with garbage and the smell of cats. Though her eyes had grown used to darkness, Lydia saw only the moth flicker of pale hands before she heard the snick of a lock going over. Hinges creaked. Ysidro said "Come" again and stepped into absolute dark.

A match scratched. Ysidro's narrow face appeared, outlined in saffron. "You need not concern yourself over rats."

He touched the flame to a pair of guttered candles in a double branch. The plaster of the walls was black with mildew, falling away to reveal underlying brick. "Like cats, they are aware of what we are and know that though it is the human death we need to feed our minds, we can derive sustenance from the blood of any living thing."

He lifted the branch. Twin lights called twin ghosts of shadow, merging and circling in a strange cotillion as he led her toward the back stair. "Anthea and Ernchester sleep seldom at the house on Savoy Walk these days. It is best to let memories lie. She scarce ever hunts this early in the night, but it may be that she has gone to her dressmaker."

Lydia checked her watch again as they passed through a downstairs hall: peeling silk wall covering, doors blackly ajar. "I suppose this close to Christmas there'd be one open . . ."

"If one has money, mistress, one always finds those willing to sell their sleep and their leisure. I have visited my bootmaker at midnight and never found him but that he was consumed with delight."

"What do you tell him?" She couldn't imagine her aunt Harriet's modiste keeping open past seven for Queen Alexandra herself.

Ysidro regarded her with eyes turned amber by the ruddy light. "That I will have none of this foolishness of two-colored shoes, nor buttons up the side." He turned to the room at the top of the stair. "So."

Like Ysidro's house, the chamber held little furniture, and that furniture old. A tester bed with a curving footboard stood against the rotted wall panels, the counterpane as faded as the silk paper downstairs; on the other wall, a blackwood armoire, stained, chipped, thick with dust-choked carving and mottled with water damage. Its doors stood open. Petticoats, corsets, stockings lay across the bed, and with them—separated by the length of space that would have accounted for a large portmanteau—two dresses Lydia immediately recognized as unsuitable for travel, one because of its now-unfashionable leg-o'-mutton sleeves, the other because it was white, a color no sane woman, dead or Undead, would wear on a train.

"She's gone after him," Lydia said, opening the armoire doors. The only dresses there in the current fashion were the decolleté silks and sumptuous velvets of evening wear. No waists, no skirts—Lydia peered shortsightedly into the lower drawer, and Ysidro handed her eyeglasses back—and no walking shoes. "She packed in a hurry . . ."

She halted, frowning, as her eyes adjusted to the sudden clarity and she realized that the tops of the dressers were in disorder: scarves, sleeves, kerchiefs caught in drawers that had been hastily closed.

"The place has been searched." Ysidro, who had passed swiftly into the other room, returned, moving his head as if scenting the air. "Living men, days ago, before she packed, I think. The air still whispers of their tobacco and their blood." He crossed to the bed, studied the garments lying there. All the colors, as far as Lydia could tell in the low amber radiance of candlelight, that a dark woman would wear; everything of the highest quality—Swiss cotton, Melton wool, Italian silk. They were cut for a woman of Lydia's height, with a waist like a stem and breasts like blown roses.

"*Her* clothing." Ysidro turned a chemise over in one gray-gloved hand. "None of his. I like this not, Mistress Asher." He let the silk slither away. "For many years now it has only been love of her that has kept him on this earth. She is the strong one. He hunts in her shadow, brittle, like antique glass."

"Might that be reason in itself?" Lydia turned from the dresser, where an ivory hair receiver and ivory-handled scissors spoke of other pieces of a matched toilet set now vanished: brush, comb, mirror. A glove box lay open, gloves of all colors lying like dried and flaccid spiders where they had been spilled.

Ysidro lifted a brow.

Lydia went on hesitantly, "Might he be fleeing her?"

"To such sanctuary as the Austrian Empire would afford?" He moved around the corner of the bed, touched the imprint on the dusty counterpane where the portmanteau had rested, and his nostrils flared again, seeking clues from the alien scents of the air. "I would not have said so. She loves him, guards him; she is all in all to him."

He paused for a long time, his face half turned from her, inexpressive as the level softness of his voice. "But it is true that one may hate one's all in all at the same time that one loves. This was something . . ." Another pause, debating; then he went on, "This was something I never understood as a living man."

He met her eyes, expressionless, and she could not reply.

After a time he said, "The Calais Mail departs Charing Cross at nine. I doubt we can prepare swiftly enough to make tonight's. Meet me tomorrow night at eight on the platform, you and your maid. I shall wire my own arrangements to Paris beforehand; I can—"

"I'm not taking a maid!" Lydia said, shocked.

Ysidro's brows lifted again, colorless against his colorless face. "Naturally, she shall know nothing of me, save as a chance-met companion on the train."

"No."

"Mistress Asher—"

"This is not a matter for discussion, Don Simon." Frightened as she was at the thought of traveling to Vienna—of dealing with one or possibly several vampires—the thought of journeying in company with one unnerved her still more. And as for putting Ellen or anyone else in similar danger . . .

"I came to you for advice in dealing with vampires, specifically with Lord Ernchester. There isn't a great deal of reliable information on the subject, you know." She saw the flare of genuine exasperation in his eyes behind the vampire stillness, and rather to her own surprise it didn't frighten her as it had.

"But I would not take *anyone*—certainly not a woman who's been my friend and servant for nearly fifteen years—into that situation without telling her what kind of danger she may be facing, which, on the face of it, is impossible."

"A woman of your station does not travel alone."

"Nonsense. My friend Josetta Beyerly travels by herself all the time. So does—"

"*You* will not." Ysidro's voice did not grow louder, nor his expression change, but she felt his irritation like a wave of cold off a block of ice. "In my day no woman traveled alone, save peasants and women of the streets."

"Well, when I encounter a roving band of paid-off mercenary soldiers between here and Calais, I'll certainly wish I'd taken your advice."

"Don't talk foolishness. You might trace Karolyi but you would never get near Ernchester, and it is Ernchester to whom I must speak on this matter."

"You're the one who's talking foolishness," retorted Lydia, though she knew he was right. "This is the twentieth century, not the sixteenth. I will certainly appreciate whatever advice you can give me . . ."

"Advice will gain you little against either Karolyi or Ernchester. If you wish to warn your husband of his danger, you must travel with me—and travel I will, to prevent Charles from doing this thing, whatever his motives."

Lydia was silent for a moment, unnerved beyond words at the thought of such a journey but remembering how utterly unprepared she had been to encounter him in the crypt. "If you must," she said slowly, her dream of fanged white faces returning to her. "Thank you . . . but I am not taking my maid into the situation she'd face if we meet Ernchester, and I'm not exposing her to the chance of finding out inconvenient things about you. Which she'd do," added Lydia. "Ellen's got an inquisitive streak, and she's smarter than she appears. I won't do that to her."

"Hire one for the journey, then."

"So that you can kill her when the journey is done? And kill me, too, for that matter?" she added, her mind making a tardy leap to the ultimate danger of traveling with the dead. She knew too much already—even her admission of knowing where his lairs lay had violated the lines so carefully drawn when James and Ysidro had parted a year ago in the burning house on Harley Street.

He needs a human companion, she thought, in his search for Ernchester, someone who could deal with such problems as might overtake him when daylight was near; and he needs someone who knows James well enough to track him, to guess his movements, and through him, Karolyi and Ernchester.

She'd told Ellen and Mrs. Grimes she was visiting her cousins in Maida Vale. It would be weeks before she was even missed.

She kept her eyes on his, positive she resembled nothing so much as a myopic rabbit attempting to stare down a dragon.

Slowly, the vampire said, "You need have no fear of me, mistress. Nor will your woman, so long as she keeps from asking about that which does not concern her."

"No."

James had told her of the vampire ability to touch living minds, a cold grip, the dreadful sensation of steely will. But his power extended to blanking and smothering thought, to diverting attention ... not to changing resolve. It was a predator's power, a spy's and a fugitive's, not that of one who must negotiate with humankind. She saw that realization dawn in his eyes, and his mouth tightened with annoyance.

"If we are to be companions in this enterprise, I will not have you traveling alone abroad like a jauntering slut," he said. "I think your husband would agree with me in that."

"What my husband thinks is my husband's business, and neither yours nor mine," said Lydia. "And I would rather be taken for a jauntering slut than betray a woman who's dependent on me. And if it doesn't suit you, I'll travel by myself."

Ysidro bent and kissed her hand, his lips like silk left outside on a dry night of hard frost. "*Bon voyage,* then, mistress. And *bonne chance* in your dealings with the Undead."

With a sensation like waking up, Lydia found herself alone.

It was not, in fact, terribly late to be abandoned in a completely unfamiliar part of London. Though the fog had thickened and the night was growing colder, the streets were still populous, albeit with foreign laborers from the sweatshops that abounded in the neighborhood and with sailors who seemed to accept Ysidro's outdated presumption that a woman on her own was a jauntering slut, at least as far as Lydia could understand their idiomatic references to Master John Thursday and pintle jigs. Evidently, Josetta's suffragist doctrines had yet to penetrate this far. Lydia made a mental note to let her know.

As she had guessed, she wasn't far from the river, and on the broad, electric-lit thoroughfare of the Embankment, she had no trouble in finding a cab to take her back to the small hotel near the museum where she had left her luggage.

Taken in the balance, she thought—removing her gloves and unpinning cook's nondescript hat—she was more glad than sorry that Ysidro would not be accompanying her to Vienna. People *did* travel alone, of course, and there was no reason why she shouldn't, Ysidro's antiquated notions notwithstanding: The world abounded with policemen to be appealed to, porters to be tipped, cabs, guides, travel bureaus, quality hotels with obliging managers, and shops in which to purchase anything she might forget to pack. The lack of a maid would engender certain difficulties, of course, but that was what hotel chambermaids were for.

It was unlikely she would catch up with James before he reached Vienna, but with luck, his cautious nature might keep him out of immediate peril until she could arrive and apprise him of the fact that he was dealing with a double agent—if worse came to worst, she could inform whoever was in charge of the Vienna Department that Dr. Fairport's sanitarium in the Vienna Woods was the likeliest place to search for a clue to James' whereabouts.

If whoever was in charge wasn't taking money from the Austrians as well.

From what James had told her, that was at least a possibility, and Lydia wondered how on earth she'd be able to tell.

Forcing down her sense of panic again, she reviewed such of her luggage as she had unpacked for the night: peignoir, two pairs of slippers—the prettier but far less comfortable ones in case any of the hotel staff came in—rose water and glycerine for her hands, distilled water of green pineapples to alleviate the incipient wrinkles Aunt Harriet had always assured her excessive reading would bring on, silver-backed hairbrush, comb, toothbrush, nail file, curling irons, frizzing irons, hairpins, several sets of underwear, corsetry, petticoats, an array of silver table knives whetted to as deadly an edge as silver would take, and a .38 caliber revolver containing the silver bullets she had had made last year.

Lydia had felt like the heroine of a penny dreadful, packing that along with the talcum, rice powder, rouge, lotions, and perfumes.

There was also the market basket that she'd bought in Covent Garden that afternoon, containing thick braids of garlic bulbs, packets of aconite and whitethorn, branches of wild rose. She wreathed her pillow with them and hung them in the single window of the unheated little back bedroom, and as she undressed and unlaced herself—there were disadvantages to staying in hotels where she was unlikely to meet anyone she or her family knew—she turned over in her mind her other options.

Confide in one of her friends and take her as a companion? Josetta understood politics and feared nothing but, Lydia knew from experience, wasn't particularly practical: she always seemed outraged at being arrested for suffragist activities which, though certainly necessary for the overall strategy of that movement, flagrantly violated the law. Her other close friend, Anne Gresholm, wiser and more intelligent, had lectures and students of her own to tend to, and her health was not good. In any case, the danger remained the same. Lydia was also aware that she had a certain amount of sufferance from Ysidro as long as she told no one of the existence of vampires. If she violated that secret, or if Josetta or Anne guessed—which they surely would—she could not answer for their safety or her own on their return.

Go to Ysidro, then, and ask him to accompany her after all? It would only resurrect the issue of a maid. She wouldn't endanger Ellen, and a chance-hired stranger would be in the same peril and might be more inquisitive and less reliable to boot.

Lydia sighed, slipped the revolver under her single, paltry pillow, and at length drifted into sleep among blankets strewed with wolfsbane, railway timetables, and guidebooks to the eastern reaches of the Austrian lands.

It must be the smell of the garlic, she thought, aware that she was dreaming and that the dream was far more vivid—lurid, even—than anything she had dreamed at home. *The garlic, or that house in the fog . . .*

She stood on the terrace of a tall mansion, a glory of half-timbering and ornamental stone, with a moon-drenched garden maze on one hand and lighted windows of many-paned glass on the other. Looking in, she saw courtiers in the stiff velvets, the soft-glowing pearls of Elizabeth's reign. They were dancing, and she could hear the swift and complex run of the music: hands linking, farthingales flouncing, the men all wearing little Shakespearean chin beards and looking silly beyond description in tights and trunk hose and bulging peasecod doublets, the women in skirts hooped out like kitchen tables and in collars of upstanding, wired lace.

A woman stood near the windows, whom Lydia noticed because she was wearing modern garments, a plain brown serge that didn't fit her particularly well and certainly didn't become her. She was plain-faced, with a slightly receding chin, of medium height, and rather pear-shaped without being fat; a wealth of curly black hair lay loose upon her narrow shoulders. Sometimes when Lydia's eyes left her and returned, she'd be wearing Elizabethan clothing, dull-colored and worked high to the neck. A servant's gown, or a poor relation's. Her small hands fussed with the jet buttons of her sleeves.

Then, very softly, Ysidro spoke.

"You would think, the way they danced, they'd wear something more suited to the exercise, would you not?"

His voice was so quiet Lydia wondered that she could hear it through the glass and over the music. She saw him then, standing at the brown woman's side. His black velvet doublet, his knee-length breeches, his high, supple boots, harked just enough to a later period to avoid the inherent ridiculousness of male Elizabethan garb without appearing anachronistic, and his hueless hair seemed warmer in the torchlight, darkened almost to honey. The girl replied, inaudibly, but it made Ysidro laugh, as if he were playing the part of someone else. Can't she see it? wondered Lydia, terrified. *Can't she see what he is?*

For a time they stood shoulder to shoulder watching the dancers in their fairy-tale costumes, the vampire and the girl.

Lydia's dreams changed, fleeted. She saw them again, this time in another garden, wide parterres of topiary and *tapis verte*, when he taught the dark-haired girl to waltz in the moonlight under the blank eyes of marble gods. Saw them later kiss beneath the gargoyles of an archway, among crowded houses built on a bridge, torchlight and lamplight from the windows above them red as jewels in Ysidro's eyes. Through another window—two windows, for Lydia herself was in a dark room across an alley that plunged sixty feet down into a canyon of night—she saw Ysidro lying wounded on the girl's sparse bed, the girl bending over him in some kind of old-fashioned garb, knotting dressings over a sword cut in his chest that would have killed a living man. Ysidro moved his hand a little, and the girl bent down to press her lips to his.

"You are different from all these others," she heard him say, in the curtained embrasure of a palace window, the sound of violins like fragile perfume amid the talk and laughter of dancers. Palace of Versailles, Lydia guessed vaguely from the cut of Ysidro's plum-colored silk coat. "How sick I have grown of them, through all eternity. I had not thought to find a woman like you." He raised the girl's hand to his lips.

"We have known one another, loved one another, down through endless time." He wrapped the girl in the dense velvet weight of his cloak as they stood alone in winter-locked woodlands, moonlight shiny on a meringue of snow beyond the barred shadows of the copse in which they stood. The girl's hair was disheveled, her gown torn, and Lydia knew that Ysidro had rescued her from some peril, and that the bodies of dead men lay out of sight in the gully by a winter-silent stream. Lydia's own feet were cold in shoes wet with slush as she stood behind a tree with the wet weight of her skirt sticking to her ankles. "Do you not remember?"

The girl in brown—it was the same brown dress as before, with the puffed sleeves and wide collar ten years behind current mode—whispered, "I remember, Simon. I remember . . . everything," and their mouths met in the zebra moonlight.

No! cried Lydia, and though her breath swirled in a diamond cloud, she could produce no sound. *He's lying to you! He's going to kill you!* Horrified, she fought to run toward them, but black thorns caught her skirts, held her back. She tried to pull free, and the branches cracked beneath her fingers like dried insects. She woke to find herself clutching the bony fragments of hawthorn twig that lay on her pillow.

Lydia took the two o'clock train for Paris. Even after that strange farrago of romantic interludes by moonlight faded from her dreams, she kept waking with the icy sense that a slender shadow with yellow eyes waited just outside her door. By the time she was awake, bathed, laced, dressed, packed, powdered, perfumed, made-up, and had fixed her hair—no small accomplishment without a maid—and considered herself fit to be viewed by the public, she had missed both the morning trains. Never again, she thought, will I stay at an inconspicuous hotel just to avoid questions from my family. She reached Paris shortly after nine that night, missing the train to Vienna by an hour and a half—it left from another station in any case—and registered, travel-weary and aching, at the Hotel St. Petersbourg that Thomas Cook and Sons had obligingly contacted on her behalf the day before.

Paris, at least, she knew from her days of debutante shopping and educational sightseeing, and later from medical conferences. Her French was good, and she understood how to handle herself in this milieu. Perhaps, she reflected, the journey would be easier than she feared, as long as she took everything methodically, one step at a time, like a complicated dissection or a series of analyses of unknown secretions.

Again she slept badly, her dreams filled with the dark-haired girl in brown and Don Simon Ysidro rescuing each other from the cardinal's guards and trading kisses on the sands of moon-soaked Moroccan deserts. Waking in the darkness, comforter drawn up to her chin, she stared at the slits of reflected street-lamp outlining the shutters and listened to the voices of the café down in the street below, wondering where James was and if he was all right. Milk wagons were creaking in the streets when she finally slept.

The Vienna Express didn't leave until seven-thirty that evening, so there was plenty of time, not only to pack and dress properly and have the hotel maid fix her hair, but to do a little shopping at the Magasins du Printemps, which lay just down the street.

She was buttering a croissant in the almost empty dining room and speculating about the pathology of Don Simon Ysidro's fingernails—clearly there had been an organic change of some kind, so the physical side of the vampire syndrome did not involve complete cellular stasis—when she heard the solitary waiter murmur, *"B'njour, m'mselle,"* and glanced up to see another woman enter the room. Even at this distance and without her spectacles, Lydia deduced this woman to be harmless: tallish and slightly stooped, she moved with the uncertainty of one who feels herself to be half a foreigner even in her own country, let alone in a land where she doesn't speak the language.

The next second she frowned, wondering why she thought she recognized her. There was something familiar about her, and as the woman drew near and came a little more into focus, Lydia realized what it was.

She was wearing a brown dress with the puffed sleeves and wide collar fashionable in the nineties.

Lydia set down her coffee cup.

"Mrs. Asher?" The woman stopped beside her table, fidgeting her hands in mended gloves, a look of anxiety in her blue eyes. She was about twenty-three, much more awkward than she'd been in the dreams, and, like Lydia when Lydia knew nobody would see her, wore eyeglasses. "Don Simon told me I'd find you here."

FOUR

A WALTZ from Tchaikovsky's *Nutcracker* ballet had been popular in Vienna the year Asher spent in and out of that city. Closing his eyes to the lulling rock of the train, Asher could hear it again, drawing in its colored wake the bright glimmer of gaslight in the Café New York on the Opernring during Carnival season, the sparkle of snow on the pavements, the slurry patter of French and Italian and Viennese German all around. Court gossip and psychoanalysis, music and politics and whose wife was betraying whom. Thirteen years later it was still as clear as yesterday.

Young matrons in their masks and costumes questing nervously for unspecified excitement. Uniformed officers, gay in swords and spurs and braid.

Françoise.

"Nothing here is as it seems," she had said the night he walked with her to the café after a St. Valentine's Ball given by her brother; and that, at least, he had known was true about himself.

She was a thin-faced woman of his own age, his own height; though to be thirty-five and almost six feet tall, and of a strong cast of feature, had always been something only considered attractive in men. Her brother was a director of the biggest bank in Vienna and owned farms, vineyards, blocks of flats in the Seventh District. His wife, the second daughter of a baron, had been trying for years to marry Françoise off in diplomatic circles.

Asher wondered if she had ever married. Had ever trusted another man.

"People pass the days away in cafés like this, sipping coffee, reading the feuilletons, watching the world go by." She moved one shoulder in a graceful shrug, her smile rueful and a little sad. She was a biscuit-colored woman, but the emeralds in her earrings caught sparkling echoes in her eyes. "Outsiders think it's all very relaxed, very gemütlich, but it's really because most of the people here live in one-room apartments, they and their families together, and they can't stand the smell of cooking and dirty diapers and the arguing of their children. So they come here and look leisured and carefree because that is exactly what they are not.

"We here in Vienna have a hundred separate degrees of nobility and bureaucrats, titles and order and neatness and rules, and underneath, the Slovenes and Serbs and Czechs and Moldavians and Muslims are all clamoring to have their own nations, their own schools, their own languages, their own crowns. They bomb and shoot and riot and scheme with the Russians and the British and whoever else they think will help them break free."

Her big hands in long gloves of ivory kid darted, as if forming illustrative patterns that Asher could not see. He had first encountered her at a Twelfth Night ball in his guise as a professor of folklore. Folklore was always popular in Vienna, the more bizarre the better, and in exchange for arcana on Japanese werewolves and Chinese milkweed fairies, Asher had met a number of the aforesaid Serbs and Czechs and Moldavians and was beginning to find out just who they were scheming with on the subject of riots, bombs, and freedom from Austrian control.

He hadn't really needed to seek out Françoise a second time. But he had.

"When we complain," she went on, "it isn't really a complaint. When we weep, it isn't necessarily out of pain; and when we dance, it isn't always for joy. Yes isn't really yes, and no is seldom no, and the palaces you see mostly aren't really palaces, and everyone talks about everything except what really consumes their thoughts."

Her dark brows drew down over those bright green eyes as she considered him, skirting the brink of questions that she wasn't sure she wanted answered or even asked.

"We don't always know whether what we're seeing is real or a mask."

Asher's eyes had met hers, and he hadn't known what to reply.

I spoke to you last week to find out which of your young officer friends are deepest in debt.

I'm here to learn things that could get your armies defeated, your country disgraced, your friends and nephew killed.

I think I love you.

He wasn't sure just when that last had happened.

For a time they regarded one another without masks. Even now, looking back on it from the edge of dreaming, Asher didn't know what he would have said, had she asked him then.

But she smiled and put her mask back on, and held out her hand. "It's the 'Waltz of the Flowers,' " she said. "Do you dance?"

He had never been back to Vienna.

He pulled himself brutally from the edge of sleep. It was too early to sleep. The lights of Paris were barely behind them: St. Denis, Gagny, Vaires-sur-Marne spilled firefly glints into the indigo dark. Asher sipped the café noir he'd tipped the porter to bring to his private compartment—the compartment he'd managed to secure at the last possible moment, leaving himself again, he reflected dourly, with only five pounds in his pocket.

But on the Paris-Vienna Express it was imperative that he travel first class if he wanted access to the car where Karolyi and Ernchester would be. He knew himself incapable of remaining awake another night in second class. In first class he would be safer, less likely to be seen by either Ernchester or Karolyi.

Karolyi.

Nothing here is as it seems to be.

That same Carnival evening he'd seen Karolyi surrender a dance with the most attractive heiress in Vienna that season to go outside and stop a carter from whipping his horse. Françoise's comment had been, "Laying it on a bit thick, no?" And, to Asher's raised brow: "You must have noticed he only does such things where others will see." Asher had noticed, but to his knowledge, no one else had, save Françoise.

He hadn't had time to telegraph Lydia. Nor Streatham, telling him Cramer was dead.

Streatham would have left his office at six anyway, Asher reflected sardonically, and wouldn't be back till twenty minutes past nine in the morning. Dear God, had it only been that morning?

When he closed his eyes, he could see the brassy-haired prostitute, back arched like a bow above the seat of the chair, flopping and kicking her legs as her body gave up its life.

Could see the dark glitter of Cramer's blood where the rats had gnawed his face.

He feared his dreams, but they drank him in, like water flowing down into darkness.

He thought, *I've been in this room before. When have I been in this room?* Beyond shrouded windows rain streamed down, sodden and heavy; if there had been furniture in the room once, all had been cleared, but for a table at one end. Shawled with drippings, the guttered stumps of candles burned in tall holders, two at the head, two at the feet, and their light made daffodil thumbprints on the velvet pall that draped one end of the table like a thrown-back counterpane and winked in the jeweled leaves of a coronet set in the black cloth's midst. The dream had the taste of very distant memory, and he somehow knew that it was deep, deep in the night.

A woman lay on the yellow marble floor before the table, like a second pall dropped by a careless servitor, awkward in corsets and bum rolls and strange pennoncels of ribbon. Her hair was black, except where the candle flame breathed on it a cinnamon light. Its puffs and volutes, like those of her clothing, were in tangled disarray.

"Anthea." Another woman came down the room's length,

passed within touching distance of Asher, or where Asher would have been had any of this ever really occurred. "Anthea, you must come to bed." Even drugged with sleep, Asher identified the longer vowels in *come* and *bed*, the elongated *ou*, and thought automatically, *Late seventeenth century*. This new woman also wore black. Against ebon lace cascading from high combs, her face seemed lifeless, her eyes swollen and red. " 'Tis long gone midnight, and the mourners away to their homes." She knelt in a sighing waterfall of back-draped skirts and touched the prone woman's arm.

"How can he be dead?" It was a deep voice for a woman's, low but very clear. There were no tears in it, only a tired wonderment, as if she really wanted to know. The odd thing was that Asher recognized it but remembered a modern pronunciation, unlike the one she used now.

"I don't . . . I don't feel as if he were. Did I walk up the stairs, would he not be waiting at the top?" A ribboned fontange snagged in her hair, tilted drunkenly as she raised her head, then slithered to the floor unheeded. Though he was at least twenty feet from her, Asher knew her eyes were the color of last autumn's oak leaves, matted at the bottom of a pool.

"I felt so, when my Andrew died." The other woman put a hand to Anthea's side to help her up. Anthea rose unsteadily, tall and wholly beautiful though her clothing was askew from lying on the floor. The flesh of her breasts rose in creamy mountains above the flattening of her bodice, and small shadows marked the paler line of her collarbone, the curves of her broad-set cheeks. "Believe me, my darling," said her friend, "he is dead."

Slowly, like a very old woman, Anthea stepped forward, reaching to touch the velvet pall where, Asher realized, a coffin had lain. Her voice was very small, like a child's. "I don't understand what they expect me to do without him."

She turned and walked the length of the room, as if she did not see her friend who followed in her wake. Certainly she did not see Asher, though her black skirts brushed the tips of his boots and he smelled the musky blend of ambergris, funeral incense, and womanhood that sighed from her clothing. Her

tall lace headdress lay on the floor where it had fallen, like a
broken black rose.

"Steffi, darling, you do realize how *dreary* you are when
you're jealous?"

Asher jolted awake, sunlight in his eyes, his neck stiff and
the gentle, persistent rocking of the train still tapping in his
bones. He slumped back into the corner of the seat again and
listened as Steffi—whoever Steffi was—rumbled some reply
in harsh Berlin *hoche Deutsch* as he and his baby-voiced Viennese girlfriend passed down the corridor outside, toward the
restaurant car presumably. Asher reached up and switched off
the still-burning electric lamp above his seat, then pressed the
porcelain button to summon a porter. When he ordered shaving
water—accompanied by a tip he couldn't well afford—Asher
asked the time.

"It is five minutes past ten in the morning in Vienna, sir,"
said the man in Italian-accented French. "Ten minutes past
nine in Paris. Myself, I should put local time at quarter of ten."

Asher, who had reset his watch to Paris time but had been
too exhausted to wind it last night, set it again. "Have they
done with serving breakfast?"

"They will have by the time m'sieu has finished shaving."
The porter touched his cap. Venetian, Asher guessed. Dark, but
with the extraordinary sensual beauty that even the crones of
that ancient republic possessed like a birthright. "I could bring
m'sieu a little something."

Asher handed him another silver two-franc piece, reflecting
that porters on the Vienna Express would undoubtedly pocket
anything from dollars to piastres. "You wouldn't happen to
know whether the Hungarian gentleman who's traveling with
the Englishman is still in the restaurant car, would you? Not,"
he added, holding up his hand, "that this matter need be mentioned to either of them."

The Italian's dark eyes brightened with interest, and Asher
added another franc. "A matter of family business."

"Ah." He nodded knowingly. "The Hungarian and the
Englishman, their light burned on throughout the night, though

of course because the curtain was closed I could see nothing of what passed within the compartment itself. But I know that they did not summon me to take down the bunks, and this morning when I go in to *ranger* the compartment, still they have not been slept in." He glanced meaningfully up at Asher's pristine bunk. Asher had locked the compartment door upon entering last night, and if this man had knocked, had slept through it.

When the porter—whose name, he said, was Giuseppe—returned with hot water, a breakfast tray, and coffee, he brought also the information that the Hungarian Herr Feketelo was no longer in the restaurant car. Following breakfast, Asher made his way unobtrusively down the corridor, banking on the fact that Karolyi, like his traveling companion, would sleep during the day. His own compartment was near the head of the coach, close to the accordion-fold bridge leading into the restaurant car. The compartment shared by Karolyi and Ernchester, according to Giuseppe, was close to the tail end. The next car in the train, Asher had already determined, was the baggage car.

It was sealed, but Asher had dealt often enough in duplicate seals and keys—and had seen enough of the sheer preternatural physical strength and agility of vampires—to know that this would present Ernchester no difficulties.

Asher expended several more francs from his dwindling resources on arrangements with Giuseppe to have his lunch also brought on a tray. It was certainly a more comfortable way to see Central Europe, he thought, than dodging around the Dinaric Alps with a price on his head, dogs—and Karolyi—on his trail, a pocketful of incriminating serial numbers from Swiss bank accounts, and a bullet in his shoulder. He listened to the voices passing in the corridor and kept his own curtain closed, watched the dark trees and fairy tale villages of the Black Forest rise and fold themselves over the lift of the Swabian Alps, with the higher gleam of white in the distance that marked the true Alps growing nearer as the train bent southward. At Munich the Express stopped for half an hour to add two second-class cars and another *wagons-lits* that had come down from Berlin, and Asher risked a dash to the station telegraph office to send two wires, one to Lydia telling her of his altered plans, and one to Streatham, informing him of the death of his agent.

He remained angry over that, not so much at Ernchester and Karolyi—it was, after all, a game they all played—but at Streatham, for assigning the least experienced of his men to a job that he should have known was dangerous. And, though he knew there was nothing else he could have done, at himself.

Crossing the great floor of the station under the weak gray daylight of the glass ceiling, Asher tried to remember who was in charge in Vienna these days. Perhaps no one he knew. Streatham had been right about the reorganization, of course. Fairport, at least, would still be in Vienna, unobtrusively operating his safe house out at his sanitarium in the Wienerwald, peddling rejuvenation to bankers and stockbrokers' wives, fussy and trembly with his ill health and his cotton gloves and that fanatic glint in his pale blue eyes.

Asher smiled, recalling the three days he'd spent with that comic-opera hypochondriac, journeying to some remote Czech village so Fairport could interview a peasant brother and sister who were contemporaries of his own great-grandparents, and so Asher could trace local variations of the verb *byti* or *biti*—and have a look at a forest road leading into Saxony that, for no good reason, had been widened and repaired with funds from Berlin. The old man hadn't taken off his gloves for the entire trip, had warmed the snow water of the streams because it was better for the liver, and had brought his own food, his own sheets, his own soap. The local peasants had shaken their heads and given him names of their own—"the laundry maid" and "Grandmother English"—and the innkeeper at one village had taken Asher aside and gravely asked if it were true that in the City—meaning Vienna—they had doctors who could cure people of such ailments. Asher had been hard put to explain that Grandmother English *was* such a doctor.

He grinned at the memory and settled into his compartment again with a feeling of having successfully dodged through a complicated obstacle course. In addition to sending the telegrams, he had purchased the *Neue Freie Presse* and two spring-operated children's toys: a bear that clashed cymbals when wound with a key; a donkey whose four legs moved so that, if carefully balanced, it would more or less walk. He put them through their paces on the table, deeply and gravely entertained.

Other passengers were reboarding, armed with fresh books, magazines, newspapers, candy, or pastry. Through the window he glimpsed the man who had to be the jealous Steffi and his fairylike Viennese girlfriend, her arms full of fresh flowers, and smiled a little at the capacity of humans to believe what they wish to believe.

There was a beautiful dowager in an impeccable Worth suit, trailed by a cowed-looking maid and three little black French bulldogs; a white-bearded gentleman with the face of a warrior monk, and a boy who might have been his grandson or a servant hurrying in his wake. Karolyi, clean-shaven and fresh, a winter rose in his buttonhole, strode lightly along the platform, pausing to remove his hat when he spoke to a shabby girl selling peanut brittle. Asher saw by the girl's face that he'd considerably overpaid her, and remembered the brassy-haired whore again, tied to her chair. He wondered if the police had found her body yet.

Why Ernchester?

His mind gyred back to the question as the train rocked into motion once again.

Why an Englishman at all? Had the Vienna vampires refused to cooperate with an Austrian offer? Not as odd as it might sound: the Viennese, in Asher's experience, had their own rationale for doing things, an idiosyncratic frivolity that could encompass any reason from Czech or Hungarian—or Serbian or Moldavian or Venetian—nationality to a personal opinion that the Emperor was an old fuddy-duddy whom they disdained to serve.

And indeed, whatever promises the government made, Asher knew the vampires were right to guard their anonymity. Having been a spy for seventeen years, he knew too well that no government—certainly not his own—could be trusted to keep any promise it made.

It still didn't explain why an English, rather than a French or a German, vampire had been approached.

Or had they? He paused in the act of dismembering the key-wound bear, a half-farcical vision rising in his mind of the sealed baggage car stacked high with coffins and trunks in which slumbered the vampires of Paris; of himself, strolling innocently into the restaurant car to face table after table of chalk-white, bone-thin faces and a sea of eyes that burned like actinic flame.

When it came down to it, what the hell was he going to do once he reached Vienna? Try to hand the problem over to another incompetent and reluctant Department head? Get some other young novice killed?

He unfolded his bunk, undressed, and slept again, to wake from uneasy dreams with the sensation he'd had in dealing with vampires before, of having had his mind momentarily blanked. In silence he swiftly rolled from his bunk, the compartment around him lit only by the yellow glow from the passage leaking around the edges of the curtain. It showed him an empty compartment—certainly there was nowhere to hide, for there was barely room for one person, let alone two—and he pressed his face to the edge of the door, moving the curtain just enough to see past it.

Karolyi and Ernchester were walking up the corridor, Karolyi speaking with eloquent gestures of his white-gloved hands, Ernchester expressionless, very small and thin beside him.

"It does not do, you understand, to spend the entire journey in one's compartment. For one thing, the porters gossip."

"I see no reason why the prattle of groundlings touches us." Ernchester's voice was so low as to be almost inaudible, and Asher wondered why the elongated *ou* and open-ended *ea* rang so familiar in his ear. Who had he heard recently, he wondered, speaking with that archaic inflection? "There is nothing in this 'train' "—he spoke the word as if it were foreign to him—"of interest to me. If, as you say, we shall be in Vienna some days . . ."

They passed beyond his hearing. Asher found his watch, angled it to the slit of incoming light. It was a few minutes past six-thirty, Vienna time. Karolyi must have just released Ernchester from the baggage car, once more replacing a seal with a duplicate. It was the subtle touch of the vampire's mind on all those in the car that he had felt in his sleep. Outside Asher's window the Alps glimmered eerie blue under the stars.

He dressed swiftly and stole down the corridor, listening for voices in the other compartments. Silence reigned. Most of them, he guessed, were already at dinner. The lock on Karolyi's compartment yielded readily to the wire tools he'd constructed from the innards of donkey and bear. He searched deftly, thoroughly, though he knew Karolyi wasn't a man to leave information lying around. No notebooks, no letters, no addresses. A great deal of money in the valise, which Asher opened after carefully inspecting its lock and frame for bits of hair, wood chips, or gum; he abstracted two hundred florins in notes and also two of the dozen or so duplicate baggage-room seals.

Under the false bottom Asher found ten small boxes of wax and wood, which contained impressions of keys, probably to the baggage car—possibly to all baggage cars in use on the line. Asher pocketed them and replaced the clothing. By the time Karolyi noticed they were gone, they'd be off the train.

The valise also contained two folded Personals sections of the London *Times* from successive dates, and these he dared not take away with him. Time was passing swiftly; he didn't have time to scan them, knowing that there would be no mark on the advertisement. He made a note of the dates, folded them as they had been, and replaced the valise above the velvet seat.

A traveler's chess set stood on the table, its men neatly ranked for a game. Ernchester's old-fashioned, fiddlebacked greatcoat hung near the door beside Karolyi's wide-skirted one; Asher checked the pockets quickly, wondering where the vampire would stay once they reached Vienna.

Back in his own compartment again, he rang for the porter, ordered dinner brought to him, adding with a wink and a couple of francs that he was indisposed. "You wouldn't have the English *Times* on board, would you?"

"Certamente, sir," Giuseppe said, drawing himself up indignantly. "All the newspapers we have for our first-class passengers, of the latest editions."

"How about last Saturday's? Last Friday's, too, if possible?"

"Hmm. That I don't know, m'sieu. I shall ask, shall look about the porters' rooms . . ."

"Discreetly," Asher said. "You don't need to bring me the whole thing. Just the Personals." He raised one eyebrow and tilted his head wisely, and the porter bustled away with the air of one who sees himself an experienced international intrigant.

And perhaps he was, thought Asher. In his position he'd have the opportunity. In any case Giuseppe returned with a much-battered copy of Saturday evening's Personals, retrieved from the porters' lavatory, and Asher spent the next half hour scanning it for whatever message had arranged the meeting between the vampire and the Hungarian.

> *Olumsiz Bey—Front*
> *steps of British*
> *Museum, 7.—Umitsiz*

Asher had to read it twice before he realized it was what he sought.

Olumsiz was Turkish for *deathless*—or perhaps *undead*. *Umitsiz*, for *hopeless*—or perhaps for the British form of the name *Wanthope*, the collateral name of the Earls of Ernchester, one of several under which Charles Farren had many years ago willed property to himself.

Curious. Why Turkish? Asher folded the paper, slipped it into his valise. *Deathless Lord. Without Hope. Want-Hope. Wanthope. Deathless Lord . . .*

Quite clearly Ernchester and Karolyi wanted to conceal their transactions. That would fit, if the other London vampires—who must surely read the Personals, nights being long for the Undead—frowned on an alliance. Would Grippen, the Master Vampire of London, know Turkish? Ysidro would, thought

Asher, oddly uneasy at the memory of that bleached Spanish
hidalgo who had, against the wishes of all the other London
vampires, first sought his help. The Ottoman Empire had been
a formidable power in the sixteenth century. It was conceivable
that Ysidro, a courtier and sometime scholar, would know
some of its ancient tongue. Conceivable, too, that the earl
would. Certainly likelier than, for instance, Hungarian, which
in that era had been the language of barbarians and herders,
people without power in the West. Any of the other London
vampires would almost certainly know German or French.

A Viennese or Hungarian vampire who had been made in
the sixteenth or seventeenth century would very probably
know the tongue of the armies that had repeatedly overrun
his land.

Asher looked at the top of the paper again. Saturday, October 31—and no copy of Friday's paper. What, he wondered,
had the summons said that made Ernchester so anxious to conceal his movements from the other London vampires,
including his wife?

Who was it who called himself the Deathless Lord?

Even at ten in the evening the Vienna Bahnhof was the swarm-
ing center of the comings and goings of an empire. Stepping
quickly from the train before it had even come to a complete
halt, striding along the platform to mingle with the crowd,
Asher felt the stab of homecoming—*nost-algia,* the pain
of remembering. There was no city in the world quite like
Vienna.

There were backcountry Jews in black caftans, tallis, and
side curls being resolutely ignored by their frock-coated Ger-
manic Reform co-religionists, Hungarian *csikos* in high boots
and baggy trousers, a tattered rainbow of Gypsies. There were
the Viennese themselves, ladies bundled in linen traveling
coats and veils to guard against smuts, brilliantly uniformed
men who might have been Lancers or postmen, children
clinging to black-clothed governesses, and students in bright-
colored caps. French, Italian, singsong Viennese German as

unlike as possible from the tongue of Berlin blended with Czech, Romanian, Yiddish, Russian, Ukrainian . . .

The air was redolent with coffee.

Vienna.

Illogically, as he made for the stand where the fiacres would be ranked—where Ernchester and Karolyi would head the moment the customs officials were through with their luggage—Asher found himself holding his breath, fearing that somehow, impossibly, he would meet Françoise.

He had dreamed about her, in his uneasy sleep that afternoon; a dream threaded with waltzes. She was walking along the Schottenring, past the marble and stucco and gilt of the great blocks of flats, through the crystal light of a spring evening. She looked not as she had looked thirteen years ago, but as she must look now, her hair almost completely gray, and lean as certain cats get as they age; rather like a cat in a gray walking suit tabbied with black lace.

I'm sorry, Françoise.

As he watched her, he had been piercingly aware of the ornate bronze gratings in the walls at sidewalk level, brushed by the gunmetal taffeta of her skirt. There was movement in the darkness, he realized, movement beneath the pavement under her feet; whispering in the shadows, eyes in the dark. Waiting only for the coming of night.

They were in Vienna as well.

Françoise, get out of there! he tried to shout. *Go to your home, light the lamps, don't let them in. Don't speak to them, when they meet you on the pavement . . .*

But because of what he had done, thirteen years ago, she could not hear him or would not heed. She walked on, and it seemed to him that gray mist drifted up through those bronze gratings and breathed after her down the street.

He shook the recollection away. It was not likely that he would meet her—she might not even live in Vienna anymore—and in any case, the love between them was past and done. And there was nothing for which he would trade the prospect of living the rest of his life with Lydia, that copper-haired, bespectacled nymph.

But still there was that ache in his heart whenever he heard the "Waltz of the Flowers."

"Herr Professor Doktor Asher?"

He turned, startled, halfway to the cab stand, his first thought, *Not now!* Karolyi and Ernchester would be along in minutes . . .

Two brown-uniformed Viennese policemen stood behind him. Both bowed.

"You are the Herr Professor Doktor Asher who has just come from the Paris-Vienna Express?"

"I am, Herr Oberhaupt." The old Viennese custom of bestowing titles on everyone dropped immediately back into place, along with the lilting, slightly Italianate Viennese accent. "Is there a problem? I presented my passport . . ."

"No, no problem with the passport," said the policeman. "We regret extremely that you are wanted for questioning in connection with the murder of a man in Paris, a Herr Edmund Cramer. Will you be so good as to accompany us to the Rathaus?"

Shocked, for a moment Asher could only stare. Then a string of Czech curses caught his ear, and he looked around in time to see a couple of porters loading an enormous, brass-cornered trunk onto a goods wagon, observed by Karolyi and the Earl of Ernchester. Karolyi happened to turn his head and for a moment met Asher's eyes.

He tipped his wide-brimmed hat and smiled. The last Asher saw of them as he was escorted out of the station, spy and vampire were making their leisurely way to the rank of cabs.

FIVE

"WE knew each other in a former lifetime, you see." Miss Margaret Potton looked up from picking at a loose thread on the button of her left sleeve, and behind lenses as massive as Lydia's own—had Lydia been wearing them in so public a forum as the Hotel St. Petersbourg's dining room—her blue eyes had a look of wary defiance. "Many lifetimes. It's as if I always knew, all my life. All my life I must have been having those dreams, only to forget them absolutely, completely, in the morning."

" 'Must have'?" quoted Lydia, trying to keep her fury at Ysidro out of her voice. "When? If you forgot them that completely, how do you know you had them 'all your life'? Do you honestly remember any prior to last night?"

The small mouth set stubbornly. "Yes. Yes, I do. Now."

Lydia said nothing. *That cad!* was all that came to her mind, and she thought, *Surely there's a more descriptive word than that. James is a linguist. I must ask him about it.*

Miss Potton looked up again and set her shallow chin. "That is, I knew I had dreamed something important. I always had the knowledge that I was dreaming about something—something beautiful, something critical, something that would change my life. Only I never remembered, until last night."

"I've never heard anything so idiotic in my life!" All the lurid dreams returned to her, love, rescue, waltzing on moonlit

76

terraces, she witty and he laying his reluctant heart at her feet. "Last night he wanted you to *think* you remembered. Because it was convenient for him . . ."

"No." A beetroot stain blotched thin cheeks. "Yes. In a way. Because he needed me." She returned to picking at her sleeve button. "When he came to me last night—when I woke in the moonlight and saw him standing there at the foot of the bed—he said he would never have crossed my life again, would have forced himself to stay away from me, for my own good, except that he needed me. Needed my help. You don't understand him."

"And you do?"

"Yes." She didn't look up.

Lydia drew in her breath, but she felt obliquely that if she came anywhere close to her true feelings, she would probably scream, and that obviously wouldn't do in the dining room of the Hotel St. Petersbourg. Rage at Ysidro drowned her fear—her fear of him, of Ernchester, of the vast uncharted ocean of the world outside university research.

The word she wanted, she realized, was *vampire*.

Miss Potton raised her head and went on, "I understand that his kind need people they can trust. He told me they will seek for years for a human being large enough of spirit to accept them for what they are, in whose hands they dare to lay their lives. I was . . . he and I were . . . This was how it was between us for . . . for many lifetimes in the past. He said he always knew where I was, but deliberately never contacted me in this lifetime, because in a former life I . . . I was killed in his service."

"That's the most ridiculous—"

"That's all you can say." Miss Potton regarded her with a steady, pale, fanatic gaze. "But I remember it. I've remembered it all my life in dreams. I just—didn't recall it until last night. And he needed me again, he needed someone, to journey to Vienna . . ."

"He needed a duenna for me at half a day's notice!" cried Lydia, appalled. "I don't know which is worse, that kind of old-fashioned absurdity or what he's done . . ."

"He is an antique gentleman," Miss Potton said calmly.

"He is a killer! Not to mention a bigoted Catholic and the most unconscionable snob in shoe leather, and you're a fool if you believe—"

"He isn't bigoted!" The waiter came, bringing a cup of café au lait the size of a soup bowl. Miss Potton looked up at him anxiously, as if fearing he would demand payment of her on the spot. Only when he left again without a word did she turn back to Lydia, an eager intensity illuminating her face. "During the Massacre of St. Bartholomew's Day, in the wars of religion in France, Don Simon had a Huguenot servant who sacrificed his life to keep him from being burned by the Inquisition. Later he and I saved that servant's family, got them on a boat for the Americas . . ."

Lydia stared at her, unable even to reply. Even at the distance of the table's width, Miss Potton was a blurred figure, in her brown wool frock made for someone else and badly altered. Her squashy black velvet hat—startlingly similar to the one Lydia had borrowed from her cook—was years out of date. The spectacles hadn't made it into the dreams.

"But I . . . I *know* I've dreamed about it before. All of it. Running along the beach, minutes before the first, fatal gleam of dawn; Don Simon turning back, sword drawn to hold the cardinal's men at bay while I got Pascalou's children into the rowboat. The way the sea smelled, and the mewing of the gulls."

Straight out of Dumas. And unforgivable. Lydia tried to stir her coffee and gave it up, for her hand was shaking too badly. For all her careful training in the social niceties, in fashionable flirtation and dinner conversation, she had always regarded the majority of humanity as a slightly alien species, possessors of fascinating circulatory and endocrine systems but, with a few exceptions like James and Josetta and Anne and Ellen, detached from herself and her concerns and largely incomprehensible. She had, literally, not the slightest idea of how to go about warning this poor silly child, talking to her, reaching her through the vampire glamour of dreams.

"Miss Potton," she said at last, in a voice kept level only by years of deportment lessons, "please thank Don Simon for me, but tell him that I'm a grown-up woman and quite prepared to travel by myself. I don't need a lady-in-waiting, as he seems to think. And I don't need him. But if you'll take my advice—"

She saw Miss Potton grow rigid at the word and realized despairingly that she must have said the wrong thing. But she couldn't think of anything else to say. "If you'll take my advice, go back to London." It only made her sound patronizing, she thought in despair. "Have nothing further to do with Don Simon. If you dream about him again, pay no attention. If you see him in the flesh—"

"I can't go back." Her small, stiff mouth wore a smirk of triumph. "I gave Mrs. Wendell my notice yesterday morning at breakfast. I'd been up, packing, since three, since Don Simon came to me in my room, spoke to me, woke me from all those years of dreaming. I told her to find someone else to look after her nasty children, for I was done with such things forever."

Lydia could just imagine how her aunt Harriet would have greeted such an announcement from Nana over her lightly buttered toast and China tea some rainy morning . . . Not that Nana would ever have done anything so irregular. The poor girl would never get another job. Done with such things forever indeed!

"I have no family," Miss Potton went on, with that same oblique pride. "I have put myself, my fate, into Don Simon's hands, as he has put himself into mine. And it feels . . . right. True. Good."

"*Anything* would," Lydia argued, startled, "after spending— how many years were you with Mrs. Wendell?—looking after someone else's children."

The young woman's mouth flinched, and as she averted her eyes, Lydia caught the quick shine of tears. Her first anger was subsiding, and Lydia could see that this awkward girl was only a few years younger than she, and as homely. But Miss Potton had never learned to use fashion and artifice to conceal that fact—or had never had the money to do so.

No wonder Ysidro had found her an easy target when he'd

gone questing through London that night, looking for someone whose dreams to invade.

"I'm sorry . . ." Lydia fumbled at the words. But of course once words are said, there is no *I'm sorry*.

Miss Potton shook her head. "No," she said, and took a sip of coffee to steady herself. Her voice lost some of its melodramatic ring. "No, you're right. I've been wanting for years to get out of there, to find something else. David and Julia really are the most horrid brats. But that doesn't mean that what Don Simon told me is any the less true. I think I was looking for a way out because I *knew* there was another possibility. As if the memories of those other times, those other lives, though I couldn't recall them, were alive within me, telling me there was something more."

"They were not." Lydia felt like a monster, wresting a cherished new doll from a child's hand on Christmas morning, breaking it with a hammer before those disbelieving blue eyes.

But there was a scorpion in that doll. A white mantis, thin and stalky and preternaturally still, watching from the shadows with terrible eyes.

"A year ago Ysidro told my husband that vampires can read the dreams of the living," Lydia went on slowly. "Ysidro is a very old vampire, a very skilled vampire—one of the oldest still in existence, in Europe at any rate. Obviously, he can do more than just read dreams. The—The task I need to perform in Vienna requires his help, and what's at stake is sufficiently important to him that he wants to go with me, but he refuses to do so unless I conform to his medieval standard of womanly conduct. I'm surprised he didn't insist that I bring a chaplain and an embroiderer as well. He picked you because he thought he could get you to leave everything behind and go with him— go with me—at a day's notice."

Miss Potton said nothing but looked down again, picking at a small mend in the finger of her glove.

"Go back to London," Lydia said. "Tell Mrs. Wendell that you had to deal with the affairs of a wastrel brother or a drunken father, and even if she's found another governess, she'll probably relent enough to give you a character for your next post. *Don't do this.* Don't let Ysidro do this to you."

Miss Potton still said nothing. A motorcar went past on the Boulevard de la Madeleine, popping and sputtering like a company of American cowboys on the rampage. Somewhere a tram horn blatted.

"This isn't any concern of yours. Tell Ysidro that he's . . . he's welcome to join me in my journey, but that I *will not* bring a third party into it, either of his choosing or my own . . . Though you probably don't even know where he's staying, do you?"

"No." She had to guess at the word from the movement of Miss Potton's lips.

"No." Lydia remembered the hidden trapdoors, the new locks, the house, the square that was no longer on any London map. She picked up her handbag and brought out a slim roll of notes. "Take this and go back to England this afternoon."

Miss Potton stood up, straightening the back that had long ago acquired the mousy stoop of the downtrodden. "I don't need your money," she said quietly. "I trust Don Simon will take care of me."

And she walked from the room in a dignified rustle of skirts.

Lydia reached the Gare de l'Est at seven. Too sick at heart to visit the *magasins* for which Paris was famous, she had nevertheless forced herself to walk down the Rue St. Denis to the Halles Centrales—the great central produce market of the city—and purchase garlic, wolfsbane, and wild rose. As she walked along the platform toward the Vienna Express, trailed by two porters with her hatboxes and trunks, she reflected that it must have taken astonishing courage for Margaret Potton to resign her post as governess, pack her few possessions, and cross the Channel to a land where she'd probably never been and had only an academic acquaintance with the language; to walk into the dining room of a foreign hotel and up to a complete stranger and announce, "I know all about the journey you're making, and a vampire has sent me to accompany you."

She wasn't sure she could have done it.

To save Jamie?

It was, more or less, what she was doing now.

Lydia drew a deep breath.

Under ordinary circumstances her reaction to Miss Potton's revelation would have been bemused incredulity. People did and believed the most extraordinary things, which was one reason why Lydia had always been far more comfortable as a researcher. But she felt responsible for Miss Potton, for Ysidro's deadly lures, and it was depressing to realize that she could describe in detail the workings of that child's thymus without having the slightest idea of how to bring her to her senses.

It occurred to Lydia, belatedly, that her most effective course of action would have been a blank look and a cold "I *beg* your pardon?"

She could only hope, now, that Miss Potton would return to London . . .

To what?

Would Ysidro even let her return?

Damn him, she thought, renewed fury wiping out her sense of helplessness. *If he harms her, if he dares to harm her . . .*

But again, the inner voice whispered, *What?*

Miss Potton had made her choice.

And she had made hers. She was going to Vienna to deal with the vampire earl—and goodness knew what other vampires, not to mention the slippery intrigues of the Foreign Office—alone.

One step at a time, she thought.

If Jamie had wired her Monday from Munich, he must have reached Vienna Monday night. Today was Friday. Last night she had telephoned Mrs. Grimes from Charing Cross Station and ascertained that nothing further had been heard from him. Four days, she thought, with Dr. Fairport, potential traitor and seeker after immortality; four days with the hazards of Ernchester and Ignace Karolyi, and who knew what besides.

The porters loaded her luggage into the van, to be sealed for the journey to Vienna, and carried the smaller portmanteau and two hatboxes and an overnight case to the compartment Mr.

Cook and Company had booked for her, whose number she could probably have ascertained for herself had she been willing to squint a little. After her interview with Miss Potton, she had checked the hotel's copy of Bradshaw, seeking a train to Vienna that left before sundown, but though there were plenty of trains that would eventually take her there, via Zurich or Lyons or Strasbourg, none was faster than the Vienna Express. And speed was of the essence. James was in danger, trying to work with a flawed tool that could turn on him at any moment.

Or a prisoner already.

Or . . .

She put the thought from her.

The compartment was a comfortable one, embellished with rosewood paneling, velvet upholstery, and electrical light fixtures shaped like frosted lilies. Alone, Lydia unpinned the jade-and-eggplant fantasia of her hat and settled into her seat, gazing out the window at the impressionistic flower bed of color, shadow, and light that was the station platform, seeking, she realized, for the sturdy brown blob, the clumsy stride that would be Margaret Potton. After a moment she opened her handbag and fished forth her spectacles, a little startled, as always, at the sudden sharpness of people's faces, the lettering on the signs. According to the booklet on the little table before her, dinner would be served in the salon car at eight-thirty, but between anxiety about James and the obscure fear that even yet she would encounter Ysidro, she doubted she would feel much hunger. Her head ached, and she realized she hadn't eaten anything since the three-quarters of a croissant she'd consumed before Margaret Potton had entered the dining room at the hotel.

She watched through the window until the train began to move. Then she settled back and closed her eyes, and breathed a sigh.

Jamie . . .

"If I may say so, mistress," murmured a voice like the sudden slide of silk over unexpecting bare skin, "you make yourself difficult to look after. Were I your husband, I would school you."

Lydia whipped around in her seat, stomach lurching—anger, fear, and, against her will, a deep flash of relief that she'd have some kind of help and advice. Her relief angered her still more, and she replied tartly, "Were you my husband, I would demand a separate establishment." She pulled off her eyeglasses and slipped them behind her hat.

He stood in the doorway, ivory and shadow. As in his tomb, only the slender hands, the gold ring, caught the light. Behind him, spectacle lenses flashed in the corridor.

"You behold it." He stepped inside and his small gesture took in the rosewood, the velvet, the frosted lily lamps.

He had fed. She could see the faint color that stained his white face and close mouth, so that he appeared more nearly human in the staring light.

Sickness filled her that she had ever felt relief. That she had ever asked help or advice of such a thing.

"Miss Potton has taken a compartment at the other end of the carriage," Ysidro went on. "It would be our pleasure, would you join us there for cards."

Lydia stood up, slender and straight in her traveling dress of carnation faille, jet and amber glittering. "Send her home."

"I've already told you I don't have—" began Miss Potton, and Ysidro raised a finger.

"This is not possible."

"Will it not be possible after we return from Vienna?" Lydia's face was almost as chalky as the vampire's. "Are you going to kill her when you're safe in London again? And me, and James, to secure the secrets you hope to stop Ernchester from telling the Austrians?"

His expression did not change, but she was aware of thoughts passing through the sulfur-crystal mazes of his eyes. Thinking about options? she wondered. Or only about what kind of story she was likely to believe?

"You have admirably guarded the secrets you learned a year ago," he said after a time. "They are no more believable now than they were then. And I believe Miss Potton as capable of keeping them as yourself."

The train lurched a little, going over the points; lights cascaded past the window. In the corridor a small dog barked furiously and a woman crooned, *"Là, tais-toi, p'tit malin!"*

"I understand that dinner will be served at half past eight." Ysidro's fingers moved toward the folder on the table but did not touch it. Like everything about him, the gesture was minimal, as though long years had wearied him of all but the smallest symbols of what had been human mannerism, human expression, human speech. Lydia was suddenly reminded of the worn stones of a field circle in a pasture near Willoughby Close, her childhood home, like the white stumps of teeth protruding from olive turf.

"I suggest you ladies partake, if so be your wish, and return after to Miss Potton's compartment. Do you play picquet, mistress? The most excellent of games, and the representation in little of all human affairs. I assure you," he added, saffron gaze meeting the brown, "that neither you nor she has aught to fear of me."

"I never did," Margaret said from the doorway. Ysidro did not so much as shift his eyes.

Lydia said, "I don't believe you."

The vampire bowed. "This news breaks my heart."

And he was gone. Margaret, who no more than Lydia had seen him go, looked startled, then hastened away down the corridor without so much as an excuse, leaving Lydia standing alone.

Miss Potton returned half an hour later, tapping gently on the curtained glass. Lydia, who in the intervening time had neither resumed her spectacles nor taken from her portmanteau the issue of *Journal des Études Physiochemiques* she had brought for entertainment, turned from a somewhat blank contemplation of the lights fleeing by in the darkness and said, "Come."

The governess stepped inside, holding to the doorway as if afraid of rebuke. She'd dispensed with her deplorable hat. Her hair, tightly prisoned in pins on the top of her head, was the one thing about her that was truly as it had been in the dreams, thick, heavy, silky, and black as night.

I did call her a fool, thought Lydia, seeing the hesitation in the other woman's eyes.

But she is *a fool!*

But telling her so again would not break Ysidro's hold on her.

Lydia took a deep breath, rose to her feet and held out her hand. "I'm sorry," she said. "I don't trust him, but that's no reason to . . . to be angry with you."

Miss Potton smiled tremulously in return. She had envisaged, Lydia realized, a journey in company with a frozenly hostile traveling companion, reason enough to look wretched. "You can trust him, you know," she said, her blue eyes widening with earnestness. "He is a true gentleman."

And a multiple murderer who hasn't been human for at least four hundred years. "I never doubted that," Lydia said. "Is he there?" She nodded down the corridor. When Margaret bobbed her head, she went on, "Would you wait here for me? There's something I need to say to him in private."

He was playing solitaire. An abacus, a small calculating machine, and a notebook lay on the table beside the spread of the cards. Four decks. The corridor lights made wan mirrors of his eyes. No light burned above the little table where he sat.

"You summoned her for me, because no lady travels alone, is this correct?"

The pale head inclined. In the near dark she had the impression of a skull surrounded by the spider strands of his long hair.

"Then the corollary would be that no lady travels with a known killer?"

"You've lain with one every night for seven years, mistress," replied the nearly soundless voice. "In my time ladies traveled with them regularly, quite sensibly, I might add, for protection." A white hand, almost disembodied in shadow, laid card upon card and shifted a column; flicked a bead in the abacus; made a note.

"In your time," Lydia persisted, "was it not customary for

gentlemen to respect the wishes of the ladies with whom they traveled?"

"If they were not foolish." He turned a card, made another note.

"I won't have you killing while we're traveling together."

Another card, colors indistinguishable in the cinder-colored gloom. He did not look at her. "Unless it be for your convenience?"

Lydia stood for a time, her breath coming fast. Then she turned and strode down the corridor to the restaurant car, leaving him alone turning cards in the dark.

SIX

"My dear Asher, a terrible mistake . . . a terrible mistake." Dr. Bedford Fairport fidgeted with the cuffs of his gray cotton gloves and flinched away from a stout blond policeman who came through the station-house duty room with a musically inclined drunk in tow. Much was made of Vienna's reputation as "The City of Music." Asher wondered whether this was what its enthusiasts had in mind. The drunks with whom he had shared his cell the previous night had both sung, though not always the same songs. One was a Wagnerian, the other a disciple of Richard Strauss. It had been a long night.

"Mistake, hell." Asher closed his valise, having satisfied himself that its contents—including the key waxes and counterfeit baggage-room seals in the secret pocket—were untouched. A uniformed clerk offered him a release to sign, then a paper for Fairport. "Karolyi must have seen me when I got off to telegraph Streatham in Munich. I suppose I should be glad it isn't worse."

"The honorable Herr will be staying with Herr Professor Doktor Fairport?"

Asher hesitated; Fairport said, "Yes, yes, of course. Not an imposition at all, my dear Asher," he added, as the two crossed the worn black marble floor and emerged into the chill, misty sunlight of the Ring. "In fact, since I've agreed to be responsible for your conduct, I'm sure the police wouldn't have it any other way. It will be quite like old times."

Asher grinned a little wryly, recalling the clean, small bedroom above what had been the old stables at Fruhlingzeit, the sanitarium tucked away in the quiet slopes of the Vienna Woods.

"You must have spent an appalling night!" Fairport twittered. "Hideously irresponsible—I shall write to the *Neue Freie Presse* about the ghastly misconduct of the police in putting simple witnesses wanted for questioning in the general cells! You could have caught anything in that cell, anything from tuberculosis to smallpox to cholera!" The old man coughed, and Asher remembered that Fairport had had tuberculosis—and smallpox—as a child. His milk-white skin was still marked with it, like ancient chewings of mice.

He did not look well now. But then, Fairport never looked quite well. Thirteen years ago, when he first met Fairport, Asher had been surprised when Maxwell—then head of the Vienna section—had told him the doctor was only fifty-four. Prematurely stooped, prematurely wrinkled, prematurely white-haired, he had the air of an almost-invalid that Asher did not consider much of an advertisement for his sanitarium.

The Viennese apparently thought otherwise. They flocked to the isolated villa and paid huge sums for "rest cures" and "rejuvenation" by means of chemicals, electricity, and esoteric baths. Looking down now at the bent little man beside him— even straight he wouldn't have topped Asher's shoulder by more than an inch—Asher wondered if Fairport's preoccupation with reversing the effects of age was part of his fury at the encroaching dissolution of his own body.

Fairport must be nearing seventy now, calculated Asher, and forced himself not to offer his help as the old man hobbled along the pavement. His face had the shrunken exhaustion of years, his hands—encased as always in the gray cotton gloves he bought by the dozen, washed after wearing once, and discarded weekly—trembled uncontrollably. Lydia, he found himself thinking, would have diagnosed something or other on the spot.

Even under clouds, Vienna had the air of brightness he recalled; the clifflike labyrinths of buildings cream or gold or brown with their pseudomarble garlands, their putti and grimacing tragedy/comedy masks; gilded ironwork, tiny balconies, great somber doors guarding flagstoned courtyards inside.

A short distance along the Ring a smart brougham drew up beside them, the black body of the closed coach varnished and gleaming, its brass hardware polished like gold. A big man wrapped in a coachman's long coat and muffler sat on the box, frowning under a simian brow ridge while a footman, equally tall, sprang from the rear platform to open the door. Asher reflected that the sanitarium must be doing well if the old man could afford this kind of turnout.

"You'll want a hot bath and a good rest, I daresay." Fairport gestured away his footman's proffered arm with a wave of his cane. "Thank you, Lukas . . . I've telephoned Halliwell—he's the head of the Vienna section these days, do you remember him?—to let him know you're in town, but this evening, if you're feeling up to it, will be early enough."

Asher considered. It was mid-morning, the mists from the canal barely diffuse in the bright air. Though they stood on the threshhold of winter, the cold seemed not so raw as that of London or Paris, the damp not so bitter. The air had a soft quality, like rose petals. In the Volksgarten a few hardy citizens sat behind the line of chain and potted trees that demarcated the terrace of a small kaffee haus, and Asher had a flashing recollection of true Viennese coffee and the concentrated sinfulness of a Creme Schnitten. Fruhlingzeit Sanitarium, isolated among woods and vineyards, was restful and silent but about an hour's drive from the outskirts of the town.

"If you don't mind," Asher said slowly, "there are things I need to do here. Someone I need to trace, without delay."

"Karolyi?" Fairport's almost hairless white brows formed little arches in the fish-belly forehead. "His addresses are quite well known. A town house in Döbling and a flat on the Kärtnerstrasse . . . I assume you're not interested in that ancestral castle at Feketelo in the Carpathians . . ."

"No." Asher shook his head. "No, someone else, someone whose name I don't know. And it may take me a little time in the Rathaus to find the records."

He knew it would have to be done, and his mind leaped ahead, calculating how long it might take and when the sun would set. He thought he would have time to do the thing in safety, but with an almost subconscious gesture he rubbed his wrist to feel, through glove and shirt cuff, the protective silver links.

"If I may abuse your hospitality so far, I think what I need to do is, first, find myself a public bath and get cleaned up, then start my search in the records office. How late might I come out to Fruhlingzeit without disturbing anyone to let me in?"

Fairport smiled, a dry little V-shaped quirk. "My dear Asher, this is Vienna! My staff remains active until nearly eleven, and I'm frequently at work in the laboratory until midnight. Right now there's no one staying at the sanitarium—we had some electrical troubles early in the week—so there's no trouble about that."

He fished in the pocket of his old-fashioned frock coat and produced a latchkey. "If you don't see a light in my study or the laboratory, simply let yourself in. I'll have the old room ready made up for you, the one looking out onto the garden at the back, you remember?"

Asher smiled. "I remember."

His smile faded as Fairport climbed into the brougham—the footman Lukas had to help him—and drove away into the shifting traffic of the Ring, brasses winking like heliographs.

He remembered.

He remembered sitting for hours in the window of that whitewashed room, looking down into the overgrown courtyard whose high wall formed only a nominal barrier against the whispering high-summer woods, reading over and over the three telegrams he'd found upon his return from the mountains. Remembered not wanting to know what they told him.

All three had been from Françoise, sent on successive days. All three had asked for an immediate reply. But he'd seen her at the Café New York—his shoulder tightly strapped and a hefty dose of Fairport's stimulants in his veins—earlier that day. She had mentioned the telegrams in passing, but said they were nothing much.

It meant that she'd been checking on his movements in the period of time in which he was supposed to be ill rather than away.

It meant that she suspected him of leading a double life.

It meant that he was a footfall away from being blown. With Karolyi returning to Vienna in a matter of days, he knew what that would mean.

She'd been perceptive enough to see through Karolyi's imitation of an innocuous young idiot. Why hadn't he thought she would see through his own impersonation of scholarly harmlessness?

He'd sat by the window until the long summer afternoon faded and the white roses on the garden wall dwindled to milky blurs, until he had been unable to read the printing on the dry yellow telegraph forms, though he had by then memorized what each had said. He knew what they meant. He knew what they meant he had to do.

He pushed the memory aside now. When he recalled Viennese coffee and Creme Schnitten, he had automatically thought of the Café New York. Though he guessed Françoise had not entered its doors since the summer of 1895, either, he knew he'd look elsewhere for those small pleasures.

Françoise had been right about cafés in Vienna. It applied equally to public baths. Though not as ubiquitous as cafés, they were plentiful and good for the same reason. Most apartments in the overcrowded city lacked hot water; thousands of families still relied on communal pumps in the halls, communal toilets in the courtyards. But the Viennese were a clean people, cleaner in Asher's experience than the Parisians, for all the French fanaticism about keeping their windows spotless. Certainly the jail cell he'd occupied last night had been far from the pesthole of Fairport's imaginings.

The Heiligesteffanbaden was a veritable emporium of cleanliness, and heavily populated even for a Tuesday morning. Workingmen, students, bearded bourgeoise, and stolid *hofrats*

scrubbed conscientiously in pink marble tubs, under the solici-
tous eye of the usual host of marble and mosaic angels and the
usual Viennese hierarchy of Herr Oberbadmeister, Oberbadmeister, Unterbadmeister, and the *garzone* who collected the
towels. Asher visited the barber next door to be shaved,
changed into the shirt and underclothing he'd bought on the
way from the Prefecture of Police, paid a quick visit to a man
he'd known back in '95 who cut keys, and felt much better,
though the clerks at the Rathaus looked askance at his rumpled
jacket when he asked to examine wills and title documentation
of the older dwellings in the Altstadt. He guessed he would
have enough time to do what he needed to do, if not before
dark, at least before the crowds thinned from the streets.

As both scholar and spy, Asher had long ago learned that
human beings reveal the true workings of their souls when
their attention is on something that consumes them to the
exclusion of their usual desire to make an impression on
others—and that something is usually property. He had, he
reflected dryly, witnessed a particularly unappetizing modern
example of that very phenomenon in the wake of his cousin's
funeral three days ago. In their preoccupation with who's
going to get what, people forget to cover their tracks: banking
records, wills, probates, leaseholds, account books can yield a
startling amount of information to someone with time at his
disposal and a high tolerance for dust.

Asher started with the oldest palaces of the Altstadt, those
exuberantly decorated masterpieces of white stucco whose
baroque façades could barely be seen because of the narrow-
ness of the ancient city's alleys, matching ownership records
with wills, wills with death notices and, more importantly,
birth notices; doing sums on every page of his notebook and all
around the margins of the *Times* Personals, the only other
paper he had in his valise. He found himself heartily missing
Lydia, not out of romantic considerations, but simply because
she was a good researcher and would thoroughly enjoy this
chase.

He left around two for a sandwich, but it was only when one
of the several bespectacled young clerks came to his table in

the reading room and said apologetically, "If it please you, Herr Professor Doktor, this building is now closing," that he realized the windows were pitch-black and that the electric lights had been on for nearly an hour and a half.

By previous arrangement, Artemus Halliwell was waiting for him at Donizetti's café. The head of the Vienna section was in his mid-thirties, untidy, bearded, bespectacled, and enormously obese; Asher remembered him from the London statistics department. Behind small oval slabs of glass, Halliwell's pale green eyes were like *cabachon* peridots as he listened to Asher's account of his journey.

"So this Farren thinks he's a vampire, eh?" Halliwell carved a neat fragment of *backhendl* and popped it into his incongruous rosebud of a mouth. "I suppose that's how he came into your purlieu in the first place, is it?"

Asher nodded. In a sense it was actually true.

"You get some of that in Vienna, though not as bad as Buda-Pesth. When I went west into the mountains only last year, there was a tizz-woz in one of the villages about a man who was supposed to turn himself into a wolf. I'm told in parts of the Black Forest no one will talk to you, sell you anything, give you directions to anywhere, if you kill a hare."

He dabbed his lips with his napkin and the ubiquitous Ober appeared, asking with folded hands if everything was all right.

"I think you should know," said the fat man, when the Ober had effaced himself again, "that there's been a bit of a stink."

Asher felt his nape prickle. He'd been around the Department long enough to recognize that carefully neutral tone. "Oh?"

"Streatham's doing." He made a dismissive gesture with his fork. "Naturally. Always wás a bloody fool. He's made to-do about that boy Cramer's death with the French authorities, ranting about British citizens and treaty rights—just as if our offices weren't in flat violation of any treaty's assertions of good faith. The thing is, the French have washed their hands of the whole matter, contacted the Vienna police, and are demanding your return under escort on the first available train. I held them off for a day, saying I hadn't any idea where you were," he went on, raising a staying hand against Asher's protest. "But whatever you've learned today at the Rathaus, you'd probably better pass along to me."

"Idiot," Asher said dispassionately, while his mind raced ahead. It was close to eight; the streets would remain crowded enough to protect him until ten at least, possibly later, and in any case he doubted that vampires could detect an intrusive interest in their lairs from a single walk by a casual observer.

But even in a single walk-past he could tell a great deal, particularly which of the several houses on his list of possibilities was the likeliest haunt. Enough information, at least, that whoever took over wouldn't be going into the job defenseless, as Cramer had done.

"And what was it," asked Halliwell, "that you went to the Rathaus today to find?"

Asher considered for a moment, then said quietly, "Vampires."

Halliwell's tufted brows went up.

"Are there people here who believe in them?"

The Vienna chief gestured with his fork again. "There's always muttering among the Gypsies. The waiter at my café swears he saw a vampire on an old gate tower connected to a house in the Bieberstrasse—used to be part of the ramparts." He shook his head. "*My café*. I sound like a Viennese. Caught myself calling this place *my restaurant* the other day, same as I'd talk about my club at home."

"I don't know." Asher looked around him lazily, soothed by the atmosphere of the place, the slight shabbiness of the oak panels, the soft flicker of the gaslight and the all-pervasive smell of goulash, and scratched a corner of his mustache. "Isn't one's café here a little like one's club in London?"

"The hell it is." Halliwell surgically excised another morsel of chicken. "At a club you have a vote on who gets let in the door. Here anyone can come in—*and* does." He glared across at a party of uproarious young subalterns in the sky-blue coats of the Imperial-and-Royal Uhlans. "The wine's atrocious, and I think if I hear one more waltz, one more operetta, one more Mozart concerto, I'm going to open negotiations with the

Turks to re-invade, and this time I'll make damn sure they win. Has Farren been to Vienna before?"

"I haven't been able to find that out," said Asher. "Not under his own name, anyway." Which might or might not be true, but was probably true enough for this century. "I have an idea he'd hide out in a house reputed to be haunted or connected somehow with . . . odd rumors."

Halliwell nodded, thinking, and the Ober returned with the Herr Ober in tow, to collect the polished ruins of Halliwell's *backhendl* and Asher's *Tafelspitz*, and to solicitously attempt to interest Halliwell in dessert with the air of a man who fears his client will collapse from starvation if not attended. Halliwell issued instructions as to the composition of an *indianer* with an attention to detail that seemed to delight the Herr Ober's soul, then turned back to Asher as the two waiters bowed and took their leave.

"I've heard of the Japanese doing that in the Chinese war," said Halliwell. "Headquartering in haunted houses in Peking."

Asher nodded. "I was there," he said. "And yes, they did; complete with mirror tricks straight off the Paris Opera stage. It may be harder to pull off here . . ."

"Not as hard as you think." There was a small commotion in the doorway—two other young officers, brave in gold braid, with bright-clothed girls on their arms, and all the rowdy subalterns calling out greetings—and Asher saw Halliwell's bulging eyes cut briefly, unobtrusively, in that direction, making sure the noise did not represent potential danger. Not a reaction one would expect from a fat gourmand ostensibly preoccupied with his pastry.

His eyes returned to Asher. "There's a lot of country people in Vienna, in off the farms to the east: up-country Czechs and Hungarians and Romanians and what-have-you, come to work in the sweatshops after spending the first part of their lives, to all intents and purposes, in the sixteenth century. People who live in the Altstadt don't interfere if there's a big old palace that's shut up day after day—it's part of the neighborhood, and one would never risk incurring the displeasure of a baron. But newcomers from out of town—they get inquisitive."

"And which big old palace," Asher inquired, "are we talking about?"

Halliwell grinned and fastidiously removed a mote of powdered sugar from his whiskers. "There's three or four. One on the Haarhof is supposed to be haunted, and there's a seventeenth-century *palais* on Bakkersgasse where people claim to have seen lights. All the Hungarian waiters in town swear the baroque *palais* built over the ruins of the old St. Roche Church on Steindelgasse is inhabited by vampires—it's actually owned by a collateral branch of the Batthyanys—and there's a house in Vorlautstrasse near the old ramparts where four or five people are said to have disappeared over the course of the last ten years. All of them have perfectly legitimate antecedents, by the way, winter palaces of landed families who have larger places out in the country."

"Any belonging to Karolyi?"

"I think the Bakkersgasse *palais* belongs to the Prague branch of the family. Not to our bird. It's a huge clan." Behind the spectacles the pale eyes danced, as if pleased he'd anticipated the thought. "Will you need help?"

Asher hesitated. The bloodied ruin of Cramer's face came back to him, glistening gruesomely in the reflected light. Gummed with blood, the silver chain had crossed the huge wounds on the throat. The shopkeeper in the Palais Royal had sworn the chains were pure silver. More likely tourist trade trash, the thinnest wash over pewter or lead. The boy probably hadn't even heard Ernchester approach.

"I haven't much to send with you," Halliwell went on. "Streatham's an ass, but he was right about that. Everything's been cut since the end of the war. Still, if you need a man . . ."

Beyond the gilt-framed windows of Donizetti's, passersby hurried along the pavement, greatcoats bundled tight about them. Mist had risen again from the Danube Canal, blurring the outlines of apartment buildings whose grandiose central staircases led to dreary attic rooms shared by cobblers, embroiderers, Obers, and Herr Obers and their wives and children and Uncle Tom Cobbley and all. Between the buildings the shadows lay deep in narrow passages leading to the heart of the ancient city, where sunlight fell only at noon.

One of the possibilities on Asher's very incomplete list of suspect properties was on the Steindelgasse: *said to stand over the crypt of old St. Roche.*

"No," Asher said softly. "No, I think I'll be all right on my own."

The palace in the Steindelgasse was typical of the great town houses of the nobility in the old city: five floors of massive gray walls, wedged between an ancient block of flats and the town palace of some count of the Montenuovo family that was illuminated like a Christmas tree for a ball. Looking up, Asher could see the tall windows of its first-floor salons ablaze with gaslight, which partly illuminated the narrow street; crystal chandeliers were visible, and a portion of a god-bedecked baroque ceiling.

The Batthyany palace was utterly dark.

Curious enough in itself, thought Asher, pausing before the heavy archway of the door. A number of the old noble families boosted their incomes by renting out the ground floors of their palaces for shops and the topmost floor or two below the attics out for flats. Certainly there were people coming and going through the great gate of the Montenuovo *palais* who were not of the upper crust. The other buildings Asher had looked at since parting from Halliwell, in the Haarhof and the Bakkersgasse, had been dark as well, lacking even spectral lights, and like them, this one had a slightly dilapidated air. The obligatory marble atlantes that upheld its shallow porch and heavily carved window frames were uncleaned, though Asher was interested to note that the hinges and ironwork on the door were free of rust.

The building was clearly the oldest in the street.

Hands in armpits for warmth, Asher strolled slowly past the enormous doors. It was later than he had intended to be still abroad. Fog and deepening cold were thinning the passersby, and he heard eleven strike from the Domkirche a few streets away. He noted the shutters behind the windows' iron bars and the lack of recent wear on the pavement before the doors, and turned to fix in his mind the irregular shape of this narrow lane, orienting himself in the tangle of little streets that lay between the cathedral and the old Judenplatz. Within the gate would lie a broad passageway or possibly a sort of columned porch opening into the central court. Not a large one, judging by the frontage, but the building might be far longer than it was wide.

He walked on, seeking a way to circle the block. Away from the lights of the apartment blocks and the Montenuovo town house he felt his nape prickle with his old instinct for danger, but if he was going to be shipped back to Paris in the morning, the least he could do was arm his successor with some knowledge of what he was getting into.

He turned down a short lane, his boots splashing in thin puddles. The small iron lamps that burned high on the walls here were the only lights, feeble through thickening fog. He turned again, reflecting that this part of the old city was as bad as the London waterfront. Worse, in some ways, because the uniformly high walls closed in like a canyon, shutting out even the sight of spires or chimneys that could be used as landmarks.

There was no one in sight around him. He thought, *Finish this up and get out.*

In another narrow street off Tuchlaubenstrasse he identified what he thought was the back of the Batthyany Palace, no more than a slip of older masonry between two apartment blocks set at an odd angle; there was a little postern door there whose iron handle he knew better than to touch.

A footstep splashed in water, close behind him. Asher turned and threw his back to the wall, lashed out as a dark figure laid hands on him from one side even as he heard the panting approach of another man. His fist jarred on the bony angle of a jaw. The man lurched back and Asher spun, his second attacker seizing his arm; he grabbed the man's hair with his free hand, yanked the head sharply against the stone of the wall behind him, twisted his body from the drag of the grip. At the same time, his mind registered tobacco and sweat and dirty clothes, the sound of breath and the warmth of snatching hands. Pain slashed his side even as he hooked the one man's feet from under him, slammed aside the hands clutching at his throat, smashed his fist into the other's face.

He could barely see them in the dark between the buildings, but broke for where he thought they weren't. Someone clutched the skirts of his greatcoat but couldn't hold. He fled, stumbling, bruised his shoulder on the stone of a corner, fell where his foot caught a pothole in the broken pavement. He caught himself against a wall and pain seared his side again, and he realized that one of them had had a knife.

He turned down what he thought was a lane back to the Seitzergasse, but the dirty glow from a window high and to his right showed him a blank wall. He pressed himself back into a corner where the shadows were darkest, reached to whip the knife from his boot as panting and footfalls echoed loud in the narrow space before him and he saw the blur of what might have been faces and the glint of edged steel.

Then a hand like the mechanical jaws of a trap caught him above the elbow, and another, corpse-cold and strong as death, covered his mouth. He was dragged backward, down, into damp cold that smelled of wet stone, earth, and rats, and the dim arch of paler darkness blinked from existence as the door was kicked shut.

The smell of Patou perfume filled his nostrils, covering a dim exhalation of putrefying blood.

A woman's voice said in his ear, "Don't cry out."

Asher was silent. Even if the silver protected the big veins of his throat and wrists, a vampire could still break his neck, and he knew what was in the darkness beside him.

The hands left his arm and face. He listened, wondering how many of them there were.

There was no sound of breath, of course. After a moment a silvery rustling, like infinitely thin metal fragments rubbing against each other. A woman's taffeta petticoat.

He thought, *She spoke English.*

Then the scratch of a match.

He blinked against the needle-bright golden light that suddenly outlined a colorless hand, a papery white face, and touched with cinnamon threads the black mass of framing hair.

Brown eyes met his, reflective vampire eyes, but still the color of brown leaves at the bottom of a winter pond.

It was, he realized, Anthea Farren, Countess of Ernchester.

"I do not understand the how of it," Ysidro said.

He had taken off his gloves to deal the cards, and now he held up his hand, slender and white with long fingers like the spindles for bobbin lace. Lydia observed again the quasiony-chogryphosis of the fingernails and the fact that the musculature showed no abnormal development, though she had seen this man wrench apart iron bars.

"It's my theory that it is a virus, or more probably a complex of several viruses." Lydia sorted her cards: ace, king, ten, eight, and seven of hearts; queen, jack, seven, and ten of spades. Almost no clubs—a nine—queen and jack of diamonds. Darkness fleeted past the train windows. Around them the first-class carriage had slipped slowly into silence.

"Because the cells of the flesh are themselves altered?"

She paused, a little surprised that the vampire knew what a virus was, then remembered all those medical journals in his house. Playing cards, and conversation, had insensibly lessened her fear of him—she wondered if he had chosen the absorption of a new game for that reason, or simply because, like her aunt Lavinia, he wanted a partner for the journey.

"It's one way of accounting for the extreme sensitivity of the flesh to things like silver and certain herbs," she said after a moment. "Not to mention photocombustion."

"Do we really need to talk about this?" Margaret squirmed uncomfortably, never lifting her gaze from the flying crochet needle and the lacy snowflakes of antimacassars overflowing the workbasket on her lap. After two or three tries at learning picquet, Margaret had retreated to her needlework, fighting to remain awake so as not to be left out of Ysidro's conversation, though she had very little to add. Into the discussion of railway travel, the finer points of picquet, the mathematical odds involved in card play and the structure of music—which Ysidro understood on a level very different from Lydia's superficial acquaintance—Margaret had interjected periodic observations that she hadn't been out of England before or that she had read of this or that monument or notable sight in a travel book or Lord Byron's memoirs.

She had tried two or three times to deflect the talk from the physical state of vampirism, but when she spoke now, her voice was low, as if she wanted to register a complaint that she didn't actually want the others to hear. Silly, thought Lydia, considering the fact that Ysidro could tell people apart by their breathing.

The vampire moved two cards in his hand, removed three and laid them facedown near the stock, replacing them in his hand with three others. "It may sound odd, but to this day I do not understand what happened to my flesh the night I was taken, in a churchyard near the river, as I was coming home from my mistress' . . . I always had mistresses in those days. Girls south of the river, who cared not that I was a Spaniard of the consort's entourage."

He lifted the corners of two other cards and replaced them in the stock without change of expression.

"I believe that this condition is two separate matters: the matter of the flesh, which preserves the body, not as it is at the moment of death, but as it is in the mind, molding even those who are taken old back into the shape of their living prime; and the matter of the mind, which sharpens and strengthens both the will and the senses, and gives us power over the wills, and the senses, of the living."

Lydia discarded her club and two diamonds, drew another club—the eight—the ace of spades, and the queen of hearts. After four or five games in which Ysidro had systematically bested her, she was beginning to get the hang of the game, a complicated manipulation of points in which she could almost always deduce more or less what Ysidro had in his hand, though as yet the information did her little good. As a teacher, he had endless patience, gentle without being in the slightest bit kind. He had dealt with Margaret's total absence of card sense and her inability to follow or remember rules with a matter-of-factness that had, oddly enough, almost driven the governess to tears.

"It is the blood that feeds the flesh," Ysidro said. "We can—and do, at need—live upon the blood of animals, or blood taken from the living without need of their death. But it is the death that feeds the powers of our minds. Without the kill, we find our abilities fading, the cloak of our illusion wearing threadbare, our skill at turning aside the minds of the living shredding away. Without those skills we cannot send the living mind to sleep or make others see what they do not see, or bring them walking up streets they would not ordinarily tread in moments of what feels, to them, to be absentmindedness."

Margaret said nothing, but her needle jabbed fast among the flowery lacework in her hands.

He gathered his cards. "Those, by the by, are our only powers, Mr. Stoker's interesting speculations aside. Personally, I have always wondered how one *could* transform oneself into a bat or a rat. Though lighter in weight than a living man, I am still of far greater bulk than such a creature. But in the speculations of this man Einstein I have found considerable food for thought."

"Do you cast a reflection in mirrors?" Lydia had noticed upon coming into the compartment that a scarf—one of Margaret's, presumably, blue with enormous red and yellow roses printed on it—had been draped over the small mirror, and the curtains drawn tightly over the dark window glass.

She recalled her own ghostly image in Ysidro's huge Venetian mirror draped with black lace.

"We do." Ysidro made his discard. "The laws of physics do not alter themselves for either our help or our confusion. Many of us avoid mirrors simply because of the concentration of silver upon their backs. Even at a distance, in some it causes an itch. But chiefly, mirrors show us as we truly are, naked of the illusions that we wear in the eyes of all the living. Thus we avoid them, for though we can still cast a glamour over the mind of a victim who glimpses us in reflection, the victim will usually be troubled—unaccountably, to him—by what he sees or thinks he sees. We are not overfond of the experience ourselves. Four for quart in spades, ten high."

They played cards until long past midnight, as the lights of

Nancy flashed past the window and then the Vosges rose under their starless shawls of cloud. Still fascinated but nodding with weariness, Lydia finally returned to her own compartment, but, as she had feared, could not sleep. A little light strayed through the curtain from the corridor, a comfort, like the elephant-shaped *veilleuse* that had burned in her room when she was a child. Once, a shadow passed that light, and she lay awake for some time, imagining Ysidro drifting like a soundless specter along the train, sampling the dreams of the lady with the little dog, of the pair of brothers who'd asked to share the dinner table in the restaurant car with Lydia and Margaret, of the conductor in his chair and the kitchen boys in their bunks, like a connoisseur tasting different vintages of wine.

She wondered what Margaret and Ysidro had to say to one another in the course of the night.

SEVEN

"HAVE you seen him?"

Lady Ernchester tilted her stub of candle to spill a few drops of wax onto the stonework of an elbow-high niche, then propped the light upright in it. The flame steadied and broadened, touching first her face with its deceptive warmth, then the stiff, sad features of a small stone image of the Queen of Heaven in the niche itself, fouled with rat droppings and the trails of slugs. The light penetrated farther, to show them in a sort of vestibule at the foot of the crooked stairs down which Anthea had led him. The walls and ceiling groins of brick and stone had lost most of their covering plaster, and earth floor filled the air with a raw exhalation of damp. Opposite them a door into another chamber had been bricked shut, but not the long windows on either side. Looking through, Asher could see that the room, far deeper and higher than the one in which he stood, was filled with human bones.

He leaned against the wall, the pain in his side suddenly turning his knees to water. When he pressed his hand under his coat, he felt the hot soak of blood.

"You're hurt . . ."

She stepped forward and caught his arm; her hand pulled back and he staggered, for her fingers had accidentally brushed the silver chains where they ran under the cuff of his shirt. For a moment they stood looking at one another in the candle's wavering light.

"Wait here for me," she said. He heard the rustle of her petticoats but did not see her depart.

He sank down onto the windowsill, leaning against the rusted iron bars. His head swam, but losing consciousness was something he dared not do. The bones behind him rose in heaped mountains, losing themselves in a distance of utter night. A faint scratching clatter: movement among the piled skulls, and the glint of tiny eyes.

A plague crypt, he thought. Easily as large as the one under the cathedral, though probably deeper in the earth. In the faint glow of the candle the bones were as brown and shiny as ocean stones.

Get thee to my lady's chamber, thought Asher dizzily. *Tell her that though she paint an inch thick, to this end will she come . . .*

Unless, of course, she chooses not to die.

For some reason Lydia came into his mind, and he shut his eyes. *To this end will she come . . .*

"Here." A hand touched his shoulder, swiftly withdrawn. She stood at his side again, his valise in her hand. "Take off your coat."

The attacker's knife had slit the heavy wool and the lighter tweed of the jacket and waistcoat beneath. Shirt and waistcoat had absorbed most of the blood; had he not been wearing the greatcoat, he would probably have been killed. As it was, the wound, though painful, was superficial—he could move his arm, though he knew it would stiffen, and his breathing was unimpaired.

With an exertion that left him light-headed, he stripped to the waist, the air shockingly cold against his skin. He remained seated in the embrasure while she moved away from him, to the opposite side of the vestibule under the Virgin's niche, where she tore the bloodied shirt into neat pieces as if the tough linen had been cigarette paper. As she worked, she spoke in the quick, jerky voice of one who seeks to preserve herself from what silence might bring.

"Have you seen him?" she asked again.

"I saw him at Charing Cross Station," he replied, "talking with a man I knew to work for the Kundschafts Stelle, the Austrian secret service."

She glanced up, eyes flaring wide with shock. They were the color of mahogany but no more human than a raptor bird's. In the small saffron light her lips were colorless as the pallor of her flesh, pallor somehow mitigated—or explained—by the mourning black of her clothing. Her hair, upswept into the style Lydia called a Gibson Girl, seemed to flow out of the darkness of her clothing, garnet-tipped pins gleaming in it like droplets of blood.

"*Talking with* someone?"

"Why does that surprise you?"

"I had thought . . ." She hesitated, looking at him for a moment; then, as if not daring to linger on the dark glitter of blood on his side, her unhuman eyes returned to her work. "Our house was searched, you see. Ransacked by men while I was out." From the reticule at her waist she withdrew a square of yellow paper, folded small, and crossed the room to hand it to him with bloodstained fingers, then moved quickly back away. "That was on the floor when I came back."

Asher unfolded it. It was a railway timetable. Sunday night's seven-thirty boat-train was circled; a strong European hand had added, in the margin, *Vienna Express*.

"He was gone by the time I came back that night," said Anthea, digging in his valise for the small flask of whiskey there. She soaked an unbloodied fragment of shirt in it, braced herself almost imperceptibly before stepping near enough to touch him again. Asher raised his arms against the top of the window in which he sat, that the silver on his wrists might not come into accidental contact with her ungloved hands. The whiskey stung coldly in the wound, the smell of it almost covering the raw whiff of the blood.

"In wintertime, when dark falls by four, I often go on errands, to buy newspapers or books. I have a dressmaker who keeps open for me. Ernchester will sometimes stay all the night

through in his study, reading, even on those nights when I go
out later . . ."

She stopped herself visibly from saying *to hunt*. But Asher
saw it in the shift of her eyes. Her hands were icy against his
bare flesh, and she worked quickly, holding the bindings in
place with small bits of what little sticking plaster he'd had in
the valise in case of emergencies. His blood dabbled her fingers, garish as paint on ivory. Cold breathed over his ribs from
the bones within the crypt, chilling him further.

She went on, her words swift, like a woman talking in the
presence of a man whom she fears will seduce her. "He used
to go out walking. I thought it was only that. So I went out
again and, when I returned, found the place rifled, smelling of
human tobacco and human sweat, and that was on the floor. I
thought . . . I thought that he had been taken away."

Her dark brows pinched together as she pinned the final
bindings in place. "I would have known it, had he . . . had anything befallen."

Asher remembered his dream. *How can he be dead?* she
had asked. *Did I walk up the stairs, would he not be waiting at
the top?*

Even then she had known.

"And you didn't go to Grippen?"

Anthea shook her head. "Since last year—since the rift
among us concerning you and your knowledge of us—there
has been uneasiness among the Undead of London. Grippen has
gotten other fledglings in place of those who were killed; has
summoned to London older fledglings of his as well. Me, he
never trusted. Indeed, I . . . until you spoke of the Austrian, I
could not be sure that this was not of Grippen's doing. But for
that reason I dared not go to Ysidro, either."

She handed him one of the new shirts he had bought, then
took the whiskey flask and stepped quickly away, pouring the
liquor on her fingers and meticulously, repeatedly, almost
obsessively wiped from them all trace of his blood. While she
did this, he put on his shirt, resumed his tie, his jacket, his coat,
moving slowly for his vision sometimes would suddenly gray,

but she did not offer her help. In the dark of the crypt, rat shadows flickered among the bones.

"At a certain distance I can feel my husband's mind. Sense his presence. I did not . . . I dared not wait." She raised her eyes to his. "Might he have gone to this Austrian because he was fleeing the Master of London?"

"He might," said Asher. "But I suspect Grippen had nothing to do with it. Come." He picked up his valise. "Will you go with me for coffee?"

They went to LaStanza's on the Graben, luminous with gaslight and bright with the pastel frocks of the dancers. Anthea had donned, over her cold white fingers, a widow's black lace house mitts, and produced from a corner of the crypt's vestibule a plumed hat bedighted with veils that further hid—and heightened by contrast—the whiteness of her flesh. She must have left it there, thought Asher, when she went to rescue him from his attackers in the alley. The scent of her hair on the silk had evidently been enough to keep the rats from coming anywhere near.

"I have been afraid for Charles for years," she said after the Herr Ober took their orders. "Part of it was Danny being killed—the man who had been our servant since the days of the last King George. Burned up in the light of the sun. Some would say, a fit end for such as we." She glanced quickly at him, challenging, but Asher said nothing.

"Part of it was the death of the city that he knew. Not all at once, as when the fire took it, but little by little, a building demolished here, a street torn up there that the Underground might pass beneath. A word or expression would fall out of use, or a composer die, whose work he loved. He used to go every night to concerts, listening with joy to the new men, to those light airs like clockwork flowers, and then the strength, the passion that came after . . ."

A waiter brought them coffee: for her, "dark with skin"— one had to be specific when ordering coffee in Vienna—for him an *einspanner*, black coffee, whipped cream.

"Is it passé now, the waltz?" She put back her veils and raised the cup to her lips, not drinking, but breathing deep of the bittersweet riches of the steam. On the dance floor women floated weightlessly to "Tales of the Vienna Woods," their gowns like lilies of saffron, rose, pale lettuce-green; the black clothing of the men a delineating bass note, the officers' uniforms jeweled flame.

"I think so." He remembered dancing with Françoise. She'd been gawky as a scarecrow to look at but never missed a step, as light as a bluebell on a stem. "Not with people my age," he went on. "But the young and the smart are doing things like the foxtrot and the tango."

"Tango." She savored the unfamiliar word. "It sounds like a New World fruit. Something whose juice would run down your chin. I shall have to learn it one day." Her eyes returned to the dancers, quickly, as if avoiding a thought. "The waltz was a scandal when first I learned it. And so I thought it, too." She laughed a little at herself. "Ernchester still enjoyed dancing in those days. Grippen mocked at us. For him all things are only to serve the kill. But we'd go to Almack's Assembly Rooms or to the great ton balls during the Season. He . . . was not always as you've seen him."

"Did something change him?" His voice was low, under the music, but she heard, and past the wraiths of her veils her glance crossed his again. Then she looked away. "Time." She traced the ear-shaped curve of the cup's handle, a gesture that reminded him of Lydia when she had something worrying her. Her eyes did not meet his. "I wish you could have known him as he was. I wish you could have known us both."

Silence lay between them, save for the music and the swirl of silk and slipper leather. "Do you read the Personals?" asked Asher, and the question startled her out of the reverie into which she had slipped. He started to reach down for the valise on the floor between their chairs, but the bite of his wound stopped him; he gestured to the newspaper visible in the bag's open mouth.

"Or more to the point, does your husband?"

"We all do." She leaned to withdraw the folded sheets. "We follow families, names, neighborhoods for years, sometimes decades. To us, chains of events are like the lives of Balzac's characters, or Dickens'. The nights are long."

Asher unfolded the section and touched the advertisement he had seen.

"Saturday's paper," he said. "His departure was arranged in advance. *Umitsiz* is Turkish for *hopeless*—a variant, I think, for *Want-hope*. Does Ernchester know Turkish?"

"He was part of the legation King Charles sent to Constantinople, before we were married. He was away three years. To me it seemed eternity."

A wry smile brushed her lips as she considered the irony of that, and she added, a little shyly, "It still does, you know, when I look back."

Then she frowned and held the railway timetable beside the few short lines of type, as if comparing them. "But why?" she asked at last. "What could they have said to him—this Olumsiz Bey—to make him come here without a word to me? Even without Grippen's support, we have wealth and a place where we are safe. Men searched the house, yes, but it was night when they did so—they could not have overpowered him, even had he returned to find them. At night men are easy to elude. Charles knows London's every cellar and bolt-hole. Even if he knew Vienna once, cities change with time, and those changes are perilous to those whose flesh the sun will destroy. What could he have been offered?"

"I suspect the men were only agents of someone else." Asher folded both paper and timetable again. "Ysidro told me once that the Undead usually know when someone is seeking them. You know nothing, guessed nothing, of the men who searched the house?"

She shook her head. "There had been no . . . no unknown faces seen too many times, no footfalls passing where none should be."

"Which means that someone told them about the house."

The waltz had finished. On the platform the orchestra was putting up its instruments. A woman, small and gray-haired and dumpy, laughed as her white-bearded gentleman friend swept her up into an extravagant cloak of golden fur. Anthea turned her head to watch them, and in her eyes Asher saw an expression of almost sensual delight, a softening, as if she had drunk wine.

Karolyi? Asher wondered. An attempt to make sure the earl's wife didn't stop him from coming? But would Karolyi have known of the power struggle between Anthea and Grippen that would rob them of the master vampire's support?

Karolyi had certainly hired the toughs who attacked him tonight. They had probably followed him all day, waiting their chance. That meant he'd better pick the toughest-looking fiacre he could find and warn him of trouble once they got into the isolated lanes and vineyards of the Vienna Woods.

The Ober appeared, Lady Ernchester's black cloak on his arm. Putting it around her shoulders brought Asher a stab of momentary agony, and she turned quickly.

"You're in pain." Her fingers were cold still, though she'd warmed them on the cup. "I'm sorry, I didn't think."

"It just took me by surprise," he said. "I'll take you to your lodging."

A tulle of fog suffused the gaslight on the Graben to dim haloes, blurred the swags and statues of the façades. Here and there a window still glowed, where maids, having unlaced their mistresses, brushed their hair and handed them nightdresses and prayer books, now locked up jewels or brushed dirt from slippers, or laid final fires for the morrow before creeping to cold beds themselves. The air was ice, the leafless trees friezes of unreadable runes passed by only a few final, home-hurrying shadows.

"Dr. Asher."

He paused in his stride and saw, again, her face turned half away from him in confusion.

"I know no honest woman asks a man to come back to her rooms with her, to stay with her the night." Her fingers stirred at the buttons on his sleeve. "And I understand that it's the stuff of farce for me even to care about such conventions. Old habits die harder than you think. But . . . will you do this?"

She raised her eyes to his as she spoke. Oddly, Asher felt no sense of danger. He remembered how carefully she had wiped the blood from her fingers and the stammer of her nervousness that hurried to fill the silences of the dark crypt. It crossed his mind to wonder if she had inhaled so deeply of the coffee to cover from herself the smell of his blood.

Yet he had no sense that she was influencing his mind, laying upon it the vampire's glamour that blinded victims to their danger. Which might only mean, he thought, that she was very, very good at what she did.

Into his hesitation, she continued, "Save for one thing only, traveling alone on that train was the most terrifying thing I've ever done." They moved on along the wide street, two isolated figures in the thickening brume. Beside them the Plague Pillar ascended in an astonishment of cherubs, saints, and clouds, white in gaslight and shadow. "I only just reached the hotel room in Paris in time, and I was terrified that sleep—the unbreakable sleep of the Undead—would overcome me where I stood in the street. They must have thought me a madwoman, hurrying the porters to take my trunks into my room and then pushing them all out and locking and double-locking the doors. And even when I was alone, the fear near overwhelmed me. How could I know that I'd wake with the setting of the sun again and not burn up screaming through some chambermaid's prying or greed?"

Her step quickened and her hand tightened on his arm, the memory of that terror making her fingers, for a moment, crushing iron.

"And it was worse, shipping the trunk the following night," she went on. "Sending myself like a parcel, falling asleep to the rocking of the train, trusting to fate. Not knowing if I'd ever wake. They say we don't wake, should our darkness be violated by sunlight—that we burn up in sleep. But who knows?" Under the veils her face was calm, but there was a flaw in her voice, and she drew her cloak close about her, as if even her Undead flesh felt the cold. "None of us are ever there, to see it happen to another. Even in utter blackness, the sun submerges our minds. Sometimes we hear and know what happens about us, but we do not wake."

They reached the door of her hotel, a splendid mansion

whose lower stories comprised the palatial residence of some wealthy family, but whose marble stair led to a far humbler lobby on the upper floor.

Anthea paused in the columned shadows of the entry-way. "A year ago Ysidro hired you—forced you—to be his servant. To do for him in daylight what he himself was unable to do. And you did it honorably."

His breath mingled whitely with the fog that had floated through the outer gate behind them. Her words had produced no such clouding. "I had no choice."

"We all have choice." Her gaze met his in the dim light from the chandelier of crystal and gilt. "I can only ask you. Stay with me in the room until the sun sets again. Please."

Lydia had once calculated how many human beings the average vampire killed in a century. If he were the man he once had been, Asher thought, he would have said yes, then later thrown open the trunk lid and let the sun reduce such a murder-ess to dust.

Perhaps because she had saved his life, he would only have said no.

The clock on St. Stephen's was striking two, and like courtiers repeating a sovereign's joke, clocks on churches and monasteries throughout the Altstadt took up the chime. He would be alone, awake, with this woman for hours before she would be with him, alone and sleeping, trusting him as he must trust her.

If it weren't all a trap, to get him to a place where he could not call for help.

But surely the crypt had been that.

He told himself it was because he needed to find Ernchester, something he could not do without a vampire's help. But he knew that wasn't true.

"Very well," he said.

"He ceased to care at all, about anything, fifty, maybe sixty years ago." Anthea removed her hat, and despite the renewed slash of pain in his side, Asher helped her off with her cloak and the jacket beneath it. Her frock was Norwich silk, its ruffles glittering with star fields of jet. "Music, watching people—not for prey but just for the curiosity about how they live their lives—it all meant less and less to him. Like that fairy book that came out a few years ago, where a man's limbs are replaced, one by one, by magic with limbs of tin, until suddenly he realizes he has no heart and is no longer a man." She passed her gloved hand across her eyes, the smooth skin of the lids pinching at the memory of pain.

"You're thinking that all those fifty, sixty years, when his life meant less and less to him, still he prolonged it by killing two and sometimes three men a week. There are things that can't . . . be explained. It's easier than you think, to fall into . . . habits."

"I'm not thinking anything." He remembered Jan van der Platz's blood on the barn wall, the shocked hurt in the boy's eyes just before Asher pulled the trigger.

She lighted the lamp on the heavy table. Asher wondered if she had been aware of the brassy-haired prostitute's death agonies, and it occurred to him that this woman had probably seen worse. Maybe done worse herself. The small chamber, copiously decorated with swathes of peacock feathers and dried flowers and smelling vaguely of carpets, had not even been fitted with gas, much less electricity. The topaz light made the vampire's face more human, lent color to her cheeks and a kind of life to her eyes, and brought forth cinnabar glints in her hair. Asher remembered again his vision of her lying on the floor of what he realized now was the old Ernchester town house in Savoy Walk, the house where first he had met this woman—where she had saved him from the Master of London's wrath.

"I'm sorry to have provoked this division," he said. "To have robbed you of whatever support Grippen would give."

She shook her head. "It's been decades coming. Maybe centuries. He wanted Charles—and the houses and land that would give him a system of bolt-holes. We had no living child, and there are ways of manipulating even entailed property, to keep a good part of what you own. Grippen lost much in the Great Fire, and afterward the city was greatly changed. I kept the property tied up in trusts, so Grippen couldn't own them outright. But it was only a matter of time before he would come to an end of needing Charles. Vampires do not kill vampires, but . . . I suspect in any case he would not have helped.

"Who is this Karolyi?" She took off her mitts, and her long nails glinted oddly in the lamplight.

While she plucked the jewel-headed pins from her hair, Asher told her about his early acquaintance with Karolyi in Vienna. "He's continued in the diplomatic corps, I understand. Young men of his class do, with only minimal qualifications. I know he's been responsible for the deaths of at least two of our agents over the last ten years, but it's never been proven."

"How would he have known about my husband?" She paused, brush in hand. "He may be ruthless, yes, clever and dangerous, but it would not have told him how to find a London vampire. Only another vampire could have done that. And why would he have chosen a London vampire to . . . to bring here? The masters among the Undead are jealous of their territories. They do not tolerate vampires who are not their fledglings and subservient to their wills. Ernchester knows this."

"That may be part of Karolyi's plan." Stiffly and clumsily, Asher began to sponge with cold water at the blood in his coat, and Anthea said, "I'll do that," and took it from him. Now that the shock had worn off, he felt very tired, the pain in his side settling into a dull ache. He was glad to sit quietly on the room's overstuffed brocade settee.

"What he wants your husband for is less clear," he said after a time. "Maybe he wants your husband because he *isn't* a fledgling to some local master, here or someplace like Bulgaria or Greece. That's what I need to find out. It may be he wants your husband to make a fledgling who can be put to Karolyi's uses. But whatever he planned, he had to get your husband out of London because of Grippen."

"Yes," Anthea said softly. "Grippen would know."

She walked to the doorway between that chamber and the next, the movement of her shadow summoning vague blinks of light from the brass fittings of the trunk that filled most of the space not already occupied by the four-poster bed. Her hands, straying in the lace at her throat, were like lilies, ringed with solitary gold.

"When a master vampire begets a fledgling," Anthea said slowly, "he . . . he takes the fledgling's mind, the fledgling's consciousness and personality, into his own being, for the time it takes that . . . that fledgling's body to die. Once death is complete, once the . . . the changes to the vampire state have begun, then the master breathes that mind, that soul, back into the changing body once again. But not all of it. And what is breathed back is . . . stained. Altered. Just a little."

The marble profile remained averted, sienna eyes staring blankly into distance.

"No," she said. "He wouldn't use Charles in London. Grippen knows . . . everything. And he has been watching us. Maybe waiting for his chance. I hate him."

She shook her head, moved her shoulders as if to shed a weight of thought. "I have hated him since the first night Charles brought me to his house. Elysée de Montadour, the Master of Paris, is not so old or so powerful as Grippen, but she would sense it, I think, if a strange vampire came to Paris. Still, they could have gone to Rouen or Orléans to make their plans. The vampires of those cities perished in the confusions of the last German war. Such a journey would have been safer, would not have involved travel by day . . ."

"Do you know the vampires of Vienna?"

"No." She crossed to the window, spread back its teal-green velvet curtains, with their treble fringes of gold and tassels like double fists. "I feel them . . . feel their presence. As they feel mine, without being able at once to see where I am. They know I am here."

Her fingers traced the fringe, the fabric, drinking of the texture as they had drunk the shape and texture of the porcelain cup. The dim light from the street below edged and transformed her face into a song of gold planes and black.

"I feel . . . everything. This new city that seems to bleed music from its very stones . . . When I saw the men pursuing you, I'd been walking about the streets for nearly an hour, just glutting myself on new tastes, new smells, the voice of a river that isn't the Thames. All those new dreams and thoughts and sensations hammer around me and in me and at me. I feel as if every cobblestone has a diamond underneath it, and I want to run through the streets gathering them up like a greedy little girl."

The colorless lips curved in a half-wondering smile, and Asher remembered her watching the dancers in the café, drinking the smell of the coffee, the music of the waltz. "I know I'm in danger. I'm afraid, and I know I should be more afraid than I am. I could die in moments, just because I don't know the right place to hide, the right turning to take. But it's so beautiful."

She half wrapped the curtain around her, the lush color startling against her face, like a silver icon or a painting by Klimt.

"This is all so new to me, wonderful and strange. It's the first time, you understand, that I have left England. The first time since . . . since I became what I am . . . that I've been out of London. It's been nearly two hundred years, Dr. Asher. I traveled a little after I thought Ernchester was dead, visited a sister in the north. But in my mourning I had no taste for it and only wanted to return to what I knew. I mourned for a long time."

Asher had seen a portrait of her, done when she was over sixty in her mortal life. She'd put on weight, and her hair had grayed, and the raptor eyes that flashed copper in the rosy lamp flame had been dead, resigned, filled with a kind of hurt puzzlement, as if she had never ceased to ask, *How can he be dead?* In the painting she'd worn the broad gold band that gleamed now on her finger.

"A vampire traveling is . . . horribly vulnerable."

"And yet you came."

She smiled, a human smile, the full, pale lips hiding the fangs. "I love him," she said. "To my last breath—and two centuries beyond."

Lady Ernchester had instructed the management of the hotel that she was not to be disturbed by chambermaids. She was an actress, she had said, and likely would be out most of the night, sleeping in the day. When she told Asher this, during a discussion of how words were pronounced in her early girlhood while she mended the slashes in his jacket and greatcoat, he closed his eyes briefly, imagining the concierge's reaction to this request.

But in fact when Asher later heard the chambermaids chatting in Czech and Hungarian in the corridor, none even tried the door.

Asher had tried to remain awake through the night, talking of philology and folklore with the vampire countess—her imitation of her nursemaid's Wessex dialect had been both hilarious and fascinating—but the ache of his wound, loss of blood, and exhaustion had claimed him. The voices of the chambermaids woke him in mid-morning, to find a heavy sunlight slanting through the chinks in the teal-colored curtains. He lay back on the settee again, trying to formulate an article in his mind—countryfolk of Anthea's day had pronounced the *y* or *e* at the end of such words as *hande* as a sort of aspiration, though they no longer spoke an *e* as *a*, and they would walk across a field rather than meet a pig in the road. But how on earth could he claim he'd had an interview with a contemporary of the Cavalier poets?

In time the voices of the chambermaids faded and the upper floor of the old *palais* fell silent. A heavy silence, broken only by the far-off clatter of a tram in the Schottenring and the distant threads of a hurdy-gurdy. He thought again of the woman sleeping, sealed within her double trunks, trusting his word that he would remain through the day and see that she came to no harm. Over the centuries she had killed . . . how many?

I wish you could have known us as we were.

Was all vampirism a craving to hold to the sweetness of a vanished youth, a desire not to have the good years, the dream years, slip away in the flowing stream of time?

I love him, she had said. *I knew he could not be dead.*

Who had loved the men, the women, the children whose lives she had traded for the continuance of her own?

He sighed and leaned the bridge of his nose on his knuckles, twisting at the problem again as a fish twists on a hook. She trusted him. And indeed, only through her could he hope to find Ernchester now, to keep him from selling his services to the Hapsburg Emperor, if he hadn't already. What had Karolyi offered him? Safety from Grippen? Why not tell Anthea, then? Why not bring her to Vienna with him?

Who had searched the house, who had known of Karolyi's plans, and for what had they been seeking? Who was Olumsiz Bey?

A transliteration for the Master of Vienna? Who might, after all, be Turkish himself. The whole area had been overrun as late as the mid-seventeenth century, and it was conceivable that the Undead in this most cosmopolitan of cities might not be Austrian—or even European—at all.

And what, above all, was he going to do when he *did* find Ernchester. Kill him?

He knew already that he would never sleep easy again if he didn't kill Anthea as well.

With a soft, oiled click, a key turned in the lock. Asher's mind fumbled tiredly for the Hungarian for *This room is not to be disturbed* as he rose and crossed to the door, which opened to reveal Bedford Fairport.

"Asher!" The little man blinked in surprise and adjusted his spectacles as if Asher were some trick refraction of the light. "What on earth . . . ?"

Deportation telegram, thought Asher automatically, his mind still sluggish with sleep. And then, *How did they trace me . . . ?* He was mentally framing what he was going to tell Halliwell about the layout of the Batthyany Palace when, with panther quickness, Ignace Karolyi stepped around the side of the door and put a knife to Asher's throat.

Fairport bleated, *"No!"* as the blade gashed like splintered glass. "Not here!"

The ape-browed coachman and two burly thugs Asher had never seen before were already in the room and closing the door. One of them caught Asher's elbows behind his back, thrust him against the wall; the other walked straight to the window to pull the curtains shut. Blood from the small cut on his neck burned hot on Asher's skin, but Karolyi had already turned his attention elsewhere, though the blade remained cold against the flesh.

"Find it."

Asher tried to turn but was pushed against the wall again. Over his shoulder he saw Fairport staring at him in a kind of aghast astonishment; one of the thugs took the medical bag out of Fairport's hand, opened it and pulled out a paper of sticking plaster, which he slapped over Asher's mouth. With his free hand Karolyi took something from his greatcoat pocket, a silk scarf, with which the thug tied Asher's hands. Probably the same one, thought Asher, he'd used to strangle the woman in Paris.

Only then did Karolyi take his knife from Asher's throat, sheathe it in an inner pocket of his jacket. The man who'd been holding Asher's arms kicked him roughly behind the knees, thrusting him to the floor, a minor theater of operations while the others pushed through the doorway into the next room. Asher tried to cry out, a warning, protest, appeal against the hideous vision of them prizing open the double lids of the trunks . . .

Then he realized that Anthea was perfectly safe.

It was Karolyi who'd had her house searched—probably Karolyi who'd written *Vienna Express* on the timetable.

He'd had her followed here from the station.

"This has to be it," he heard Fairport say in German.

"You're not gonna check to see?" asked the coachman.

Fairport squeaked protestingly; Karolyi said, "Let it be, Lukas," his voice casual, but the henchmen stepped quickly out of the room. "Did you think she would not follow?"

"To tell you the truth, I didn't know."

Asher turned his face against the thick, dust-smelling carpet, saw them standing together in the doorway, the old man looking up into Karolyi's face like a retriever who's just lugged in a pheasant nearly its own size. He thought, *Fairport's a double*. Something about the distance between them, the tilt of Fairport's head, told the whole story. *Has been a double for years.*

On reflection he supposed he should feel anger, but he

didn't. It was something that happened in the Great Game, like stray whores being strangled or those who learned too much getting shot.

Karolyi looked down at Asher with an expression of rueful half amusement. "So tell me, Dr. Asher—was it just coincidence that you were the man assigned to follow me? Or was Ernchester wrong in believing that the British are not also using the Undead?"

Asher inclined his head. He reflected that it might even be the truth.

Karolyi laughed. "Not many, I daresay. They're good, rational, God-fearing, Church of England, university men in your Department. Civilized, the way they tried to civilize me all my life." He came over and squatted beside Asher's shoulder, slim and soldierly even in the impeccably cut brown suit he wore. A hot blade of sunlight flashed across the gold and ruby of his cravat pin, red and gold repeated on his signet ring.

"But being raised in the mountains does something to you. I suspect I got from my Moravian nurse, at the age of five, what you got from years of comparing legends and collecting odd facts that don't fit into the curricula of Oxford and Innsbruck. Was that why they picked you to follow me? Surely they don't think I'd miss a familiar face?"

Unable to reply because of the sticking plaster, Asher only met his eyes. *You know I'd never answer your questions anyway,* his look said, and the full, red lips curved in a mocking smile.

"Well, I admit I didn't realize it *was* you in 'ninety-five until I saw you in the Munich train station. Our good Dr. Fairport kept that little secret from me back then." Karolyi stood up. Behind him, the two thugs carried Anthea's trunk to the door which the coachman Lukas held open; Fairport stood by, watery eyes flicking nervously from the trunk to Asher and Karolyi. "You know, I'd have thought you'd have been promoted past field agent by this time. You always struck me as being smarter than that. But maybe that was luck."

He took his gloves from his pocket, started to put them on but glanced down again at Asher and returned them to the pocket again. A small gesture, but Asher knew at once what it meant.

White kid was expensive, and blood would not come out of it.

"Remember my instructions, Lukas ... *all* of my instructions ..." he called out, and then turned with an admirable casualness to say, "Dr. Fairport, perhaps you'd best go with them."

Fairport nodded, his gaze behind the massive spectacles glued to the trunk as the stevedores maneuvered it through the door. "Of course," he breathed, "they can't appreciate ... Klaus! Klaus, please, a little more gently!"

He's forgotten I'm here, thought Asher. More furious than frightened, he made a muffled noise that might have been Fairport's Christian name.

By the way the old man flinched, Asher knew he'd guessed right. Absorbed, fascinated, obsessed by the prospect of taking a vampire alive, Fairport *had* forgotten. Had forgotten what Karolyi did with those inconvenient to him, if he'd ever known. The old man turned back, not quite in time to catch Karolyi smoothly withdrawing his hand from the front of his coat.

Asher met Fairport's eyes, forbidding him not to guess what was going to happen the minute he left the room. The old man's eyes, pale blue and tiny, distorted behind enormous rounds of glass, flinched away. *Damn you,* thought Asher, *if you're going to let him kill me, at least admit to yourself what you're doing . . .*

"You'd best supervise them," Karolyi said gently, nodding after the departing men. *You don't really want to see this, do you?*

Karolyi's eyes met Fairport's, held them, and Asher understood the unspoken barter: *If you don't want to have anything further to do with vampires, of course that can be arranged, too . . .*

Fairport turned uncertainly, as if Karolyi had implied that only his intervention could prevent the three stevedores from heaving Anthea's trunk out the window or riding it down the stairs like a bobsled.

Then he turned back. "Someone, er—might have seen us come in," he said hesitantly. "They'll certainly have seen the name on the van." He looked apologetically down at Asher and twisted his hands in their gray cotton gloves, as if that were the best he could do. Asher wanted to kick him.

Karolyi fetched a long-suffering sigh. "Have you chloroform in your bag, then?"

Fairport went to his instrument case, but the tremor of his hands, increased by nervousness, spilled the chloroform as he tried to pour it onto the cotton pad. Karolyi strode over to steady him, and in that moment Asher twisted his wrists against the hastily knotted scarf. The silk wasn't like rope, with rope's matted fibers; one knot tightened hard while the other slithered and loosened. As Karolyi turned back with the drug-soaked cotton in hand, Asher chopped hard with his legs at the Hungarian's ankles, pulled free one arm from the scarf, rolled to his feet and bolted for the door.

Karolyi, who had caught his balance on Fairport's shoulder, threw the fragile old man aside and flung himself after, shouting at the same time, *"Stop, thief!"*

Coatless, unshaven, unknown to the hotel and still mute from the sticking plaster over his mouth, Asher could only redouble his speed down the front stair, swinging himself over the banister and down to the next flight as two stout porters in brass-buttoned green uniforms pelted up to meet him. He kicked his way through a rickety French door to a balcony that ran around two sides of the building's central court, scrambled down a rain gutter to the court where a red and white van, Lukas at the reins, was just lurching into the carriageway to the street. He veered as the coachman drew rein and one of the thugs dropped off the back to meet him, ducked through a door into kitchen quarters, dodged past two startled cooks and a scullery girl, and out again into a lane, pursued by cries of *"Dieb! Mord!"* and hammering feet.

The cramped, medieval streets of the old city seemed filled with pedestrians, either retreating from him in alarm or joining in the pursuit. He struck someone, blundered against a market woman and a postman with his parcels, ducked down an open gateway into another court and through another kitchen as half a dozen young officers in the blue and yellow uniforms of the Imperial-and-Royal Hussars sprang up from a table at a sidewalk café and streamed joyously after him, hands to their sword hilts and spurs rattling on the pavement.

He dodged into another gate and raced up the shadowy stairs, while police, guards, and passersby sped past him and into the courtyard, looking for a kitchen door or postern through a shop—finding it, they roared on through, while Asher pulled the sticking plaster from his mouth—with a certain amount of damage to his mustache—and, when they were gone, descended the steps and walked out to the pavement of the Dortheergasse again.

The ache in his side was breathtaking, and under the bandages he could feel the warm seep of blood. Gray afternoon cold cut through his shirtsleeves. He fought a wave of dizziness as he hurried toward the crowds on the Graben, feeling in his trouser pocket and praying there was something there besides his handkerchief.

He was in luck. He'd paid for the coffee last night with one of Karolyi's ten-florin notes and, owing to the pull of the wound in his side, had put the change in his trousers rather than the inner pocket of his jacket. It was enough, maybe, to get him a jacket at the flea market in the Stephansplatz if he wasn't too fastidious, and a tram ticket out of the immediate area, to somewhere that he could hide.

EIGHT

ASHER remained on the Prater until nearly four, to give the hue and cry time to subside.

He had a late lunch at one of the rustic cafés that lined the Volksprater's bridle paths, consuming Czech sausage and *buchty* with one eye on the broad, graveled way that led from the organ grinders and carousels around the great Ferris wheel off into the gray and rust fastnesses of the old Imperial hunting park. Once he caught a glimpse of the brilliant cobalt jackets of the Imperial-and-Royal contingent of his pursuers among the thin trees and heard their faint hallooing as they searched.

England, when war comes, I think you'll be safe on the Austrian front at any rate.

But his inner smile faded at the thought of Ernchester, no longer now entirely a volunteer. If there were any stipulations in the deal he'd made with Karolyi, any acts he wouldn't perform at the nobleman's behest, the rules had changed. Or would change, when they told him they held Anthea prisoner.

He shivered in his rag-fair coat.

How long had Fairport been a double? he wondered. According to Karolyi, as far back as the flap over the smuggled Russian guns. It wasn't as unusual as it might seem to outsiders that Fairport hadn't blown him to Karolyi then. The fact that Fairport was passing the odd fact along to the Kundschafts Stelle from time to time didn't mean he was entirely their man.

Doubles—particularly men like Fairport—were frequently masters of self-deception, as Asher knew from having dealt with them. They always kept things back, from either side, sometimes for the most bizarre and absurd reasons: He remembered an American missionary in China who hadn't warned him of an impending rebel attack because he didn't want a Chinese patron of the mission to learn that his—the patron's—son had a mistress in the quarter of Tientsin through which the rebels were expected to come.

And perhaps Karolyi hadn't asked it of him, judging the matter too small to waste a trump on information he could learn some other way.

Even in retrospect, however, the thought of how close he'd come to dying as his Czech mountain guide had died made Asher shudder.

Fairport's research was already an obsession back in the nineties. Top quality materials, facilities, research journeys were always expensive, and Fairport was not a wealthy man. The best agents, Asher reflected, were those without any weak points, any handles upon which an enemy could grip.

Like Karolyi. Smooth, hollow men for whom the Job was all.

He glanced back at the self-consciously rustic kiosk where the waitresses huddled out of the cold, and wondered if Halliwell could be trusted.

Fairport might not be the only one in Karolyi's pay. Better, certainly, to wait until six and leave a message at Donizetti's, arranging a meeting. If he could stay out of sight until then . . .

But after six it wouldn't matter.

Not to Karolyi.

Though Asher was already fairly certain what he'd find, he strolled to the kiosk and bought that day's *Neue Freie Presse*. On the back page he found a small lead line:

LACEMAKER'S BODY FOUND IN WIENERWALD

Scanning the brief copy, his eye picked out the words "drained of blood." The name of the vineyard near which she'd been found was familiar, a quarter hour's drive from Fruhlingzeit.

So. He stared blankly in the direction of the gay-colored

midway, the shooting galleries and Punch and Judys, the panopticum where the murder of the Czar was on view in wax for the edification of schoolboys. A fleer of music blew from that direction, a distorted jingle of pipes and chimes, and then was gone. "The Waltz of the Flowers."

So.

A lacemaker. Like the prostitute in Paris, a woman no one would miss.

Of course Karolyi would pick a woman.

Ernchester would be there until sometime tonight.

Fairport was disposable. Even the knowledge of a scheme to use vampires was disposable. As Karolyi had said, most men in the Department weren't going to believe it anyway.

What could not be disposed of—what he himself could not relinquish—was Ernchester.

Today—now—Asher knew where the vampire earl was, where Anthea would be. Knowing Fairport—and Fruhlingzeit—were blown, they'd move tonight and, like true vampires, fade into the mists, leaving only a little blood and a muttering of rumor behind.

A fiacre drove by on the path, the coachman whistling briskly. The afternoon light had turned steely and cold. Asher shivered again and blew on his hands.

There was, of course, always the option of taking the first train back to Munich—cadging a ride in the baggage car, at this point, but Asher had done that in his time. If Burdon were still the head of the Munich branch—if there still *was* a Munich branch—he could at least get enough money to go back to England. Tell them Fairport was a traitor, Karolyi was in league with—well, a very dangerous man—and wash his hands of the business. Go home to Lydia, who might very well have sent him a wire at Fairport's . . . None of this was his affair anyway. He had done all he could be expected to do.

But that left Anthea in the hands of Karolyi.

And he knew where Ernchester was today. That was the crux of the matter.

There was a telephone in the kiosk. Undoubtedly the police could trace him through the exchange if he phoned Halliwell—

he'd dealt with the endless polite chatter of Viennese telephone operators too often to think the transaction could be accomplished quickly. And the delay of a night in jail meant that Ernchester—and Anthea—would vanish untraceably.

When he'd taken a seat at this table, half screened from the path by a hedge, there had been two or three other brave souls sipping coffee and gazing contemplatively over the slaty waters of the canal. Now he was alone. Across the river the clock on St. Stephen's struck three.

Unwillingly Asher got to his feet, thrust his bare hands into his pockets, and after a cautious glance up and down the path for signs of pursuit, headed back along the Haupt Allee for the Praterstern, where with his last few pfennigs he could catch a tram at least partway to the Vienna Woods.

It was not long after the coming of full dark that Asher realized he was being followed.

He took the tram as far as Döbling, then climbed the winding road through thin rust-and-pewter woods past Grinzing. Moving kept him a little warm, though his side hurt at every step and he had to stop repeatedly to rest on the low rock walls that divided woods or vineyards from the road. He was sitting thus, trying to get his breath after a particularly steep patch of road, when he heard the church clock in that storybook village chime five.

Now and then a farm wagon passed, and once a motorcar full of homebound seekers after pastoral calm, but as the twilight clotted under the trees, such things became few. A small wind cleared the clouds; a shaved silver coin of moon floated in a halo of ice. By six it was utterly dark.

That mattered less than it might have, for Asher knew the road. Toiling upward with the ache of fatigue dragging at his bones, there were times when he felt he'd never been away. He didn't even have to look for the Fruhlingzeit Sanitarium's gateposts of ivy-covered stone. The slope of the road told him exactly how far yet he had to go.

He listened for the sound of human pursuit. But that was not what he heard.

He would have been hard put to say exactly what it was he did hear, or what he felt, that told him they were in the woods behind him. Perhaps, had he not come so close to death at their hands—or the hand of those like them in Paris—a year ago, he would not even have known he was being stalked.

But he knew. A touch of sleepiness at his mind, in spite of the wind eating through his holed coat and the ache of his wound. A sense that it wasn't really necessary to look behind him, or around him, at the woods. And then, when a single breath of moving air sighed from the cinder-colored darkness among the trees, the sweetish stink of blood.

He didn't slow his step, or quicken it, not daring to let them see he knew, but he did wonder what he was going to do. He was nearly at the drive that turned into Fruhlingzeit, and the drive, at least, would be watched by Karolyi's men. He'd have to leave the road then. The silver on his throat and wrists would buy him a few seconds, but they wouldn't save him from a broken neck. The road before him lay deserted.

On the whole they moved without sound, but it was late in the autumn, and beneath the pale stems of the beeches the brown leaves mounded thick, and dead fern and ivy rustled and whispered with the passage of unseen feet.

He stopped on the edge of the road—he'd been keeping to the shadows along the ditch in case Karolyi had patrols on the road—and took his watch from his pocket, angling it to the moonlight, then closed it with a click and, under cover of slipping it into his pocket again, unhooked the fob from his belt. A quick motion wrapped the chain twice around his middle finger, so that when he drew his hand out again—and tucked it under his armpit, as if for warmth—he carried the rounded disk of silver cradled out of sight in his palm.

It wasn't much, but it would have to do.

He sprang across the ditch, scrambled a little up the bank, wondering if they could hear the sudden heavy slamming of his heart. The Vienna Woods were thin. Beneath a summer canopy of leaves he doubted he could have navigated by night, but with the trees bare, the familiar shapes of beech and sycamore were just visible by the latticed pallor of the moon.

There was no way of telling how great a force of men Karolyi had at the sanitarium. It would take only one to spread an alarm.

Provided he lived to get anywhere near the walls.

What had Anthea said? *The masters among the Undead are jealous of their territories.* He remembered, too, that pitiful fledgling Bully Joe Davies back in London, glancing in terror over his shoulders: *They'd kill me, they would—Grippen don't want none in London but his own get, his own slaves . . .*

Had they, too—whoever *they* were—read that tiny mention in the *Neue Freie Presse* about the dead lacemaker and known that another was hunting on their territory, killing in such a way as to rouse the suspicions of the rulers of the day?

Or did they simply recognize his heartbeat, Asher wondered, the smell of his blood, as those of an intruder who had been snooping around the walls of their palaces last night?

Asher walked as quickly as he dared, moving purposefully. Once he heard the leaves rustle, and some sound that might have been a taffeta petticoat, but his senses screamed at him that there were more than one. Like sharks they followed him, slipping unseen through the abysses between the trees.

White glimmered ahead. Black veins of ivy traced it: the rear wall of Fruhlingzeit. Above it bulked the house's steep roofs and stuccoed walls, the golden ochre hue so characteristic of Viennese houses grubby in the dark. Most of the windows facing the woods were shuttered, but lamplight from those facing the court outlined what had been the stable, since converted into a laboratory and therapy room. Asher had always suspected that the aged cats and dogs—and the occasional Viennese businessmen—upon whom Fairport experimented showed improvement because of the therapeutic massage, good food, and careful tending that went with "magnetic induction." There was a sort of crypt under the stable, Asher remembered, where Fairport's generator was housed among stores of carbolic, ether, kerosene, and coal.

Nearer the wall he smelled the smoke of a guard's cigarette.

The trees pressed close around the back of the property. From the concealment of an oak he could see the window where he'd sat all that long ago afternoon, planning how to get himself out of Vienna and betray Françoise in the most painful possible fashion in the process.

Then he turned his head and saw a woman standing beside him.

The hair lifted on his nape. He had not heard one single sound.

She was beautiful, like something wrought of moonlight, flaxen hair piled high, but snagged and tugged by the branches until its tendrils floated around her face in a glowing halo; light eyes, gray or blue, etiolated and transparent. Her dress was moonlight, too, some oyster shade, colorless as a web, and the luster of satin flickered along its sleeve as she lifted her hands. Her eyes filled with longing and sorrow and desire.

Asher felt his mind shutting down, warm yearning for her flooding heart and thoughts and groin, even though, in the shadows of those waxen lips, he saw the curve of fangs. It didn't matter. All that mattered was that he wanted her, as desperately as he had wanted Lydia before they were married, as desperately as he had wanted the pretty shop girls of Oxford when he was a student and frantic with a boy's nascent lusts. Against his will a sort of drunkenness filled his mind and he found himself reaching for her, filled with the irrational conviction that kissing her, touching her, would not matter, that it would be all right, the way one thinks in a dream.

As if from some tremendous distance he saw himself, his mind protesting but unable to connect its thoughts with his actions. Her hands touched his face, cold even in their gloves of shell-colored kid; they slipped over his ears and down to his neck, and his own hand felt rough and cold on the taut silvery cloth of her side.

Then her mouth twisted in a snarl, wide, like an infuriated cat's. The glamour snapped away as her hands jerked back from his collar, where even through fabric and leather she felt the sear of the silver underneath. Asher gasped, waking, it seemed, to find her mouth inches from his throat, her grip already like iron on his arms. Before she could move, he struck her cheek with the silver watch palmed in his hand, twisting away from her even as she screamed—shock, pain, fury, like a cheetah's scream, or a demon's in hell.

He flung her from him, bolted for the wall. She screamed again, and from the corner of his eye he saw her collapse to her knees, clutching the side of her face, screaming over and over as she clawed at the flesh. Something—some darkness— flashed among the trees, and he felt a smothering sleepiness crush his mind like gloved iron. He thrust it from him, scrambled up and over the wall as men's voices cried out somewhere close, dropped into the rosebushes below instants before the first of Fairport's servants pounded around the side of the house. He rolled into the shadow, hiding the pale blur of his face, and they ran through the garden to the gate. The moment the last was gone, he flung himself across the narrow space of gravel and bare thorn to the door under the stair.

Then other men were in the garden, calling to one another. He heard Lukas the coachman's name, and someone called something about "Herr Kapitän . . ." presumably Karolyi's regimental rank.

The screaming had stopped. But they'd all be busy for some time.

Ten minutes, he thought—striding down the stone-flagged passageway to the kitchen—while everyone dashed madly around the perimeter of the wall. Longer, if they had as few men as he thought they did, or if they found anything. He tripped the lever behind the scullery cupboard, slipped down the narrow stairway it revealed. More than once he'd taken Slav nationalists or Russian messengers down this way, to keep them unseen by Fairport's patients.

God, how the blond woman had screamed!

At the flea market he'd purchased wire to make another picklock; his hands shook while he winkled the lock at the bottom of the stair. It was an old-fashioned tumbler type, and he could have picked it in his sleep—he'd warned Fairport about it a dozen times . . .

Seventeen years with the Department, he was interested to see, had not inured him to that old chivalric voice within him that protested that there were things that a gentleman did and would not do even in defense of his life: kick a man when he was down or render what was euphemistically called a "foul blow" in a fight; shoot a man in the back; lie on sworn oath; forge another's name.

Shoot a sixteen-year-old boy who trusted you.

Steal money from a woman who loved you.

Strike a beautiful girl in the face with a handful of substance that you were reasonably certain would react upon her like vitriol.

Evidently the fact that had he not done so, she would have killed him within seconds was of no importance to those old voices of his childhood: his country-doctor father, his grim-faced uncle, his tutors at Winchester and Oxford. He still felt an utter swine.

Did he think she was any different from Anthea?

The pawls of the lock snicked back. As he opened the door, dim gaslight from the scullery above showed him a strange gleam on the lock plate. Asher braced his foot in the door to keep it from closing—it was, as he recalled, heavily springed—and lit a match for a better look.

On the inner side, the lock was silver.

The smell of fresh-sawn wood filled his nose, and beneath it, the smell of blood.

His nape prickled again, and he stood still, listening, barely breathing. Then, slowly, he turned the catch to keep it from locking again, raised his lucifer higher and held it up into the room within.

Silver flashed in the seed of phosphor light. Where he had known only a small underground chamber equipped with bed, chair, and chamber pot, he now saw a glittering grillwork of silver bars that stretched from side to side not three feet from the door. Where the base bar of electroplated steel held them across the floor there were curls of sawdust, yellow and new.

Behind the bars, eyes caught the reflection like the eyes of a cat.

Asher blew out the match as the flame scorched his fingers. Frail, twice-reflected light from the stairway showed him a pale face, pale hands as they approached the bars, the white of a shirtfront and an old-fashioned stock.

A voice spoke out of the darkness. "Have you come for my capitulation? I told you I'd do anything you asked. Isn't it enough that you've betrayed me, lied to me? Was it necessary to . . . to do what you did?"

There was a pause, while Asher stared blankly into the darkness, and the strange eyes gleamed back at him from behind the silver bars.

Then the voice said, "Dr. Asher. The doctor of languages from London. Don Simon said you had been a spy."

Asher's mind made a tardy jump. "That wasn't your wife's voice you heard," he said.

One of the white hands moved; Ernchester pressed it for a moment to his mouth, closed his eyes, like a man trying to still something within himself.

Asher went on quickly, "It was another vampire, a woman, who attacked me just outside the walls. Do you know where they keep the key?"

Ernchester shook his head. "Fairport keeps it," he said after a moment. As Asher had heard on the train, his accent was far less modern than his wife's, the flat vowels making it sound very American. "Where is Anthea? They said they had her . . ."

"I don't know."

"Find her. I beg you, take her out of this place . . ."

Asher stepped to the bar, examined the keyhole of the small doorway set in the lattice. It was a Yale cylinder type, and unlocking it was far beyond the capacity of a piece of wire. At the back of the barred area he could see a trunk, like a block of shadow. In front of it the earl seemed very small in his shabby, swallowtailed coat, his gay red-and-yellow waistcoat and strapped pantaloons, a ghost wrought of dust, a mummy that sunlight would shatter.

"I'll be back."

As he turned to go, he saw, lying on the bench beside the outer door, the lace mitts Anthea had worn at LaStanza's and a red ribbon from which depended a black pearl the size of a pea. It had been around her neck when she'd lain down in the trunk that served her as a traveling coffin. They must have brought them in, to show him that they had her indeed.

What had the original deal been, he wondered as he mounted the hidden stair to the scullery above and pushed the shelves to behind him. A lure, to bring him into their power for something he'd never have consented to do? What? Ernchester had certainly gotten on the train at Charing Cross of his own volition, had been a free man when he'd murdered Cramer. Asher's jaw tightened bitterly, remembering that large young man's ingenuous grin. He should shoot the boy's murderer, not risk his own life setting him loose.

He remembered again as he climbed the stairs to Fairport's office with quick silence—staying by the wall so the treads would not creak—why he had come to hate the Great Game.

A lamp burned in the office—inconveniently, because one of the curtains was half open, and it meant careful maneuvering not to be seen from outside as he approached the desk on his hands and knees. He'd heard no one in this wing of the house. He had only minutes before they returned and started searching in earnest, and Ernchester was right in that he must, above all, release Anthea. While Karolyi had her, he had the vampire earl, whether or not the man was actually in his possession. The fact that Ernchester had jumped to the conclusion that the dreadful scream he heard had been hers told its own story.

They are killers, he thought, in a kind of baffled rage at himself. *Over the years Anthea has done to thousands of men what that woman nearly did to me. Why should I care?*

But all he remembered was the face of a woman in a portrait, plump, weary, gray-haired, in mourning for a husband who had died thirty years before. *How can he be dead?*

Among the litter on the surface of the desk—Fairport, though not as bad as Lydia, was an untidy housekeeper—Asher recognized the folded copy of last Friday's *Times.* Beside it lay a yellow envelope containing two train tickets.

Paris to Constantinople, by way of Vienna.

Constantinople?

A thought came to him. *Isn't it enough that you've betrayed me, lied to me?*

Crouching on the floor beside the desk, he removed the handset from the telephone and cranked the Vienna exchange.

"Here Vienna Central Telephone Exchange," came the operator's cheerful voice. "A very good evening to you, honored sir."

"And a very good evening to you, honored madame," replied Asher, who knew that it never did anyone any good to try to hurry a Viennese telephone operator. "Would you be so kind as to connect me with Donizetti's café in the Herrengasse, and ask them to let me speak with the Herr Ober, please?"

The floor vibrated with a door closing somewhere. Feet passed quickly along a downstairs hall. Seconds fell on him like shovelfuls of earth filling a grave.

"Certainly, honored sir, it would give me great pleasure."

He heard her voice, distantly engaged in formal greetings and elaborate social chat with someone at Donizetti's, asking at length for the honored Herr Ober, there is a most honored Herr who wishes to speak with him if his duties will allow him time, and, more closely, voices calling from the courtyard outside the windows. ". . . found nothing . . . someone there . . ." Minutes, he thought, and they would begin to search the house.

"Ladislas Levkowitz at your service, honored sir."

"Herr Ober Levkowitz, I realize it's a tremendous imposition on such a busy man as yourself, but would the British Herr Halliwell have arrived for dinner yet? Could you be so kind as to let him know that Herr Asher wishes to speak with him on a matter of some urgency? Many thanks . . ."

Asher cradled the handset against his face, rose to his knees and with a swift glance at the window made a quick review of the rest of the desk. Three or four green-covered notebooks contained interviews with octogenarians in the Vienna region, and others much farther afield. A thick bundle of invoices for glassware and chemicals connected with experiments on the blood of these ancients proved, at a glance, that Fairport's expenses were far greater than the sanitarium's profits could possibly cover. In the back of a drawer was a thick wad of torn-open envelopes of the stationery of the Austrian Embassy in Constantinople, each containing a dated slip with amounts written on them—large amounts—and signed "Karolyi." The dates went back two years. There were half a dozen keys, none of which would fit a cylinder lock of the type on the silver lattice's door. A crowbar, he thought. There'd be one in the generator crypt if he could get to it.

Dammit, he thought, *stop chatting with the Herr Ober and come to the telephone . . .*

"Set the receiver back in the cradle, Asher."

He turned his head. Fairport stood in the office doorway, a pistol in his gray-gloved hand.

NINE

ASHER didn't move.

"I'll use it," Fairport warned. He came slowly into the room, circling wide to stay out of Asher's reach and keeping the pistol pointed, until he was close enough to the desk to stretch out his free hand and push down the cradle, breaking the connection.

Asher settled from kneeling to crouching again beside the desk, his legs gathered under him, the handset still dangling from his grip. "Even against one of your own countrymen?" It was the cant of the Great Game—honor on the playing fields of Eton and God Save the King. But the Game was one Fairport had been playing for years as well, and there was a chance he would still think in its terms. And Asher was curious about the terms in which he *did* think.

"This matter goes beyond country, Asher," said Fairport softly. He backed a little, out of immediate arm's reach. "It's all you can think of, isn't it? All that sleek brute Ignace can think of. Like savages, both of you, tearing up volumes of Plato to stuff into cracks in the roof to keep the rain out. What we have found is the greatest revelation, the greatest discovery, in the history of mankind, and all he can think of is how such a man can be used in Macedonia and against the Russians in Bulgaria—and all you can think of is how to kill such a man,

139

that the balance won't tip against you in the 'Great Game.' You don't understand. You refuse to understand."

"I understand how much damage a man like that can do, if he allies himself with any government. And I understand the kind of fee a government would pay such a man."

Fairport looked completely blank. Then, when Asher raised his brows, the old man flushed an unhealthy, blotchy pink. "Oh. Oh, that. I'm sure it's a condition that can be rectified with proper medical investigation . . . I've found astonishing virtue in yogurt as a food of longevity, and in Chinese ginseng. They won't always be drinkers of human blood . . ."

"I'm sure that lacemaker Ernchester killed last night would be glad to hear it," Asher replied grimly, though some objective corner of his mind had to fight not to laugh at the image of Lionel Grippen, Master Vampire of London, supping on a dish of yogurt and ginseng tea. "And don't you think there might be vampires who're as fond of the taste of human death as they are of human blood?"

The old man's mouth flinched. "That's the most revolting thing I've ever heard! They can't possibly be . . . No one in his senses could be. They'll welcome that liberation as much as any drunkard would welcome the liberation from drink. And in the meantime there are the physically and socially unfit—"

"You mean traitors?" No other sounds in the house, though there was a dim clashing of shrubbery as someone passed by under the window. If he could disarm him without a shot being fired, there might still be time.

Fairport drew himself up. "I am not a traitor," he said with dignity.

Asher sighed in genuine disgust. "I never met a double agent who was."

"I have *never* passed information along to Baron Karolyi which would hurt any of our contacts or our agents . . ."

"How would you know?" Asher demanded tiredly. "You know nothing about politics, you barely read a newspaper, or at least you didn't when I was here. You don't think, if he can make a deal with vampires—if he can blackmail Ernchester into creating other vampires, fledglings loyal to the Austrian government—they won't eventually be used against us here? Or back at home?"

"That won't happen!" Fairport cried. "I won't let it happen! Asher, Karolyi is only a means to an end. These petty politics, a handful of military secrets that are going to be useless in three years, they're a small price to pay for the knowledge, the learning, that will free man, finally, from the grip of age, and debility, and death!

"Asher, look at me!" He gestured like a frustrated child with his miniature fist. "Look at me! I've been an old man since I was thirty-five! *Sans teeth, sans eyes, sans taste . . .*" He shook his head. "And every day for the past twenty years I have dealt with men who, like me, have felt that cold, awful terror of knowing their bodies are failing them. Men stumbling as they try to outrace the Pale Horse. I've tried everything, traveled to the far corners of the world, seeking out those who have conquered age—trying to find what it is that makes the body fail, that cripples us, blinds us, deafens us, renders us white-haired and flatulent and impotent and brittle."

Behind his thick lenses the blue eyes glittered suddenly, and genuine venom seeped into his voice. "What it is that wears out some while others continue to gorge and rut and dance into their eighties, their—"

Asher struck, thrusting off his long legs like lightning, smashing aside Fairport's gun hand at the same moment he drove a fist into the little man's chin. He struck with all he had, to carry him across the distance between them quicker than Fairport could react and shoot, and the impact hurled the professor back and to the floor, as if Asher had struck a child. There wasn't time to think or regret—in another moment Karolyi or one of the footmen might enter, and at that point Asher knew he would die. Karolyi, unlike Fairport, was not a man to justify or explain.

He scooped up the gun, transferred Fairport's key ring from the old man's coat pocket to his own, pulled free the old man's four-in-hand and used it to bind his wrists behind him, then stuffed Fairport's handkerchief into his mouth for a gag. He took another moment to drag him behind the desk, keeping low still, out of the range of the windows . . . Really, he thought, half regretful, the man had always been out of his league . . .

And smelled smoke.

Gray smoke was rolling along the ceiling of the upstairs hall.

Asher cursed. He would almost certainly be caught if he tried to get Fairport out of there, but there was nothing for it, and the man's halfhearted interference back at the pension in Vienna had almost certainly saved his life. He glanced out the long windows behind the desk, ascertained that there was no one visible in the gardens below, and kicked them open, dragging the little man out onto the balcony where the fresh air would revive him and he'd be able to hump himself down the outside stairs. Then he ducked back inside. Crimson reflections on the bare boughs showed him where two or three of the downstairs rooms were already in flames, and, even as he watched, he saw yellow light flare in the dark windows of the old stable building.

Arson, thought Asher in alarm. *Two places at once. Who the hell . . . ?*

He flung himself down the stairs, Fairport's gun in hand, the smoke already tearing his eyes and eating at his lungs. Under the stucco the old house was mostly wood and would go fast. Downstairs the smoke was worse, the heat pounding on Asher's face and making him dizzy as he raced along the corridor to the scullery. As he ran he thought, *If this is Karolyi's work, why let Fairport stay free? Or has Anthea somehow started this?*

The coachman's body lay in the scullery door. His eyes and mouth were both wide in a look of utter shock. His collar had been torn open, his shirt pulled back to reveal the hairy masses of neck and chest. Wounds bulged like tattered white mouths from ear to collarbone, but there was almost no blood.

Asher felt as if his heart shrank and turned to ice in his chest.

He crossed the scullery, looked swiftly out the rear door to the yard and saw what looked like another body in the shadows under the outside stair. Smoke seared his nostrils, weighted his rib cage. He couldn't tell if there was a smell of blood or not.

Not Anthea. And not Ernchester.

The others. The vampires of Vienna.

The ones who had followed him here.

Sweat was rolling down his face as he shoved back the shelving, ran down the stair into the cellar's cool abyss. He struck a match as he thrust through the door at the bottom; Ernchester, pacing the silver cage like an animal, wheeled, his eyes flashing in the tiny speck of the flame. "They're here," he said hoarsely. "I feel them. The house—they've fired the house . . ."

He flicked through the barred silver door the moment Asher had it open, twisting his body so as not to touch.

"Anthea!"

He started for the door, then turned back, catching Asher by the elbow in a grip that came close to breaking the bone. "Did you find her? She isn't in this house, I'd have known, I'd have felt her, read her dreams . . ."

Asher recalled something Ysidro had said to him once, about being unable to sense the presence of people deep in cellars through the muffling weight of the earth.

"She'll be in the crypt under the stable."

Flame light poured down the stairs, bloody on the earl's face; a thin face and not particularly an aristocratic one, with an indefinable air of age despite the fact that, like Anthea, he appeared to be no more than thirty-five. Asher did notice, as they raced up the stairs into the choking inferno of the scullery, that at no time did sweat break from the smooth skin of the vampire's brow.

Asher crossed the yard at a run, but the vampire earl was ahead of him, moving with an insectile, weightless speed, huge bounds like a gazelle. Ernchester stopped, however, in front of the burning stable, hands raised before his face and his blue-gray eyes sick with horror and shock.

The earl followed him without question, however, circling the building to the rear, where the flames were less. Asher drove his boot through a cellar window, dropping into what had been a boiler room. The place smelled of dirt and damp brick, and the thin, sickly odor of kerosene that lifted the hair on Asher's neck. He dug another match from his pocket, scratched it on the wall behind him. There were barrels of the stuff, ranged along the wall beyond the hunched black monstrosity of the generator itself. He heard the earl whisper, "God's death!" behind him, and pointed toward what looked to be the door of a closet, nearly invisible in the shadows by the coal bin.

"Through there. We have a few minutes. The fire's just caught."

The door was locked. Ernchester ripped the entire mechanism—lock plate, handle, bolt—free of the wood without visible effort and threw it clanging to the brick floor, then vanished like a moth in the darkness.

Asher had been in the crypt many times. Like the subcellar beneath the scullery, Fairport used it to conceal people who weren't supposed to be in Vienna or who had to leave the town in a hurry. Because of its remoteness from the main house—and the patients who usually resided there—it had also been used for meetings, if instructions had to be passed along with minimum risk of being seen.

He'd felt his way halfway down the boxed-in stairway when yellow light glowed at the bottom. Through the doorway he saw Ernchester setting on the table a newly lighted oil lamp and turning back to the coffin trunk that filled half of the room.

"She's in here," the earl said softly and knelt beside the trunk. He passed his hands along the lid, pressed his cheek to the leather. His eyes closed. The flesh around them rumpled and compressed, like an old man's. Then he moved his head and looked up over his shoulder at Asher, standing in the doorway. "Can you take an end?"

It was awkward, getting the trunk around the corners of the stair. Even in the few minutes they had been in the crypt, the air in the boiler room had heated, and the smoke there was growing thick. Like the house, the stable was wood, the roof and walls went up like tinder. When they dragged and manhandled the trunk upstairs, they found the ground floor suffocatingly hot, filled with blinding smoke under a vicious rain of cinder and sparks. Asher coughed, gasping for breath, his grip on the trunk slipping. As his knees gave under him, he wondered suddenly what chemicals Fairport had in the laboratories here and what fumes they might be adding to the miasma of smoke.

He tried to get to his feet, and fell.

Above the roaring of the fire overhead he heard the scratch of the trunk's brass-bound corners as Ernchester—unbreathing, undead, desperate to save his wife at all costs—dragged it toward the door and safety.

Black unconsciousness rolled over Asher like a wave. He tried to stand, then realized that the air was a little cooler down near the floor. Inhaling was like trying to breathe kerosene. *Kerosene,* he thought dizzily. *When the roof goes, it'll take the floor with it, and the whole place will turn into a furnace . . .* The thought that he'd probably be killed by the falling roof before the kerosene scattered the building over half an acre of the Vienna Woods was not much of a comfort. At one point he thought he was crawling, but a moment later realized he was lying with his cheek to the superheating linoleum of the floor, a fallen cinder burning the back of his left hand.

Hands as cold and strong as machinery took hold of his arms, lifting and dragging him as if he were a bale of sticks. The smell of smoke seemed stronger outside, perhaps because his lungs were working again. He stumbled, trying to get his feet under him, and clutched at the shoulders that supported his arm.

He felt them flinch.

Silver, he thought. The chain on his wrist would sting through Ernchester's coat.

The trunk lay just within the compound gate. It was still shut. Ernchester must have turned back the moment he'd dragged it out of range of the fire.

"She's asleep."

Asher raised his head, his brown hair hanging in his eyes, his face burning in the cold air under a film of sweat, soot, and grime. Ernchester knelt beside the trunk, one arm resting along its lid, the reflection of the flames imparting gory color to his narrow face, glittering in his close-cropped fair hair, his haunted, weary eyes.

"Drugged, I think," Ernchester went on softly. "That is . . . as well. Thank you."

Asher looked back across the gardens. The front part of the main house was in flames. The rear wing, where Fairport's office and his own rooms had been, was still intact. By the flaring light two bodies were clearly visible on the gravel paths.

He fumbled in his pocket for Fairport's keys, found two that would open the trunk's heavy latches. Ernchester touched his hand lightly as he would have opened the lid. "Not yet. The air will revive her, and I don't think I could stand that. I won't do that to her." The earl straightened his back, though he remained kneeling, one hand atop the other on the lid of the trunk. "Take her away from here. Go with her back to England. Take her out of this place. I beg you." He closed his eyes. "I beg you."

Firelight picked out the sudden lines around his eyes, the set of the thin lips—a face no one would notice, thought Asher, except that it was not a nineteenth-century face, much less one that belonged to this newborn era. The muscles, the speech, the expressions that had formed the mouth and chin and the set of the cheeks were all from some earlier time, and the years had not changed them.

"I can't repay you," he added softly. "I won't be seeing you, nor anyone known to you, ever again. I will owe you this favor, this boon, for all of time. But please make sure she gets home all right. Tell her—" His voice did not break but halted for a moment, almost as if he sought words. "Tell her that she is all that I ever wanted, and all that I ever had."

Then he raised first the outer lid, then the inner, to reveal the woman sleeping within.

The living dead, they had been called. By the fevered glare of the firelight she looked, indeed, both alive and dead: waxen, still, unbreathing, with her dark hair scattered about her, the linen of her gown not whiter than the flesh it covered. And beautiful, thought Asher. Beautiful beyond words.

Looking up, he saw Ernchester's face, without expression, as though all expression had grown too much to be supported under the weight of endless years, save for his eyes.

Ernchester bent a little to touch his wife's cheek, then leaned down to kiss her lips. To Asher he said, "She'll wake soon. Tell her that I love her. Always."

Yellow light flared higher as flames ran along the roof of the main house. Asher turned, startled, in time to see a spindly figure move on the balcony, work and thrust itself to its feet, wobbling and off balance. Disheveled white hair caught the light, and the lenses of his spectacles made great rounds of burning amber as he turned his head. Staggering, Fairport began to descend the stairs.

Asher shouldn't have been able to hear it under the roaring of the fire, but he did. Thin, silvery laughter, like the breaking of wafer-frail glass, and beneath that, the obscene toad-croak of a bass chuckle. They seemed to hover on the balcony, and on the stair, not quite touched by the fire's light, as if visibility were something to be put on or off at will, but at one point Asher thought that one of them wore a dress the color of web and moonlight.

Fairport cried under the gag and fell, rolling down the stairs. They floated after him, half-seen migraine visions of alabaster faces, shining hands, eyes that caught the light as had those of the rats among the bones of St. Roche. At the foot of the steps he tried to get to his feet, falling heavily and trying again, and they ringed him, like porpoises playing, flickering shadows of a force he had entirely underestimated, following him as he scrabbled and heaved along the ground.

They let him get quite some distance before they began to feed.

With a roar, the roof of the stables fell in, curtains of flame leaping higher, yellower, beating upon yet somehow failing to completely illuminate what was happening in the court. Then a deeper roar, like a battery of eight-inch guns, and the earth jarred underfoot as the kerosene went up. Beside Asher, Anthea cried out, "Charles!" and sat up suddenly, her brown eyes wide with terror.

Asher caught her hand. Her gaze met his, clouded with old dreams. "The stones. The stones exploded with the heat." Then she flinched and turned her face away, and Asher realized that for a moment she had thought she was still in London, many years before, when the whole of that city burned.

She said again, "Charles," and when she looked at him then, her eyes were clear.

"He's gone."

She started to rise, and he closed his hand hard on hers, drawing her back and knowing he had no way to hold her if she simply wrenched herself free. She could have broken his wrist, or his neck, with very little effort. She looked at him again, questioning and pleading, her black curls a cloud around her face and shoulders, the flame a soaked gold in her eyes.

"He told me to take you back to England," Asher said. "To see that you reached there safely. He said that he would not see me—and, I presume, you—again. He said that he loves you, always and forever."

In the courtyard the vampires had sunk down in a ring around Fairport, whose frantic noises had risen to a muffled crescendo, then ceased. Asher wondered what he'd do if Anthea vanished, as Ernchester had, flickering away like a ghost in the woods to seek him. He'd never make it back to Vienna.

For a moment he thought she would. Then she, too, glanced across at the dark shapes in the firelight. Just for a moment her pale tongue slipped out and brushed her lips.

But when she turned to him, her eyes were a woman's eyes. "Do you know where he's gone?"

Asher stroked a corner of his mustache. "I don't know," he said, "but I can guess. And my guess is: Constantinople."

TEN

"THURSDAY." Lydia stared blankly at the newspaper by the glare of the station lights. "Thursday night. We were still in Paris."

Margaret whispered, "Oh, my God," through hands pressed to her mouth.

"I thought . . . I thought I'd have a little more time to catch up with him. That things wouldn't happen so quickly."

Ysidro reappeared at their side, trailed by a laconic individual in a Slovak's baggy white britches who, at his command, loaded Ysidro's trunk and portmanteau, Margaret's satchel, and Lydia's voluminous possessions onto a trolley that he pushed away in the direction of the doors. The vampire tweaked the newspaper from Lydia's hands, and read.

DOCTOR PERISHES IN SANITARIUM FIRE

Early yesterday evening the well-known sanitarium "Fruhlingzeit" burned to the ground in a conflagration of epic proportions, claiming the life of the man who had made it his life-work and monument. The body of the most distinguished English specialist in rejuvenatory medicine, Dr. Bedford Fairport, whose work has contributed to the comfort and healing of hundreds of men and women in Vienna over the past eighteen years, was found in the smoking ruins by police constables and firefighters in the early hours of

Friday morning. According to the Vienna police, foul play is suspected. The bodies of a coachman and a laborer were also found.

No patients were present at the sanitarium when it burned, Dr. Fairport having temporarily closed the premises last week. The distinguished Herr Hofrat Theobald Beidenstunde, of the Imperial-and-Royal Austrian Coal Board, undergoing treatment for a nervous condition at Fruhlingzeit last week, states that Herr Professor Doktor Fairport requested that all patients return to their homes due to repairs on the foundations of the main building. Complete financial recompense was made to all patients so affected.

It is believed that the fire started in the laboratory where a generator was positioned too close to stores of kerosene, and later spread to the main villa. However, since all three bodies bore marks of violence, arson is being considered as a possibility. Further investigation by the Vienna police is under way.

"Behold an Englishman," murmured Ysidro. "The good Hofrat Beidenstunde should thank his stars he was reimbursed. The old Queen would never have approved such request for funds." He folded the newspaper and bestowed it in the pocket of his cloak.

"Victoria?" Margaret Potton asked in surprise.

"Elizabeth. There is nothing there which proves your husband's fate, mistress. This way."

The Slovak was waiting for them in the square outside, on the seat of a gaily painted wagon. Ysidro helped the two women in—lifting Lydia with unnerving ease from the pavement—and without wasted words they proceeded into the winding network of high-walled ways that made up the most ancient part of the Altstadt.

"Who—besides Fairport—would Jamie seek out in Vienna?"

"Three years ago it was a man named Halliwell." Ysidro turned his head, as if listening for some sound below or between the myriad voices and threads of stray music that clamored all around them on the bustling streets. "I have no more recent knowledge than that, nor am I sure where the Department has its headquarters these days. The embassy would be the place to inquire. Say that you seek your husband, that you wish to speak with Halliwell."

"They won't be there on a Sunday," Margaret pointed out worriedly.

"At least we can rent a carriage and go out to the ruins of the sanitarium." Lydia brought the newspaper up close enough to her nose to make out something other than vague blocks of gray. "It may not say anything about Jamie, but considering it was Fairport I came to warn him against, the coincidence is a little marked. I expect we could find the address in a city directory."

"I expect every jehu in the town will know its location," Ysidro remarked. "From what I know of human nature, the place will have been trampled by curiosity seekers ere the ashes cooled."

Palaces crowded them on all sides, the darkness patched and painted by a thousand glowing windows whose reflections gilded the scrollwork of doorways with careless brush strokes of light, the faces of the marble angels rendered curiously kin to Ysidro's still, thin features as the vampire turned his head again, seeking whatever it was that he sought.

The wagon drew up before a tall yellow house in the Bakkersgasse, like an excessively garlanded wedding cake in butter-colored stucco. Ysidro accompanied the two women inside, watching as the Slovak unloaded Lydia's trunks, portmanteau, satchel, and hatboxes, but when that was finished, he returned to his own luggage, still on the cart, and drove away with it into the darkness. An hour later he returned, afoot and uncommunicative as ever, for picquet in a salon that was a miniature Versailles above a shop selling silk.

"I made arrangements ere departing London," he said, shuffling the cards. "It is necessary to know the existence of such places, which can be had in any city for a price. You will find a cook and chambermaid at your disposal in the morning, though they speak no English and little German. Still, I am assured that the cook is up to the most exacting of standards. Certainly, for English, she will suffice."

Margaret said, "It's too good of you . . ."

"Assured by whom?" Lydia wanted to know.

Ysidro picked up his cards. "One whose business it is to know. You are the elder hand, mistress."

Ysidro's estimate of human nature proved a distressingly accurate one. When Lydia and Miss Potton arrived by rented fiacre at the smoke-stained wall around what was left of Fruhlingzeit Sanitarium the following afternoon, they found at least five other carriages there, the drivers seated comfortably on the low stone wall across the road chatting among themselves, and a large number of fashionably dressed men and women prowling around the trampled weeds or engaged in argument with a couple of sturdy gentlemen who seemed to be guarding the gates.

"I do not see that you have the authority to turn us away," a slim man in an overemphatic waistcoat was saying as Lydia hesitantly crossed the road. "I do not see this at all."

"Can't do anything about that, sir." The sturdy gentleman pushed back his flat cloth cap and remained blocking the entry. Even through the comforting blur of myopia, the glimpse of blackened rafters and fallen-in walls was horrible, and the smell of cold ash lay thin and gritty on the chill air.

"I shall write to the *Neue Freie Presse* about this."

"You do that, sir."

Lydia stepped forward hesitantly as the slim man stormed away to rejoin his party by the carriages; the sturdy gentleman fixed her with a jaundiced eye and said, in not-very-good German, "Nobody allowed in, ma'am."

"Is . . . is a Mr. Halliwell here?" asked Lydia. If Dr. Fairport were officially an agent of Britain, it stood to reason the burning of his sanitarium would not go uninvestigated by the Department. It only surprised her they'd still be at it three days later. She saw the man's stance shift at the sound of the name and said, "Could you tell him a Mrs. Asher is here to see him? Mrs. James Asher."

Without her spectacles, Mr. Halliwell proved to be a magpie behemoth, a series of circles of blacks, whites, pinks, and gleaming reflections that resolved itself at four feet into a heavy, pugnacious face and brightly humorous green eyes behind small oval lenses. A big damp hand gripped Lydia's while a second patted it moistly; the little clusters of would-be sightseers across the road glowered at this favoritism.

"My dear Mrs. Asher!"

"My friend, Miss Potton."

Halliwell bowed again, an awesome sight.

"Strange business. Deuced strange business. Your husband didn't send for you, did he?" He glanced down sidelong at her from his height, but she noticed his voice was barely above a whisper.

She shook her head. "But the telegram he sent me on his way here gave me reason to believe that he might be in trouble. He . . . he wasn't here when this happened . . . was he?"

The green eyes narrowed. "Why would you think he was?"

"Because . . ." Lydia took a deep breath. In broad daylight and in front of half a dozen argumentative Viennese, she thought, they couldn't very well drag her away in a closed carriage. She said, very softly, "Because he said he was coming to Dr. Fairport. And because I have reason to believe Dr. Fairport was in the pay of the Austrians."

His glance flicked across the road, then to Miss Potton—discreetly out of earshot—and back. "You don't happen," he said equally quiet, "to have mentioned this to anyone else?"

"No. Not even to Miss Potton," she remembered to add, mindful of her companion's safety. "But I think it's true. I take it," she went on slowly, "that you haven't spoken with Dr. Asher on the subject."

Halliwell fingered his short-clipped beard, studying her as if matching the eggplant taffeta of her gown, the mint and ecru frills of her hat, against other things. Lydia wondered how James could possibly have played at spies for as long as he had: This business of not knowing what to say or whom to say it to was both wearing and unnerving. Presumably, Ysidro would come to her rescue if Halliwell were a double agent also, provided Margaret had the wits to run for it . . .

But if Margaret had been foolish enough to believe Ysidro's farrago about previous lifetimes, goodness knew what she'd do in a crisis.

"I'm inclined to agree with you," the fat man said abruptly. "And I was starting to think so before you turned up. Just the fact that the Kundschafts Stelle hasn't let us into this place until this morning tells me there's something fishy, though of course we can't come out and say the man was working for *us*."

He glanced again at the loitering tourists across the road. "Would you ladies be so good as to meet me for dinner at Donizetti's on the Herrengasse this evening at eight? We'll be able to talk there." He nodded back toward the burnt-out shell of the house, where another man could be seen slowly picking his way through the mess of collapsed beams and bricks. "I can tell you now no one's found any trace of your husband . . . and what we *have* found is not anything a lady should see."

"God knows what the Kundschafts Stelle found before they let us in." Halliwell's small, rather womanish mouth pursed as he removed his gloves. In the saffron-drenched Renoir of color that was Donizetti's without spectacles, he seemed to fit in, becoming curiously invisible in a way that he hadn't in the unfamiliar environment of open air and bare woods. He reminded Lydia rather of some of her uncles, who grew like fleshy pale pot plants in their London clubs and never emerged into the light of day.

"I'll tell you the truth, Mrs. Asher—if your husband were at Fruhlingzeit when it burned, nobody's said anything about it to us. They've had the place closed off for two days. It was twenty-four hours before they even let the police in. Typical. When the Emperor's son blew his brains out twenty years ago, taking a seventeen-year-old girl with him for reasons best known to himself, the original story was that he'd died of 'heart failure.' Government agents and the girl's own uncle propped her corpse into a carriage with a broom handle up her back to keep reporters from learning two bodies instead of one were found at the scene. How did your husband know this Farren fellow, and how did you find out about Fairport?"

At this point the table captain appeared again, waiter and boy in tow, and a long and Byzantine discussion ensued concerning the concoction of *Tafelspitz* and how the *canard Strasbourg* was prepared this evening, and the relative tartness of the sour cherry soup. Rather to Lydia's surprise, Margaret, who had all day been her tongue-tied self, plunged into the conversation with the absorbed interest of a fellow gourmet, winning the approval of both Halliwell and the table captain— the Herr Ober, Halliwell called him—with her opinions on capers and *beurre brûlé*. It was, Lydia reflected, an entirely new side to her traveling companion than she had so far seen.

Only when the little train of servitors was gone did Halliwell turn back to her. Lydia, after a moment's pause to collect her thoughts, sketched a bowdlerized version of the telegrams she had received, the articles they had prompted her to read, her realization that Fairport would certainly be interested in Ernchester's pathology and almost as certainly would be working for, or with, Karolyi. "I don't know what, or how much, of Farren's abilities are connected with his belief that he is a vampire," she concluded carefully. "But I know Dr. Asher considered him a very dangerous man, dangerous enough to warrant his dropping everything to pursue him to Paris to keep him from selling his services to the Emperor."

"Hmm. For which he got small thanks from old Streatham, I daresay. How did you know to come to me? Asher didn't know my name until he arrived."

"A friend of my husband's," Lydia said, not sure whether she was telling the truth or not.

"Your husband had dinner with me in this café Tuesday night," said Halliwell. "There'd been trouble in Paris, one of our operatives was killed. Your husband seemed to think this Farren had done it, but word got to the police that your husband had something to do with it, even before the French police sent for him. Karolyi's work, of course. Asher spent the night in jail, which isn't as uncomfortable as it would be in London, and was going to stay the night at the sanitarium after he'd had a look around the Altstadt Wednesday. That was usual—the place was a safe house. Your husband had stayed there before."

"And did he?" She picked a little at the delicate crepe on the plate before her, her appetite gone.

"I gather he didn't. Fairport showed up at the firm in the morning asking if Asher had been heard from."

"That might have been a blind."

"I don't think so." Halliwell dabbed his mouth with the delicacy of a maiden lady. "He sniffed around for information, which I don't think he'd have done if he'd had him under hatches. He wasn't that clever. Later in the afternoon he came back saying Asher was wanted by the police, which I knew already, and why didn't I go talk to them? He hung about and wasted my time and asked a thousand questions and went with me to the station, which is just what he'd have done if he were a double and waiting for Asher to try telephoning, though that may be hindsight on my part. If I were Karolyi, I would have shot him for it. Personally, I never thought old Bedbugs had enough red blood in him to work a double game. At about seven that night Ladislas—the Herr Ober—came to my table and told me a Herr Asher was on the telephone for me, that it was urgent. By the time I got there, the line was dead. About two hours later we got the first reports of the fire."

"Oh," Lydia said slowly. "I see."

"Do you?" The green eyes glinted sharply at her. "I don't. None of us do. You're thinking Asher might have started the fire . . ."

"Well," Lydia pointed out, "my husband always said that one *should* burn the place down after killing someone . . ."

She regarded Halliwell with startlement when the fat man burst into delighted laughter. "It's true," she protested. "It isn't as if there were other houses around to be damaged."

"My dear Mrs. Asher," he chuckled, "I can see why old James married you."

"Well," she said, "it wasn't for my domestic talents. But I don't think, if James had started the fire, anyone would have found enough of two bodies to identify them. He's usually much more efficient than that."

"No." Halliwell's round face grew suddenly grim. "And I can't picture your husband killing them the way these men were killed."

He glanced apologetically across at Margaret—digging her way happily through a towering castle of chocolate and whipped cream—and lowered his voice. "According to our sources in the Kundschafts Stelle, they were ... horribly wounded. Bled almost completely dry of blood. They must have been cut in the house itself and later dragged into the open. I can't imagine your husband, or any sane man, doing that."

Lydia was conscious of Margaret putting down her fork, her hand suddenly shaking.

Halliwell went on, "And there were more than three bodies found. There were at least five, two of them so badly burned they couldn't be identified; and they haven't even finished digging out the building where the kerosene blew up. Bedbugs had a room underneath it, which we used for a hiding place for whoever was inconveniently connected with the local socialists or anarchists or Serbian nationals. If Asher was a prisoner, he'd have been held down there."

Lydia looked again at her untouched dessert. She felt cold inside. She'd been a fool, she thought, not to guess that the newspaper would lie. She'd been a fool to think she could overtake him in time to prevent disaster. She said again, "I see."

"We found plenty of evidence of the kind of man Farren is, if he could take out five men like that, as well as evidence of what he thought he was. Fairport had fitted up a safe room with silver bars—vampires are supposed to hate silver, aren't they? But we haven't found any trace of your husband."

She took a deep breath. "And Farren?"

Halliwell shook his head. "No sign of him, either. Our connections in the Kundschafts Stelle tell us they were watching the Bahnhof for your husband all evening—the police really *were* looking for him that day—so it's doubtful that he left town that way."

He reached out and clumsily patted her arm. "That doesn't mean he's come to harm," he said. Lydia looked quickly up at him.

"For all I know, they're still looking for him. God knows what Karolyi told them about him. I've asked, and they're being damned cagey. And he could have left town on the Danube ferries or taken a tram and walked to another station. Anything. It may be he's simply hiding out."

"Maybe." Lydia remembered one of James' digressions on how easy it was to get out of a town that had become temporarily too hot.

Then she thought about the burned skeleton of the sanitarium and the stink of charred wood still hanging in the chilly air, and her heart sank, as if with sickness or shock.

"In the meantime, you can do me a favor, if you would, Mrs. Asher. Your husband said you were a medical doctor?"

She nodded. "I have a medical degree, yes, but I mostly do research on endocrine secretions at the Radcliffe Infirmary. The few women with practices all seem to go into what they call 'women's medicine'—and *still* have trouble making a living at it, I might add. And I've never been terribly interested in what my aunts referred to as 'the plumbing.' Did you need something looked at?"

He mopped up the last of his Sacher torte and gazed regretfully at the polished white porcelain plate. Then he propped his glasses, frowning. "None of the laboratories survived—they were all directly over the kerosene stores—but we do have Fairport's notebooks from his study. The place was pretty badly charred, but those we managed to recover. He was a British citizen and be damned to who paid the rent on the sanitarium. I suspect the Kundschafts Stelle's going to want to see them eventually, but if you'd be good enough to have a look through them and tell us anything that it might be worthwhile for us to know, I'd appreciate it. I have them here."

He held up a battered leather satchel, overloaded and strapped together with rope where its buckles would not hold.

"We'd like to know what he was working on. If you still have your list of his articles . . ."

Lydia nodded. "Aging," she said. "Blood. Immortality."

Halliwell grunted. "No wonder he fell for Farren."

"Yes," Lydia said quietly. "No wonder."

In light of the articles she had read, Fairport's experiments—with blood, with saliva, with mucus, with the chemistry of the brain and the glands—came into crystalline focus.

The man who seeks to live forever, Ysidro had said.

He was right, she thought, turning over the cryptic notes while Margaret dozed in a welter of crocheted snowflakes. He was right.

Bedford Fairport was quite clearly a man possessed with the fanatic determination to discover whence came the deterioration of age, and an even greater determination to learn how to reverse its effects.

In the article in which he had mentioned Ignace Karolyi's donation of the sanitarium and funds, Fairport had spoken of his own "premature aging." Lydia had encountered reports of such progeria dating from the sixteenth century, and was of the opinion that some unknown vitamin deficiency or breakdown was responsible. She pushed up her spectacles on her forehead, rubbed her eyes. Of course he would grasp at rumors of immortality.

A glance at the reagents and vitamin solutions told Lydia that his experiments had been appallingly costly. He'd used orangutans as subjects two dozen times in the past few years, and Lydia knew from her own experiments how expensive the animals were. Unnecessary, too, she thought. In most experiments with deficiency syndromes, pigs seemed to work just as well. A double check showed her that he used orangutans to repeat experiments done on pigs, refusing to take what were, to her eye, quite clear failures as anything more than individual variations in data. Toward the end he'd taken to rerunning additional tests on everything, insistently investigating smaller and smaller points, like a man clutching at straws. Even if Fairport had private funds, he'd have to be staggeringly wealthy to continue such work as long as he had.

And she knew that if he had family money—if he'd been connected to one of the wealthier families in England—her aunt Lavinia would have steered her toward him at some point in her own Oxford days as a potential reference, partner, or colleague.

He'd betrayed James. Taken him prisoner. *They haven't even finished digging out the building where the kerosene blew up . . . If Asher were a prisoner, it would have been down there . . .*

James might have gotten out of town, she told herself defiantly. The police were looking for him. He could have taken a tram, as he always said was best, or a ferry.

Bled almost completely dry of blood . . .

Tears fought their way to her throat, and grimly she forced them back. *We don't know anything yet. We don't know.*

"An entire notebook of the historical and folkloric."

The soft voice nearly startled her out of her chair. Looking up, she saw Ysidro sitting opposite, a green cloth-bound ledger open before him. Past the vampire's shoulder the mantel clock was visible, and Lydia was mildly surprised to see that it was now close to three in the morning.

"I hadn't got that far." She reached back to twist her heavy braid into a less schoolgirlish knot. The cook—an excellent woman of broad smiles and a completely incomprehensible language—had left Sacher torte, bread and butter, and a succulent bunch of Italian grapes, should either *dziewczyna* suddenly find herself in peril of starvation before morning light, and the smell of the coffee warming on the little primus stove was heavy in the room. "And folklore would only be speculative. Even so-called 'historical' personalities—rumors about Ninon de l'Enclos and Cagliostro and Count What's-his-name in Paris . . ."

"Scarcely speculative at the end." Ysidro turned the ledger, slid it across the table to her, hands like old ivory in the lamplight.

Old man who lived to be a thousand, related the wandering

script. *Brzchek Village. Woman who lived to be five hundred (wove moonlight). Okurka Village. Woman who used moonlight to make herself beautiful forever. Salek Village. Man who made a pact with devil, lived forever. Bily Hora Village. Woman who bathed in blood, lived five hundred years. Brusa, Bily Hora, Salek.*

She looked up, puzzled. "It sounds like the sort of thing James does—talking to storytellers and grannies and old duffers at country inns."

"I expect Fairport observed the way James went about his questioning and turned it to his own usages." He tilted his head, moved the pile of invoices so he could read the top sheet. His pale eyebrows flexed. "One can, in any case, see the trend of his mind. But orangutans? I have spoken to those who saw James leave this city."

Her breath drew sharply; Ysidro watched her in stillness for a moment, his head a little to one side, like a white mantis, and again his eyebrows flexed, though it was impossible to read the expression in his eyes.

"Walk with me, lady." He rose and held out to her his hand. "The Master of Vienna has given me leave to hunt in this city, if so be that I am circumspect. Should he see us in company, he will know you as a sojourner, and think us chance-met and you harmless prey."

Lydia glanced back at Margaret's snoring form as Ysidro handed her her coat. Even through the gloves he drew on, and the kid that covered her own hands, his flesh was icy. Automatically, though no one would see her, she removed her spectacles, slipped them in her pocket. The card games had broken her of the habit of hiding her eyeglasses in Ysidro's presence; he had seen her, she reflected, at her four-eyed ugliest and did not appear to mind. Perhaps it was only that he had seen many others worse than she.

He led her down the gilt and marble staircase and through the bossed bronze of the inconspicuous door to the pavement outside.

"You saw the Master of Vienna, then?"

"Count Batthyany Nikolai Alessandro August—and his

wives. He has ruled Vienna, and indeed the greater part of the
Danube Valley, since the days when men still fought the Turks
on the banks of the river. As well that he and I are both con-
versant in the old French of the courts, for German I know only
from books. It was not, you understand, a language spoken by
anyone of breeding in my day; one reason that I made a point
of being elsewhere until the Kings of England learned a more
civilized tongue."

Lydia hid her smile. She'd heard him speak German to the
Slovak and to the cook. One thing she had learned about
Ysidro in the past few days was the depth of his snobbery.

Around them, Vienna slept, a drowned Atlantis at the
bottom of a lightless sea. Shutters of wood and glass ac-
cordioned over the bright cafés, and even the dormers of the
servants, high at the tops of the canyon walls, were closed eyes
sealed in dreaming.

"Your husband injured Batthyany's youngest wife," Ysidro
went on as they walked. "He did well to leave Vienna. He
was seen at the train station boarding the Orient Express for
Constantinople . . ."

"Constantinople?" Lydia said, startled.

"Even so. A most curious choice."

"But who . . . who saw him? If it was one of this Batthyany's
vampires . . ."

"Another wife," Ysidro said smoothly. "Who perhaps had
reasons of her own for wishing ill to the fair German beauty
who had—until James evidently burned her face with a handful of silver—been the count's fancy. The German beauty—
Grete, her name is—slew at least two of the groundsmen at
Fruhlingzeit in the hopes that their blood would speed the
healing of her wound, but it will be some time before she is
anything but hideous. Indeed, for some time to come Batthyany's coterie must hunt with the greatest of care, for fear of
attracting notice by the police—another reason it is as well that
your husband left Vienna when he did. Count Batthyany spoke
of revenge, but his eldest wife—Hungarian, as he is—seemed
pleased."

They turned a corner, coming clear of the tall walls to a

cobbled expanse where the cathedral rose suddenly before them, like a black and white fish skeleton in the wintry moonlight. Mist lay thin about its feet, stirring with their stride; the air stung the inside of her nose when she breathed.

"Was it the vampires who killed Professor Fairport, then?"

"Of course." Ysidro's head turned at some small sound across the pavement. A young girl emerged from the cathedral's porch and hastened across the square to the concealing dark of the lanes beyond, drawing her shawl over her head as she went. The Spaniard watched her, speculatively, out of sight.

"Batthyany was enraged, you understand, at any other's fledgling entering his domain," he said, turning back to Lydia. "And doubly, that any would ally himself with mortal governments, and so bring such governments into knowledge of the vampires. He considered the burning of Fruhlingzeit—and the death of the men involved—sufficient warning. His intent was that Ernchester die too in the conflagration, but says that the earl has departed also from Vienna. According to his eldest wife, your husband was accompanied on the train by a female vampire whom they found upon the premises, who claimed that she had been kidnapped and held prisoner by Fairport. Indeed, Batthyany and his countess helped this woman take horses from the stable and load into the wagon her traveling coffin, by the light of the burning house. With horse and wagon she would have easily returned to Vienna in time to be on the train."

"Anthea?"

"It would seem. And my guess is that your husband lay alive in that coffin. He could not have escaped, else."

Lydia kept her face from showing the inner shudder she felt at the thought, but even as it went through her, another part of her mind was busy piecing together implications. Around her in the blanched moonlight the whole city seemed to lie in a drugged dream of mist and shadow, still with a stillness like death.

Ysidro's world, she thought. The fag end of nighttime. The sense of being the only one left alive.

"That means—it must mean—Ernchester has gone to Constantinople."

"Even so," Ysidro agreed. "According to Batthyany's countess, Anthea claimed that she had been used as hostage to force Ernchester to the will of Karolyi and Fairport. It implies, of course, that Ernchester did not come to Vienna of his own accord, and so they hunted him no further."

"But James saw him get on the train with Karolyi of his own accord," Lydia said, puzzled. "After Karolyi was dead and Ernchester freed, why would he flee?"

"The fact that Charles got on the train of his own accord," Ysidro said softly, "does not mean that he did so of free will. And it would explain what has troubled me from the start. Ernchester is not a politician's choice—that slut Grippen has lately got in St. John's Wood is stronger to the hunt and the kill than Charles. But someone knew enough about him to know that he could be ruled. That a threat against Anthea would bring him. That to hold her would be to guarantee his conduct."

"Would Karolyi know that?"

"Evidently."

They had reached the house in the Bakkersgasse again. Unwilling, perhaps, to give up possession of those dark streets that were their sole dominion, Lydia and Ysidro sat as if by unspoken agreement side by side on the marble rim of the small fountain before the house. The gaslight wavered on the surface, made watching pits of the eyes of the bronze emperor above the water and touched the lower half of Ysidro's face, giving the effect of a carnival mask through which fulvous eyes gleamed like marsh fire as he spoke.

"Will you return to London, mistress? The trap here is sprung."

Lydia hesitated, feeling for one minute the overwhelming desire for the comfort of the things she knew, the world of research circumscribed by the university's walls. But she knew perfectly well, as the thought of it formed in her mind, that only *a* trap had been sprung.

"It isn't . . . it isn't over yet, is it? Whatever started this. Not anywhere near it."

"No."

Frightening as it had appeared in the beginning, Vienna hadn't been so bad.

"Would it be of help to you for me to go on to Constantinople? Because that's what I would prefer to do," she added, seeing the swift thought behind the Spaniard's eyes.

"It would be of help in finding Ernchester, yes." He frowned, as at some unexpected thought. "I would not have you undertake unnecessary risk—yet you know your husband's thought, and the legitimacy of your inquiries will help in the search for the heart of this matter."

He paused again, considering, and there was, Lydia thought, just the smallest trace of surprise in the enigmatic eyes.

"Curiously enough," he went on, "Charles has been in Constantinople. This was many years ago, but there might be some there who knew him when he—and possibly they—were living men."

"But it doesn't make sense—" Lydia pulled her collar closer about her face. "—if vampires are all as—as jealous of interlopers as the Count Batthyany is. That is . . . are they?"

"Mostly," said Ysidro. "Burning Fruhlingzeit as a warning was one of the milder expressions of displeasure I have encountered. Master vampires are not to be jested with when they conceive their territories in threat. Yet only a vampire could have summoned Ernchester to Constantinople. Only a vampire would know the threat that would bring him. Only a vampire would know that, of all the vampires I have met, Ernchester is one of the few capable of love."

ELEVEN

"Do vampires not love?"

Ysidro looked up from tallying his points. Lydia had scored sixteen for eight through king in hearts, with the nine making up a quart; Ysidro, by not declaring a sequence in diamonds, had managed to win most of the tricks, including the last. It hadn't saved him.

They had spent the day among the ancient basilicas and rose farms of Adrianople, owing to Ysidro's flat refusal to travel during the hours of light. Now the rough hills of Thrace, through which they had creaked with maddening slowness all of last night, seemed, as far as Lydia could tell, to have evened out. The train was a good one, German built and fitted, but even this first-class car smelled of garlic, strong coffee, tobacco, and unwashed clothing. On the platforms of Sofia and Belgrade, Lydia had observed that the farther east one got, the more casual railway personnel seemed to be about the presence of livestock in passenger cars. At Adrianople, earlier in the evening, she'd seen a Bosniak family casually load two goats into the third-class carriage, the father holding the long-fleeced kid in his arms and stepping back politely to let a bearded Orthodox priest climb on ahead of him, while farther down the platform people passed crates of chickens in through the windows.

Aunt Lavinia had always said that travel was broadening. Lydia suspected this was not what she meant.

The noise in the other first-class compartments seemed to be lessening, though in the corridors the tobacco fug still lay thick. Miss Potton, after her usual stubborn struggle to play a game in which she had neither aptitude nor interest, had fallen into a doze at Ysidro's side. For nearly an hour the only words exchanged had concerned the lay of the cards and the trading of points, but Lydia suspected that the governess was as jealous of those as she was of other conversations Lydia and Ysidro had.

The wheels clacked steadily, like mechanical rain. Ysidro finished his tally, the steel nib of his pen scratching softly on the cheap yellow pad, the friction of his cuff on the tabletop a dry whisper against Margaret's stertorous breath and the occasional bursts of laughter or speech audible through the compartment wall.

It was a long time before Ysidro replied.

At length he said, "As humans understand it?"

"How do humans understand it?" Lydia gathered the cards, turned them in her hands. Living half by night—half in the sunken silences of darkness—had given her a small degree of understanding of something Ysidro had mentioned early on, that vampires' senses were far more sensitive than those of humans. With blackness pressing the window and gloom thick beyond the circle of the gas burner's solitary light, every sound, every sight, seemed portentous, fraught with meaning beyond the simpler shapes of day.

"You said back in Vienna that Ernchester was a rarity among vampires, because he is capable of love. I wondered what that actually meant."

"As with the living, among the Undead love means different things to different individuals." He turned his head, champagne-colored eyes resting briefly on the woman who snored beside him in her muddle of yarns. After a moment her head lolled more heavily and her breathing deepened still further; she slumped against him, and with a fastidious care he leaned her into the other corner of the seat. In the five days it had taken them to work their way south via local trains—for the Orient Express only left Vienna on Thursdays—through Buda-Pesth, Belgrade, Sofia, Adrianople, waiting sometimes for most of a day for the next train that departed after sunset—Lydia had been occasionally aware of the highly colored romantic dreams that illuminated Margaret Potton's sleep. In all of them Ysidro had been a vampire, outrageously Byronic in black leather and pearls, with daggers sticking out of his boots.

In all of them, love had been implicit. His professed, passionate love for her, bonding them, drawing her like a silver rope into love for him.

Whatever love is, Lydia added to herself. It would hardly do, at this point, for Margaret to hear any true opinion of Ysidro's on the ability of vampires to love.

"It is not unlikely, or even infrequent," Ysidro said, "for those who have the capacity to love others more than themselves to also have the will to make the transition from the living state to that of the Undead." The train jostled around a curve sharper than those found in northerly or westerly Europe. Ysidro put a gloved hand on Margaret's shoulder to keep her steady—perhaps to keep her from waking. He touched her carefully, even with gloves. His hands, Lydia knew, were cold as bone these days. She could tell when he had fed, and she knew he had not hunted in Vienna.

"It is unusual, however, for such a one to survive long after the deaths of those for whom they care. In many cases, friends or relatives constitute the vampire's early victims or fall prey to them in the course of the years. For those vampires who do not avail themselves of the convenience—and the odd comfort—of this resolution to immortality's riddle, there is often a sense of disorientation when family and lovers age and begin to die. In my experience those capable of loving seldom make successful vampires."

In the juddering glare of the gaslight, his face had the appearance of a skull in the ashy frame of his long hair; Lydia wondered whether he had always looked so or whether he had thinned and wasted in the past five days. Margaret stirred in her sleep, and Ysidro turned his face to look at her again, unreadable indifference in his gaze. There was long silence before he spoke again.

"You understand that having become vampire myself at the age of five-and-twenty, my experience of human love is . . . incomplete," he went on, as if the matter were not one for his concern. "In this case, what love actually means is that someone—one of the Constantinople vampires, or one who has been in contact with him or her—would know that a threat to harm Anthea—by human agency, perhaps, or with the understanding that if human means proved ineffective, vampire agents would not be far behind—would bring Charles to heel. The vampire mind is an endlessly subtle one, and Charles knows the extent of their abilities to manipulate circumstance. Even were Grippen willing to defend Anthea, defending against a sufficiently determined attack might lie beyond his powers. For his own safety, Charles would not care, but as Dryden said, we give hostages to fortune when we love."

He moved his hand, turning it as if revealing a hidden card. "I would guess that the sack of the house was an effort to take her hostage once he had departed, to prevent him changing his mind."

"But if the Sultan wants a vampire," Lydia said, puzzled, "and if he's been in touch with one in order to know about Ernchester in the first place, why go to the trouble? Aren't there plenty of vampires in Constantinople? At least from all the legends James hears, Greece and the Balkans have to be stiff with them."

"Perhaps the vampire who spoke of Ernchester to Karolyi—or to the Sultan, if it was he who sent Karolyi—is now dead. We cannot know how long ago it was, and there have been upheavals in the city recently. Of a certainty, he—or she—would be dead, did the Master of Constantinople learn that there was a plot afoot to bring an interloper into his city. And it may be that whoever has sent for Ernchester feels that he would be more easily controlled than any under the sway of the Master of Constantinople. In this he would be correct."

Ysidro stretched a hand like gloved bones to part the window curtain. "Behold."

It was not like Paris, not like Paris' glittering carpet of gaslights. Softer lights and fewer—amber, citrine, topaz, red as the juice of blood oranges—jeweled the long spine of hills that made the city and lay in spangles of isolate flame in the nearly unseen movement of the sea. The train swung around a great curve. A many-towered gate loomed in the darkness, archways strung with yellow electric lights that cast reflections on a tree-filled ditch and a massy wall stretching into the night. Lydia gasped in surprise—she'd heard of the walls of Constantinople but hadn't quite realized that the Byzantine ramparts would still be standing, watchtowers intact.

As the train slowed, the lights from its windows caught the black-glass combs of choppy sea beneath the railway embankment. Where the land curved, the old sea wall rose above the tracks, dark houses with outthrust upper floors growing from the ancient masonry like mushrooms from a riven oak.

Ysidro produced a gold pocket watch. "Twenty of one," he said approvingly. "Only two hours late. Excellent, for the Ottoman lands."

After coming into Sofia four and a half hours late, with the sky like wet slate and Margaret in hysterics as if she, not Ysidro, would be destroyed by the light of the dawn, Lydia could only be thankful. On that occasion, while the Sofia train lurched and stopped and started all through the shelterless hills of Thrace, Ysidro had grown quieter and, when he spoke, more incisive. Though Lydia did not know exactly how much light was necessary to trigger the photoreactive properties of the vampire flesh, she gathered that they had reached the Terminus Hotel in Sofia, and Ysidro had taken his usual leave of them, with only minutes to spare.

This had led to a furious and not very coherent scene with Margaret, in whose aftermath Lydia still felt embarrassed. The younger woman had accused Lydia of "not caring anything about" Ysidro, of "using people up like old dishes, and then throwing them away when they break." When Lydia had pointed out that at any time Ysidro could have retreated to his coffin trunk and trusted the girls to get him to safety, Margaret had screamed, "If you'd ever had anything to do with earning your own living, without having everything you ever wanted just handed to you on a silver plate, you'd have learned you can't treat people that way when they're trying to help you!"

In view of Ysidro's relations with Margaret, this had struck Lydia as so outrageous that she'd simply said, "Oh, stop behaving like an idiot," and had gone into the suite's single bedroom and closed the door. She'd been far too exhausted by her own fears to remain awake long, but during the few minutes she'd spent stripping off her outer clothing, petticoats, and corsets, she'd heard Margaret sobbing hysterically in the parlor. When she emerged, not much refreshed, hours later, it had been to see the governess sprawled unprettily on the sofa, face flushed, shirtwaist off, and corsets unlaced, sound asleep.

They'd made up after a fashion, as traveling companions must, but their never-easy relations remained strained. Now Margaret mumbled, "You should have waked me sooner," when Lydia shook her.

"We're here. Constantinople." She didn't mention that Ysidro had done his best to keep the woman asleep.

Margaret pulled a comb out of her handbag and straightened her hair, with nervous glances at Ysidro as if he hadn't seen her in rumpled slumber for many nights. Only then did she turn to the window and say in disappointment, "Oh. You can't see anything."

Across tumbled onyx water a long curve of lights glimmered as if a congregation of shepherds had kindled watch fires on the point. Here and there, close to the tracks, reflected light showed a thumb smudge of honey-colored walls, but for the most part the city was dark. The high, dark backbone of the land was studded by minarets and domes under the gibbous moon's waning light: the embodiment of formless dreams, a dark suggestion of labyrinth hoarding darkness within.

No, thought Lydia. You didn't see it. You drank it, and it left you filled with an indescribable sense of hunger, and loss, and grief.

"They called it the City of Walls," Ysidro said softly. "The City of Palaces. Like a Kipling treasure guarded by a cobra, they have fought over it, or feared it, for all the long centuries since the emperors departed from Rome. Not even those who won it, who dwelled in it, ever knew it all."

Like James looking at the towers of Oxford, thought Lydia, and calling them each by its name. Did he name in his heart each dome, each quartet of spires, against that lambent sky? "Were you ever here?" Margaret edged possessively closer to him, took his arm—though Lydia knew he hated to be touched—and looked into his face.

Ysidro smiled, for her. "Once," he said in a voice that promised her new dreams. Over her head his eyes met Lydia's, enigmatic, and looked away.

The train chuffed to a stop at a small station beneath the beetling towers of an old fortress gate. Up close the ambience was anything but exotic. The station was Western, stuccoed and painted the same ochre hue so common in Vienna, and by the harsh electric lamps Lydia saw the grannies and goats, the gentlemen in red fezzes and black coats, the Greeks in full white pants and the Bulgarians with their crated chickens and straw suitcases, get on and off with the leisured air of those who know the train isn't going anywhere in a hurry. The stink of slums and tanneries was thick hereabouts, and there were, Lydia noticed, a lot of soldiers in the stations, clothed in modern khaki uniforms, nothing like the colorful warriors of tales.

"Those aren't the janissaries, are they?" she asked, and Ysidro's yellow eyes developed the smallest of twinkles, like a fugitive star, at the bottom of their cold, ironic depths. Despite the insectile thinness of his face and its white-silk pallor, he looked briefly human.

"The corps of the janissaries was abolished a century ago—massacred wholesale, in fact, by order of the Sultan Murad, who wished to establish a modern army. This past July that modern army returned the favor by deposing the current Sultan and converting him by force into the type of constitutional monarch fashionable among those who like to style themselves enlightened."

"You mean there isn't a Sultan anymore?" Margaret sounded like a child who has been told on the twenty-fourth of

December that Father Christmas has been pensioned off to a villa in the south of France.

"July . . ." Lydia said thoughtfully. "The printer's deadline for my monograph on the effects of ultraviolet light on the hypothalamus was August fifteenth . . . And I never can remember whether they're on our side or Germany's. So it couldn't have been the Sultan who sent for Ernchester?"

"It may well be," Ysidro said. "He is not without power, even yet. But if he thinks to regain it by bringing in a vampire whom he hopes to control, he reckons without the Master of Constantinople."

The train lurched and began its slow, rocking progress again, the city growing above them in thick accretions of shadow, lamps, and ancient walls shrouded in vine.

"Who is the Master of Constantinople?" Lydia asked quietly.

They were all three clustered by the windows of the compartment, looking out over the inky water toward the lights of Seraglio Point and the dim hills of Asia beyond.

"In my day it was not considered a wise thing to speak his name." Ysidro turned back to the table and gathered the cards. He fumbled, dropping them; Margaret sprang at once to help him but he'd retrieved them already, slipped them into the paper band that usually encircled the pack, secreted them in a pocket of his mouse-gray coat.

"He was a sorcerer in life, a title which could mean anything from a theoretical alchemist to a student of the properties of herbs. Certainly he was a poisoner, possibly an astronomer, though one does not always keep these things up. He wielded tremendous power, before and after his death, with the Viziers of the Sublime Porte. Legends said that certain of the sultans gifted him with prisoners, that he might feast upon their deaths, though considering the size of the beggar population of Constantinople, I do not find this at all likely or necessary. And as Juvenal says, 'Foolish is he who puts his trust in princes.' Personally, I wouldn't touch any edible offered me by any of the sultans."

Ysidro put out a hand again, to steady himself on the wall as the train swung around the rocky slope of a hill and lurched into another suburban station. There were electric lights here, too, and soldiers armed with businesslike Enfields.

"It is probably best," he said, "that the master of this city not be spoken of in any terms until we are in Pera."

Another of Ysidro's gruff local henchmen awaited them in the square before the main Gare of Stamboul, this one a Greek—whom Ysidro addressed in Spanish—with the usual wagon and horses. Lydia had removed her glasses before leaving the train compartment, but the moment they were settled on the high seat and moving off through the tangle of drays, donkey carts, and foot passengers, she sneaked them back on, gazing around her in wonderment. At the foot of the square the dark waters of the Golden Horn flashed with the lights of ships moored there, and even at nearly two in the morning the lights of small boats could be seen plying between the Stamboul shore and the lamp-flecked hills of Pera on the other side.

Black streets swallowed them, and for a few minutes Lydia could no more than guess at the houses crowding above, balconies—sometimes entire upper stories—jutting overhead as if grabbing for airspace, here and there the low glimmer of lamps behind thick latticework. Cats' eyes flashed everywhere, and the smell of goats and dogs and human waste was like a curtain thick enough to be touched with the hand. Lamps in iron cages showed her the somber glory of a mosque half veiled in Stygian gloom as they passed through a square, a note of great age on the lighted threshold of a modern iron bridge.

On the bridge's other side the houses were European—or Greek, with white walls like clotted cream in the moonlight. They wound their way uphill to a tree-grown public square lying beneath a splendid Italianate palace of pale golden stone.

"The British Embassy," came Ysidro's soft voice. "I trust you ladies will present yourselves to the Right Honorable Mr. Lowther in the morning. For many years the embassies have been the true power here."

As usual, Ysidro had wired ahead for lodgings, this time a pink-washed Greek-style house whose stone-flagged arch led into a court shaded by a massive pomegranate tree, staffed by three thickset Greek women, evidently a mother and two daughters, who smiled and replied *"Parakalo—parakalo . . ."* to everything Lydia said.

As at Belgrade, Sofia, and Adrianople, once Lydia's trunks and portmanteaus and hatboxes and baskets of herbs were carried upstairs, Ysidro climbed into the wagon once more and disappeared to some secret lodging of his own.

"You can't ask him to continue what he's doing."

Lydia turned, startled, the moss-green velvet of her dressing gown weighting her arms. Tomorrow she'd present herself, not only to the Right Honorable G. A. Lowther, but, armed with Mr. Halliwell's letters of introduction, to Sir Burnwell Clapham, the attaché in charge of what were nebulously referred to as "affairs." It was entirely possible, she thought, that Jamie would be there, or Jamie would be somewhere close. *Oh, yes, Dr. Asher. He arrived last week . . .*

Please, she thought, shivering inside. *Please . . .*

Margaret stood awkwardly in the doorway of the single large bedroom the two women would share. As in Vienna, in Belgrade and Sofia, it was not by their choice—even had relations between them not been strained, Lydia would have preferred to be spared her companion's nocturnal sighs and mutterings in dreams. But in no house had more than one bed been made up, nor could the servants anywhere be induced to do so. In the small connecting chamber, Lydia had already found the dismantled pieces of a massive four-poster that looked as if it had been ordered from Berlin at the height of the Gothic craze. Its sister ship filled most of this room, the bright pink-and-blue local work of its coverlet incongruously gay; the dressing table, mirrored armoire, and marble-topped washstand had clearly been ordered en suite, and though the room was large, with a bay projecting over the street, they gave it a cluttered feeling, jammed and awkward.

At least, thought Lydia, they weren't strewn with the porcelain knickknacks featured in their Belgrade lodgings, and the

whitewashed plaster walls were free of garish oleographs of
Orthodox saints.

She turned from the armoire, the robe still in her hands.
"What?"

"You forbade him . . ." Margaret hesitated, and her wide
blue eyes shifted as she sought another word. "You forbade
him to hunt," she said at last. "As a condition of letting him
travel with you, of letting him protect you." Her voice stammered and she twisted at her black-gloved hands. "Now that
we've reached our destination, you really don't have any right
to continue . . . to continue . . ."

Frozen in mid-motion, Lydia only stared at her, too shocked
to speak.

Margaret, who had clearly hoped that she would say something and spare her the completion of her sentence—and in fact
the completion of her own thought—trailed off uncertainly,
and for a moment there was only the clutch and jerk of her
breath. Then she burst out, "You don't understand him!"

"You keep saying that." Lydia crossed to the bed and
dropped the robe beside the nightgown the maid had laid out,
and began to unbutton her shirtwaist. The tiny pearl fastenings
of the sleeves were awkward, but she'd dismissed the servant
after she'd unpacked for them, and didn't know enough
modern Greek to summon her back. She wondered what the
servants had made of the silver knives and silver-loaded gun
among the masses of petticoats, skirts, shirtwaists, lingerie,
and dinner dresses—wondered, too, if she could communicate
to them a request to purchase garlic, whitethorn, and wild rose
on the morrow. Or as Ysidro's servants, would they refuse to
obey such a request?

Margaret reached out and took her by the sleeve, her face
bracketed with lines of distress deepened by the lamps' heavy
shadows. "You can't forbid him to hunt!" she insisted desperately. "It isn't as if he . . . as if the people he . . . he takes . . ."

"You mean 'kills'?"

She flinched from the word but lashed back almost at once
with, "It isn't as if they didn't deserve it!"

Lydia only stood for a time, her fingers still on the pearl buttons but her task forgotten. When she spoke, her voice was very quiet. "Did he tell you that?"

"I know it!" The governess was on the brink of tears. "Yes, he told me! I mean, I know—I mean, in the past—in past lifetimes—in dreams I've had about our former lives together . . . And don't tell me they're all lies," she veered away suddenly, "because I know they're not! I know you think they are, but they're really not! They're not!"

She flung herself in front of Lydia when Lydia tried to turn away, her face red, blotchy as if with the approach of tears. "You see, if a vampire doesn't . . . doesn't hunt to completion . . ."

She was still avoiding the word "kill."

"They feed on the energy, the life, the vital force!" she went on in a rush. "It's the life they take that gives their minds the powers they need to protect themselves!"

"You mean to kill other people?"

"You're starving him to death!" Margaret cried. "Robbing him of his powers to defend himself from danger, now, here, where the peril is the greatest! That's why vampires take so long to hunt, or at least why *he* takes so long to hunt, he told me, because he's hunting the streets of the city to find a thief, a murderer, a . . . a blackguard who deserves to die! You know the world is full of them. He's hunted that way for hundreds and hundreds of years! It's only from those kind of people that he takes the life he needs! And he's too honorable to go against his given word to you . . ."

"Did he ask you to speak to me?" Lydia's voice was as cold to her own ears as the silver on her neck.

"No." Margaret sniffled and wiped furiously at her eyes, fighting not to break down in front of this slender auburn and white reed of a girl, this spoiled heiress-beauty with her waist unbuttoned to show the heavy links of silver chain, row upon row of them, around the stem of her throat.

"But I can see!" she sobbed. "Every day I can see. You beat him at cards all the time now . . ."

"I've had a week of continuous practice," Lydia pointed out.

"You could never beat him if he weren't fighting to keep the other powers of his mind intact! To preserve himself . . ."

"Thank you very much." Head aching with weariness—for it was close to three in the morning—Lydia stepped around her. It was true that Ysidro had grown very gaunt—true, too, that a week ago he would never have dropped the cards, never would even have allowed the girls to see him gather them.

He could not mask things from them as he had. Or was he saving his strength for other matters?

"Margaret, do we need to talk about this now? I'm tired, you're tired, I suspect you don't mean everything you're saying—"

"How can you be so blind!" Margaret went on frantically, unheeding, following her back to the bed. "Can't you see? He can't turn people's minds aside in the train stations like he used to, or listen down the train cars, reading their dreams . . ."

Lydia's overwrought temper snapped. "Or put little scenes of dancing the waltz—which wasn't even *invented* in the six-teenth century—into yours? I'm sorry," she said immediately, as Margaret burst into a storm of tears at this brutally accurate accusation. "I shouldn't have said that . . ."

"You don't understand!" Margaret shouted wildly. "You don't understand him! All you care about is finding your boring old stick of a husband and helping him play spies, and you can't see the great-souled, noble, lonely, tragic hero you're destroying!"

She blundered from the room like a bee trying to get out of a potting shed. Lydia heard the banister creak as she stumbled against it, heard the running judder of her footsteps descend the two long, C-shaped flights of stairs.

"Margaret!" She grabbed her spectacles from the dressing table and ran after her, catching handfuls of taffeta skirt to race down the steps, the tile of them cold under her stockinged feet. Below her she heard the door bang, and she followed, appalled, into the covered carriageway in time to see the heavy outer gate swing shut on its hinges.

"Margaret!" Through her concern she thought obliquely, *Well, that does it for this pair of stockings*—even in the rela-tively clean suburb of Pera the streets were nothing to explore unshod. Two small sconces illuminated the courtyard behind her, and the candle before a saint's icon in a niche flecked the underside of the carriageway's brick vault with wavering light. Past the gate the street was like a cave a thousand feet beneath the earth.

Lydia stopped on the threshold, as if that abyssal dark were a chasm gaping before her feet.

Margaret gasped somewhere, and there was a suggestion of movement, pale in blackness. The shred of moonlight picked out a white face, like a skull's, a scrap of spiderweb hair. A moment later Lydia's eyes, adjusting, made out the white hands, holding Margaret by the wrists. Margaret threw herself wordlessly to his chest, clutching and weeping.

Ysidro must have spoken, so softly Lydia did not hear. Lydia herself had been exasperated to the slapping point with Margaret's clinging, mooning, and silent reproaches, but she had never seen the vampire anything but patient and understanding with the woman he had made his slave. Of course he understood her, thought Lydia bitterly, watching as Ysidro bent his head to listen to some muffled, hysterical rant; watching Margaret's skinny hands grab at his sleeves, his shoulders, the long folds of his cloak. If he hadn't understood her, he couldn't have baited the trap.

Illuminated only by the frail gleam from the window above, they seemed figures in a distant stage show, almost like a dream. Margaret flung back her head, gazing up into Ysidro's face, then with a passionate gesture she ripped open her shirtwaist, baring her throat and her white, soft-fleshed bosom. "Take me!" Lydia heard her gasp. "Even unto death, if that is what you need!"

What Ysidro replied Lydia didn't know. But she saw him draw the edges of Margaret's shirtwaist together, put his hands on her shoulders, speaking quietly as she bowed her head. When he began to guide her back along the lane to the gate once more, Lydia retreated soundlessly into the courtyard, concealing herself in the dense shadows of the pomegranate tree, so that Margaret would be spared the embarrassment of knowing that the encounter had been observed. For a moment they stood framed in the carriageway's arch. Ysidro must have said something else, for Lydia saw Margaret nod and push up her eyeglasses to mop her cheeks. Then the door shut behind her as she went in.

Lydia heard nothing for a time, though she knew that Ysidro had not gone inside; and indeed, moments later, the dimmest crack of light showed when he opened the gate again and stood for a moment looking out. That slit vanished; he emerged into the courtyard like an errant ghost and crossed to her hiding place as if he had seen her all along.

"I could wish her to have reserved such theatrics for another place and time."

"Yes." Irritated as she had been with Margaret, her greatest anger still lay toward him. She folded her arms against the cold. "It's a nuisance, isn't it, when people decide to feel more than you've scheduled them to feel?"

"It is." He might have been agreeing that today was Saturday. The moon was sinking; only the glow from the votives by the kitchen door showed her the garden before them. "Yet the dreams she dreams are not all of my making. And I admit I will feel safer to know that the two of you sleep in the one bed, which I trust you will hang about, as you did in Sofia and Belgrade, with those stinking weeds you have carried with you since Paris."

The chilly breeze from the Asian hills stirred the last leaves high overhead. A stray breath of it flared the votive lights, showing her briefly Ysidro's face, eyes darkened by shadow to skull-like sockets and cheekbones hollowed to bruises. Remembering what he had said about mirrors, Lydia wondered suddenly if he was actually thinning away before her to a wraith of ectoplasm and bone, or if what was thinning was simply his ability to make her believe that she saw him other than he truly was.

"The Galata slums at the base of the hill and the high streets of Pera with their embassies and their banks, they all smell of vampires." The flame repeated itself, cold yellow crystal in his eyes. "Standing just now on the steps of the Yusek Kalderim, I stretched forth my mind across the Golden Horn, and the city lies under such miasma as I have never encountered before.

The minds of vampires, the mind of the master, other minds . . .
I can smell them, heft them like silk in my hand. But everything is blocked, shadowed, wreathed in illusion and decep-
tion, as if every card on the board were down-turned, and one
had to wager all one had on a hand of three."

He frowned and turned to look once more at the gate. Invol-
untarily Lydia stepped closer to him, her anger forgotten. "Are
you sure? You've said yourself you aren't as . . . as able to
perceive . . ."

A wry line sketched itself in the corner of his mouth, the
echo of a living man's ironic smile. "A regret, mistress? A concern for the fact that you have asked me not to kill to preserve
my own life, only to discover that such abstinence may prevent
me from preserving yours?"

She studied his face a moment, trying to read something in
the twin sulfur glints of his eyes. They were like a dragon's in
their hollows. "No," she said. "A concern, maybe, but not a
regret."

"No," he echoed softly. "A lady worthy to her bones."

It was, she realized, the first time he had spoken to her of her
stipulation.

Then he shook his head and looked back to the gate and the
inky, pitch blackness that lay beyond.

"And Jamie?" She found she could barely speak his name. It
was hard even to ask, for fear Ysidro would tell her what she
had dreaded for days to hear.

His brow flinched, just barely, in a frown. "If he is here, he
is not in Pera." There was almost hesitation, an unwillingness
in his voice. "If he sleeps on the Stamboul shore . . ." He shook
his head. "No, my perceptions are impaired, but this is not a
matter of degree. This—shadow, this—blurring that lies over
the city . . . it is something that emanates from the vampires
themselves. An obscurity, gathered to hide aught within it. A
fog, as they say the Undead can summon . . ."

His smile had been—almost—a living man's smile. The
shadow in those dragon eyes was suddenly, fleetingly, a living
man's fear. "Tomorrow night will be soon enough to cross, to
walk and listen in the darkness, to see what more can be

descried at nearer quarters." He drew his cloak more closely around him, a subconscious gesture, the white of his gloves against the dark wool like frost on black rock.

"But it is clear to me that something very strange is taking place in this city, and I had rather our romantic friend had not cried aloud, even in English, regarding hunting and killing and the drinking of blood. I think it best such things not be spoken of, not even here in Pera. Not even by light of day."

TWELVE

THE voices of the muezzins woke Asher: "There is no God but God; Mohammed is His Prophet . . ." He knew the words, but could not tease them from the somber roll of sound.

Arched windows had at one time opened all along the room, five times the length of its narrow width, but centuries ago these had been bricked shut. The windows in the drums of the five shallow domes above were, as far as he could ascertain, barred with silver, though it was hard to be sure. By day he heard no voices, no clip of donkey hooves or creak of wheels from below, and only occasionally and far off, the barking of Constantinople's infamous dogs. Now and then the wind would bring him a street vendor's cry in sawed-off Romaic Greek. Day or night, the closest sounds were the squawking of the seagulls and the yowl of cats.

Through the lattice the sky was the color of tiger lilies, the light momentarily a soft and fading salmon hue on the blue tiles that ringed the domes.

Asher did not face Mecca—though he'd deduced in what direction it lay—nor repeat the words intended by the muezzin, but sitting among the cushions and blankets of the divan, he prayed. He was very frightened.

The light in the room had deepened when he finished, bleeding away to shadow. Because of the domes, the room filled with darkness from the bottom up. In the center of the floor the rectangular, blue-tiled basin of what must have been a fountain or fish pool seemed fathoms deep in the gloom, a horror from which anything might emerge. Asher scratched a match that he took from his pocket, to light the wick of one of the few bronze lamps that still occupied the serried ranks of niches in the wall. The glow did little to dispel the dreadful brooding dimness. He reached for his watch to wind it, as was his habit, but of course it had been taken, along with the silver chains that had protected his wrists and throat.

He dressed and washed, and stowed the bedding in which he'd slept in one of the room's shallow cupboards, listening all the while to night fall within the silent house. In full dark—enough so that a white thread could not be distinguished from a black, as the Koran said—he heard the key turn in the old-fashioned lock.

He moved as far from the door as he could and deliberately willed his mind not to feel, not to succumb to the odd, lazy distraction of the vampire power. Still he did not see them enter the room. He had the vague impression that he had dreamed once about standing in a darkened gallery, watching a door inlaid with brass and ivory as it began to open . . .

But it seemed to him that one moment he was stepping back against a pillar, and the next, they were all around him, binding his wrists behind him with narrow silk cord. Their eyes in the lamplight were the eyes of rats, their flesh dead clay on his. They had not fed.

"So who are you, Englis?" asked the one who had been pointed out to him last night as Zardalu. Beardless, boneless as an empty stocking, he had red-painted fingernails and a Circassian's bright blue eyes. "Yesternight I took you for one of the Bey's *mikaniki*, and I thought, This is one he intends to make one of us, to look after this thing they make in the crypts, this *dastgah*." His eyes slid sidelong at Asher under painted lids; and knowing they could hear it, Asher tried to calm the pounding of his heart.

"And now the Bey has given us other instructions concerning you. What are we to think?"

"You really think he'd join another to us for the sake of one of his experiments?" Jamila Baykus—the Baykus Kadine, she had been called, stick-thin with a strange, disheveled wildness that was somehow very like her namesake owl—put her head to one side and considered him with enormous demon eyes. Half her hair was braided or curled, dressed on jeweled combs, the rest hanging in a huge malt-colored tangle to her thighs. Pearls were caught in it, like shells glimpsed in a jetsam of kelp; she had a necklace of rat bones and diamonds around her throat. "Is that what you are, Englis?" The finger she reached up to touch the underside of his chin—for she was no taller than a twelve-year-old English girl—was like a twig brought in from out-of-doors, icy with the ice of the night.

"*He* said we weren't to question him." That was Haralpos, a one-eyed tough who had been a janissary. He held up a scarf, fine cotton, creased and filthy and patched with dark stains.

"And did he say I was not to question *you?*" Asher had studied Persian and enough Arabic to approximate the thick Osmanli they spoke and make himself understood.

Zardalu's eyebrows tweaked into circumflexes of malicious delight, and his fangs gleamed in a smile. "Oh, what a clever Englis. Of course you may question us. Who are we but your fellow servants of the Deathless Lord?"

"*He* said silence," Haralpos insisted. The dark Habib and the voluptuous and silent Russian girl, Pelageya, stirred uneasily. Asher knew of whom the janissary spoke and knew the others had a right to be uneasy. "*He* said to walk in silence, like the fog. Would we have this infidel cry out to be saved?"

"Would it do me any good if I did?" countered Asher. He turned to Zardalu, whom he sensed to be the most dangerous of them, and asked him, "What *dastgah* is this?" The word meant a scientific apparatus, which could mean anything from an astrolabe to a chemical experiment.

"How should I know that, Englis? The Deathless Lord has put up silver bars across the cellar which lies beneath the old baths that are no longer used. He has veiled the place with his mind, to keep us from thinking about it, even as he has veiled this entire city." The sweet alto voice sank lower, and as the vampire leaned close, his hair and clothing breathed patchouli and decay.

"He has veiled the place, yet still we feel the cold of the ice that he has men bring in during the day for his experiments. We smell the *naft*, the *alkol*, the stinks of what he does . . . even as we hear the footfalls of the workmen, down below in the crypts, as we sleep. Does he think we do not?"

"Come," Haralpos said impatiently. "Now." He reached out with the scarf, and Zardalu touched his wrist.

"Our friend James has said—may we call you James, Englis?—that he knows better than to cry out. The Bey will surely punish us if he escapes, and so even an escape's attempt will mean—oh, not death—" His cold knuckle brushed the scars under Asher's ear. "—but surely some unpleasant experiences with tweezers, or water, or hot sand." The red nails clinched suddenly hard on the earlobe, cutting stronger and stronger like the grip of a machine, Asher gritting his teeth, shutting his eyes, forcing his mind away from the pain. Just when he thought the claws were about to tear away the flesh, Zardalu released him and smiled a fanged smile as he opened his eyes once more. "And he knows he will not escape."

There was blood on Zardalu's nails. The vampire held Asher's gaze with his own as he licked them slowly clean.

They led him out into an open gallery two floors above a courtyard paved in stone. An old *han*, or caravansary, Asher guessed as they descended the long flights of tiled steps. A solitary lamp burned in a wall niche at the bottom of the flight, outlining the arch of a short passageway that led through and down into an octagonal vestibule whose mosaic floors, though long defaced, still showed parts of Byzantine figures. He had crossed that vestibule yesterday afternoon, in the midst of the men who had surrounded him in an alley of the market district, a knife pressed to his back. They had said nothing to him, but had not needed to. The age of the place, as much as the absence of lamps from the niches and mirrors from the walls, had told him what house he had been brought to.

* * *

Last night in the flickering lamplight of the upstairs chamber, Olumsiz Bey had said to him, "It is unfair to keep you utterly a prisoner, when my house has libraries and baths and amusements for an intelligent man." Asher had been lying on the divan then, bound hand and foot and more frightened than he had been in his life.

"But the House of Oleanders is an ancient house, and a large house. There are rooms in which no lamp has been kindled for a great many years, and my children come and go freely in the dark." The Bey gestured to the fledglings with his right hand, coarse and square and covered with rings whose jewels had been carved long before the faceting of gems was devised. In his left he carried a weapon that Asher had not seen him set down, a halberd five and a half feet long whose naked eighteen-inch blade was wrought of shining silver, honed to a razor's keenness and backed along its spine with slanting teeth like a fish's ribs.

"Thus I believe it best that Sayyed here go with you." The Deathless Lord's wave brought forward an impassive servant, one of the three who had kidnapped him yesterday. "I think," the Master of Constantinople had added, as the living servant drew a knife and cut away Asher's bonds, "that you will find he is your best friend."

Asher understood. For several hours Sayyed had stood in the doorway of the library, watching him while he explored the inlaid cupboards and read the titles of the books within them— Arabic, German, Latin—by the light of a dozen lamps and candles. The servant made no comment when Asher had taken a volume of Procopius' *Secret History* and a bronze candlestick back to his room with him, and that was as much as Asher had sought to accomplish. The candlestick was ornamented with tendrils of vine wrought of bronze wire, which Asher had pried loose to work into picklocks as soon as the sun was up.

The interview with Olumsiz Bey was in his mind now, as Haralpos bound his eyes with the dirty scarf and he was guided along, bound and blind and surrounded by whispering voices of those the Bey had warned him to avoid. In his mind, too,

was the silver weapon the Bey had carried, and what it meant
that he carried it.

Asher tried counting turns and footsteps, and concentrated
on the feel of the ground underfoot. But as the Bey had said,
the house was a large one and composed, from what little
Asher had seen, of several old *hans*, minor palaces of Turk or
Byzantine construction. They passed through two open courtyards—or one courtyard twice, for the brick underfoot felt the
same—up and down steps, through a place where water
splished thinly under his boots and another where loose boards
rang hollowly, though only with his own tread despite the cold
grip of hands on his elbows. It did him no good to count steps
and turnings, for it seemed to him that he woke, like a sleepwalker, to find himself on his feet outside, with the stink of
the Constantinople streets in his nostrils and the barking of the
dogs louder in his ears. Eerily, he had no sense of the vampires
around him. It was as if he walked alone, save that their hands
were on his shoulders, his arms, his neck, and that now and
then they spoke.

"Can you see the Bey making such a one into one of us?"
Haralpos' deep voice was close in his ear as they made their
way down a steep street toward the sounds of the harbor. "An
infidel who tinkers with machines? He has grown picky, the
Deathless Lord. He has not brought one into our ranks since
Tinnin came to grief."

"Tinnin was a scholar," breathed a voice he recognized as
belonging to the Baykus Kadine. "A Nubian *philosophe*, like
those in Europe in those days, insolent even to kings . . . Ah,
but sweet. Sweet. He knew the wherefore of those experiments, not just tinkering with the bits of metal and wire."

"Perhaps our James knows the wherefore as well?" Zardalu
purred. "Perhaps our Bey does not trust us?"

Rising ground steep under his feet, then steps—somewhere
seagulls yarked. The House of Oleanders lay a stone's throw
from the government ministries on the shoulder of the Second
Hill, but the market quarter between the Place d'Armes and the
mosque of the Sultana Valide was one of the oldest and most
tangled districts in the town. As in many Islamic cities, after

the prayers of nightfall the inhabitants retreated to their houses and barred the doors; the Undead and their captive walked unopposed.

"High time he trusted someone," Haralpos grumbled.

"He didn't trust Zarifa, either," the Baykus Kadine said, her voice like weed stalks and bones. "Nor Shahar, and you saw what came to them. It is a deep game he plays, our Deathless Lord, and deeper now with this new little pet." Her nails, inch-long claws on those skinny child's hands, flicked his neck.

One of them must have felt him listening, sensed his mind, for it seemed to him almost that someone blew drugged smoke into his thoughts, so he had to fight to remain even a little aware of his surroundings. His mind drifted, hazed with strange impressions and alien smells, but when it cleared, the salt tang of the sea and the mournful clang of ships' bells was gone, replaced by livelier chatter in the distance and the music of the Gypsy quarter. They were making for the walls.

He told himself if they were going to kill him where the Bey could not see, they would surely have done so already.

It didn't help.

Steeper ground, ankle-breaking potholes and rock under-foot, and the occasional brush of broken stonework against his shoulders. Once, someone pressed a hand to his head, making him duck. Then cold sea wind, and the rustle of trees. When his eyes were unbound, he could make out all around him the pale shapes of funerary steles, like clustering finger bones in black blots of tree shadow, and the heavy loom of stone *turbe* tombs. The moon had not yet risen, but stars glimmered feebly, so he could barely glimpse the hueless bulk that reared behind him: old watchtowers, decaying ramparts, a fosse thick with weed and shadow and the ghosts of men who'd died defending the walls. Black on black, touched only by the frailest of lights, the city's hills offered domes and minarets to an iron sky.

Only Zardalu stood beside him, smiling a little. His old-fashioned clothing—pantaloons, tunic, pelisse of black velvet—glittered with jewels.

"Now you will walk a little among the tombs, James, my friend, no?" Effortlessly the painted nails slit through the cords around his wrists. Under the rouge and the paint on his eyelids, all rendered to dark smudges by the night, the white face was like something from a horrible dream, equivocal and boneless as the rest of his body. He shook back his long hair, dressed in womanly curls, and earrings flashed wetly in it. "Parade yourself, as those Undead who find themselves in this city must, in politeness, parade themselves that the Deathless Lord may look on them and give them his leave or no to hunt. I hope," he added, with a corpse's widening grin, "that you understand the rules."

"I think I do." Asher rubbed his wrists. Though smooth, the cord had been drawn tight and his swollen fingers were nearly numb. The thought of trying to make it back to the city walls, of playing hide-and-seek among the ruined passages of the abandoned towers with those who could see in midnight-black, had only to be framed to be discarded at once and utterly. Something flicked at his hair, like a sigh. He spun as if it had been the touch of a knife point, but there was nothing to be seen.

Zardalu laughed, a soundless gapping of the rubber mouth. His fangs were long and pointed, like a wolf's.

"So who are you in truth, Englis?" he asked softly. "And who is he whom the Bey thinks will risk himself to come to you? Since the waning of summer he has said, 'Find him and kill him.' Now he says, the one who comes to the Englis, bring that one to me."

He gestured around him at the crumbling *turbes*, the steles with turbans—or stylized veils—carved on them leaning every which way, as if a giant child had randomly stuck a thousand thousand enormous matchsticks in the unkempt grass. "Are you his servant? Or is it some secret that you know?" The blanched eyes, dirty ice in the starlight, seemed for a time to be the eunuch's only reality, the rest of him a thing of smoke and dreams. Asher felt on his mind the narcotic pressure of the vampire's power, an almost impossible weight of sleep.

"I don't know what you're talking about."

"Who is this interloper, Englis? And what has it to do with the *dastgah* and the silver bars that guard the way to the crypt?"

With an effort, Asher pushed the soft cloudiness away. "If your master is going to punish you for asking," he said, "I think it would behoove me not to answer."

Zardalu flung up his hands in an exaggerated mime of amusement, but his anger was palpable. "Behold the wise man!" he cried, soundless as the night wind. "Now all he needs is a little bell, like the goat they tie to summon the tiger."

Asher felt the grip of his mind and tried to throw it off again, tried to follow where the tall vampire went, but could not. It was as if he woke suddenly again, standing alone in the frost among the rotting tombs.

They were all there somewhere, he thought. Zardalu and Jamila Baykus; Haralpos and Habib and Pelageya: watching him. An ambush. A trap. Anthea had told him of the strange condition, a sort of mental spell she sensed over the city, that prevented her from feeling the presence of any other vampire—the work, she had said, frightened, of a great master or masters.

As he walked cautiously among the tombs, groping where the somber cypresses blotted even the wan glow of the sky, he sought to absorb as much of this landscape as he could. Had Anthea fled their lodging after his disappearance to hide in such a place?

Or had his encounter with the men of the Sultan's guard, who had picked him up in the courtyard of the Mosque of the Bajazid, been engineered to leave her unguarded?

Then why kidnap him less than an hour after his release, before he had even returned to her? Why use him, as he was being used now, as bait?

Was it for her, even, that the trap was set?

He stopped to rest on the low flat tomb of some prince or noble, like a marble bench inscribed in flowing Arabic script and terminating in a narrow stele surmounted by the figure of a turban. The turban signified a man. The fact that it was depicted as tilted to one side meant the dead man had been strangled by the Sultan's order. The marble was starred white where bullets had struck it when the army came through here to their final battle with the Sultan's forces in July.

And that final battle, he thought, had abruptly terminated whatever power Olumsiz Bey had held in the Sultan's court—almost certainly financial, since the entire country was in pawn. With Abdul Hamid's imprisonment in Yildiz while the Committee of Union and Progress thrashed out how to get a Parliament elected and bring the empire into the twentieth century from a standing start in the sixteenth, the Bey had needed to find someone else to send to England, to conduct Ernchester here.

For whatever reason he wanted the earl here in the first place.

Something moved among the black trees, but strain his eyes as he would, he could make out nothing. A rat or a fox—though if rats fled the smell of Anthea's hair upon her bonnet, it was unlikely they'd venture close to the silent watchers among the trees.

He slipped off the tomb and moved on.

Tombs clustered all the length of the land walls, from the seven-towered gate of the Yeni Koule to the mosque at Eyoub. People came here to pray in the daylight, but the *turbe* themselves were undisturbed.

Somewhere close dogs howled.

His personation of a goat in a tiger hunt lasted for what he calculated was almost two hours, judging by the moon's progress among the clouds. From the dark city the muezzins' final cries ascended, that deep, haunting wailing that is like no other sound on earth. In time, across the water, a church bell answered from Pera, small and clear.

Was it Anthea they thought would appear? Or Ernchester? Or just possibly someone else?

By what Zardalu had said, Asher wasn't sure they knew exactly who it was they expected to trap.

Anthea, he thought, *fly this place. Go away.*

Then Zardalu was walking toward him, across open ground with the ashen grass surging around his pantaloons. When he bound Asher's wrists again and wrapped the scarf over his eyes, his hands were warm.

"You serve a heartless master," said the eunuch. "Or maybe

by this time he's found himself another servant, clever or no. Did he promise you everlasting life, James? They all do, you know."

"Even the Bey?"

"Ah. An impudent infidel, no less."

Asher could hear the smile in Zardalu's sweet whisper. "Just curious."

When they passed the city walls this time, there was no sound in the streets, save the crying of the gulls. Zardalu kept one hand on Asher's elbow, the other on the back of his neck, and the smell of fresh blood and the reek of death drowned out both the smell of the muck underfoot and the vampire's perfume.

Only when they were, Asher estimated, coming over the Second Hill again did he hear other voices and steps drawing near. A man mumbled, "Beloved ... beautiful fairy ..." in harsh-sounding Romaic Greek, and on the air, like the vapors of poisoned flowers, Asher heard the silvery flicker of vampire laughter.

"She's found a treasure, our Pelageya," Zardalu's voice breathed in his ear. "How is it, *sagir sayyat*? Did you find a strong bullock to trap in your nets?"

The Russian girl laughed, a soft, thick tickling that, in spite of himself and all he knew, went straight to his groin, as if the woman leaned naked in his arms.

They stopped. There was the sound of a key in a lock, impossible to tell what kind of key—the man with them muttered drunkenly, swearing eternal love, promising feats of ecstasy that would have his newfound adored one crying out with gratitude, and all the while around him Asher heard the whisper of unholy mirth—Haralpos, Habib, the Baykus Kadine. Their voices were a fleeting susurration, now before, now behind, as he was guided through a doorway and down long uneven stairs, worn in the center and incredibly deep, to a place that smelled of water and stone.

"That little beggar Habib's got won't be missed, but what of that bullock of yours? He looks well-fed."

"And if he is? He's an Armenian, she found him in the Kara

Geumruk. The Sultan is quicker to avenge Gypsies and Jews than such folk . . ."

"But is he sober enough to give us sport?" Zardalu's drawling voice was petulant. "Well enough to steal sleeping beggar children for El-Malik, but after a night sitting in a graveyard, with only one wretched tramp sleeping behind a tomb, I want a little sport."

"El-Malik entertains his infidel *makaniki*." He could almost see the Russian girl's lazy shrug. "I can smell the coffee from the street. This one will waken enough."

El-Malik. The master, the king. The Master Vampire of Constantinople. And while they were talking, a sharp turn at the bottom of the stairs, two of his own steps, and the brush of a curtain against his face, right turn, wildly uneven brick underfoot and the sudden throat-catching stink of ammonia and chemicals, and a blast of cold.

And far off, inarticulate with agony and horror, muffled as if behind some barrier of wood and iron, the sound of a man's voice.

"I came on one of the *makaniki* the other night, as I was returning early," Zardalu was relating lightly, turning, Asher thought, so that his hand slid from neck to shoulder. Had it not, he thought the vampire must have felt the prickle of the hairs at the sound of that horrible, distant despair. "A fat little infidel like an *asure* pudding, with spectacles on his nose, so . . . He backed against the wall by the rear gate, holding his little hammer out like this, staring around squeaking, 'Who is that there? I hear you . . . You cannot get away . . . Come show yourself and I will not hurt you . . .' " while the unfortunate Armenian youth mumbled endearments and Asher measured in his mind a narrow stair that wound around itself three times, then the echoes of some open room, and more stairs. Cobbly pavement of small stones underfoot, then of bigger ones, like cannonballs, in an open space where grass grew between blocks. Right, and a locked door . . .

They stopped, suddenly, in a room with a bare wooden floor. By their silence Asher knew why.

"Nothing?" The voice was brown velvet, roses, and gold.

By the shift of Zardalu's grip, Asher knew that he bowed. "Nothing, Lord."

In his blindness he heard the dense rustle of silk, but only when it was close enough that he could smell coffee, incense, ammonia . . . blood.

"Yet you have done passing well. Habib, my sweet, is that *sarigi burma* for me? What a dirty little thing she is. And ah, Pelageya . . ." Asher could almost see him bow, and there was a momentary scuffle, the swish of clothing and a stifled grunt of terror as the young man suddenly, belatedly, realized that he stood in the presence of smiling death.

A hand like animate steel brushed the side of Asher's face, almost in a caress. The scarf was slipped aside. Eyes that had once been coffee-dark but had been bleached, by a trick of the vampire state, to a garish and unnatural orange blinked into his by the glow of oil lamps close overhead.

Olumsiz Bey stepped back.

He was as tall as Asher—six feet—and nearly as thin, but his shoulders stooped, giving the narrow, hairless head an uptilted angle like a tortoise's. The nose was an ax blade such as might have hewed the lipless mouth into existence with a single stroke, but it was not an unhandsome face. In one ear he wore a huge chunk of amber, as orange as his eyes, in which an ant was trapped, so big that Asher could see the curve of its serrated jaws; one almost expected to see other insects locked in the frozen prisons of his real eyes as well.

"It is probably well," Olumsiz Bey said to him in the flowery Osmanli of the court, "that you return to your chamber now, Scheherazade, and remain there for the balance of the night. The tales we will tell tonight are not for the ears of the living."

Asher's eyes went past him to the fledglings, grouped closely now around a husky young man with a prominent nose and dark, thickly curling hair. The young man was staring around him, growing horror struggling against wine and whatever glamours Pelageya had laid upon his mind, taking in the rich garden of blue and yellow tiles in the hall and the way darkness waited in every corner. Asher took it in, too, printing it in his mind . . . Habib, a coarse and powerful vampire who seemed to be special friends with Haralpos, carried, as Asher had deduced, a sleeping beggar girl of twelve or so, holding her against his shoulder as if she were an infant.

"Sayyed has already taken food thither for you," the Master of Constantinople went on. "And books—if you will pardon my presumption in choosing them for you—to beguile with old legends the passing of the night. There will be . . . a little sport here." His smile had a flex, a curve to it, like a reflex that his eyes had long ago forgotten or had never known. He gestured with his right hand, for his left never loosened its hold on his silver-bladed weapon, which glittered whitely in the many-hued glow of the bronze lamps overhead.

The eyes of the fledglings threw back that glow, cats waiting to be fed.

The Armenian boy made a little noise of terror and tried to pull his arms free of Pelageya's grip and Haralpos', but he could not. Asher smelled urine as the boy pissed himself. He would give them the run they wanted, Asher thought bitterly, through all the dark galleries of that accursed house.

And all the while he repeated silently to himself, *A cobbled courtyard beyond this place, smaller cobbles, right through a door, across a hall, down a narrow stair and then another twice as deep . . .*

The place of silver bars, where Zardalu said the *dastgah* was, smelling of chemicals . . .

And a voice that screamed its despair to the dark.

There was only one person he could think of whom the Bey would hold prisoner behind silver bars.

"My children forget themselves sometimes in their chase."

He jerked his mind back—the Bey must not guess his abstraction.

"Yes, I really think it best if you remain in your chamber, and if any call out to you, save me alone, I suggest that you do not answer. My darling . . ."

The Bey's jeweled right hand caressed Zardalu's cheek.

There was an impassive flicker behind the sapphire eyes, nothing more.

"I will take this one back to his chamber. Have Habib bring the child to my own room." He held up the scarf that had covered Asher's eyes, extended it to his fledgling once more. "Be so good as to conduct my other guest of this evening back to the usual meeting place. Remember, I will know it if the slightest ill befalls him. Indeed, I shall know it if you so much as speak to him, as you did to this one, and he to you." The smile again, cold as his grip. "And I will not be pleased. Is this understood?"

Zardalu bowed again, bending his long boneless form so that his black curls fell forward over his shoulder and swept the wooden planks of the floor. "This is understood, Lord."

"Come." Olumsiz Bey beckoned to someone who had stood all this time in the gloom of the room's inner doorway, and switched to German, perfectly contemporary and without accent or inflection. "This man will take you outside. I guarantee that you need not fear him."

"I have no fear within your house, or anywhere that I walk, under your protection, my lord." Ignace Karolyi stepped from the darkness, his light brown Saville Row suit as incongruous in that setting as a khaki-uniformed Tommy with an Enfield would have been at Marathon. He stopped before Asher for a moment, regarding him with sudden, narrowed speculation in his wide-set brown eyes. Then he turned back to Olumsiz Bey and bowed.

"I trust that I am forgiven, my lord, and that terms between us can still be reached?"

The Bey regarded him with strange eyes, holding his silver weapon before him, the edge glittering in the light. "This remains to be seen. As all things do, it rests in the hand of God."

THIRTEEN

"I DON'T see why he can't come with us." Margaret Potton stepped down from the embassy carriage at Lydia's heels, and, trailed by a Greek footman, hurried in the wake of the formidable Lady Clapham, a tall, thin, horse-faced individual whom Lydia had guessed at once to be the headwoman of the British diplomatic community in Pera. "You could introduce him as your cousin. When you told Sir Burnwell that you had a cousin here in Constantinople, I thought it was a good idea."

"I told him that in case we have to produce Ysidro in an emergency," Lydia replied, patient and somewhat bemused, but without anger. "I don't think a diplomatic reception at the palace qualifies." Ahead of them, half glimpsed between strolling ladies in tulip-skirted ensembles and coal-scuttle hats that would not have been out of place in Paris or Vienna, Lady Clapham paused in the doorway of Mademoiselle Ursule's and looked back for her two charges. Lydia almost expected her to snap, *Step along, girls, spit-spot . . .*

"I don't know," Margaret said. "I think it would be nice for him."

Lydia shook her head but was spared further discussion by conjunction, in the doorway of the boutique, with her guide and hostess for the shopping trip and the modiste herself, a middle-aged and firmly corseted Belgian woman who apprehended instantly the difference between Lydia's two-hundred-guinea, Alice-blue raw silk and Margaret's outdated brown wool, but varied not a whit the warmth of her smiles of greeting to both. It did cross Lydia's mind, as Lady Clapham explained to Mlle. Ursule what they'd come for, that Ysidro might have some difficulty these days in passing himself off as a living man.

Margaret was staggered at the news that it was for her benefit, not for Lydia's, that they had made the excursion to the fashionable European shopping quarter along the Grand Rue. "Silly goose," Lady Clapham declared, not unkindly, as the governess turned pink with pleasure. "Of course you'll accompany Mrs. Asher tonight, and you certainly can't wear what you have on."

Lydia felt slightly relieved at this confirmation that other people—older and in positions of social authority—were far more tactless than she.

Much as it annoyed Lydia to admit it, Ysidro had been quite right. In Constantinople as in Vienna, Margaret Potton was her mantle of respectability, her mere presence making it entirely unnecessary for Lydia to say to anyone, *As you see, I am not a jauntering slut.* Her presence had certainly worked its intended magic at the embassy yesterday afternoon. Without Margaret, Lydia guessed she would still have been admitted, would still have had her queries answered . . . would still have spoken to Sir Burnwell, stooped and gray and with the slightly puffy face of an intermittent sufferer of kidney problems . . .

But only the presence and respectability of a companion had brought Lady Clapham into the office, holding out her hands and saying, *My dear, I'm so sorry . . .*

So sorry.

Cold closed around her again, dimming the voices of Mlle. Ursule, Lady Clapham, Miss Potton, as if the small, neat, and extremely Parisian room with its powder-blue satin wallpapers and gilt mirrors was at the end of a very long corridor.

Wednesday. James had been missing since Wednesday afternoon.

"Which one do you like, my dear?"

Lady Clapham's voice pulled her back to the present. The

dressmaker had spread out on the table two gowns, one straw-yellow with an overgown of white georgette, the other fawn-and-white-striped mousseline de soie trimmed with pink silk. "I think that's up to Miss Potton," Lydia said, manufacturing a smile with an effort and stepping close to get some idea of how the dresses actually looked. Miss Potton turned red and pale and pink, and blotchy combinations of all three, and finally settled on the mousseline de soie, for which Lydia then bought a pair of white satin slippers, kid gloves, and a thin gold chain with a pendant of rose quartz and earrings to match.

"You really shouldn't have," Margaret said softly when, later in their bedroom, Stefania Potoneros was lacing her into the gown. "I mean I . . . it must be terribly expensive."

It hadn't been, in terms of higher fashion, reflected Lydia, putting on her spectacles to turn and look over her shoulder at the girl. Mlle. Ursule had expertly graded ranks of gowns for all occasions, and the fawn and white silk, however pretty, was designed to be no competition whatsoever for Lydia's point lace and baby ribbons. But to a girl without a family, who had spent any number of years in the dreary confines of the typical governess' quarters, it must seem like Cinderella's ball dress.

"I can't . . ." Margaret stammered. "I can't repay you . . ."

"Good heavens, no!" Lydia said. There was a silence, Margaret undoubtedly remembering—as Lydia remembered—the hysterics in Sofia, the furious outburst upon their arrival the night before last. A little awkwardly, she explained, "It's nothing, really. I mean . . . what's the point of being an heiress, and putting up with uncles and aunts telling you how to live and who you have to marry, if you can't . . . can't buy someone a present now and then? And I know it helps to have the right thing to wear."

"I thought if you were an heiress, it meant you could do what you wanted," said Margaret as Lydia barely touched the eiderdown puff to her cheeks, then leaned forward until her nose nearly touched the glass to inspect the results in the mirror.

Lydia shook her head. "Well, I don't know about other

heiresses. My father and his two sisters had a terror of fortune hunters, and my life was . . . rather restricted at times."

I'll not have you turning my money over to a scoundrel, had been her father's exact—and oft-repeated—words.

Not, *A man who only marries you for money will make you wretched.*

Not, *How do you expect such a man to fit into the life you want to make for yourself?*

I'll not have you turning my money over to a scoundrel.

His money, even should he die.

She rubbed the rouge on her fingertips, smoothed the tiniest hint of a blush along cheekbones and temples, seeking the perfection that had been her only protection against everything they could do.

"It couldn't have been that restricted, if they let you go to Oxford," said Margaret. She picked up the powder puff, turned it cautiously over in one square, disapproving hand. "Do all heiresses learn to use cosmetics like this?"

"Only if they have a nose like mine." Lydia squinted at the effect of the rouge, then licked the end of her eye pencil and began careful shading along the upper lashes. "James—he was a friend of my uncle Ambrose, the dean of All Souls—arranged with one of the pathology professors to help me borrow money under another name. I begged Uncle Ambrose not to tell Father, and I'm not sure he would have agreed if he'd known I was studying medicine. It was exhausting, going back and forth by train and concealing sessions when my tutor came down to town. Fortunately, our place was near Oxford—Willoughby Close—and Father spent weeks at a time down in London. If my mother had been alive, I could never have done it."

"What did they do when they found out?" Margaret asked, blue eyes wide with alarm.

"There was a row," Lydia said evasively. Why, after eight years, did her father's cold fury still hurt? "Would you like to try this?" she added, seeing the other woman's hand stray to touch the rouge pot, the lip rouge, the several types of powder and skin food indispensable to the artifice that Lydia regarded as her armor against the world.

"C-could I?" Margaret stammered, turning pink again. "I know I shouldn't—the sisters at the orphanage all said that ladies don't use such things . . ."

"Well, I never met a lady who didn't," Lydia said with a smile. "It's just that there's a trick to doing it so that nobody notices. Here."

The transformation was not a startling one, but having spent years compensating for what she considered her own short-comings—a slightly aquiline nose, too-thin cheeks, and un-fashionably shaped lips, to say nothing of a preference for knowledge above society gossip—Lydia knew how to apply rouge and powder to reduce the impact of the other woman's shallow chin and snub nose, and to give her better cheekbones than she'd been born with. At the end, staring into the lamplit glass, Margaret breathed, "Oh . . ." in a kind of wonderment, the blue eyes widened and deepened, the pale, pretty face surrounded by raven masses of curls as it had been, Lydia knew well, in her dreams. "Oh, thank you!"

She fumbled for her eyeglasses.

Lydia laughed. "You aren't going to wear them to the reception, are you?"

"Of course." Margaret settled them firmly on her nose, even as Lydia was removing her own to be helped into her gown by the maid. "If people don't like me in my eyeglasses, that's just too bad." She blinked mildly at Lydia as the Greek maid laced her expertly up the back. "Thank you," Margaret said simply. "Thank you so much for doing this for me. I've never been beautiful before."

Lydia smiled a little and shook her head. "I'll teach you how to do it, if you'd like," she said, stowing her spectacles in a silver-mounted leather case and making a final inspection of herself in the mirror. Stefanie's sister Helena had come to the door twenty minutes ago with word that Sir Burnwell and Lady Clapham were waiting downstairs with the carriage; they should, Lydia guessed, arrive at the palace in fashionable good time.

She worked her tight kid gloves onto her hands and surveyed Margaret once more, pleased with the results in spite of the glasses. She had done her best—the fact that Miss Potton was her companion was no reason not to make her as beautiful as she could be, though she knew girls of her own year as a debutante who would dispute that—and she suspected that her companion's raven hair and tourmaline eyes made her prettier than herself.

"Margaret," she asked, as they collected reticules, fans, shawls, and keys, "what are you going to do when you return? To London, I mean? I could help you . . ."

"Oh, I'll leave that to Don Simon," Margaret said. "My fate is in his hands."

She smiled happily and followed Lydia down the stairs.

The reception was held in a medium-sized pavilion in the inner garden court of the old palace of the sultans, flanked by plane trees and surrounded by a colonnade of shallow, green-tiled domes. The Sultan himself had not occupied the Topkapi Palace for a good fifty years, but the new government—the Committee of Union and Progress—used it for state functions, and this three-room suite, though a little small for a reception and rather stuffy with its low, coffered ceilings and Western-style crystal chandeliers, was at least unhallowed by any sort of Imperial tradition.

"Ambassador Lowther hardly knows whom to speak to these days," Sir Burnwell confided to Lydia as gorgeously caparisoned palace servants divested them of coats and cloaks in the doorway of the kiosk's small service room. "It's like the old story about the seer who was right half the time, but one never knew which half. The C.U.P. holds power in patches, but nobody knows which patches they are."

"At least under the old Sultan one knew whom to bribe." Lady Clapham brushed straight the folds of her periwinkle and gold chiffon dress, and nodded approvingly at both the younger members of the party. "Don't worry, my dear," she added more quietly to Lydia. "If there's anything to be found about your husband, we'll find it here. I know at least someone who saw him Wednesday afternoon. I hope he's here . . . Russians have such an Oriental idea of time."

She led the way into the main hall, where the reception line moved slowly past the bearlike Talaat Bey, the new lord of this place where the sultans had reigned for five centuries, and the Romeo of the new army, the beautiful Enver Bey. The room was crowded with men and women dressed in the height of European fashion—most of them fair-skinned and all of them speaking French—and servants in old-fashioned turbans, slippers, and pantaloons bearing silver trays of refreshments. Lydia noticed Miss Potton craning her neck, looking around her, presumably in the hopes that Ysidro would have followed them here after all.

"Andrei!" Lady Clapham called out and moved into the crowd, returning a moment later with a hunter-green colossus on her arm. "Prince Andrei Illyich Razumovsky, of the Russian Embassy; Mrs. James Asher. His Highness is an acquaintance of your husband, my dear. He was the last one to see him after that affair with the Sultan's guards Wednesday, weren't you, Andrei?"

"The Sultan's guards?" Lydia raised her eyes to the man who towered over her, the impressionistic glitter of bullion, buttons, epaulets, fringe, and a beard of still-brighter gold resolving themselves into a good-humored, handsome face and bright blue eyes as the prince bent to kiss her hand. *Slavic facial angle,* Lydia thought automatically. *Brachycephalic. Cranial index about 82. I really* must *stop seeing people in terms of their internal structure . . .*

"There was little harm done," the prince said in beautiful Oxonian English and offered her his arm. Lydia followed him back out into the colonnade, where electric lights had been incongruously strung from pillar to pillar. A few men stood at one end of the arcade smoking—Lydia caught the acrid whiff of tobacco, but at that distance they were little more than a clump of black forms spatchcocked with the white of shirtfronts.

The day had been a cold one, and few ladies, bare-shouldered as she was herself, ventured into the sea-chilled darkness.

"Your husband had lodgings here in Stamboul," the prince went on when they were out of earshot of the smokers. "Most Europeans prefer to stay in Pera, of course, particularly since the coup. There haven't been riots among the Armenians in the past week or two, but fighting in the streets between the Greeks and the Turks can't be stopped. Your husband . . ."

He gazed down at her for a moment from his great height, and Lydia could see him asking himself what he could, in discretion, ask her. The look in Lady Clapham's eyes when she'd said, *An acquaintance of your husband,* had told her exactly what this "junior attaché" did in the Czar's service.

"I know that my husband came to Constantinople to ask the advice of . . . certain friends." She laid the same emphasis on the last words and met his eyes. The corners of them crinkled in a little smile. *Yes, I know my husband was a spy and you still are.* Presumably, she thought, Lady Clapham wouldn't have introduced them that way if Russia was an ally of Austria. Whose side was the Ottoman Empire on?

"Ah," he said. "As you say, Madame Asher." His smile widened. "Then you know that he probably had his reasons. You wouldn't happen to know what those were?"

She shook her head. "I only knew that he might be in trouble. Sir Burnwell told me he arrived in Constantinople a week ago yesterday, and that nobody's seen him since Wednesday afternoon."

"And what sort of help did you believe you could be?" He spoke kindly, but she could see something else in his gaze. *Just because we're allies,* Jamie often said, *doesn't mean we're on the same side.* She felt panicky again, as she had in Vienna, panicky and unable to make a correct choice.

Forcibly, she put the panic aside. "I thought I could recognize the man who might betray him," Lydia lied, with what she hoped was calm. "I don't know his name," she added, and went on at once, "But what happened Wednesday afternoon?"

Razumovsky looked as if he might say something else, but changed his mind. Probably, thought Lydia, because he thought it likelier he'd get more information later if he gave a little himself. He might even actually like Jamie—he looked like the sort of person Jamie, and in fact she, would and could like.

"As I said, he had lodgings on the Stamboul side of the Horn." The prince lowered his voice and glanced along the colonnade to the group of smokers again. None looked in their direction, but the prince guided her down the short flight of marble steps that led to an arched tunnel beneath the pavilion, and so through to the dark gardens beyond. "He told no one where they were, and when I saw him, he had the look of one watching over his shoulder. On Wednesday men from the palace intercepted him by the Grand Bazaar, sent by the High Chamberlain, they said—though anyone could have bribed him to do so." He grinned reminiscently. "I've bribed him to do similar things myself."

"And he sent to you for help?"

"We've been friends a good many years," said the Russian. "Sir Burnwell would probably have complained to the army first, or the C.U.P., and been put off for God knows how long. Semibarbarity has its advantages. I came here—where the Chamberlain and in fact the Sultan still hold a good deal of power—and blustered and shook my fist. Shook my country's fist, which frightened them even more. Already the Sultan is playing off the people against the army, trying to rouse them in a countercoup, for he wields power as the head of the Mohammedan faith, you know. If it comes to it, the Chamberlain and his master are going to need support."

Lydia shivered, remembering a scene glimpsed from the window of the embassy carriage as they'd clattered along one of the few streets in the old city wide enough to admit such a vehicle: three men, dark-haired and hook-nosed, in the khaki uniforms of the new army, beating up an old man outside a half-closed shop. A muttering crowd had gathered, but no one had dared interfere; the old man had only put his hands over his head for protection, as if he knew perfectly well that begging for mercy or asking for help were equally out of court.

"They brought him out in a short time," Razumovsky went on, stroking back the surge of his golden mustaches. "As I'd suspected, they were holding him in the guardhouse here, which means it was the Chamberlain who'd been bribed. He had been knocked about a little, nothing serious."

"I hope he put proper antiseptic on it," Lydia said, and was startled when the prince burst into laughter. "I mean," she added hastily, realizing how that had sounded, "I'm quite shocked, of course, that he was hurt, but if he *will* get into danger . . . What had he been doing?"

"Apparently—he did not tell me this, but I found it out through palace contacts of my own—questioning storytellers in the markets. That was how they knew where he would be."

"Storytellers." *Old man who lived to be a thousand . . .* The wandering script of Fairport's notebook sprang immediately to her mind. *Woman who lived to be five hundred (wove moonlight).*

"You tell me why," said the prince.

Lydia only shook her head, though a numbness started behind her breastbone and seemed to spread to fingers, lips, toes. Stress on top of hypothermia, she thought. And then, a small inner voice like a child's, *Jamie, no . . .*

"You're cold, madame." The prince put a warm hand to the small of her back and led her up the steps again, toward the brighter lights at the other end of the arcade. "We were walking back to his rooms in the Bajazid when an Armenian boy came up to him. I didn't hear all the boy said, but I know he said, 'My master told me to show you the place.' Jamie took his leave of me . . ." He shook his head.

Did he look well? she wanted to ask. *Did they take his knife when he was arrested, and did he get it back? Did you see if he still had the silver around his neck, on his wrists?*

It was conceivable, she thought, that the Sultan's guards had stolen it. The ones she'd seen at the palace's outer gates looked capable of relieving a dying man of his shoes.

Under her corsets her heart seemed to be pounding uncomfortably fast.

"Your palace contact didn't happen to say which storytellers, did he?"

Razumovsky stopped, gazing down at her again. Men had

appeared in the colonnade, Europeans in bright colors that had to be uniforms. By the way they were looking around, Lydia guessed they were the prince's own attachés.

"Mrs. Asher," he said quietly, "Constantinople is not a good city. It is not a safe city, especially now, with the army in power and turning things upside down, and it has never been a good city in which to be a woman. I have been making inquiries of my own about James. When I hear anything, even of the smallest, I will send to you at once."

"Thank you." Lydia clasped the broad, kid-gloved hand. "I can't tell you how much I appreciate that. I can't . . . there are reasons I can't tell you how I know . . . what I know. But any help you can give me . . ."

"On this condition." Razumovsky brushed at his mustaches again. His glove buttons had diamonds in them that twinkled like tiny stars. "Something tells me I do not need to tell this to you, but I will anyway. *Do not investigate anything alone.* Not anything. Call on me for help at whatever hour. Is there a telephone where you're staying?" She shook her head. "Then send a page. Do you understand? If I can't come, I'll send a servant. You don't need to tell me or him or anyone where you're going, but *don't go alone.*

"Sir Burnwell and the embassy staff are good men, but they haven't been here as long as I. Moreover, they are perceived as being on the side of the C.U.P., and against the old powers. In any case the German businessmen who've advanced money to both sides hold more power here than either my embassy or yours. When you go about the city, take someone with you—someone besides that silly girl of yours, I mean—and don't assume that you can get away with anything safely. This isn't England. There," he said, and led her back toward the lights, the smokers, the door with its tall guards in their billowy pantaloons and turbans of orange and red. Not until they were inside and he had fetched her champagne and a cracker of sour cream and Russian caviar did he excuse himself, and two minutes later she saw him—or at any rate someone his height with a gold beard and a uniform of hunter-green—deep in conversation with Enver Bey himself.

FOURTEEN

THE room was more crowded than before. During her conversation with the prince, Lydia had been dimly aware of lights passing among the trees and hedges as servants conducted newcomers along the paths from the enormous outer court. Scanning backs, Lydia identified the asymmetrical mauve volutes of her patroness' gown in the midst of a dark cluster of male suiting. As she approached, she heard the guttural babble of German and made out references to track miles, rolling stock, gauge widths, and Krupps that told her that Lady Clapham had fallen among the businessmen, but in any case Lady Clapham held out her hand to her with the air of a somewhat long-toothed Andromeda greeting a schoolgirl Perseus in ecru lace and pink ribbons.

"My *dear* Mrs. Asher," she cried. "May I present to you Herr Franz Hindl? Herr Hindl, Mrs. Asher. Now if you'll please excuse us, Herr Hindl, I promised to introduce Mrs. Asher to Herr Dettmars ... You're a godsend, my dear!" she added in a low voice as the stout, fair-haired gentleman who had shaken Lydia's hand was left behind with considerable celerity. "*Such* a bore." She steered her into one of the smaller rear chambers of the pavilion, just as crowded and if possible more airless than the long front room. "Do I have the appearance of a woman who will perish if she does not receive accurate information concerning the differences between soft-coal hummer furnaces and hard-coal base burners?"

Lydia paused to study her with mock gravity. "Turn 'round," she instructed, and with a straight face the attaché's wife did so.

"Only a little in the back," Lydia replied after due consideration.

"I'll wear a shawl over it, then," promised Lady Clapham. "I am suffocating. Was Prince Razumovsky able to give you any information about your husband, dear?"

Lydia nodded slowly. "He told me my husband was doing some kind of research, talking to storytellers in the markets. Did he—Dr. Asher, I mean—mention this to you?"

"That isn't what brought him to Constantinople, surely?"

"No," Lydia said. "But he does research in such things wherever he is. He's a folklorist as well as a linguist."

Lady Clapham sighed resignedly and poked at her untidy, graying coiffure. "Well, better than one of those lunatics like my brother, who goes about taking rubbings off tombs. Not even in heathen parts but in places like Wensley Parva and Bath Cathedral. *And in hunting season!*" She shook her head wonderingly and picked a cracker of caviar from a servant's tray as if the man had been a table. "Yes, he did ask about storytellers. Burnie told him about the old fellow who sits in the street of the brass sellers in the Great Bazaar. Did His Highness offer you his help? I thought so. Just make sure you have Miss Potton with you at all times and you should be quite all right. Where *has* Miss Potton got to?"

Lydia gazed around the small chamber. Though without her eyeglasses most men in crowds looked alike—except James, of course, whom she would know anywhere under any circumstances, and human Christmas trees like Prince Razumovsky—she could generally spot women by the colors and shapes of their dresses. But there was no sign of the fawn-and-white silk among the crowd, no ink blot of black curls glistening in the sharp yellowish light. She remembered Ysidro remarking last night, *I may be somewhere thereabouts,* and

Margaret's desire to see him at the reception . . . And the more so now, to show him her newfound beauty.

"She may have gone into the gardens." The image of Margaret, in improbable Georgian panniers and wig, waltzing with Ysidro on the terrace of some dream mansion, floated through her mind.

"She'll freeze," Lady Clapham predicted. "Oh, my dear, there's someone I *do* want to introduce you to . . . absolutely charming, and such a cut-up . . ." She was already starting to lead her toward a man who had just entered the smaller room. Another uniform, this one scarlet, heavily braided with silver and ornamented with, of all things, a leopard skin over the shoulder, set off dark hair and a stance that told her at once, without being near enough to see his face, that he was as handsome as Apollo and knew it. All Adonises, she reflected—or was that Adoni?—seemed to stand in the same way. She wondered if anyone had done a study on the subject. Not that anyone but a woman would notice, of course . . . ". . . member of the diplomatic community here and an absolute charmer, even if he's never going to rock the world with his intellect. Baron Ignace Karolyi . . ."

"Excuse me," Lydia said hastily. "I think I see Miss Potton and I really do need to . . . I'll be back in one moment . . ."

"Really? Where . . . ?"

But she dodged away into the crowd.

Fortunately, a doorway connected that room and the other rear chamber of the suite. Lydia ducked through, wove her way to the door leading back into the main salon, and worked back with what speed she could—given a visual range of less than a yard, though the brilliance of the man's uniform helped in avoiding him—to the double door leading into the colonnade. The cold was sharp. Wishing she'd had time to fetch her cloak, Lydia hurried along the black and white cobbled pavement to the stairway passage in which she'd taken refuge with the prince, and gathered her point-lace train in hand to descend the sloping tunnel to the terrace beyond.

Once certain she was out of sight, she pulled her spectacles from her handbag and settled them on her nose.

What had been an impression of leafy blackness and swimming spots of color resolved itself suddenly into a sable
wonderland of cypress and willow that sloped down to the
indigo shimmer of the sea. Bare boughs or somber leaves were
illuminated from below by a rainbow lace of colored lamps,
which outlined paths and terraces like dim-burning jewels
dropped on velvet.

To her left the lights traced terraces, stairways, the eaves of
pale shut-windowed pavilions in a flickering web of ruby,
azure, honey stars . . . and at the top of a flight of marble steps
she saw one star was missing. A lamp had been taken.

Margaret. She didn't know why she was so sure. Gathering
her train more firmly, she hastened along the terrace and up
those pale steps to the gap in the line of lights.

A gem-latticed darkness of marble pavements and low box
hedges spread out before her at the top, rimming deep stands of
lawn and trees. The pavement led her around to the locked
doors of the two pavilions overlooking the lower gardens. Past
the second pavilion's door a low arch of very old bricks
pierced the wall, marble steps leading down again, through a
vaulted tunnel, to the terraces below.

Had Margaret seen Ysidro in the gardens? Or only a shape
she thought might be his?

She turned back to scan the colonnades, the elaborate pavilions above and behind her, but saw no movement there; neither
was there any sight of the pale mousseline de soie dress in the
semiwilderness of trees and long grass that lay between her
and the sea. She pulled a handkerchief from her bag to shield
her fingers from the heat, then picked up another lamp, the
brass base beneath the bowl of ruby glass hot through both
cloth and glove. One of the innumerable wild cats that lived in
the half-deserted shrubberies stared at her for a moment, then
poured itself away into the darkness.

What am I doing? wondered Lydia, half in disgust, as she
descended the marble steps. *Two minutes after the handsome
Russian prince warns me "Don't investigate alone," I'm off
like the heroine of a cheap thriller . . .*

But something about the shadowy darkness of the palace,

deserted once the activity around the kiosks had been left behind, filled her with fear for the sake of the younger woman. The sight of Karolyi had shaken her, and she did not think she dared either wait or go back.

The red light of the lamp caught in the curves of an iron lion posted in what had been flower beds. On a tangle of overgrown rosebush, Lydia glimpsed white threads where a petticoat hem had caught and been pulled free.

There was a door, hidden in the shadows of the three high vaults of ancient brick. It stood open. For a long time Lydia hesitated in the narrow aperture, one hand pressed to the stone jamb, the red-glowing lamp raised to look within. The stagnant pool a few yards behind her seemed to breathe cold over her bare shoulders, an echo of the damp chill that lay before her in the dark.

Little did she know, quoted Lydia from the aforesaid cheap thriller, in an effort to push back the dread whispering at her heart, *what horrors lay crouched in wait for her.*

But it was only a stone stairway—used, she thought, but not recently, save for the wet tracks vaguely outlined on the upper step or two.

A woman's slippers.

Idiot, idiot, idiot. She wasn't sure if it was Miss Potton or herself to whom she referred.

At the bottom of the stairs, another open door, and a cavern vast and lost in shadows, where the ruby stain of her lamp smudged pillars, incredibly old, rising out of obsidian water to the brick vaulting of the ceiling low overhead.

Of course, Lydia thought. All those pools in the gardens had to be watered from somewhere.

A walkway stretched along one side of the cistern, vanishing very quickly into darkness. Heart beating hard, hoping she'd find Margaret soon, she started along it.

"This is not a wise thing, mistress."

Ysidro's voice was barely louder than a cat's tread in the dark behind her, but somehow it didn't startle her. It was as if, for the second or two before he spoke, she knew he was there. Turning, she saw him on the walkway, dressed, as the men at the palace reception had been dressed, in black morning coat and gray-striped trousers, colorless hair framing a dead man's face.

Her breath escaped in a shaky sigh. "Coming to Constantinople was not a wise thing," she said. "I wondered what you had in that trunk of yours. Did you bring a top hat as well?"

"It is where I can reach it, should I choose to enter the pavilion."

He stepped closer and took her hand, guiding her along the path above the sable pool. The light seemed to follow, like a fish in the depths. Cold as she was, his hand on her waist was colder.

"The sultans used to bring the ladies of the harem up this way, when they watched polo or archery from the kiosks on the terrace."

"Have you found any trace of her?"

"She did not pass you, then?" In the evenness of his voice she read his irritation. He knew whom she meant and what had happened. Then, "My concentration has been on other matters. It is difficult . . ."

The uninflected words might have been a complete sentence instead of a broken beginning, but Lydia knew what he stopped himself from saying to her. They stood for a moment face-to-face in the open door of another stair, with the lamp between them, as they had stood in the stairway of his London crypt. The blood-hued light made him more alien still, and she had the curious sensation that if she closed her eyes his features would shift and be no longer the face he was always so careful to show the living, but the face he turned away from mirrors in order not to see himself.

"It's my doing." She wondered what else she could say. *I'm sorry I asked you not to kill innocent strangers on the streets, in the train, in the corners of this palace?*

In time he said, "No. My own, for supposing I could have my way without price. I will survive it."

Another silence. Lydia remembered Margaret's white breast the night before last when she'd torn open her bodice on the empty street. She had to ask, though she knew it was none of her business. "Are you drinking her blood?"

"It would do me no good," replied the light voice, but he seemed unsurprised by the question. "It is the death we need to feed the mind's power. At this point it were too easy to kill her, did I but taste of her blood."

I should be afraid of him.

And it *was* her doing.

"It is no easy thing," he went on, as if he had read her thought, "to see myself in the mirror of your honor. Let us hang a shawl before it, as I do the mirrors in my house, and deal with commonplaces as we find them. You're cold."

She realized, as he guided her up the long flight, that she was trembling.

She had no impression of him leaving her side after they reached the door at the top, but somehow he had a shawl in his hands, heavy silk with a hand like cream as he draped it around her shoulders. "This is not a safe place to walk." He stretched his fingers in the direction of the lamp and in some fashion snuffed the flame without touching it. They passed into a court-yard barely wider than a hall, stairways going up and down into impenetrable night. Dark lay like the seal of death, so that he had to guide her, his fingers tombstone marble through the thin kid of her glove and his.

"I saw her footmarks when I returned to the cistern stair," he said. "They were unclear, and I had to look on the walkway to be sure she had not passed that way going out." He paused and added something Lydia knew enough Spanish to identify.

"You chose her because she was stupid," she reminded him softly. "Stupid and loyal. What she feels for you was your doing."

"It is one matter to follow a husband whom you know to be walking eyeless and unarmed into treachery." They passed into a chamber, crossed layers of dust-thick carpet and ascended a rickety stair to a balcony enclosed by lattice—down another stair and so out again. "You sought advice in the matter, recognizing your limitations, and his. It is another matter to pursue needlessly one to whom you will be naught but a liability, only to tell him what he already knows.

"This is no safe place, not for her to walk, nor for us to call out, nor to hold aloft lamps that she may see their light."

"This is the harem, isn't it?" The name conjured images hopelessly romantic to Lydia's mind, but the room they entered—and indeed, all the rooms along this lightless slit—even unfurnished, seemed poky and cramped in the filtered rays from some other wing of the building. The walls were plain plaster, unpainted, dirty and mildewed. The divans were lumpy and far lower than Lydia had pictured from storybooks, about the thickness of a good mattress. The carpets were threadbare, smelling of mice and rotted perfume.

"I thought the palace hasn't been used since the fifties."

"Not as the Sultan's residence." The voice might almost have been the exhalation of dust from the carpets underfoot. "It was the center of government until last July. But a part of the old seraglio is where he put women who belonged to his father or his grandfather, or girls who failed to please him. Here they dwell still, with their servants—fewer, but much as they used. In the heyday of this place they slept, four and five to a room, the ones who did not catch his fancy, seeing no one but the eunuchs and each other, seldom even seeing the sun."

In the almost dark she saw him touch the wall in passing. "They lived upon opium, many of them; opium and intrigue. The walls here sweat with their pettiness, their boredom, and their tears."

His eyelids lowered and he tilted his head, listening. "There," he whispered. He guided her with swift and weightless stride down a stair as steep as hell's abyss and so dark she couldn't see the steps thereof. Later on, safe in her own bed in Pera, Lydia wondered a little at her absolute trust in him, her willingness to step forward in utter darkness, propelled by his hand. Not, she thought, that Ysidro would have given her any choice.

Margaret stood in the midst of a large chamber that once had a sunken pool in its center, now only an oval of shell-edged shadow. Marble lattices covered the windows on three sides; a divan circled the chamber, and slanting squares of light no bigger than tea sandwiches strewed the dirty and mouse-ravaged cushions. The whole room choked of mildew.

She had no lamp in her hands now, as if she'd set it down somewhere and left it forgotten. In the checkered glow from the windows her face was blank; behind the thick lenses of her spectacles, her eyes were those of a sleepwalker.

She looked beautiful, as she had looked in her dreams.

Lydia found herself alone in the tiled entryway looking at Ysidro as he turned Margaret's head gently, so that he could see the exposed—and unmarked—whiteness of her throat.

"Margharita," the vampire whispered. The girl startled like one waking.

Then Margaret's breath drew in a hoarse gasp, and she flung herself on Ysidro, clutching him with desperate, grabby hands. The next second, past his shoulder, she saw Lydia, like some bespectacled, prosaic ghost with her train a cascade of lace over one kid-gloved arm, her shoulders draped in the faded web of an old silk shawl. Margaret backed quickly. "I . . . are you all right?" It wasn't to Lydia that she spoke.

"Indeed." The vampire inclined his head politely. "Less so than I had been, had I not come back to this place to seek you, however. It were foolish of you to follow me, Margharita, for your reputation's sake alone, and your safety's. And mine, and Mistress Asher's, too, coming to find you here. Now let us return, ere our absence causes remark; and I warn you, do not come after me thus again."

His voice never rose above its usual even key, nor did its tone change one whit from the polite phrases of his accustomed speech, but Lydia cringed inside as if at sarcasm or curses. Margaret's cheeks flushed dark and she looked away, and for a moment Lydia had the impression she would have fled, plunging into the unknown labyrinth of the deeper harem, had not Ysidro laid an imperative hand on her arm. Her voice trembled as she looked back at him with tear-filled blue eyes. "I was only afraid . . ."

"Afraid?" He smiled his chilly smile, manufactured, Lydia guessed, to cover the remainder of his anger. Still, the impact of it was startling, the echo of an astringent charm that had been the living man's. "That I should find peril here beyond my capacity, from which you could save me?"

No expression, no inflection; he had been dead, Lydia recalled, a long time. But still she guessed the smallest twinkle of banter, far back in the sulfur-crystal eyes.

Margaret didn't. She only hung her head and snuffled, and suffered Ysidro to take her arm and lead her through the maze to the perilous cistern stair, and thence back along the terrace where the harem ladies had gone to their lord. As they passed through a vast court above a terrace and pool, where shuttered windows hovered tier upon tier above their heads, Lydia thought she saw the glow of a lamp left under one of the ramshackle stairways, and made to turn aside.

"Leave it," Ysidro said softly. "It will only draw those we have little desire to meet."

Lydia removed her spectacles again and folded the shawl inconspicuously in the cloakroom before reentering the diplomat-crowded salon. She concentrated, through the remainder of the reception, on avoiding an encounter with the straight, graceful figure in the crimson uniform of the Hungarian Life Guards.

"You watch out for that Razumovsky, mind," Lady Clapham said to her as they were getting into the carriages. "*And* watch that girl of yours."

Startled, Lydia turned to regard Margaret, being helped by servants into the embassy coach. Soldiers clustered in the small square, torchlight throwing sharp flares on their rifles, for warning had come of sporadic fighting among the Armenians in Galata that might spread to Stamboul.

"I really don't think we need worry," she said. "I happen to know her heart is . . . otherwise engaged." To someone, moreover, infinitely more dangerous than a Russian nobleman.

"I mean watch what she says." Her Ladyship drew Lydia a little farther back into the darkness of the gate. The shadows of the soldiers wavered drunkenly across the vine-grown brick wall opposite, behind which the silent domes of the Aya Sofia slept in the dark.

"And what *you* say. Razumovsky isn't a fool, and he knows perfectly well your husband didn't come to Constantinople to interview storytellers. That treaty the King signed won't cut much ice if the Czar sees a chance of getting a point ahead of us, either here or in India."

Lydia sighed, reassured her hostess and shook her head inwardly as she took Sir Burnwell's hand to ascend to the coach. At least everyone in the world had cardiovascular systems and endocrine glands, and there wasn't any argument over those. For a moment she thought longingly of the Radcliffe Infirmary, where things were safe and in their places— *was* Pickering keeping proper graphs of the long-term weight gain of those subjects? She had no idea what she'd tell the editors of the *Journal of Internal Research* about her article. *I'm sorry, I had to go to Constantinople to rescue my husband from vampires.*

But without Jamie . . .

She shook her head. She would find him.

She had to find him.

FIFTEEN

"WHAT was it you were afraid of, in the seraglio?"

Ysidro did not turn. Upon bringing the women back to the house on Rue Abydos, he had uncharacteristically made sure that Margaret got safely to bed, then gone to the floor below to sit in the parlor's projecting bay, a sort of balcony that overlooked the front door. For nearly an hour Lydia had been aware of him there, as, still in her evening frock, she drank the aromatic tea Madame Potoneros brewed for her.

It was late, close to three. The near-riot in the Armenian quarter had forced a long detour through the market district to the old Mohammed Bridge; even then, winding their way up the steep Rue Iskander, they could hear the distant cries, the breaking of glass, the shots. Sitting quiet between Margaret and Lady Clapham, Lydia had pulled her cloak closer and wondered if she'd ever feel warm again.

There was still no emphasis, no rise or fall, to his voice. "So you, like Margaret, suppose me to have been in peril? I thought better of you, mistress."

"Well, I do know you're perfectly capable of avoiding any twelve saber-wielding eunuchs out to protect the Sultan's name from dishonor. So what *were* you afraid Margaret had encountered?" She thought it through, then asked, "Another vampire?"

He tilted his head a little. Late-risen moonlight edged his

profile in watery milk. "Her name is Zenaida. I went to the seraglio to speak to her, before ever I knew Margaret had followed."

His hands, lying one atop the other on the window's sill, seemed about to move, then subsided again into quiescence, the echo of some gesture pared away by time. "She has been there a long while, and no longer recalls the name of the Sultan for whom she was first bought in the markets of Smyrna. Perhaps she never knew it. Like most of the Sultan's women, she was cunning but stupid, and uneducated as a peddler's donkey. She told me many of the odalisques still think she is a living woman, some forgotten Sultan's *kadine*."

"And you think she may know something about . . . about Ernchester? Or James?" He sat on an old chest that did service for a low table in the bay; she leaned against the corner of the wall. The windows were open behind their lattices, and listen as she would—she could not keep herself from doing so—she did not now hear any sound from the slums that lay all along the foot of the hill. Smoke still gritted in the air.

"That," the vampire agreed quietly. "And other matters."

He gazed for a few moments more in apparent disinterest through the carven screens to white walls and tile roofs. The City of Walls, with its minarets and domes, its markets and its filth, was no more than a great shoulder of rucked velvet across the water in the night.

Then the yellow mantis eyes shifted to hers. "My senses, my perceptions, my ability to touch the threads of thought and scent and heat which move upon a city's air—these have suffered from lack of their proper feeding. Nonetheless I should be able to feel some of what takes place in the lives of night-walking things. If not from here, from the gatehouses of the palace where I stood tonight, from the hill of the Aya Sofia, where all the dreams of the city come together like light in a glass. And I do not."

Lydia pushed her spectacles up onto her nose. She'd taken off her gloves and her pearls, and the silver shone on her throat and wrists like looped links of ice. "And the last thing you needed was a couple of silly heroines to look after," she said, rueful and shy.

His head moved again, once, and his eyes met hers with that brief flicker of human amusement. In the street below a dog barked, the gruff shrillness picked up in another alley, and another, as all that starveling horde felt called upon to comment and reply. Ysidro waited them out, listening as if he could distinguish some clue within the sound.

"I walked in Galata last night when I left you here," he said in time. "I crossed the bridge to Stamboul and sought out the other quarters where the Armenians live, down seaward of the Burned Column and in the poorest quarters along the walls. It is there, you understand, that the vampires will hunt, among those whose deaths the Turks count as less than the scraps I feed my cats. The miasma was thick there, the sense of diverted attention, of watching through smoke, though the night was clear. It was like the veil we lay over human eyes and human minds, but the veil was of a different quality, a different texture, wrought to shield a different kind of mind.

"There is war between vampires in this city."

Lydia recalled the elaborate precautions in Ysidro's London house—or one of his London houses—and it occurred to her that human incursion might not be the only threat against which he protected himself.

"You think one of the Master of Constantinople's fledglings is ... rebelling against him? Trying to overthrow him? And summoned, or blackmailed, Ernchester here to help him?"

"It could be that," agreed Ysidro. "It can happen so, though as a rule a master as old as that of Constantinople will show more care in who he makes into his fledgling. Or a newcomer has arrived from the outside, in flight from his or her own master vampire, and seeks to take over mastery of Constantinople himself. This he will find no easy matter."

"Ernchester?"

He made a conceding movement with his eyebrow that three hundred years ago might have been a shrug and a gesture. "In truth I find that a morsel hard to swallow, particularly given the fact that he must have known the master of the city in life. Yet war there is. Charles plays some part in it . . ."

"And since Karolyi knows about it," Lydia said thoughtfully, "he's going to try to make of it what he can. Would it have been he who was behind James' . . . disappearance?"

"I think it likelier he engineered this incident with the palace guard." Ysidro's white hand moved upon the windowsill. "Behold the timing of it. He was taken up in the morning, when a living man would have the most time to question him or to act in his absence. He was taken up, too, outside the Grand Bazaar, where he is known to have been speaking to the tellers of tales. So his dwelling place was unknown. Karolyi did not reckon on James' friendship with your golden barbarian, and he did not have time to get him into his own hand before he was released. I think," he added, "that this Karolyi knows something of what is taking place, but not all. And I think that if it was his goal to get James into his hand, rather than simply to kill him, it was to find Anthea through him."

"So they were still together."

"So it appears." His hand moved in the shadows again, and Lydia saw that he had wrapped a thick cashmere lap robe over his morning coat, as if to ward off the chill of the autumn night. "In two nights' wanderings I have found no sign of Anthea hunting, and Zenaida has seen nothing of a strange woman in her own quest for midnight blood. This could mean that Anthea is in hiding somewhere, or that she has been taken, either by Karolyi or by the Bey, the master of the city . . . or by this adversary, be he rebel fledgling or interloper. And where Charles may be . . ." He shook his head.

"It is an ancient city, and very great. Veiled as it is—and Zenaida says this mist or illusion settled upon it shortly after the gunfire and riots of the army coup, not that she had the smallest knowledge or interest in the Sultan's overthrow—there are an infinity of places to hide. Zenaida says that she knows not where the Bey is, nor knows she of any other vampire. She says that she does not mind, never having cared for the dominance of the Bey."

Lydia gazed in silence for a time into the night beyond the

lattices, the moon-soaked city and the silver-flecked waters that lay between. At last she said, "And she knew nothing . . . would know nothing . . . of Jamie?"

Ysidro made no reply.

My master told me to show you the place, the boy had said.

"Would it help to find the hiding place of the master of the city?"

He gave her a glance of inscrutable irony, as if to say, *As you found mine?* "He will have many, you know. In a war among vampires, he will be moving his sleeping place nightly."

"I understand," Lydia said. "But it will give us a starting place, and if we find out what we *can* find out, clues lead to other clues. About Anthea or Ernchester, or . . . or Jamie."

"Always provided Jamie is not lying with a cut throat at the bottom of the harbor."

"If I were willing to accept that without further investigation," retorted Lydia, "I might as well go back to London."

He inclined his head, though whether in mockery or apology she did not know.

"Anyway," she went on after a moment, "I obviously don't have Jamie's training in questioning storytellers, aside from not speaking any . . . is it Turkish they speak here?"

"Turkish and Greek in the streets. Arabic among the scholars, Osmanli at the Sultan's court."

"Since there doesn't seem to be any central depot of records, I think I'm going to have to have tea with German businessmen and ask them about native clients, and try to spot some kind of oddity in payment. My German isn't wonderful, but last night most of them seemed to speak very good French. I wonder if I can get on the good side of someone at the Banque Ottomane? Or the German Orient Bank?"

She straightened her shoulders, the words themselves giving her courage; she spoke as if sorting a hand of cards, seeing what she had and what she needed. "Extensive use of middlemen and corporations that don't seem to have any raison d'etre beyond paying the bills of one or two households; payment in gold or credit rather than silver; clients who either never appear at all or only appear after dark. That sort of thing. The purchase of housing that has some kind of multilevel cellars or that's built over old crypts, like that cistern we passed through. Maybe corporate credit funneled through the palace with instructions not to check too closely into bona fides?"

She fell silent, watching his face, which was without expression. His silence lay on her heart like plates of lead.

Then he said, "Did we but find one of his bolt-holes, it could be watched. Not a safe occupation, even with the illusion which veils this city, but as you say, clues lead to other clues, and it is clear to me that more than finding Charles, more than finding Anthea, it is necessary to learn what is happening in this city. If Karolyi is here, there is still bargaining going on."

Behind them the mantelpiece clock chimed four; seagulls cried in the darkness outside. Ysidro went on, "You have catalogued already those things I will alter in my own arrangements, when I gain London once more. Quest among your German businessmen for word of purchase of either a great quantity of silver bars or silver-plated bars. If there is war among the vampires of this city—if the master of the city seeks to summon and imprison Ernchester—he will need a place to put him. And seek also," he added, "for someone using the roundabout financial methods of which you speak to purchase and install modern central heating in one or more old houses."

"Central heating?" The absurd picture rose to her mind of the cloaked and sinister West End stage Dracula deep in conversation with Herr Hindl about soft-coal hummers and double-heating, self-feeding base-burner anthracite models, only ninety-seven marks plus shipping costs . . .

"If there is a challenge to the Bey's power, chances are good that it is because the Bey himself may be growing . . . tired. Brittle. Losing his grip. A thing one seldom considers of the Bey," added Ysidro, "but a possibility. It happens, in time, even to the Undead. When this chances, vampires suffer cold and joint ache. Winter is coming on. This city will be under snow. A master fighting for his position, refusing to admit the drag of darkness in his soul, might well heat one or more of his bolt-holes for his own comfort, particularly if it has been his custom to use the living as servants."

He had been watching the darkness of the street. Now he turned his attention fully toward her again, a ghost-shape in the gloom. "You understand," he said, "that though clues of this kind may lead us to Ernchester or to the heart of this affair with Karolyi, you may not find your husband, mistress."

She looked down at where the moonlight lay on the shawl over her arms. "I understand. I'd been hoping," she went on after long silence, her voice low, as if speaking to herself, "that when I went to the embassy yesterday afternoon—Saturday afternoon—that Sir Burnwell would say something like, 'Oh, of course, he's staying right across the way at the Pera Palace.' And the day would finish with Italian ices on the terrace and telling stories in bed half the night."

She drew the shawl's long fringes through her fingers, to keep them from trembling.

"You have never been alone, then."

It wasn't what she had expected him to say—if anything at all—but it was true. She nodded without looking up.

"Well, I felt I'd been alone for years and years, before I knew him. But I expect most children feel that way. And I knew him—I mean, he was in and out of Uncle Ambrose's house—when I was fifteen, sixteen. I don't remember a moment of falling in love with him, but I remember knowing there was no one else I'd rather live with. I remember crying because I knew they'd never let me marry him. I was underage. And he wouldn't ask. He didn't want me to be hurt in a family row. He didn't want me to lose my inheritance over him."

"I daresay your father put his own interpretation to that." The soft voice was like the wind flowing down an empty hall. "What happened?"

"Father disinherited me over my studies. Jamie was away in Africa. That was during the war. Someone . . . someone said he was dead. I was terrified because I didn't know if I could succeed in an actual practice. Most women have a terrible time. My research is sound, but pure research would be out of the question, and I . . . I didn't know if Jamie was coming back. But without him I didn't care, really, what became of me. When he came back he asked me to marry him because I hadn't any money, and Father permitted it. Then later he changed his will again."

"But you never thought of giving up your study?" The vampire sounded amused.

Lydia raised her head, shocked. "Of course not!" He was regarding her, she found, with a curious, unreadable intentness in his sulfurous eyes. For a moment she thought he would speak, but then like a ghost he seemed to withdraw a little from her.

"In truth," he said, "we can only do what we can. I spoke not to crush your hope, mistress, but only to warn you that not all grails are found intact. Nor, indeed, found at all."

"No," Lydia said softly, "I understand. Thank you."

He rose. She held out her hand to him, as she would have to a brother if she'd had one, or a friend. After a moment he took it, his thin hand emerging from the dark folds of his lap robe like Death's, oddly bereft of its native scythe, fleshless knuckles and fragile bones dry as bleached bamboo under her touch. She'd taken down her hair while drinking her tea; its natural straightness had almost destroyed the remains of earlier curls, so that it lay in unswagged cinnabar heaps on her shoulders and back, like seaweed on a beach after a storm.

With her free hand she propped her spectacles again, a schoolgirl's gesture.

Remembering it later she had the impression that he'd said something else to her—or maybe just spoken her name—and that his cold hand had brushed her face, pushing back the flame of her hair from her cheek. But that wasn't clear to her, as if she'd dreamed it. Perhaps, she thought, she had.

It did occur to her that it was not at all like Ysidro to be concerned whether her hopes were crushed or not.

The street of the brass sellers lay four or five aisles in from the main entrance of the Grand Bazaar, according to the dealer in attar of roses of whom Lydia made her inquiry . . . "Or more or less," added the man in excellent French; the beaming smile that split his dark face reminded her forcibly of a discolored and incomplete set of piano keys. "But for what does la belle mademoiselle want brass? *Pfui*, brass! It is attar of roses, the incomparable essences of Damascus and Baghdad, which delight the heart and offer the gift of sweetness to God. Only thirty piastres . . . That wretched cheating son of an Armenian camel driver is going to charge you more than fifty for a brass thimble that won't be brass at all, but cheap tin with a brass wash no more substantial than a Greek's sworn word . . . Thirty piastres? Fifteen!"

Lydia smiled, curtseyed, murmured, *"Merci . . . merci,"* and with Slavonic clairvoyance Prince Razumovsky, enormous in exquisite London-cut mufti, appeared at her side and said, "Come along, come along," steering both women—Margaret hanging back for one more sniff of a painted ointment pot— into the crowd.

"Can we go back there?" Margaret asked diffidently of His Highness. "When we've found the storyteller, I mean? True attar of roses costs ten or twelve shillings for a flask that size back home."

She craned her neck, trying to look back between a jostling pair of German businessmen and several drab-uniformed soldiers at the tiny stall with its magic rows of twinkling glass. The shopkeeper gave her another demolished smile and a wink as bright as his wares.

"My dear Miss Potton," the prince smiled through the Colchian fleeces of his beard, "twenty feet from this spot you can buy a flask that size for two piastres, if you look sufficiently indifferent. It requires practice. Hold in your mind the image of a room—a building!—filled with such flasks . . . or, rather, think of having to carry a *veddras* of the stuff—about three of your gallons—up a steep hill, and then go back for another, and another, and another . . ."

Margaret giggled and blushed, and someone else cried out in awful Greek-accented French, "Madame, Madame, here all the perfume, all best roses of land of nightingales . . . !"

The light that suffused the bewildering mazes of the Grand Bazaar was never direct, falling as it did through windows high in the vaulted ceiling, and in the pale green archways the voices of every nation from the North Sea to the Indian Ocean swirled like soup. There were no genuine spots of light, nor actual shadows, but a dizzy kaleidoscope of color that shifted too quickly for Lydia to guess at distant things—the contents of the shops they passed, the faces or nationalities of men who seemed, at a distance, to be only swirls of white or dark or colored robes. As they passed close they came into focus: swarthy Turkish men in pantaloons sitting on floors to bargain, talk, drink glasses of scalding tea; Greek men in wide white skirts and bright caps or women in close-fitting, dowdy black, arguing with shopkeepers at the top of their lungs; porters bent matter-of-factly under superhuman loads; Armenians in baggy trousers, Orthodox priests and thick-bearded Jews in black gabardine and prayer shawls. Young boys shouted offers of shoe shines or guides to the city, or dashed importantly through the jostling shoppers bearing brass trays on which rested single glasses of tea. The air was redolent of sweaty wool, garlic, carpets, dog, and sewage.

Down the aisles that branched from side to side, Lydia glimpsed wares at which she could only guess: coats of karakul and astrakhan, carpets of blue and crimson, shawls, bright-flashing glass, hanging racks of silver earrings, bolts of prosaic wool alternating with gauzy rainbows of veils. Every time a beggar came whining up to them—hideously disfigured, some of them, freaks who would have been confined to fairs anywhere in Europe—every time they passed strolling groups of soldiers who whistled and rolled their eyes, Lydia was heartily glad she'd asked the prince to act as their protector and guide.

He'd been right. This wasn't England. It would have been madness to investigate alone.

She'd slept uneasily for the few hours after Ysidro's departure, prey to troubling dreams. Part had concerned the harem, with its smelly little cells, its cramped windows blocking out all view of the city, of the sea, of the sunlight had it been day: *The walls sweat with their pettiness, their boredom, and their tears.* She'd dreamed of wandering in that darkness, looking for someone, the rooms growing smaller and smaller around her while she felt the waiting presence of something lying very still on a burst and stinking divan, listening for her footfalls with a smile on what had long ago been its face.

Once, very briefly, she'd had a fragmentary image of a Gothic tower in a thunderstorm, the lightning lurid as a carbon-arc flare over seas of churning heather, the rain pounding in a deserted courtyard—rain that somehow only barely dampened the white dress, the raven curls of the woman who stood at the tower's gate, gazing with expectation across the wilderness of the heath. Lydia, in the shelter of a broken shed on the other side of the court, had not been wet at all by the rain, though she smelled the soaked earth. She thought the woman was waiting for a horseman. Turning her head, she saw Ysidro nearby, almost invisible in the shadows, dressed as he had been on the balcony, in morning coat and striped trousers with the lap robe held close about his shoulders. His head was bowed, his color-less eyes closed as if deep in concentration, his face the face of a skull.

The dream image snuffed like a guttering candle, and wak-ing, Lydia had heard Margaret crying, muffled, angry, and hurt. Margaret had had very little to say to her that morning and would not meet her eyes. Since their meeting with Razu-movsky over a late breakfast, she had addressed all her remarks to the prince, giggling at his flirtations and responding cheerfully to his effort to draw her out.

There seemed to be storytellers everywhere. They sat on dirty rugs and blankets, swaying with the rhythm of their tales, spreading their arms, using their voices to conjure thunder, rage, love, and wonder. Children and teenage boys sat around them, listening eagerly, and even grown men and a very few black-veiled women stood with the air of those in no hurry to leave. Lydia moved toward one and peered shortsightedly at the wares in the surrounding booths. Lady Clapham had told her that each man had his regular pitch, and the man who worked the street of the coffee merchants would no more dream of shifting to the street of the slipper vendors than she herself would have considered walking uninvited into her neighbor's house in Oxford and appropriating her neighbor's nightgown and bed.

It was simply Not Done.

As she edged her way a little into the crowd, trying to see past the dark backs of the Greek ladies, a man put his hand on her shoulder and said, "Madame Asher?"

She turned, looking up slightly at the Adonis face, the beautiful dark eyes, of a tall man who moved like an athlete within his tobacco-colored suit. At this distance she could see the close-clipped mustache, the long eyelashes, the pearl buttons of his gloves as he bowed to kiss her hand. He wore a gold stickpin in his cravat, a winged griffin that seemed to regard her with a single, baleful ruby eye.

"I've seen your husband," he said quietly, and, while her breath was still stopped with shock, he added, "Permit me to introduce myself. I am the Baron Ignace Karolyi, of the Imperial Diplomatic Service. May we talk?"

He led her out of the crowd, into the dimness before a shop front where an elderly Greek sewed slippers of colored leather and gave them—most uncharacteristically for a merchant of the Grand Bazaar—not so much as a glance. It occurred to Lydia that Karolyi must have paid him in advance for his disregard.

"Is he alive?"

Karolyi nodded. Although she knew he must be at least thirty-five, he seemed younger and radiated a kind of earnest intensity, like a youthful charmer who has put his charm aside to speak of important things.

"Though I cannot guarantee how much longer that will last. He is in the hands of . . ." He hesitated artistically, studying her face, like one who debates with himself how much of what he says will be believed. And yet, she realized, he was actually watching her, trying to guess how much she knew.

Like Ysidro playing picquet, she thought, peeking at the stock cards and wondering what to appropriate and what would do him no good.

Her heart beat harder and she thought, *Jamie will die if you botch this up.*

"He is in the hands of a man called Olumsiz Bey," he went on after a moment. "A Turk. A truly evil person. Tell no one," he added quickly, as Lydia pressed her hands to her mouth and widened her eyes as Aunt Lavinia generally did before crying out in horror at the presence of death-dealing spiders or the perfidy of the children of her neighbors. "What exactly did he tell you, Mrs. Asher, that brought you to Constantinople to search?"

He must have been talking to Lady Clapham. She wondered how much that redoubtable woman had seen fit to tell him— how much she would have considered not worth the trouble of hiding.

"Oh, where, when?" She didn't expect a truthful answer to the questions and asked them to buy herself time to think, but she had no need to manufacture the panic, the desperation that she threw into her voice. She had never considered herself to be an actress, but any young lady of good society knew how to exaggerate delight or terror, or whatever other emotion was called for. A number of conversations with Margaret over the past week certainly helped her performance.

She clasped her hands to her breastbone. "Did you speak with him? Did he look well?" *Has he been in touch with his own department? Do they know I had dinner with Mr. Halliwell? Why would I have come to Constantinople if I didn't know the kind of danger he was in?*

"We did not have the opportunity to speak." Karolyi's voice was soothing, a beautifully modulated tenor with the barest trace of a Middle European accent. An eminently believable voice. "He appeared unharmed, though as I said, there is no way of knowing how long that will last. That is why you and I must talk. When you fled from me last night, I feared some rumor or calumny had reached you. I assure you, Madame . . ." He made his voice earnest, deeply concerned. "I assure you, such rumors are exaggerations, fed by the enmity of our two countries and the suspicions of men who see only threats wherever they look."

"Fled from you?" Lydia steeled herself, produced her eyeglasses from her handbag and put them on to peer at him. "Last night? Were you at the palace reception last night?"

Under the fine traces of mustache his mouth quirked, disarmed for a moment. With two quick gestures of his forefinger he smoothed the mustache, and Lydia noted the fine cut of the pale tan gloves, French kid at six shillings the pair.

"Baron!" Razumovsky's gray and golden bulk appeared from around the corner of a stall and pushed through the crowd, Margaret scuttling in his wake. Lydia's glasses immediately disappeared from her face and into the folds of her skirt. "Back from your flying visit to London, I see."

"Prince." Karolyi bowed to the exact depth required of a Russian prince rather than an English one. "A flying visit indeed, but one must dress, you know." He laughed rather vacantly and flicked the lapels of his Saville Row suit. "Are you here with Mrs. Asher?"

He believes I've been taken by surprise, thought Lydia swiftly. *If I put this off, he'll guess I had time to prepare.*

"Will you excuse us for a few moments, Your Highness?" As the Russian moved off she turned her back slightly and put her hand behind it, signaling—and hoping he saw—with her outspread fingers: five minutes.

"From what Mr. Halliwell said I gather you and my husband weren't exactly friends," she said quickly, keeping her voice fast and breathless to keep from stammering with uncertainty and dread. "But it is all really a . . . a sort of confraternity, is it not? You are all in the same business, no matter what side you're on." She produced her glasses again and put them on, well aware of the air of scholarly ineffectualness they lent to her face. "Thank you so much for letting me know! I knew—I *knew*—that Cousin Elizabeth couldn't have been wrong!"

"Cousin Elizabeth?"

"Cousin Elizabeth in Vienna," said Lydia, as if slightly surprised that Karolyi were not acquainted with her family. "She lent my husband twenty pounds a week ago Thursday night, to take the Orient Express to Constantinople. She's his cousin—his second cousin, actually—and she lives in one of the suburbs, I forget the name . . . In any case I telephoned her when Mr. Halliwell gave me the note from my husband . . ."

"Note?" The graceful eyebrows deepened in a frown.

"Telling me to return to London. Saying he was going on, he

couldn't tell me where. Mr. Halliwell did his best to convince me to go back, and I let him think I *was* going back, but I *knew* my husband was in danger of some kind! I knew it." She clasped her hands again, praying that it wasn't obvious that she was shaking all over.

"Why were you in Vienna?" He was running this over in his mind, trying to fit pieces together. Guessing at Ysidro's inscrutability had given her a greater ability to deal with ordinary human expression.

She widened her eyes. "He sent for me." *What other reason would there have been?* her tone seemed to ask. And, when Karolyi looked gratifyingly skeptical, she explained, "He telegraphed and said there were some medical notes that would need to be analyzed. I am a medical doctor, you know," she added, propping her spectacles and looking as unworldly and harmless as she possibly could. "I do research at the Radcliffe Infirmary."

"And your specialty is?"

"Rare pathologies of the blood." It was nothing of the kind, but unless Karolyi read medical journals, he wouldn't know that. It was the kind of thing they *would* have sent for her to examine, if they were dealing with vampires.

He evidently didn't, for a look of enlightenment dawned in his eyes. "I see."

"But when I reached Vienna, Mr. Halliwell told me something dreadful had happened and Dr. Asher had had to leave the city suddenly, and gave me his note, telling me to return to London. And I knew he had to be in some kind of danger, especially after Cousin Elizabeth told me he'd borrowed money from her to come to Constantinople all of a hurry. And now they tell me he's disappeared, and I don't know what to do! Oh, Baron Karolyi, if you know anything, can help me in any way . . . !"

He looked annoyed, as well he might, she thought, but he concealed it well as he patted her hands. "Calm yourself, Mrs. Asher, calm yourself. What have you been able to find out of his whereabouts?"

That, she thought, was what he wanted to know. That, and how much she herself knew.

"Nothing!" she wailed. "I came here to the marketplace because I understand he was arrested near here. I thought that some of the shopkeepers might have seen something, or know something . . ." She removed her spectacles and blinked dewily up at him. "Prince Razumovsky was kind enough to offer to escort me here, as he knows the language."

Karolyi sniffed, just slightly, and Lydia reflected that Lady Clapham's estimate of the prince's amorous nature was probably correct, if Karolyi would believe that the prince would come here to escort a woman.

"Listen, Mrs. Asher," he said, lowering his voice somberly and leaning down a little to gaze into her eyes. "His Highness may officially be on the side of the English, but believe me, he is not a man to be trusted. Whatever you chance to learn—even small details, even if they sound foolish to you—let me know at once. You and I can pool our resources; together we can find your husband."

You mean you can find the Master of Constantinople's hide-outs, she thought, a moment later watching his splendid brown shoulders disappear into the crowd at Razumovsky's approach. Still, she thought, turning with shaky gratitude to her rescuer, she hadn't done so badly. On her first visit to the Grand Bazaar, she had been able, at quite short notice, to sell an almost total stranger a complete load of goods.

As they began to move away, the shopkeeper, who until this time had remained sewing slippers in a corner, got to his feet and padded over to her, and without a word affixed to her collar a cheap brass safety pin on which was strung a blue glass bead, painted with an eye. Then he smiled and bowed, and explained something to Razumovsky at great length.

"For the Evil Eye," the prince said as he led Lydia away.

The street of the brass vendors contained, in addition to innumerable tiny shops where old men tapped and fashioned everything from plates and boxes to enormous long-spouted teapots and life-sized deer, four sellers of fig paste, a man dispensing lemonade from a huge earthenware jug on a hand-cart, a vendor of sesame candy, and a regiment of beggars.

There was no storyteller.

"Helm Musefir?" the keeper of the largest shop on the row said in response to Razumovsky's question. He was a little man with a beard the color of iron down to his middle, who had not abandoned the old-fashioned clothing with the coming of the reforms. His pantaloons were resplendent in volume and hue, his sashes fringed in tarnishing silver, his slippers purple morocco and curled extravagantly at the toe. His turban was green, pinned with an enormous clasp of shining brass like an advertisement above his brown, good-natured face, and as he spoke he fingered a loop of prayer beads in his hand. "Since Monday he is gone. My wife's cousin has a friend who lives in the room above him; he says he has not been to his rooms, neither he nor Izahk, the Armenian boy who takes care of him and runs his errands."

"Was there a reason for this?" the prince asked. When the brass seller hesitated, Razumovsky gestured to Lydia and explained in the French in which most of the vendors seemed fluent, "This good madame is seeking news that the *hakâwati shaîr* might have had for her and would deeply value any word as to Musefir's whereabouts."

"Ah." The shopkeeper bowed slightly at the emphasis Razumovsky placed on the word *value*. "In truth, I do not know. Will the good lady be so kind as to accept . . ." He held out to her a brass dish of Turkish Delight, pale green in a snowy dust of sugar. "My wife's cousin's friend is also a friend of the landlord's sister, and she says that the *hakâwati shaîr* was not in debt, nor in arrears of rent. Likewise the boy Izahk's uncle, who frequents the same coffeehouse as my brother-in-law, would have mentioned had the old man been ill. So I do not know."

Of course, thought Lydia, wiping powdered sugar from her fingers as His Highness walked her back through the teeming aisles of the bazaar, no one had seen or noticed James himself. James was like that. But it did not escape her that if James had arrived in Constantinople Saturday evening, he could easily have sought out the *hakâwati shaîr* Helm Musefir on Sunday—the last day upon which the old storyteller himself was seen.

SIXTEEN

AFTER the bewildering stinks and colors of the Grand Bazaar, tea at the Hotel Bristol was like stepping through a door and finding oneself suddenly in the south of France. For Lydia this effect was heightened by the fact that, in spite of the Bristol's excellent view of the Golden Horn, she could not see the old city. For her, the world ended a yard past Herr Hindl's broad shoulders in a light-filled sea of obscurity through which white-coated waiters swam, their silver dishes flashing like strange treasure in the late afternoon sun.

Women wearing stylish pale-hued frocks chatted with well-tailored gentlemen in French and German over Ceylon tea and crème brûlée. A small orchestra played Mendelssohn. Three children in knee pants and starchy white dresses consumed water ices under the benevolent glare of a tightly laced woman in black bombazine.

It was restful beyond words.

At the foot of the hill on which Pera stood, Lydia knew, Armenians cleared up charred beams and broken glass from the harsh retribution against their protests. Men like Razumovsky and Karolyi shifted and jockeyed for position in the background, selling guns to the Turks or the Greeks or the Arabs in preparation for a war that everyone knew was coming, and telling themselves it was all to maintain the peace. In every house in the old city, women lived in ugly little rooms like the harem, behind lattices that forbade not only the eyes of men but the sun itself, and no one raised a voice for them.

And beneath the surface moved darker shadows yet.

"Maybe it's just my being a newcomer here that makes me feel as though I've dropped into another time as well as another world." Lydia blinked brown eyes against the golden light and took a sip of her tea, dainty fingers half covered with mitts of ecru lace. "Sometimes it seems to me it's the small things, not the big ones, that make a country change from ancient to modern, the way the Ottoman Empire is doing. Like buying stoves and furnaces instead of heating their houses with braziers . . ." After three days in the house on Rue Abydos, Lydia knew all about braziers. "I expect you still have people paying you with handfuls of gold."

Hindl chuckled richly. "Ha ha, precisely so, Frau Asher. One finds the strangest things here in the mysterious Orient! You know, the other day I was called in to consult with a wealthy man who wanted to donate plumbing fixtures to the hospital attached to the mosque of the Sultan Mehmed . . ."

The ensuing story occupied fifteen minutes and had nothing whatsoever to do with furnaces, odd financial avenues, or possible wars among the city's Undead, but nevertheless Lydia found it intriguing for its contrast between the new and the old. Once she discounted her host's rather heavy-handed attempts at humor and his propensity for telling her what, as a European lady, she should and shouldn't do, she did not find it difficult to listen to Herr Hindl on his favorite subject, perhaps because her own interests had always tended to the technical. He was, at least, a businessman with contacts in one of the strangest and most varied cities in the world, and not a twenty-two-year-old aristocrat whose world began with cub hunting in November and ended at the conclusion of the grouse shoots.

With a minimum of prompting, Hindl quite happily told her about his clients, the sometimes peculiar methods of payment found in an empire whose ruler had vetoed the building of an electrical dynamo because the word sounded too much like "dynamite" and might give encouragement to anarchists . . . and, of course, a great deal about the differences in burning time between soft and hard coal and the sorts of steam furnaces available from American manufacturers as opposed to those in Berlin.

"Ah, it's a strange city, Frau Asher, a strange city!" He shook a plump, reproving finger at her. "And not one for a lady to be traveling about in alone! I hope you're not one of those lady suffragettes we hear so much of, wanting to wear pants and smoke cigarettes and make us poor men stay home and mind the babies, ha ha!"

Lydia, who would far sooner have trusted any child with James than her friend Josetta or, God forbid, herself, simply out of regard for the poor infant's comfort, refrained from saying so. Instead she angled the conversation neatly back to Herr Hindl's adventures—in which he was far more interested anyway. In time, and with genuine interest, she asked, "So there are some clients who won't appear at all? Who refuse to deal with the infidel even for the sake of their own comfort?"

"My dearest Frau Asher," Hindl chuckled, "*legions* of them!" He poured her another cup of tea. The waiter had twice refilled the hot water, and once brought the furnace salesman another plate of Italian ice. Hindl was a thickset, fair Berliner of about thirty-five whose wife and two sons had remained in Germany. He had been one of the dozen or so gentlemen who had extended invitations, not, she knew, with the smallest intent of impropriety on either side, but simply because she was a new face in a rather small Western community and—if she didn't wear her spectacles—reasonably pretty. She'd been glad when Lady Clapham, after a moment's thought, had pronounced it "perfectly all right" not to bring Miss Potton along; even gladder when the attaché's wife had offered to invite the girl for tea and cards at the embassy instead.

Margaret had—characteristically—turned her down.

"Frau Asher, if you want to hear of impossible clients, you should talk to Jacob Zeittelstein. Now, *there's* an eccentric client for you! Huge old labyrinth of a palace lost in some maze in the heart of the city, bills of credit from who knows what companies and corporations, can only work under certain conditions, won't meet with him in the daytime at all, won't meet with him under any circumstances half the time but sends these—these *thugs* who don't know to do anything but open doors, it seems; won't meet with him on Fridays, Saturdays, *or* Sundays, changes his mind, tear it out, do it over, but hurry, hurry, hurry . . ." He laughed again, and sipped his tea.

"Poor old Jacob comes away tearing out his hair and wishing he'd never *heard* of ammonia refrigerating plants."

"Refrigerating?" Lydia inquired.

"Refrigerating?" Ysidro leaned back a little in his chair and drew the soft cashmere lap robe more closely around his shoulders. A reflex, thought Lydia, left over from the days when he had body heat to conserve. She wondered if the shivering reflex persisted. What would it be, she thought uneasily, to be conscious—*unable to lose consciousness*—in a body slowly consumed with the cold of death?

"Maybe he wants to keep blood in bottles?" suggested Margaret. "So he won't have to . . . to take it from people?"

"If it's the death of the victim rather than the blood itself that feeds the vampire, refrigerated blood would be useless," Lydia replied, then wanted to bite out her tongue as Margaret flushed hotly and flashed an apologetic look to Ysidro, as if to say, *Don't pay attention to her, she doesn't understand.*

The vampire didn't seem to have noticed either Lydia's faux pas or Margaret's reaction to the possible laceration of his feelings.

"It's been tried," he said calmly. "More for the sake of convenience than humanity, I admit. Refrigeration causes blood to clot and separate even more quickly. In any case, in a city as rife with dogs as Constantinople, I can scarce imagine anyone storing blood for purposes of mere physical nourishment."

"You know, I wondered—" Lydia began, then cut herself off quickly, realizing her medical curiosity on the subject of whether Ysidro were feeding on nonhuman blood sources might be tactless in the extreme.

The yellow eyes touched hers, only for an instant, but awareness of her question, confusion, and self-deprecation all danced like an ironic star. But he only said, "I have not heard cold itself could injure the Undead, nor cause them to sleep on into the night. The vampires of St. Petersburg dwell in palaces left empty through the winter, while most of the court goes south to the Crimea, and they rise and hunt and sleep as usual. It is not an easy thing," he added, turning to Lydia with that same remote amusement, "to be Undead during the time of the white nights. But in winter they walk abroad from three in the afternoon, and sleep does not weigh them down until eight or nine in the morning. They do not feel cold that would kill a living man, though it is true that the Master of Petersburg has spoken of removing permanently to the Crimea, which tells me that he has begun to tire, and so feel the pain of cold in his joints. Still . . ."

He turned his head a little, to contemplate the stacks of ledgers and papers heaped on the table around the oil lamps that Madame Potoneros had brought in at Lydia's behest. An embassy clerk had delivered the material late that afternoon, with a note from Lady Clapham: *I won't ask what you want them for, my dear, only that if you learn anything we should know about, you'll pass it along. The red are the Banque Ottomane; the gray, the Deutsches Bank. I'm afraid we'll need them back in the morning.* The *we* amused her, confirming as it did who was really running Intelligence—such as it was—in Constantinople.

"It will be a matter of interest to see how deep the fingers of the master of the city have gone into the flesh of the empire."

"If it's the Bey that we find."

"Oh, it will be." Ysidro rose and laid aside the lap robe, averting as he did so his face from the light. Margaret scurried away to fetch his cloak, as if she feared Lydia would usurp this task that she considered her right. "Money takes on a life of its own once it enters the veins of this body they call finance. All the masters of the great cities are aware of this and make sure they have great sums of it, not hidden, but disguised as something else. This is why they are masters. I would hazard that since July, with the army coup, the Bey has been transferring his assets from the old forms—hidden stocks of gold, investment in land—to the new. It is his protection against the interloper, if interloper there be, or against a rebellious fledgling. His protection against the upheavals of the living."

"And his challenger won't have the capital base yet."

"I doubt it. Most fledglings do not realize the need for such invisible redoubts. They think immortality sufficient."

As he reached to take the cloak from Margaret's hand, Lydia saw that the gold ring he wore had slipped around his finger, turning so that the bezel faced inward to his palm, as rings do when the flesh shrinks away from them with cold, or age, or death.

"As for me, I shall pursue Anthea and Charles as the Undead pursue, listening in the streets where the poor dwell and seeking those places where the living do not walk. If James is yet alive, as this Karolyi has said, it is because the Bey needs something of him, and at a guess it is as bait, either for Charles or for Anthea. Karolyi is still bargaining, offering what he has to sell—the support and alliance of his government in these uncertain times—while feeling for other advantages."

"But why—" Lydia began helplessly, and Ysidro shook his head.

"We move in a miasma, and not entirely that of the Bey's making," he said softly. "There is some other matter afoot here, beyond a possible challenger or interloper. Treason among the Bey's fledglings, perhaps, or an interloper not of the common run. We must each search as we can. It may be that as a physician you will recognize something concerning cold as it has to do with the Undead state, which even the Undead do not know. Later, like the knights of the grail meeting upon the road, we can exchange information and see if we can read, one for the other, what each vision signifies. Do not lose hope."

"No," Lydia said, consciously steadying herself. "No. At least I know James is alive—if Karolyi was telling the truth. Though I did notice he was very careful not to say *when* he'd seen James. It might have been—well—days ago. But really, we can only do what we can do."

"An observation worthy of the sages of Athens," the vampire said gravely and, holding out his hand, took her fingers in his. "A word in your ear."

Conscious of Margaret's glare at her back, Lydia followed him out of the dining room, to the head of the stair.

He stood with his back to the vigil light, so that only its reflection touched the points of cheeks and chin and made a spidery halo of his hair. In his enveloping cloak he looked like Death on its way to the opera; his hands were, she thought, not quite steady as he pulled on his gloves.

"You have fathomed my secret," he said, the soft voice emerging from the dark, and upon it, like the trace of his antique inflection, Lydia detected the echo of a smile. "The blood of animals gives some nourishment, though it does not warm, and their deaths are useless to feed the hunger and the need of the mind. But it would not do to shock Margaret with the information that the dark hero of her Byronic fancies is currently living on the blood of dogs—and such dogs! As a physician, however, I knew the matter would consume you until you knew."

Lydia laughed, the fear and tension she had felt since that morning in the bazaar loosening its hold. "I think you're just too vain to own to it." She smiled, and Ysidro paused, his hand on the rail of the stair.

"Of course I am vain," he said. "All of the Undead are vain—too vain to admit that, like common men, we must die."

He made a move to go, then turned back and took her hand again—carefully, so as not to come near the silver on her wrist—and raised it to his lips.

As he vanished into the shadows of the stair, she said, "Be careful . . ."

She didn't know whether he heard or not.

Margaret shoved the papers she was reading quickly into her workbasket and returned to her chair as Lydia reentered the dining room. She kept her eyes downcast, but Lydia felt the sullenness of her silence, the resentment in the set of her narrow back in its ill-fitting cotton shirtwaist. She drew a pile of gray Deutsches Bank ledgers to her, but left pencil and foolscap to one side untouched.

Determined not to have another argument with her, Lydia only asked, "You know what we're looking for?"

"New corporations in July or August paid for in gold or by transfer of lands, sums transferred to another corporation or another bank monthly or quarterly." She recited Lydia's instructions like a schoolchild regurgitating some hated—and barely comprehended—lesson.

"Look for a transfer to the second corporation, or to a new corporation, in the first week of October of ten thousand marks, or twelve thousand five hundred francs, and if you see either the Zwanzigstejahrhundert Abkuhlunggeselleschaft, or any of these names—" She pushed across to her the slip of paper she'd gotten from Razumovsky that afternoon, listing the four or five names under which the Sultan's chamberlain took bribes or laundered money. "—please flag it for me."

"I understand," Margaret said with gruff impatience, and pulled the paper to her, but didn't even turn it right side up. Lydia half opened her mouth to remonstrate, then let it go. She guessed she'd have to go through whatever Margaret did again anyway, but if these ledgers had to be back in the morning, there was no time for either discussion or for Margaret to slam into the bedroom in a tantrum. She couldn't work through all of this alone.

And what could she say in any case?

The dream returned to her, of Margaret waiting in the castle ruins for a horseman who never came. Was Ysidro unable even to project the dream memories of passion to her now, the melodramatic romances that held her to him? Was he, she wondered suddenly, unable to appear in them because in them he would be the skeletal, almost insectile creature who had spoken to her with his back to the light?

If that was what vampires saw in mirrors, no wonder they avoided them, veiled them, kept them closed behind doors. If that was what the living eyes would perceive, no wonder the vampires caused the living to see—or remember seeing—nothing at all.

All of the Undead are vain . . .

"*Kiria . . .*" Stefania Potoneros appeared, hesitating, in the doorway and held out two stiff cream-colored envelopes.

The first contained a note on the letterhead of the Zwanzigstejahrhundert Abkuhlunggeselleschaft—Berlin, London, and Constantinople—typed neatly in English and signed by a secretary.

> *Mrs. Asher:*
> *We regret to inform you that Herr Jacob Zeittelstein is unable to make an appointment with you for this week, due to the fact that he is in Berlin at this time. When he returns to Constantinople on Wednesday next, he will of course be delighted to get in touch with you regarding a meeting.*
> > *Sincerely,*
> > *Avram Kostner*
> > *Private secretary to Herr Zeittelstein*

Wednesday! thought Lydia, aghast. Two days from now until he was even *in* Constantinople, let alone when he'd have time to see her, answer her questions. Jamie could be dead by then . . .

Jamie could be dead now.

My dearest Madame, the other letter read, in an elaborately indecipherable French hand.

> *It appears we have located the storyteller your husband sought. With your permission, my carriage shall arrive for you at ten tomorrow morning, though it would be well to be prepared to do some walking.*
> > *Your most humble servant,*
> > *Razumovsky*

*

"If I may be permitted to ask a question, effendi?" Asher turned his cheek to the slab where he lay, blinking the sweat from his eyes. In the still, dense heat of the tiny *hararet*—the chamber of the baths that the Romans would have called the *calderium*, or hot room—the shape of the Master of Constantinople, white as the marble that entirely formed the walls, seemed to emerge from and blend into the steam in a disconcerting fashion, so that half the time Asher was not entirely certain he could see him at all.

"It is always permitted to ask, Scheherazade." The voice of Olumsiz Bey came out of the steamy twilight, and the red glow of the braziers in the corners made twin embers of his eyes. There was dreamy, heat-soaked amusement in the deep voice as he spoke the nickname, taken from Asher's curiosity about old words and ancient tales even in the face of his imprisonment and peril. "There would be no wisdom in the world, did men not ask."

"What do you want with the Earl of Ernchester?"

It was nearly midnight. With the early fall of winter dark, Zardalu and the other fledglings had taken Asher to an immense dry cistern, like a pillared cavern beneath the city, given him a tin lantern and sent him out in that endless forest of columns. "Behave as if you searched for someone, Englis," whispered the eunuch, with his mocking smile. "Gaze about—so—put your hand to your heart, as if to calm the pangs of love." The others laughed, the thin, metallic shivering he had heard in Vienna, and faded into the darkness, leaving him alone.

So he had walked, as he had walked in the cemeteries, holding the lantern high, and the shadows of the pillars reeled and shifted with the movement of the light. The columns themselves were of all girths: thin Ionic with rams' horn capitals, and heavy, unfluted Doric worn with the marks of water. The floor underfoot was hardened mud, silted up who knew how deep. Between them night lay thick, and the cold breaths of moving air told him the place had more than the one entry the vampires had used. He was thinking how fortunate it was that the candle within the lantern was protected by glass when the flame went out, as suddenly as if covered by a snuffer.

Asher stepped back at once, putting his back to the nearest pillar and forcing closed his mind against the crushing numbness that bore down upon it. He reached for the pocket where he kept matches, wrapped in waxed silk, and his nostrils were filled with the smell of old blood and graveyard mold. A hand closed around his arm, as if the arm had been trapped in machinery; but before he could lash out with the lantern in his other hand, before he could move or think or cry out, the gripping hand was gone.

There was a kind of movement, a breathing rustle in the dark, and he pulled the matches from his pocket and lit one with a hand that shook.

He was alone.

"My dear Scheherazade." The voice was suddenly close. Asher blinked again in the steam, to see that the Master of Constantinople stood beside the marble table where he lay, naked, as was the Bey himself, but for a towel around his loins. "These are vampire matters, of no concern to the living. Indeed, I doubt the living would understand them."

"They're of concern to those who want to stay among the living." Asher sat up, his brown hair hanging lank in his eyes, and the bathman Mustafa stepped back. Asher had guessed that the Bey's living servants weren't deaf, but he had never succeeded in getting more than a few words out of any of them. When they brought him food, when they placed clean clothing in his room or escorted him to the library or the baths, they watched him with the eerie impassivity of guard dogs, as wary as if he, not they, were the servant of the night. "Was it you who had Lady Ernchester's rooms searched, after Ernchester had gone?"

"My instructions to Karolyi were to have her destroyed," the Bey said shortly. His orange eyes, gaudy as aniline dye, glittered coldly. "The woman is his strength. A man need not be a sorcerer, or a reader of dreams, to have learned that in the course of a single conversation. In the eighteen months of his abiding here as a living man, there was not a day that he did not speak of her, nor a night when she was not in his dreams. When I heard that both had been made Undead, I thought it a foolish risk on the part of the Master of London, to have among his fledglings one with such power over his mind as she."

"He disobeyed you, then."

"Stupid Magyar, to think he could defeat the purposes of the Undead." The Bey's left hand caressed unthinkingly the silk bindings around the hilt of his silver weapon—thornwood,

Asher guessed, the silk just sufficient to keep from discomfort a vampire as old as the Bey, who had toughened a little against some of the substances reactive to vampire flesh. Around his neck he wore a foot-long knife, sheathed in leather and lead. Asher guessed the blade within the sheath was silver as well. "Was it she who freed him in Vienna and killed those set to watch over his prison there?"

Asher shook his head. "It was the Vienna vampires. Karolyi had brought a victim for Ernchester to kill."

"Fool." The vampire turned his face aside, anger in his eyes. His lean body seemed almost completely without muscle, the hair of chest and armpits paled to a strange red-brown. Though the heat of the *hararet* had laid a film of condensation on the pallid skin, Asher could see not a drop of sweat. "The man is greedy, seeing only the path to his own power, and not that things are ordered as I have ordered them for reasons beyond his comprehension. And yours," he added, looking back at him.

"Then why deal with him?"

"A man is a fool who casts away a plank in a shipwreck, Scheherazade. He is impertinent, to think that I would do as his Christian emperor bids. But power, and allies, are always needful in a difficult time."

"And are the times so difficult?" Asher asked quietly. "Is that why you're hunting Lady Ernchester so diligently? Not only to control the earl, but to keep her out of Karolyi's hands? He'll go to your fledglings, you know, if he hasn't already."

A drift of moving air stirred the steam. The curtain of embroidered leather that separated the *hararet* from the *sogukluk*, the warm room, lifted aside. The man Sayyed stood there, his head—shaven like the Bey's— glistening with moisture.

"There is one to see you, Lord. A *makanik*." Except for the last word, which was Persian, he spoke peasant Turkish, the longest sentence Asher had yet heard any of the living servants speak.

"You will excuse me." The Master of Constantinople bowed deeply, turned to go, then, pausing, looked back.

"Do not concern yourself in the affairs of my children, Scheherazade," the Bey said, and the giant ant seemed to watch Asher from its amber prison on the Bey's ear. "This is not the course of a prudent man. Do not trust them. They will promise you things—escape from this place, safety from harm, even the kiss that brings eternal life. But it is all lies. They are all treacherous. They envy one another and envy the power each thinks the other might possess; and above all they envy me. But *I* am the master of the city. This city is mine, and all things in it."

He held up his silver weapon, the blade flashing gently in the dull braziers' gleam. "And do not concern yourself with Ernchester. That, too, is a course that will bring you only death."

When he had gone, Asher stretched out on the table again, gingerly favoring the dressing over the knife wound on his ribs. It was healing well; Mustafa had changed the dressing, and now, as the man kneaded and pummeled his muscles into lassitude, Asher stretched out his right arm before him and looked at it in the dim light.

The heat had reddened the scars that tracked the vein from wrist to elbow, the scars left by the Paris vampires. Among them, the fresh dark blot of a bruise was printed like a blackening stain.

Asher picked out the marks of fingers and thumb, remembering the hand that had crushed his arm in the dark of the cistern. The dressing pinching as he moved, he brought his other hand forward and laid it over the marks.

The hand was bigger than his own.

Ernchester's hands, he remembered, were small.

The fledglings had returned to him almost at once, in the silence of the dry cistern, had blindfolded him and brought him back to the House of Oleanders without a word, as they had brought him back twice now in three days from those desolate places where Anthea might have hidden. They had blanked his mind as they came through the street, so that he returned to a kind of frightened and dizzy consciousness in the octagonal Byzantine vestibule that led to the Bey's salon.

He was beginning to think that Zardalu had made a genuine mistake and let his mind be distracted while coming back into the house from that first expedition.

Zardalu and the others had departed on their own hunt after returning Asher to the House of Oleanders, and were still gone when Asher dressed again in clean linen and secondhand gray trousers, red wool vest, and a worn and slightly ill-fitting Stamboul coat. He made his way back along the corridors to his room with Sayyed padding silently behind. He knew that route now, and how the small palace of some Byzantine prince connected with one of the several *hans* that made up its wings. Twice he'd passed a doorway he guessed led into some late Roman crypt or church, and the painted room with the tiled dome in which he'd seen Karolyi was definitely Turkish.

The courtyard of the old *han* was lighted with brass lamps hanging from the colonnade before what had been deep bays of warehouses downstairs. A single lamp burned in the niche at the end of the open gallery, two floors above. Lights burned, too, in the Byzantine vestibule—Asher could see their reflection on the arched passageway.

A *makanik*, to see the Deathless Lord.

Something concerning that secret experiment, that strange crypt far beneath the house, stinking of oil and ammonia.

Near the old baths, Zardalu had said.

There were no clocks in the House of Oleanders, and the hours of darkness could be disorienting. Asher, who had a fairly good sense of time, estimated it was close to one in the morning as Sayyed turned the key in the lock and padded away, and guessed he had an hour or two in which he'd be relatively safe.

Do not concern yourself with Ernchester, the Bey had said. But he was still bargaining with Karolyi.

Except for the dry basin in the center, the long floor was a faded moss bank of carpet, four and five layers thick. Among these carpets he had concealed the picklocks he made.

He fetched them now.

The bronze candlestick, which he kept quite openly beside his small pile of books in one of the inlaid wall cupboards, had provided him not only with wire for picklocks, but with a number of candles as well. These he slipped now into the pocket of his coat. The lock was a very old single-tumbler

Banham, probably the best obtainable when put in, but that had been more than a hundred years ago. As he descended the stairs to the courtyard, he heard the voice of the Bey shouting in the salon and stopped, startled, by the vestibule passageway to listen.

"It has been three weeks, you sputum of Shaitan's dog!" That any vampire, let alone one as old as Olumsiz Bey, should give way to rage at all was unheard of, and the passion that cracked in his deep voice was terrifying to hear. "Five days since the breakdown, and still no word of the man! I tell you there can be no more delays!"

"Peace, m'sieu," came a more muffled—and understandably nervous—reply. "The man will be back Wednesday. Wednesday is not so very long . . ."

Asher hesitated, torn, sensing that whatever could so enrage the Master of Constantinople must be of paramount importance, but knowing that if he were caught standing here—much less with picklocks and candles in his pockets—he was a dead man indeed. His every instinct told him to stay, but at least, he thought dryly, moving like a shadow away from the arch, if he's shouting at his engineer he isn't listening for me . . .

The mental image of the Bey as he had seen him other nights, sitting still on the divan of his pillared salon, silver weapon across his knees and orange eyes half shut while he listened to the teeming dreams of the city around him, was a disturbing one.

Even as we hear the footfalls of the workmen, Zardalu had said. At least as long as he walked above the ground, if the Bey listened for them, Asher knew he could hear his.

The way that leads to the old baths.

Fashions in building came and went, and the House of Oleanders was at least five old buildings fused into a monstrous maze of dark rooms and decaying memories, but, Asher knew, plumbing remains plumbing. The elaborate system of pipes and hypocausts that made Turkish baths—and before them, Roman—was not a thing to be relocated lightly or far.

We smell the naft, the alkol, the stinks of what he does . . .

His mind returned to the throat-catching sharpness of the air in the crypt. A room with a wooden floor, to the left across a courtyard where grass grows between stones like cannonballs. A second flight of steps after the first . . .

He fingered the picklocks in his pocket and drifted through the House of Oleanders like a ghost.

The solitary gleam of his candle wavered over chambers hung with printed Chinese silks whose colors showed themselves briefly; over vaulting that flickered and shone with the unmistakable dusky bronze hue of gold in shadow. He passed through an octagonal chamber whose walls were sheathed, floor to ceiling, in red tile the exact color of ripe persimmons, containing only a black-and-white wooden coffee stand; an arch looked out on a court smaller than the room itself and so choked with oleander bushes that only the dim white shape of a single statue could be seen in their midst.

Near that place he found the room he sought: the small, rich chamber of painted walls and blue and yellow tiles whose bare wooden floor thumped familiarly underfoot. From it a door let into a courtyard, long and narrow and paved in blocks of worn stone the size of halfpenny loaves, through which brown grass and weeds thrust tall.

The moon had not risen. No light touched the windows in the low buildings that surrounded the court on two sides. Roman, thought Asher, identifying the heavy rounded arches, the broken fragments of marble facing and the thick, fluted columns. What looked like the rear wall of another *han* closed in the third side of the court—he could just see the edge of a dome against the midnight sky—the red and white stone walls of the Turkish house, the fourth.

Under the columned porch the blackness was profound. The smaller cobbling was uneven, familiar. Almost he felt he could quench the candle as he passed to the left, fifteen steps across the court and through the door, five steps and left again. It was difficult to see that doorway, where it stood in shadow, though it opened in the middle of a wall of faded frescoes—more oddly still, he lost control of his steps twice, passing it without being aware. Around him the darkness brooded, watching. It could, he knew, contain anything.

Or nothing, he told himself. Or nothing.

He descended the stair. Had he not remembered a second stairway, he would have turned back, for its entrance lay concealed in the niche formed by one of the shallow false archways in what turned out to be the *tepidarium* of the house's original Roman baths. A small room, faced with marble, its shallow pool long gone dry. The mosaics of the floor gleamed faintly in the moving light of Asher's candle: Byzantine, and like those of the octagonal vestibule, long ago defaced.

The second stair, as he recalled, was twice or three times the depth of the one above. If he met them now—the Bey's homecoming fledglings with their night's prey—there would be no possibility of escape.

He guessed the crypt below had been a prison, or a storage place for something more precious or more sinister than wine. The low brick groinings of the ceiling barely cleared his six-foot height, and the few rooms that opened to his right from the short passageway were tiny, sunk below the level of the floor, which was itself worn in a channel inches deep. The air—as he recalled and as Zardalu had remarked—was bitterly cold.

Dastgah. Scientific apparatus. There were Western scientific journals in the library dating back to the eighteenth century, treatises in Arabic from the days before the Moslem world had become a scientific backwater. Just exactly what was it, Asher wondered, that the Master of Constantinople was having his Western engineers build for him? That meant so much to him that its delay would rouse him to fury? That he hid from his own fledglings?

The penny-dip glow touched something dully reflective, lodged like a gleaming bone in the throat of a dark arch.

Here, he thought. The place the Bey kept hidden, veiled with his mind.

At the end of the abyssal corridor before him, Asher knew he would find that long stone stair, climbing to an outer door. But branching down to his left, his raised candle flame showed a grille of silver bars, behind which lay—what?

Or who?

Before him the tunnel extended like the bowel of night—to his left, behind the silver bars, Stygian velvet.

He wondered how much time he had left.

He had to know.

Cautiously, he moved down the short side branch.

His wan light winked on water pooled on the uneven stone floor. The corridor was extremely narrow, curving slightly; the silver bars, tarnished nearly black save around the lock where the bolt went into the stone, blocked it about ten feet from the convergence of the two passages. Beyond, Asher could make out two archways set in the left-hand wall. On one, at least, he caught the glint of a metal lock plate on a door. The smell of ammonia was overpowering; he had to fight not to cough.

They'd be coming back soon: Zardalu and the Baykus Kadine, and the others, bringing another victim to chase through the pitch-dark house until they cornered him, weeping and screaming . . .

Even locked in his upper room, Asher had heard the Armenian boy's voice for a long time.

He turned from the silver grating, back to the main corridor, and resumed his quest for the stair that led out.

There was a door, locked, that had to be it—like the doors above, he missed it two or three times, found it only by walking with his hand on the weeping stone of the wall, until what he had somehow taken three times for an angle of shadow resolved itself suddenly into an arch. This evidence of the power of the master vampire's mind he found extremely unnerving. They must have left the door open behind them that first night when they'd gone forth—or perhaps one had gone ahead of the others to open it for them.

In any case the lock was a Yale, new; a matter for a duplicate key, not a homemade shank of bronze wire.

Heart beating fast now with apprehension, he returned to the silver grille. That lock, at least, was of the old-fashioned kind, probably because the softer metal couldn't take the stress of the smaller wards. He angled the bronze wire carefully, knowing every scratch would show. Even the lugs and pins that held it to the stonework of the walls were silver.

They are treacherous . . . the Bey had said, the silver blade of his halberd gleaming in the smoldering half-light of the baths. *They are treacherous.*

His heart slamming blood in his ears, he edged his way along the buckled, puddled flagging next to the wall. A wet footprint here would condemn him to death. Straw and sawdust salted the corridor, making the going even more delicate, and the cold was arctic. He wondered if he would hear the fledglings returning. Wondered if he would know, should the Bey be watching him from out of the darkness with those leached-out ochre eyes.

"Ernchester," he whispered at the nearer of the two doors.

Both were locked. Hasps of silver, or more probably electroplated steel. Padlocks sheathed in silver, even to the bows. Silver solder dabbed over the screw heads. The locks were new—the rest, black with age in the candle's feeble light.

"Ernchester!" he whispered again. How much—how far—could the Deathless Lord hear? Not through earth, he thought. Not through this much stone. "It's Asher. Are you there? Anthea's free, she's here in Constantinople . . ."

He had almost said, *Anthea's alive.*

Listened.

Deep behind the heavy door he heard it: a groan, or a cry, that lifted the hair on his head—physical agony mingled with the blackest depth of despair. Hell, Asher thought. Such a sound you would hear if you put your ear to the keyhole of Hell.

"Can you hear me? Can you understand?"

Only silence replied. His hand trembled, fumbled at the lock, half numb with cold but unsteady, also, with the knowledge that time was now very short . . .

"I'll come back for you," he promised hoarsely. "I'll get you out . . ." *And I'll need your help,* he added as a grim afterthought, *to return the favor.*

A draft, a shift of air, and his heart stopped as if knifed with an icicle, then began beating fast and thin. Even in that first second, he pinched the candlewick, thanking God for the smell of the ammonia that would drown the smoke of a full-fledged conflagration, much less that of a single dip. That drowned, even from the Undead, the smell of his living blood.

From the dark of the corridor beyond the silver bars he heard stumbling footfalls, and a pleading breath, "My lord, be kind—be kind to a poor girl . . ."

At the edge of hearing, a tickle of obscene mirth.

"Oh, the lord you're going to will be kind." The voice might have been Zardalu's. "He is the kindest lord in the city, sweet and generous . . . you'll find him so, beautiful gazelle . . ."

In the utter blackness there was nothing to see, no way to know if they'd noticed the slight jar of the doorway in the silver bars—he'd pulled it to behind him, the hinges oiled and uncreaking . . .

He could only wait, desperately listening, wondering if the next thing to happen would be a cold touch on his neck. The staggering footsteps faded. He himself remained where he was for a long time, unmoving, dizzy with the ammonia stink and the cold that ate at his bones, before he felt his way along the wall to the bars, and so out into the corridor, wincing as the gate lock clicked behind him like the hammer of doom.

But none molested him. In time he felt his way back to the stair—painfully, endlessly, across the baths, thanking God that navigating in the dark was a skill he'd kept up from his spying days—and up to the grass-grown court, where the little light of the stars seemed bright to his eyes. As he crept through the courtyard, he heard the silvery clashing of vampire laughter from within the salon, and the young woman's voice pleading incoherently. It seemed to him, as he bolted his own door behind him and sank to his knees under a sudden wave of nervous shaking, that the sound came to him still—that, and the moaning of the prisoner behind the crypt door.

It was a long time before he managed to get to his feet and stumble to the divan, where he lay shivering as if with killing fever until the muezzins of the Nouri Osmanie cried the late winter dawn.

SEVENTEEN

"I SUSPECTED my remark about how valuable you thought the information would yield results." Prince Razumovsky slashed with his riding whip at the two curs sleeping on the marble steps. They slunk a few feet away and stretched out again in the dust of the plaza that had once been the Hippodrome, tongues lolling an incongruous raspberry against wolfish coats which, even without her eyeglasses, Lydia could tell were half worn away with mange.

Constantinople had more dogs—and, as she had seen last night, more cats—than any city she'd ever been in.

The animals seemed to operate on two different levels, as indeed, she reflected, they would have to. As Prince Razumovsky's carriage had worked carefully through the streets of the old city, where wooden Turkish houses appeared to sprout spontaneously from more ancient walls, the dogs had been everywhere, lying in the muck or against the walls of ochre or pink stucco. The cats had the overhanging balconies or shared the sills of heavily barred windows with potted geraniums, or lay on the walls and trellises of tiny cafés where Turkish men sipped tea and talked under stringy canopies of leafless vines.

"Someone always knows someone," the Russian continued, white teeth gleaming under tawny haystacks of mustache. "The good brass seller mentioned our questions to his friends at the café that night, or perhaps a beggar overheard us or the

258

man selling baklava. One of them knew a street sweeper whose sister knew the *hakâwati shaîr* by sight or had a cousin who'd heard one of the muezzins mention that a new *hakâwati shaîr* had taken up residence in this place, or one of the neighborhood children mentioned it to another child . . . It was a Syrian boy who brought me the information."

"What did you pay him?" Lydia reached for the small reticule of silver mesh that hung at her waist. "I can't let you . . ."

"An entirely negligible sum." His Highness waved dismissively. "It will support his family for two months, doubtless—or buy one member of it two days' worth of opium, if that's their choice." He held out his hand to help her over the marble sill of the narrow door.

He had been treating her all morning as if she were made of cut glass, apparently under the impression that her haggard eyes and pallor were the result of a night of sleepless worry over her husband, not a night spent single-mindedly plowing through four and a half months' worth of the investor listings of the two biggest banks in the city.

There were more than a score of corporations and investors that seemed to fit the criteria. More people than a single vampire had guessed the way the wind was blowing back in July and started transferring funds into less vulnerable forms than real estate and gold. She wondered if it were possible to obtain the long-term banking records of the oldest banks—how long *had* there been banks in the empire, anyway?—or of property holders, to see whose lives went on for a suspiciously long time before they transferred their money to equally long-lived successors. The various names under which the palace chamberlain laundered money came up again and again in everyone's accounts—and given the general level of corruption in Constantinople, it was almost impossible to track how money appeared and disappeared.

By five in the morning Lydia had a dozen names—two of which Margaret had completely missed in the Deutsches Bank records—and Margaret had long since fallen asleep with her head on her arms.

Had she not reviewed the records, Lydia suspected she'd

have had the night of sleepless worry in any event, so it was just as well she'd had work to occupy her.

"Are you sure this is all right?" Margaret asked, flushing an uncomfortable red. "It isn't allowed, is it?"

"The courtyard is free to all," said Razumovsky. "But it would probably be best if you let me speak."

The Blue Mosque was one of the greatest in the city, a place where there were always people.

That, Lydia realized a moment later, was the point.

Razumovsky led them—Lydia burningly conscious of her Western gown and the gauzy excuse for a veil depending from her stylish hat—toward the north wall of the court, where wintry light fell upon the men along the colonnade: a bearded man in a turban selling small loops of bright-colored prayer beads on a blanket; another cross-legged behind what looked like a little desk, complete with brass inkwell, standish, and shaker of sand. There was the inevitable shoe-shine boy with his little brass-bound kit. Two men in rags, sitting near the small marble pavilion in the middle of the court fingering their beads, glared at the women as they passed, but neither spoke.

The man they sought occupied a worn carpet next to the bead seller's pitch. He was conversing with a thin, elderly man in a white robe and yellow turban, but looked up as Razumovsky drew near, and Lydia had an impression of a huge hooked nose and a tangle of dirty white beard, a green blob of turban, and, when she cast down her eyes, of grimy, horny feet with toenails like a bear's claws poking from beneath his robe. He was ragged, and his clothing smelled of filth and sweat; he gave off anger and distrust like a blast of heat in her face.

"*Qabîh . . . qabîh . . .*" he muttered ferociously, glaring up at her and then past her at Margaret. "*Qahbât . . .*" He averted his face then and added in hoarse French, "An unveiled woman is an abomination in the eyes of God."

"*Maître conteur.*" Lydia curtseyed deeply. "Please forgive me. Do you call me ill names because I wear the veil which my husband gave me to wear?" She touched the thin net veil of her green taffeta hat. "Do you blame me for wearing clothing, and dressing my hair, as my husband wishes to see me adorned?"

The man in the yellow turban had stepped tactfully away, leaving Lydia, Razumovsky, and Margaret alone with the old *hakâwati shaîr*. Lydia knelt on the worn marble paving of the mosque's court, reflecting that after journeying all the way from Oxford, the bottle-green skirt needed cleaning anyway. "And if my husband has disappeared," she went on, still in French, which the old man seemed to follow well enough, "and I know him to be in danger, am I impure for wanting to aid him?" Ysidro, she thought, should hear me now.

The black eyes glittered, chips of coal. She could see the dark line of downturned mouth amid the tangled beard, hear the anger in his voice when he replied, but she saw, in the set of his shoulders, the way he drew back from her and looked, for one fleeting instant, past Razumovsky to the courtyard gate, that he was afraid.

"You are the wife of the Ingileezee in the brown clothing, the man who asked all the questions about the Deathless Lord."

Lydia nodded. She wondered how close Razumovsky was standing behind her and how much he heard. "I am."

"He was a fool," snapped the old storyteller. "To seek the residence of Wafat Sahib is the act of a fool, and a fool's fate overtook him."

"Did you tell him?"

The old man looked away. "I told him nothing," he said sharply, and Lydia knew he was lying. James had probably offered him money. With feet like that, and the characteristic roughening of pellegra on the skin of his face, he was beyond a doubt desperately poor.

"It was my boy Izahk," the storyteller went on, too quickly. "A discreet boy; one I thought too clever to be seen. But when he did not come back that night, I knew he had done that which is forbidden: he had spoken of Wafat Sahib, and that lord is not a lord to tolerate such chatter." His black eyes narrowed, and his voice, almost a whisper to begin with, sank lower still, so that Lydia had to draw close, within reach of the gusts of breath that smelled of strong coffee and rotting teeth.

"Wafat Sahib, he has been lord in this city since my great-grandfather's time and before. He knows what is said of him in the streets, even by light of day. Even for the Ingileezee to ask me, to offer me money—which of course I did not touch," he added loudly, "made me afraid. So I came here, out of the sight of the men who serve him. Now they tell me the *hortlak*, the *afrit*, the *göla*, have been seen among the tombs outside the city, walking among the cypress trees by the tomb of Hasim al-Bayad, stopping travelers who walk late upon the road and killing them in the darkness."

Ysidro? wondered Lydia, recognizing one of the words as the Turkish for *vampire*. Or had Ysidro in his search missed something, some clue? Been deceived by the concealing glamours of the vampire mind?

It was logical, she thought, for the challenger to Olumsiz Bey's power to haunt them, lying as they did outside the city walls. "Where is this tomb?" she asked, lowering her voice and hoping Razumovsky wasn't anywhere near.

"You are a fool!" The *hakâwati shaîr* flung up his arms, coal-chip eyes blazing with sudden rage. "As your husband was a fool before you! Go away, and ask no more, lest his fate befall you as well!"

"I'm not going to go there at night—" Lydia began to protest reasonably, but the old man surged toward her, slashing with his clawed and knotted hands.

"Go! Get out! I tell you that your husband is a dead man!"

She stumbled back, startled at this violence, and Razumovsky caught her; she heard Margaret squeak in alarm.

"Leave me, infidel whore!" the old man screamed. "How dare you defile the place of holiness by even the tread of your feet?"

"Really, I—"

"Come," the prince said softly and drew her toward the gate. "There's nothing more you can learn."

"I daresay," said Lydia, struggling between a sense of injury and a terrified desire to go back to the old storyteller, to try to learn more. There was something Ysidro hadn't seen in the cemetery . . . Something that occurred after he'd gone? She looked back over her shoulder, to see the *hakâwati shaîr* shouting his wrongs to the man selling beads, and though at this distance he was little more than a threshing puppet of dirty brown rags, she could tell he was pointing at her.

Sudden tears stung her eyes, born of weariness and frustration and the hurt of being criticized when she had done no wrong.

"Forgive him, madame." It was the man in the yellow turban, waiting for them in the blue marble shadows of the colonnade beside the gate. He stepped down and bowed to them, though Lydia had the impression that he was a man of some importance here. "He is an old man and believes that those who do not dress or eat or speak as his parents did were created by some other God for purposes ill to mankind."

Lydia halted, peering up at him. Above the graying beard the dark eyes were bright and kind, and not as old as she had thought. His robes smelled of tobacco, cooking, and soap. "I'm sorry if I . . . if I said something wrong. I truly meant no harm."

"He is a very frightened man, *hamam,* and frightened men are easily angered. He claims he is pursued by demons who live in this city, and he will not be alone, not even to sleep. He sleeps on the floor of the soup kitchen. Do not judge him harshly. They are real to him."

"No," Lydia said, remembering the abyssal darkness of the streets after nightfall. She had dreamed last night, in troubled sleep, of something that had passed the house, singing beneath the balcony in a high, thin, tuneless wailing that no one but she could hear. She had risen—or, later, she thought she had only dreamed of rising—and stumbled half blind to the heavy lattices that overhung the street, but she had seen nothing, or maybe just a stirring in the dark below. Margaret had rolled over and sighed in her sleep.

"He spoke of a . . . a *göla,* dwelling in the tomb of someone called Hasim al-Bayad." She pronounced the words carefully, thanking heaven for ten years of James' quiet emphasis on correct sounds.

The holy man frowned, puzzled a little, then said, "In the west of Africa—Morocco and Algiers—a *göla* is said to be a kind of female devil who dwells in desert places, with a goat's feet and the face of a beautiful woman. She lures travelers from the road, drinks their blood and eats their flesh."

"A woman." Lydia repeated the words.

Anthea Farren. And she would know what had become of James.

He nodded. "Hasim al-Bayad was the imam of this mosque—" His small gesture seemed to touch the whole of the graceful, weightless stone that towered above them. "—many generations ago. A good man whose tomb was venerated in former times, though almost none seek it out now, for it lies some distance from the Adrianople Gate, away to the north of the main road. You may know it by the remains of an iron fence around it, though it is decayed almost to nothing; but the tomb still stands. But if you value your life, *hamam*—if you value your soul—do not go to that place alone or after the sun has left the sky."

Looking into those dark, worried eyes, it did not even strike Lydia as odd that he gave his warning to her rather than to the male who clearly took the role of her protector. She shook her head and said, "No, I won't. I promise." She turned to depart, taking Razumovsky's arm again, then on impulse turned back.

"Is it permitted," she asked hesitantly, "to . . . to buy prayers to help someone? Someone who's in trouble? He's not a Mohammedan," she added apologetically, and the man in the yellow turban smiled.

"There is no greater miracle in the world than rain," he said. "And, as the Prophet Jesus pointed out, it falls on the heads of the just and the unjust alike. Give your alms to the next beggar that you meet. I will pray for your friend."

"Thank you," said Lydia.

Your husband is a dead man. It was extremely difficult to make conversation with the prince on the way back to the carriage.

Owing to the prince's consular duties that afternoon, it was not possible, he said, for him to accompany Lydia and Margaret on a tour of the cemeteries, but he insisted that they take the carriage and the footmen: "The silly louts would only sit around playing dominoes at some café in the Place d'Armes all afternoon while I'm dealing with the transport minister," he said, sipping his tea over lunch. "You ladies might as well have the use of them, provided you come back for me when you've finished."

Lunch meant the restaurant at the railway station, looking out through elaborately pillared window arches to the unkempt grass of the square. Not elegant, but the only European cuisine available without crossing the bridge to Pera again, and Margaret flatly refused to have anything to do with stuffed grape leaves or skewered bits of lamb. Lydia protested a little at the prince's generosity, then thanked him profusely, laying both her kid-gloved hands on his wrist and wishing she looked prettier. Her eyes still felt swollen and tender despite that morning's applications of ice. Her aunt Lavinia's sovereign remedy had always been leeches—applied by the disapproving Aunt Harriet or by Lydia herself, who had even at that age had no qualms about touching the things—but Lydia, though trained in their application, had learned too much about germ theory in the past few years to feel easy now about such an expedient. Certainly too much to want to apply anything purchased in Constantinople, no matter who warranted it "clean."

And she'd look even worse, she thought, once she got her spectacles on. Just as well Razumovsky couldn't accompany them on the next phase of her quest.

As the holy man had warned, the tomb of the imam Al-Bayad lay a goodish distance north of the dust-choked road that ran toward the hills of Thrace, and Lydia had to pick her way carefully among the bizarre, stunted forest of spiky tombstones, Margaret and one of His Highness' sturdy footmen in her wake. She was glad of the footman. Closer to the gate she had seen individuals or small groups of the devout, almost always clothed in the traditional Turkish garb of pantaloons, tunic, and turban, kneeling by the low-roofed stone *turbes* among the weeds, but this far out, among the rough stands of cypress and bare-limbed plane trees, there was no sign of people at all. Only the headstones, thrusting up through the weeds like splintered bones from a messy compound fracture. Even the dirt under-foot was mixed with chips and fragments.

Margaret complained constantly of the uneven footing, the dreariness of the locale, and the uselessness of the mission. "Ysidro said he'd seen nothing here," she protested, stopping for the tenth time to ostentatiously rub a "twisted" ankle, which Lydia knew wouldn't have borne her weight if actually twisted. "Ysidro ought to know."

Maybe, thought Lydia. But Ysidro had said himself that his perceptions were not what they had been. Moreover, there was always a chance that the vampire glamour was stronger than he had counted on, and subtler, masking its own existence, as it had masked her awareness of Ysidro's house in London as she walked past it three times before she finally saw it. Whether she found anything at Al-Bayad's tomb today or not, she would tell him of the place and let him take a closer look.

Against the changing hues of the sky, the tall domes of the city gleamed; the silence here away from the road, instead of seeming peaceful, oppressed her with an air of waiting, of lis-tening. The short autumn day was already beginning to fade.

I've seen your husband . . . Karolyi had said.

If he'd been telling the truth.

And the *hakâwati shaîr: Your husband is a dead man.*

There'd been a note from Karolyi this morning, asking to take her to lunch. Of course, Lady Clapham would see no reason not to tell him where she was staying. She wondered if she should go, to see what else she could learn from him, but all her instincts cried out to her to stay as far from the man as she could. She was a novice, unable to best him in the game he'd played for years.

But what if Zeittelstein doesn't come back tomorrow? she thought, faint and helpless. *What if what he tells me is no help?* The sense of holding her husband's life in her hands, of not knowing if any action of hers would save or damn him, was hideous. Maybe if she were very careful with Karolyi . . .

A man called out to her, far off, near the road. With her spec-tacles on he was jewel-clear, waving his arms in warning, but he would not approach.

She looked ahead again and saw the grayish-white square of the *turbe*, surrounded with a few grisly fragments of rusted fence.

Weeds grew thick around the marble, whispering conspiratorially in the wind. As she approached, the smell of blood came to her, thin but rank; cold as it was, flies buzzed up in a swarm from a nearly black stain on a broken grave slab nearby.

Lydia shivered. It might, she supposed, only have been a dog's. Margaret cried, "Oh! How disgusting!" and Nikolai the footman said, "Madame, is come away. Is no good here. No good."

Lydia walked up and put her hands on the tomb.

There were fresh scratches on the stone around the heavy lid, bright marble chips lying in the long weeds. Kneeling, she peered at a stain just beneath the lid's edge, hidden under the mass of marble; she thought it, too, was blackened blood.

But all of those things came to her like afterthoughts. As soon as she touched the marble, she knew.

He is here, she thought. The marble was cold under her fingertips. *He is here.* If she stood still, if she listened, if she closed her eyes, breathed slow, opened her mind, she could hear him . . .

She stepped swiftly back, almost colliding with Margaret, who had come up behind her, saying something—she realized she had been listening so deeply that she hadn't heard what.

We usually have warning of their suspicions, Ysidro had once told James, on the subject of would-be vampire hunters. *We see them poking about . . .*

She wondered now whether he had meant during the night hours, or by day, when the vampire lay sunk in deathly sleep.

Did vampires dream?

"I *said*, can we go now?" Margaret repeated sulkily. "If Ysidro didn't see anything here . . ."

A thought flashed through Lydia's mind—she knew not from where—of a dark face lying in darkness, not very far away. Of sleep that wasn't really sleep.

Of someone, or something, that knew her name in its dreams.

"Yes," she said quickly. "Let's go."

As she was turning away, a glint of red caught her eye, lying in the long grass. She didn't want to go near the tomb again, but she forced herself and saw that the weeds along this side of it had been trampled. In the grayish dust she found the track of a man's hard-edged Western shoe.

Fairly fresh, she thought. Curiously fresh, for a place that had recently acquired the reputation as the haunt of *hortlak*.

Kneeling in the dusty weeds, she cast about for more tracks and saw the bright thing that had drawn her attention a moment ago.

It was a man's cravat pin, fashioned in the shape of a griffin, with a single blood-ruby eye.

"My dearest Asher Sahib." A shadow materialized in the archway in front of him, nearly invisible in the darkness of the old *han*'s court; an angular silhouette, and the gleam of far too many jewels. At the same moment, as Asher stopped, his heart tightening in his chest, arms slipped around his waist from behind, the thin hard body of Jamila Baykus pressing against his back, like the steel triggering mechanism of some lethal trap. The stench of blood in her jeweled hair mingled with the wash of Zardalu's patchouli.

"You left our party precipitously."

"I have a weak stomach."

"*Tcha.*" The eunuch made the word almost a caress. "Pity for a beautiful young man like the one last week, maybe, or for that little beggar girl, who I admit was pretty . . . But that ugly old grandmother? I swear to you she was still complaining over being cheated out of two piastres' worth of olives in the market. Now, how can you pity that?"

Asher turned his face aside and moved to go, but the arms around his waist, thin as a child's, held him. He knew no amount of struggle would break their grip.

Zardalu stepped forward into the colonnade, laid his hands on Asher's shoulders. Under their painted lids, the long eyes glittered in the distant glint of the lamp by the stairs. There was no other light in the court, and Sayyed, who had as usual been dogging Asher's steps, had vanished at the first sound of Zardalu's voice. "Olumsiz Bey hasn't been out of the compound," the eunuch said softly, in the vampire whisper no louder than the whisper of a silk curtain on an—almost—windless night. "Has he?"

"I don't know."

"This is the eighth night that he's had us bring him his kill." Tiny breasts, sharp hipbones moved against his buttocks and back, the Baykus Kadine rising to tiptoe so that the movement of her lips stirred against the back of his neck. They were warm. "These other vampires—"

"What other vampires?"

"It is scarcely any affair of the living," Zardalu murmured, drawing close, "what other vampires. The woman we seek in the tombs and the cisterns—the man we are told to look for . . ."

"What man? Since when?"

"Does it matter since when?" The blue eyes glittered strangely in the reflected light. "I see that it does. Why does it matter? What does it tell you, clever one? Why does he fear them? The Malik of Stamboul, the Wafat Sahib, the Deathless Lord who has ruled this city . . . He could crush them like fleas under his thumbnail. So." The long hands tightened over Asher's shoulders, the pressure of the thumbs like a geared wheel bearing on the collarbone; Asher shut his teeth hard against the blinding stab of pain, kept his eyes on the vampire's before him.

"This foreign machine, built by these infidels . . . What is it? Who is it that he keeps down there, groaning and crying out in the dark hours of the night?"

"Ask him." It was impossible to keep his voice steady; the steel thumbs had found the nerves they sought, and Asher had to fight to keep his vision from graying to darkness, his mind from blanking with pain.

"I'm asking you."

"I don't know."

The pressure lessened; Zardalu moved back a few inches, his hands remaining where they were. Asher was breathing hard, the sweat flowing cold down the sides of his face, though the night was chilly.

"But you've gone to look?"

Asher managed to shake his head, wondering if they had seen him, passing the archway last night, or smelled his blood. Wondering if they had told Olumsiz Bey. He doubted it. He doubted that he would be alive now, had the Master of Constantinople known.

Zardalu grinned like a rubber devil. "For a man who went about the town questioning storytellers about the houses of evil rumor, you show a disappointing lack of curiosity. Do you know that Olumsiz Bey keeps a set of silver keys in a recess in the floor beneath the coffee table in the room of the red tiles? No? A curious thing for a vampire to keep, wouldn't you say?"

"Not something he could readily use," Asher agreed. The Jamila Baykus moved, trying to draw him with her, and he braced his feet on the broken tiles. "Not something I would use at all. I do value my life."

"Your life?" The blue eyes widened. The silvery vampire laughter shivered in the air. "Your life? Your life ends here in this court if I so wish."

"You'd go against him?" Darkness swirled on the edges of his mind, blanking his attention, confusing his thoughts, as if he moved in a suffocating dream. Deliberately, he walled his mind against it, thought of nothing, pictured iron doors closing the darkness out, sunlight burning it away.

From far off he felt Zardalu's hands shift up to his throat, heard the vampire say, "He'll be displeased, but it won't make you less dead, Englis . . ."

He thought they were dragging him, threw out his hand to catch at the arch as they drew him into the dust-smelling blindness of one of the old warehouse bays. It was like fighting in a dream, against a narcotic weight of nothingness that filled his mind. If he could only break free for a moment . . .

Then he was thrown aside, striking the wall as if someone had hammered him with a railroad tie, and his mind cleared like shattering glass. Against the reflected lamplight he saw Zardalu hurled sprawling, a bundle of sticks wrapped in a hundred pounds' worth of sequined silk, and the Baykus Kadine backing away, mouth open, hissing, her eyes glittering rat-red. In a swirl of nacreous robes, Olumsiz Bey stood over the Circassian, the silver blade of his halberd cold as a fingernail moon. His bald head swung to and fro, like a savage dog's.

There was blood on his mouth and on his clothing. Zardalu rolled lightly to his feet, face twisted into something Asher hadn't seen outside a Museum of Horrors, fangs glittering in the stretched mouth. But the next moment the younger vampire flinched and turned away, hiding his face in his hands from the master vampire's glare, and Asher felt—guessed—sensed peripherally the cutting agony of Olumsiz Bey's will.

Zardalu made a sound, thin as water twisted out of a near-dry rag. His body bent and bent, knees buckling, hands spreading, fingers stretching, trying to cover his face as his arms came up like the arms of a fractured puppet.

Softly, the master vampire whispered, "Don't be arrogant, little Apricot." Asher, slumped against the stones of the inner wall, wasn't even sure he heard the words spoken, could not have said what language they were in. Weightless as a giant cat Olumsiz Bey stepped toward the crumpled gaudy form of the eunuch, and the dim lamplight flicked on his outstretched talons, the graceful gesture of the halberd.

"Is this the little Apricot who wept in my arms when he gave up his life? The little Apricot who said to the slave masters, when they came to geld him . . ."

No . . . It came out not even as a word, only a sound.

"I remember, you know." The deep voice purled over the words, water over stones, and stronger than the stones. "You put all those memories into my hands, you put your mind, your desires—remember Parvin, your sister Parvin?—everything. And I still hold them." He crouched over his fledgling, silver-blue robes settling over the gay, amorphous clouds of silk, the silver of the blade hovering over the bare, bent neck. It was impossible, thought Asher, that he should still hear the master vampire's voice.

"The way the Kizlir Aga touched you, do you remember that? You were twelve, and you hated him, and yet your whole body responded . . ." His coarse hand fielded, easily, the vicious flail of Zardalu's claws, and with the haft of the halberd he thrust him to the pavement again, pressing him down into the marble with it, straddling him, whispering, an act more terrible than love or rape, an act of dreadful possession as each memory, each feeling, each most secret terror and need was brought forth.

It gives a terrible power, Ysidro had once told him, in that time-faded voice that denied that such a thing had ever happened to him, that anyone had ever held over his heart such hideous knowledge.

Zardalu had begun to make noises, and silently, sickened, Asher crept back through the shadows to climb at last the long stairs. Looking back, he saw in the lighted frame of the arched passage to the vestibule that the brutish Habib and his one-eyed janissary friend Haralpos were enacting a burlesque love scene with the corpse of the old woman they had brought for the Deathless Lord's supper, to the screams of Pelageya's and the Baykus' laughter.

But it was the master vampire's whispering, rather than the other and louder sounds, that seemed to follow Asher up the black stairs.

EIGHTEEN

SHE dreamt of the old seraglio again, of wandering through its cramped, lightless cells with a ledger in one hand and a lantern in the other. One of the rooms had been filled with ice, and holding the lantern aloft, she had seen Jamie, frozen in a block of it, like a fly trapped in amber.

It should have been comical, absurd, but it wasn't. His eyes were open, sunken like the eyes of the corpses the workhouse sent, and she saw blood on his neck, staining the open collar of his shirt. The ice flashed like blue diamonds when she raised her lantern, making his eyes seem to move, but she knew he was dead. Her heart twisted, slammed within her, hurting, hurting, knowing he was dead and that she'd have to go home alone.

It was her fault. She hadn't come swiftly enough, been clever enough, been brave enough . . . She had failed to be adequate, as she had failed all her life. She propped the ledger against the block, trying desperately to find his name in it, but the cold in the room made her hands shake so badly she couldn't read. He can't be dead, she thought frantically, he can't be. He's frozen in the ice, but the ice will keep him alive . . .

She woke gasping, her hands and feet bitter cold, and heard, from the other room, Margaret saying, "You hadn't found anything there, but she insisted on going anyway! As if she knew

273

more about it than you did! Just because she's got that horrid medical degree, and cuts up bodies, which makes me shudder just to think about, she thinks she knows everything! And she wouldn't even stop when I turned my foot . . ."

Under the indignation of Margaret's voice there was a brittleness that Lydia recognized as nervousness. *Ysidro,* she thought.

A moment later the vampire's cool voice responded, "Well, she is worried about her husband, and perhaps that made her careless of your comforts, Margharita? You do not recall which cemetery this was? I would not wish to waken her."

"Um . . . I can't remember . . . We went in Prince Razumovsky's carriage, after we visited this filthy mosque and she talked to a horrid old man. And anyway, if you didn't see anything there when you went . . ."

Lydia fumbled her spectacles from the bed beside her, pushed back her hair and pulled her shawl about her shoulders as she emerged from the bedroom, rumpled, creased, and slightly disoriented, wondering what time it was.

Ysidro was on his feet at once, bowing. "Mistress." The room smelled of lamb and onions. There was an empty plate of very fine red-glazed local ware, and horn-and-steel flatware. Crumbs and droplets at the other side of the table indicated that Margaret had made her meal.

Lydia shook her head, saying, "Later, thank you," when Ysidro moved toward the sideboard.

"Some wine, at least?"

But his own hand was too unsteady to hold the glass.

Margaret took it swiftly from him, poured the black-red fluid like blood in the brazen lamplight. Ysidro flicked aside the napkin from the basket on the table, tore a chunk from the bread inside. "Sop it in the wine," he suggested, holding it out to her. "A jauntering slut I can abide, but a drunken jauntering slut, never."

And Lydia gave him a quick, shaky grin.

He perched on a corner of the table. "Margharita informs me you passed an adventuresome day."

Lydia outlined to him the events of the Blue Mosque and the

finding of the *turbe* and the cravat pin. "I had the most extraordinary sensation that he was there, listening," she said. "I know you've said vampires sleep in the daytime and can't be wakened, but ... Would he have heard me—*seen* me—in dreams? Do vampires dream?"

"Yes and no," replied Ysidro, holding out his hand for the pin. "Sleep is only a term that we use for what happens to us when the sun is in the sky; I do not know another. Dreaming ..." He paused, then shook his head, very slightly, and turned the tiny gold griffin over in his hands.

"I doubt not that you have found one of the sleeping places of the intruder, the newcomer," he said after a time. "And having sensed you in his sleep, I misdoubt he will ever rest in that tomb again. Still, it is worth the visiting, to see perhaps what I have missed. There is a great strength to him, and it is not at all unlikely that he could turn my mind, my perceptions, away from him ... And it goes without saying that any place he dominates with his presence at night, Anthea will avoid. It is no chance thing that he haunts the cemeteries, that any coming or going from the city would pass him and be in danger of coming under his sway. Anthea, at least, coming in by train with your husband, would have sensed his presence and taken care to avoid him. Charles ..." He shook his head.

"He plays a dangerous game, this Karolyi." He slipped the griffin pin into the pocket of his waistcoat and stood to fetch a pot of honey from the sideboard and set it for her next to the bread. "He still does not understand what it is that he courts. Does he think to take this interloper back to Vienna and introduce him to that stodgy mediocrity in the Hofburg? The Master of Vienna will surely destroy him, as he attempted to destroy Ernchester. Or does he think to make him Master of Constantinople, forge an alliance here?"

"Could he do that?" she asked, surprised.

"He may, could he find the master's hiding place." The sparse brows pinched together, and his eyes went to the pile of notes and pencils on the other side of the table lamps. "And what did your search reveal?"

"That a lot of wealthy old Turks who'd had their money in

gold and land all had the same idea around July of this year."
She sighed ruefully and pushed her glasses up onto her nose.
"I've got a tremendous list of companies that all came into
being at the same time and don't seem to have any reason to
exist. Besides, I know from Herr Hindl that the Bey paid for his
refrigeration unit in cash."

"True enough." Ysidro lifted the lid of the honey pot,
brought up a spoonful, and let it run down again in a column of
shining amber. "Yet at short notice he would have used a bank
draft. I believe a ticket on the Orient Express is twenty pounds?
Another two pounds to London, plus the costs of hotels and
meals . . . maybe a total of sixty pounds? Find a draft of that, to
someone of Hungarian name. Even incognito, a noble will usually take one of his lesser titles. Karolyi's are Leukovina,
Feketelo, and Mariaswalther, if I recall my genealogies aright.
My guess is he will have used one of those." Ysidro covered
the honey again and stood; Margaret sprang up to fetch his
cloak, which lay like a dense black winding sheet over a
nearby chair.

She asked brightly, "Will you be back tonight?"

Ysidro seemed to settle into stillness, considering her with
eyes that looked, in the lamplight, as gold as the honey. "My
errand should take me no great time." He pulled on his gloves
and held out one hand to Lydia. "It is true that the Dead travel
fast."

It was still impossible to see him leave a room.

"Frankly, I've always wondered how they do," remarked
Lydia, spooning honey onto a chunk of bread. "And considering the fuss he made about traveling in the daytime . . ."

But the slamming of the bedroom door was her only answer.

For a moment Lydia considered knocking and asking what real
or fancied slight Margaret suffered from now. But it would
only provoke another tantrum, another spate of incoherent
romanticism about the eternal bond carried across lifetimes,
and she felt simply too weary to go through with it. Margaret
had coolly refused Lydia's offer yesterday of instruction in the
intricacies of cosmetic art. Lydia was still unsure whether she

was being blamed for Ysidro's absence from Margaret's dreams, for finding clues where Ysidro had missed them, or for some other offense entirely.

And indeed, she thought with a stirring of old anger, it was Ysidro's fault as much as Margaret's. More, in fact, for originating the whole silly vaudeville of romance and need and lies. She put from herself in disgust the concern she had been feeling for him and ladled lamb and stuffed aubergines onto her plate, cursing Ysidro tiredly for his command that for safety the girls share bedroom and bed. It was not anything she was looking forward to tonight.

The meal made her feel better. She spread out her papers again, jotting down the names Ysidro had mentioned and seeking them among the lists of drafts drawn at the end of October, but it was difficult to keep her mind on her work. She was angry at Ysidro and, she realized, hurt. Disillusioned. But what illusion had she held, she wondered, that she felt robbed of it now?

The illusion that behind those bleached, crystalline eyes still lurked a living man's smile?

Don Simon Xavier Christian Morado de la Cadena-Ysidro had been dead since 1558.

She recalled the books on his parlor chest. A dead man might read medical journals, and mathematics texts, and volumes of logic. But would a dead man read the stories of Toad and Ratty and Mole? She took off her spectacles, leaned her forehead on her hands. And why should it matter to her whether he was dead inside or alive?

In the street below, the dogs began to bark.

Lydia raised her head, startled, and looked at the clock. It was nearly three. Had she been asleep, she wondered, since Margaret's huffy departure, or had she wakened from her first sleep later than she'd thought?

Below in the street, someone pounded on the outer gate.

"*Hamam, hamam!*" cried a voice, vaguely familiar, though she could not have said from where. "*Hamam*, it is your husband! Your husband!"

She jerked to her feet, ran to the window that overlooked the street. She pushed aside the chains of garlic and wild rose that hung there, unhooked the heavy lattice; down below she could see a cluster of dim shapes in a lantern's blurry light.

"Where?"

"Your husband!" cried the man below. "Find you, he say."

The *hakâwati shaîr*, she thought. The man in the yellow turban. Catching up the lamp from the table, she paused only long enough to snatch her silver knife as a precautionary measure and then ran downstairs. They'd want money, she thought, stepping through the door out into the carriageway. As the light of the lamp jostled huge shadows over the carriageway's vaulted roof, she thought, *Good heavens, they could be thieves for all I know . . .*

She stood on tiptoe to slide back the cover of the judas in the main gate, and tried to hold the lamp so that light would illuminate the faces of those who stood outside.

There was no one in the street.

Behind her, the house door slammed.

Lydia whirled, her breath stopping in her lungs—a glance showed her that both the main outer gate and the small postern were firmly locked and bolted. The silence seemed suddenly, dreadfully alive. She strode back toward the door, cold with terror, pulling the silver table knife from her belt . . .

The lamp in her hand went out.

Instinct more than anything else made her flatten at once to the wall. Shadow moved in the dark arch where the carriageway let into the little courtyard, where fallen pomegranate leaves made spots like dripped blood in the thin moonlight; she threw the lamp with all her force in that direction and heard it strike something soft, then shatter on the pavement. In that instant she flung herself to the door, yanked the handle, and felt the heavy jar of the bolt.

She whirled and slashed at the shadow that she felt more than saw suddenly beside her. She slashed, felt it give, turn before her. For an instant crushing pressure seized her wrist, a hand hideously strong closed over her throat, and with her mind swimming in a curious, hazy dream state she saw a face close to hers: smooth, full, olive-complected, fangs gleaming behind a thick mustache.

Then he cried, *"Orospu!"* and his hand jerked away, and she cut at his face again, knowing she couldn't let him get near enough to take her by the elbow, the waist, someplace where she wasn't wearing silver. She tried to scream, but it came out thick and tiny, like a child's wailing in a dream; a vision flashed through her mind of letting him seize her, of wanting to feel those iron arms holding her, pressing her close to that iron chest.

She cut again at his face and cursed as hands seized her arms above the elbow, gasped out the worst word she'd ever heard from the grave diggers who brought bodies into the infirmary for dissection and felt the claws tear her arms, ripping through her sleeves. She kicked and slashed and cursed at the face that she saw now as if through the muzzy darkness of a dream.

There were two of them, she thought, blindly terrified, hacking and twisting against a grip like devil-inhabited stone. Two of them, two faces in the patchy moon shadows . . .

Then she was alone, leaning against the stuccoed wall with the knife shaking in her hand.

Her sleeves were torn, the blood shockingly hot against flesh that seemed to be getting colder by the minute.

I can't go into shock, she thought, from what seemed like a great distance off. *I can't let myself . . .*

"Madonna . . ." Darkness came out of the deeper dark behind her, though she hadn't heard the gate open or close—a glint of eyes and the smoke of pale hair. Cold hands seized her arms, icy despite the frost that seemed to be spreading through her own flesh. She sobbed something, she didn't know what, pressed her face to the damp wool of a cloak that smelled of dew and graveyards, as if its weight could save her from the fanged brown face that had come so close to hers.

She was unable to breathe, barely felt the cold, gloved hands that thrust her hair back from her face, touched her neck. "Are you hurt?"

The words had no meaning to her. She considered them from a great distance away, turning them—for she seemed to have all the time in the world—one way and another, like a rare bone. Was she hurt? she wondered. For a moment she floated weightless against him, conscious, it seemed, of the skeleton within his clothing, like Death in his winding sheet . . . conscious of almost nothing else. She heard him say her name, or thought she did, and looking up she saw, at some unbridgeable distance, the face of a living man.

He called her name again, and she gasped, shaken, disoriented, but alive once more, and stepped back quickly from him so that he had to catch her elbow to keep her from falling.

"I'm so sorry," she managed to say. She looked around the courtyard. Everything seemed very distant and odd, as if nothing had anything to do with her. Shock, she diagnosed. The silver knife lay on the ground at her feet, the smashed lamp beneath the pomegranate tree. She wondered how much it would cost to replace. "I didn't mean—"

"Are you hurt?"

Her blood gleamed all over his gloves from the talon rakes of her arms, but she knew he didn't mean that. "No."

"You're sure?"

She nodded and felt her throat. She'd unbuttoned her high collar before she'd taken her nap, but the chains of silver were still there, close against the untouched skin. She bent to pick up the knife and nearly fell; he caught her in his arms as if she'd been a child, and with a single, vicious kick cracked the door bolt and carried her inside.

"You're freezing." He set her in a chair in the small downstairs hall; shut the door again and put a second chair under its latch to hold it. Then he turned back to her and wrapped her in the pall of his cloak. "And afraid."

The fear she felt was only now coming into focus; she had not been conscious of much during the attack itself. She wondered why.

In the drift of light from the lamp on the landing he looked at his hands, gloved in leather and blood. With a quick gesture he tore the gloves off and threw them on the stairs, and vanished through the dark doorway into the kitchen. He came back a few moments later, coatless and carrying a pottery basin of water and another lamp, which Lydia found profoundly comforting. As he set the lamp on the hall table, he paused to listen at the foot of the stairs, and for some reason she remembered him, white-robed and barefoot, picking knacker's meat from its paper for his cats.

"She is safe," he said, his voice very soft. "They have not been inside. My apologies for the water. The boiler is long cold."

Lydia wondered what he heard of Margaret's breathing: the peaceful snuffling of sleep or the swift, thready pant of guilt and fear and feelings hideously torn? She looked across at the door bolt, but even had the glow of the single lamp been stronger, the violence of Ysidro's breaking in had shaken loose the hasp from the bar, and it was impossible to tell whether the bolt had been shot behind her when she'd gone out, or had merely somehow slipped.

He put the cloak back from her arms, pulled the remains of the sleeve free with a single flick of his hand and reached into the basin for a sponge. The wounds were little more than scratches, but smarted horribly. Lydia flinched from the water, which was, as Ysidro had hinted, stone cold.

"I saw the interloper," she said, gritting her teeth. To her own vast annoyance she had begun to tremble again and couldn't seem to stop. With grim effort she kept her voice steady. A woman in hysterics was the last thing either of them needed. Besides, he'd want the information quickly. "He's a Turk, I think, I . . . I didn't get a clear look. Here," she added suddenly, realizing how disturbing he must find the smell of blood, "I'll do that. There's some brandy in the pantry . . ."

He'd brought napkins as well, but she was unable to bind up her own arms with them and had to wait till he returned after all.

"There were two of them," she resumed, while he pinned the bandages, white fingers neat and swift and chill as the touch of death. "I think . . . I didn't see the other clearly but I don't think he was a Turk."

"Was he vampire?"

She hadn't thought of that. "I . . . I don't know."

Their voices echoed strangely in the well of the hallway, shadows leaning over them, monstrous and upside down. Ysidro left again, carrying the basin and sponge. When he returned, he held a cup of tea cradled in his hands, the smell of it gently neutral, like sunlight on grass. "They . . . they called to me from the street . . . Or I thought someone called to me from the street. They said Jamie needed me."

"I doubt there was ever anyone in the street," Ysidro said softly. "He will have felt your mind, a little, at the tomb, and with that little he could fool you about what you saw in darkness. You were right, the *turbe* of Al-Bayad was one of his sleeping places . . . He will have others."

"But you found nothing of Anthea? Or Ernchester?"

"Nothing." He went to the hall table and stood for a moment, holding his hand near the flame of the lamp there to warm it. The fire, moving in its little red-glass bowl, lent his fingers, his hair, the skull-like ridges of his no-longer-human face a mockery of sunburnt health.

"Like him, she will change her sleeping place from night to night, and his glamour will work on her mind as well, hiding him from her, even as it hides her from the Master of Constantinople—and hides her from me. If your husband is alive at all, it is because the Master of Constantinople seeks to use him as bait to trap her, for he fears her, even as Grippen does."

"Grippen?" said Lydia. "Isn't he her master, as he is Ernchester's?"

"It is not unheard of, for fledglings to turn against those that get them."

He turned his hand over. The light seemed to shine through his fingers like parchment, illuminating spidery bones. "It takes great strength, and great anger . . . but then, Anthea *is* strong. He has always distrusted her, as all masters distrust their get; and between Anthea and Grippen has always lain a most delicate balance of wariness, and power, and hate. I do not think he would have made her vampire had not he thought he would lose Charles when Anthea, still a mortal woman, died."

"So they didn't . . . they weren't made vampires at the same time."

"No. Charles was forty, Anthea thirty-three, when Grippen took Charles. Anthea was a widow for over thirty years. She had grown old when Charles finally came for her—or got Grippen to come. She hated Grippen for holding the dominance of a master over her, but she understood that it was the gate she had to walk through if she would be with Charles again. It is . . . a rather sad tale. Will you have more?"

She shook her head. As he took the cup from her, she saw how his clothing hung on him, as if there were nothing inside it but bones. The turned-back cuffs of his shirt showed wrist bones knobbed like hazelnuts under milk-white skin.

"Thank you," she said softly.

He made a move, as if he would take her hand, then stopped himself. For a long time their eyes held, and she thought, quite irrationally, *There is something else to say.*

It was he who moved his face aside, still for a moment, then turning fully to look at the door. "I will remain here until it nears dawn, though I doubt he will be back. Tomorrow the bolt of the door can be repaired, and things placed about the doorsills and the windows that he cannot pass. I have no doubt he learned from Karolyi that you were here and wanted to put you under his influence—to force you to tell what Karolyi has been trying to persuade from you, did you but know it."

Lydia shivered, thinking of the long climb to the bedroom. Even Margaret's presence in the bed beside her seemed welcome now.

Ysidro put his head a little to one side, listening. "She sleeps now." He started to speak again, then didn't, as if he, like Lydia for the moment, did not wish to raise the issue of Margaret, and his use of Margaret, between them.

There is something else, Lydia thought again as they stood together, looking at one another in the lamplight. But Ysidro turned away and settled himself in the chair she had occupied, folding his bony arms within the shirt that seemed too large for him. Lydia slipped the cloak from her shoulders, and when he took it, slowly climbed the stairs.

As Ysidro had said, Margaret was asleep. She'd loosened her corsets and pulled the pins from her hair but still was dressed, as if she'd fallen asleep huddled wretchedly on top of the covers, and in the glow of the bedside lamp her face was taut with unhappy dreams. Lydia's hands shook as she unbuttoned her torn shirtwaist, for reaction was settling on her. She had no intention of turning out the lamp beside the bed, but it was too bright for easy sleep. As she walked around to it, she saw half a dozen sheets of paper on the floor around Margaret's basket of crocheted flowers.

They were tumbled untidily, as if she had been reading them when sleep overcame her and they'd slid from the coverlet. When Lydia picked them up, she saw the handwriting, precise and black and, though the ink was clearly modern, nothing that had been seen since the days of Elizabeth.

They were sonnets.

About darkness. About mirrors. About roads untrodden stretching endlessly into night. One of them Margaret had ripped into quarters. Lydia had to lay it on the nightstand to fit its pieces together again.

And she understood.

Blood on marble—petals of a rose—
Or copper-dark upon the lion's paw;
Brightness and heat, like wine drunk red and raw.
Wine vends dreams, but life in lifeblood flows.
Thus warmth from flesh to flesh the blood imparts,
A ruby heat reviving life and mind.
Where can hunger better substance find
Than sanguine fire drawn from living hearts?
  I've seen a brightness dwells not in the veins—
  In thinking eyes, and smiles that shame despair.
  Color and heat beyond what blood contains—
  Rose and copper in cheek and lips and hair.
  But flesh that can't be warmed by such a fire
  To only blood and silence may aspire.

The papers were creased, as if they'd been wadded small— hidden in the crochet basket, she thought, or in Margaret's carpetbag. She wondered at what point Margaret had found them and pocketed them for her own.

She laid them back on the floor where they had been and turned down the light.

NINETEEN

A CURIOUS thing for a vampire to keep.

And so they were. Two silver keys, cut in exact replica of English Yales, even to the finger grips. Asher stared at them for a long time, as they shimmered in the concealed well in the red-tiled coffee room's floor.

Local work. Probably just enough admixture of bronze to keep them from bending in a lock. Reaching down, he weighed them in his hands. Even with gloves, a vampire would have difficulty holding them long enough to use. One as old as the master of the city might just manage, as he managed to hold the whitethorn of his halberd staff, to wear the thickly sheathed silver knife around his neck.

Asher's heart pounded hard as he slipped them into the pocket of his coat. As he pushed the tile cover back over the well, returned the black and white table to its place, the shadows of his single candle seemed to lean closer, silent with a terrible, listening silence in which the Master of Constantinople seemed to be standing just outside the door.

This was not the case, he knew. Olumsiz Bey was meeting that night with one of his men of business and had himself escorted Asher back to his gallery after supper and locked him in. "I apologize," the vampire said, "for my Zardalu last night. He is treacherous and insolent, like most of the palace eunuchs. He needed a good thrashing, to make him remember his love for me." The amber eyes narrowed as they studied Asher's face. In the ambiguous flicker of the pierced lamp the Master of Constantinople had seemed wrought entirely of amber, the dusky pallor of his flesh like copal, the many-pleated silken trousers and the tunic over them, the vest and the sash all warm shades of fire and honey and marigold, the fur-lined pelisse sewn with shining flecks of gold. The lump of amber swinging from his earlobe caught the light like an unnerving third eye.

"I trust you understand that he is a liar," Olumsiz Bey went on. "He never imparts information which is not aimed at starting prey."

"He's certainly told me a number of odd things about this house." Asher folded his arms, returned the orange gaze; even in his own mind the picklocks under the carpets did not exist. "Twice he's told me the way out." This was a lie, to see what the master would say. Olumsiz Bey's eyebrows bent in the middle like startled diacritical marks, and the hard mouth quirked in laughter.

"I observe you didn't go seeking. Sayyed wouldn't be difficult to overpower."

"The way he told me was different the second time," Asher said. "I've heard them talk about the games they play with their prey, chasing them through the dark here; I've heard those poor young boys and girls screaming."

Another diacritical mark, this time in the corner of those colorless lips, and Asher thought, It was not his custom then, to have his prey brought him by the others. It was something recent.

Zardalu was right.

Something was holding him to this house.

Ernchester? he wondered now, working his way carefully around the walls of the Roman court, that he would not leave a trampling in the overgrown grass. It made no sense. Why send for Ernchester now, why not a year ago, or a hundred years ago? Why not in July, when the Sultan's regime was over-thrown? If it was to ask his help against the interloper of whom Zardalu spoke, why keep him locked in the crypts? Starving, perhaps, in pain certainly—the moans were cries of the most hideous torment.

Revenge?

Asher shivered, feeling his way from pillar to pillar of the old porch, for he'd blown out his candle. The Bey's revenges would be long.

But long enough for him to summon the old earl from his moldering town house in London, from the slow crumbling of his life, back to the city where he'd spent eighteen months a living man? What ill turn would have warranted that, after almost two hundred fifty years?

And what did the interloper have to do with any of this?

What about the machine the Bey was having constructed? Or the ice Asher had seen, melting on the floor behind the silver bars?

It crossed his mind obliquely to wonder if the revenge was against Anthea, and not against Ernchester at all.

"He is not on this train," Anthea had said, coming back into his compartment while the flat lands of Hungary swept by in the darkness. That had been late the first night of the journey from Vienna. Exhausted, half sick with the coffee the porter had brought, his head aching and every clack of the well-sprung wheels reverberating as if slaved to some infernal machine inside his skull, Asher had watched her shed the long black-fringed shawl and put back the spotted gauze of veils. She seemed beautiful to him beyond words, staring at the molten ink of the window glass. The only light on the length of the Orient Express was theirs, and now and then it tossed threads of illusory fire on the wind-lashed weeds beside the track. Not even the moon remained in the sky.

"Good." Asher set aside the book he'd been trying to read, a truly dreadful account of life and love in Nero's Rome; tried to set aside at the same time the stirring within him of protectiveness and desire. He kept his voice deliberately casual. "It means we've got every chance of reaching Constantinople before him. 'The Dead travel fast,' Goethe says—but few things travel faster than the Orient Express. If he left Vienna by any other route, even by another train the minute he got away from the sanitarium, he'll still be a day behind us. Would you know, when he enters the city?"

"I . . . don't know." She turned in her fingers the pearl buttons of her glove, a beautiful ghost in her blue and violet silk dress. He remembered the moonlight vampire girl in the woods outside the sanitarium and knew this dreadful warm surge of wanting for what it was—the lure to prey. Dimmer, more distant, almost certainly without her conscious volition, still it was there. He wanted her.

"I don't know what arrangement was made with this Olumsiz Bey," she went on after a moment. "I looked at the guidebook. There are smaller stations in the city before one reaches the main gare, and this . . . this Bey, this master . . . may have planned to meet him at one of them. I don't know whether it will be safe for me to watch the main gare through the night. Perhaps he will not enter the city by train at all. Charles never trusted trains, nor the Underground of London, never liked them and never rode them. And the city itself, its sounds and smells, will be . . . different."

She fell silent, her fingers in their lacy mitts resting still on the purple plush curtain, her brown eyes staring out into the night. Seeing the night with the night's own eyes.

"Even Paris is different from London," she said at length, as if speaking to herself. "In London I know it if a policeman takes an unfamiliar turning within two miles of any of our houses. I could find Charles did he sleep in the lowest subcellar, did he walk the most obscure back way, did he haunt the steeple of St. Paul's or the warehouses of Whitechapel—given time. Vienna was more different still, chaos, a game without rules. Constantinople . . ."

She shook her head, but in her voice Asher heard the tremor, not of fear, but of excitement, of joy.

"It's strange," she went on, her voice so low that it should have been barely audible. "I should be terrified. Outside of London I'm a snail dispossessed of its shell, a rabbit with all her earths stopped. And yet all I feel is delight. The lights on the Alexander Bridge in Paris, like being inside a star; all the voices and music and scents of Vienna, making me drunk as I walked along the Ring. I know I could be destroyed in seconds, but all I wanted to do was dance and laugh and take off my hat and swing it around by its veils, just to be . . . just to be somewhere else. Seeing something new, something wonderful that I'd never seen. I don't know if you can understand that."

"Maybe not fully," Asher said. "I've never been dead."

"That's what being alive is, isn't it?" She turned toward him and reached up to pull out the jet and steel pins that held her hat to the close-folded raven universe of her hair.

Asher nodded, understanding something else about her now, and the desire he felt was softened and transmuted to pity. "You never wanted to be a vampire, did you?"

She hesitated, the hat like a dark bouquet overflowing her hands. "Oh, I did," she said. "The sharpening, the deepening, the enriching of the senses . . . one drowns in the color of silk, or the scent of coffee, or the weeping of the fiddles in distant night. Or the smell of blood, of sweat, of human fear. It is all the universe, as it never is to mortals, except maybe to a small child. It is living. And I wanted more than anything else not to leave Charles, ever. Once I came into it, I wanted it, craved it as a drunkard craves brandy." Her lips quirked ruefully; pale, Asher noted automatically. After Anthea had released him from her coffin, they had rushed onto the train with only minutes to spare, and Anthea knew well that every passenger was rich and expected at the other end, every porter and waiter accounted for.

"I gather people become vampires because they want life; they want life that won't stop, won't even pale as life does for the old." She stroked the ostrich plumes of the hat, curling them around her fingers, her eyes not meeting his. "But to be dead is to become . . . static. And that is what we all become. We do not travel because it is dangerous. We wall ourselves into our houses, our crypts, our secret ways, because sleeping in the hours of daylight, we are as if drugged. We ring ourselves with locks and traps and things that we can control, and destroy those things that we cannot. We become dead. Journeying like this . . ." She shook her head once more. "All new things are peril, peril of death—and maybe peril of death is one definition of life. Sometimes I feel that I shall never return to London again."

Asher remembered Cramer, who would have been one of the best if only he'd had the chance.

She stretched out her hand to him, her face gravely beautiful. He knew that what the moonlight girl had tried to do to him in the dappled silence of the Vienna Woods, this woman had done to thousands of men in the streets and alleyways of London: made them love her, want her, need her, with a need that brought them mindless and damned into her arms. He remembered Fairport crying pitifully as the vampire women stripped him of his clothes, ripped at his veins in tiny, shredding cuts that would not kill immediately; drank his terror and his despair as well as his death. Fairport who had only wanted to live as normal men lived.

And still he reached out and touched the long square fingers with his own.

"Thank you for coming with me," she said quietly. "Thank you for . . . for seeing that I come to no harm."

I feel as if I shall never return to London again.

Standing alone in the darkness at the heart of the crypt, Asher felt the knife-twist fear in his heart, that he would never see Lydia again.

He had thought of her often in the long prison chamber, listening to the sunset wailing of the muezzins, the constant squabbling of the gulls, the wind-whisper flight of vampire feet in the labyrinths below. He was glad in an odd way that if it was to be so—if he was going to die in the House of the Oleanders—he hadn't known it that rainy morning when all he'd been looking forward to was the emotional harrowing of his cousin's funeral and the distasteful scenes of family greed sure to follow. He'd have been solemn then, he thought, and solemnity would have completely spoiled the pillow fight early on the morning of his departure, and the giggling tussle of lace and kisses and stray medical journals.

Seven years. It should have been longer. She'd probably track him to Vienna, but Anthea had smuggled them both onto the train. It was not possible that anyone from either Halliwell's Department, or the Stadtspoliz, or the Kundschafts Stelle, had seen them board. Thin, matter-of-fact, beautiful with a breathtaking marsh-fairy beauty which she herself had been forbidden to see ... His soul ached, suddenly and desperately, with the need to see her one more time before he died. Only that, if nothing else were possible ...

He wondered if, in tracing his contacts in the Austrian city, she would somehow meet Françoise.

The tarnished silver bars glimmered dully in the light of the single candle, cold even in the comforting yellow glow. Asher set the candle down carefully on a crossbar, its base protected by a circle of paper torn from a book to preclude telltale drips of wax while he worked carefully with the twisted bronze wires of the homemade picklock. It was hard to keep his hands steady, given the cold of the November night, the ice piled here in such quantities ... the fear. The silence was a second darkness, and the smell of ammonia clutched his throat.

The silver hinges did not creak. He stepped into the low-roofed corridor, edged past the puddles of water, the sawdust and the straw.

Why ice? Absurdly, he remembered something the vampire Ysidro had once told him, about aging vampires suffering from cold. Surely all this wasn't just to make an old enemy uncomfortable? He wondered, if he freed Ernchester a second time, whether the vampire earl would escape with him at all, or whether he would, as he had in Vienna, simply let him free and cleave to the Turkish master who had summoned him.

Why?

The second door along the corridor, as Asher had already begun to suspect, opened into a cramped pitchy wilderness of coils and tubes and tanks, the harsh stink of ammonia like acid in the air. The weak firefly glow limned the words ZWANZIG-STEJAHRHUNDERT ABKUHLUNGGESELLESCHAFT on a crate.

Twentieth Century Refrigeration Company.

Freezer chests, a vacuum plant, hoses like obscene rubber entrails dangling. Glass carboys of poisonous ammonia gas gleamed like monstrous eggs. Though the floor of the corridor was wet, there were no tracks in here, no straw, no sawdust. Having gone through the installation of a new furnace in one of the New College lecture halls, Asher guessed that some part or valve had broken, and had been sent for to Berlin.

Five days since the breakdown, the Bey had screamed, *and still no word . . .*

He closed the door, locked it, wiped the silver handle with his handkerchief.

The second door's handle was like ice. The sound of the tumblers going over was that of hammers driving coffin nails, answered from within, as from the deeps of a tomb, by a profound, sickening groan.

The stench that rolled over Asher as he pushed the door inward almost physically blinded him. He shut his eyes, averted his face. *Stupid . . .* he thought the next moment. And then, *If it's this bad when it's this cold in here . . .* His breath was a cloud in the wan candle flare; the hoarfrost glistened on the stone walls, as did the ice that almost filled the crypt.

But all that was peripheral to the dark thing crawling toward him through the mess of half-frozen sawdust and straw on the floor—and to his understanding of what it was, and what it meant.

Staring down into the face—into what was left of the face— he knew everything, everything except where Ernchester was, and even that he could begin to guess.

Then his breath was shut off under the crushing grip of a fleshy hand, and he was swept backward through the door with such force that he felt his feet leave the floor. He barely had time to pull his head forward when he struck the corridor wall, not thrown into it, as Olumsiz Bey had hurled him before, but slammed against the stonework with such force as to break ribs. He cried out—he thought he cried out—as the bones knifed him within, his mind suffocated under darkness, breath driven from him and unable to return. He struck the wall a second time, pain lancing his left shoulder blade as if he'd been struck by an ax, and all the while a voice screamed at him, screamed curses in Persian and Arabic and Turkish, incomprehensible through his mounting desperation to breathe . . .

He didn't know what language, he thought the voice was shouting, "Is this what you wanted? Is this what you sought?" and the hand twisted his head, the pressure on the spine intolerable, the icy water on the floor drenching him as he lay in it. "Is this what you wished to see?"

But he could see nothing, the candle having fallen to the wet floor of the crypt; nothing except, in his mind's eyes, the livid face of the thing in the crypt. Claws slit his sleeve open, shoulder to hem, while a knee ground in his back and the terrible weight pinned him to the stone, his neck bones cracking under the vindictive twist of Olumsiz Bey's hand. His arm was torn open to the wrist, blood burning hot on the sudden cold of his flesh, and all the while the smell grew around him, mounting and horrible, waves of it, while something fell squishily against the wall nearby, dragged with a horrible, thick groaning through the pools on the floor. Something fumbled at his arm, slick and glutinous around the sharpness of teeth; he heard the vampire whisper, "Drink. Drink, my kitten, my child, my beloved . . . drink . . ."

Something that felt like a hand—or what had once been a hand—groped along his arm for a steadying hold.

Then with a retching noise the thing pulled away, rolled, crawled, with horrible sounds, back toward the door of its crypt and began to vomit. Asher thought later it was the release of the twisting pressure on his neck and backbone as Olumsiz Bey left him, as much as anything else, that finally let him faint.

He didn't think he was unconscious more than a minute or two; the jabbing pain of a tourniquet on his arm brought him back to the same inky darkness, the icy water seeping through his clothing to icy flesh, the sinking weakness of blood loss. His own blood, coppery in his nostrils, was the least horrible thing he smelled.

The cold was marginally less. The crypt door was closed.

Softly, his body aching with the careful ration of his breath, he said, "So that's why you wanted Ernchester."

"You know nothing of these things." The master's voice came shrill, slivered thin through constricted throat, constricted lungs. His hands dragged the tourniquet as if he would use it to cut off the arm he bound.

"I know you're fighting an interloper on your territory. I know you don't trust those of your fledglings you have left . . . and I know now that you've lost the ability to make more."

The nails tightened on his arms, tearing again the numb flesh.

"That's it, isn't it? You haven't been able to make a fledgling for years. Only six vampires, for one of the biggest cities in Europe? Where the government doesn't even *care* if you kill, so long as it's Armenians and Jews and the poor? Even your fledglings were beginning to comment that you were growing choosy about getting others to replace those who'd been destroyed.

"But when the interloper came, you had to make the attempt. And when you saw it wouldn't work—that you could hold the fledgling's mind alive through physical death but couldn't transmit the physical syndrome of vampirism to the body—you used your contacts with the old Sultan's allies to send for the one vampire you knew you *could* control, the one you knew whose fledglings would be yours, under your power . . ."

The hand closed around his neck again, not strangling this time, the clawed nails hooking like wolf's teeth under the bundle of nerve and tendon and blood vessels below his ear. The hard knee pressed, bracing, on his chest, like the small, blunt end of a ram. Very softly, Olumsiz Bey said, "I . . . could . . . kill you . . ."

"If you didn't need me for bait," he said, barely able to whisper against the dig of the claws. "Bait to trap Anthea, and bait to trap the earl. If Ernchester isn't with the interloper already."

The hand released his throat. Wet silk passed over his bare

arm, the side of his face, as the vampire stood. Then Olumsiz Bey kicked him, like the deliberate blow of a hammer, again and again like a man smashing rocks, and in a very short time Asher fainted again.

TWENTY

"THERE is no God but God, and Mohammed is the Prophet of God." The voice of the muezzin pierced the sodden fog of Asher's dreams like golden wire. "Come to prayer. Come to prayer."

Anthea, Asher thought, trying to surface, then slid back into velvet chasms of unconsciousness. He could see her on the train, her profile a milky coastline against the window's obsidian sea. "Ernchester has never trusted trains," she said, and then her pale face, her white hands, turned to the marble bones of the grave steles beyond the Adrianople Gate, the dark of her dress and hair to the black cold of night.

Through brittle moonlight he saw a man walking, small and stooped in his old-fashioned clothing, but moving from gravestone to gravestone with the flitting lightness of the vampire. In the open ground he stopped, like an indrawn breath. Asher felt the presence of the shadow without seeing it, but in his dreaming it seemed to him that he smelled again the rank mixture of blood and mold that had overwhelmed him in the darkness of the dry cistern. Ernchester moved, turning as if to flee, but as he turned, the shadow was before him.

The air stirred with vampire laughter.

Do you think his favor is now off this man, and he is ours?

The voice slipped into the dimming scenes of his dream, as

if the wind had said it, but he knew what it was. He fought, panicked, to wake, struggling back out of the abyss.

"Did he want him dead, he'd be dead, not here," grumbled the voice that he recognized as one-eyed Haralpos.

"Wake him," the Baykus Kadine giggled. "Wake him up and ask."

Wake up! he screamed at himself. *Wake up, they're all around your bed!* Sleep was a black velvet pillow over his face. Maybe his body realized that if he woke, he'd hurt.

"Maybe he should be kissed," Pelageya said in her deep voice, "like the damsel in a tower?" Something that might have been fingernails trailed across the bare skin of his chest.

The whispering blurred, blended. He thought he saw the dim golden outline of the open door to the corridor outside, the sub-aqueous flicker of the pierced brass lamps, but he could not see the vampires around him at all. Only the red glint of their eyes.

"Maybe he knows where the Bey has gone?"

"What makes you think he might?"

"Someone had to bring him here . . ."

"We have to find him . . ."

"And tell him what?" Zardalu demanded scornfully. "That some worthless Armenian dog has been found with his throat slit?"

"Bled . . ."

"In a church . . ."

"The man was a priest . . ."

"Then he deserved it, whoever did it to him."

"He wasn't the only one. There was the old fig seller in the Koum Kapou . . ."

"He is getting insolent, our Shadow Wolf." Zardalu spoke the name in Turkish, Gölge Kurt, the words harsh and guttural in the flow of his court Osmanli. "Now our Bey must come out of this foolish hiding, must walk the nights again and stop crouching here with his *dastgah* and his *almanya* infidels . . ."

"And if he doesn't?"

"That kind of murder is stupid, senseless, leaving his kills to be fallen over. No wonder the Bey has told us to find this intruder Gölge Kurt, to kill him . . ."

"What do you expect of a peasant who thinks he's a soldier because some other jumped-up peasant has put a gun in his hands?"

"We must find the Bey . . ."

". . . find him . . ."

He didn't know if they'd ever really been there. It seemed to him that he woke with a kind of start to find the chamber empty. The door still stood open, outlined in gold, and against the plastered walls the patterned spots of the lamp still wavered like an insubstantial scarf.

You know nothing of this matter, Olumsiz Bey had said.

And Charles, *I love her unto death, and beyond.*

He thought he knew where Olumsiz Bey could be found, and his heart turned over, sickened with shock and pity.

"There is no God but God, and Mohammed is the Prophet of God." The voice of the muezzin echoed dimly through the window lattices, as the ridiculously overdone grandeur of the Constantinople sunset bled to death in the west.

She could barely keep her hands steady, so it wasn't easy to achieve a proper symmetry of her coiffure. And in any case, thought Lydia, keeping her mind on what she was doing as if it were a dissection—with a kind of cool, inquiring deliberation—in any case her hair had never taken the fashionable curls necessary for a coiffure à la grecque. In her current mental state she'd be lucky if she didn't singe half of it off with the curling irons.

She was trying not to look at the envelope marked with the Hapsburg crest, lying on the table beside her.

Not that she needed to. She knew every word of the few lines written inside.

If you would save your husband's life, meet me at the Burned Column at 3:00 today. One close to you is a servant of the Bey—tell no one, but do not fail or your husband will be dead before dawn. Trust me. Karolyi.

Trust me.

Lydia had seen the Burned Column two days ago, when Razumovsky had detoured past it after the excursion to the bazaar. It stood—a massive monument of Byzantine porphyry, its bronze horseman blackened by ancient smoke—in the center of the old market district, a labyrinth of courtyards, alleys, warehouses, and crumbling, disused baths in the most ancient part of the city.

It was exactly the place she would choose for a kidnapping, if the victim were to be snatched up and quietly chloroformed. When the note arrived that morning, her immediate thought had been, *What on earth does he take me for?* He must have realized, she thought, that she would be of no use to him, and was in a position to interfere with his plans.

The certainty that she was right hadn't made it any easier, during tea with Lady Clapham, to listen to the embassy clock strike three.

And if Herr Jacob Zeittelstein wasn't at the reception of Herr Hindl's Turkish partner tonight—if he hadn't returned from Berlin as expected that afternoon—she didn't know what she would do.

It was Wednesday night. James had been missing for a week.

She closed her eyes, her hands trembling so much that she had to lower them, the iron cooling in her grip. *Dear God, let me find him,* she prayed. *Dear God, show me another clue if this one fails . . .*

Ice, she thought immediately. She seemed to hear Razumovsky saying, above the clamor of the Grand Bazaar, *Someone always knows . . .*

If Herr Zeittelstein had gone to Berlin to fetch a piece for the refrigeration plant, it stood to reason Olumsiz Bey would be buying ice. It might take a few days to trace . . .

I can't afford a few days! she thought despairingly. *Jamie can't afford a few days!*

There was a noise behind her. She opened her eyes with a start, the distorted panic of too little sleep flooding her . . .

Margaret stood reflected in the mirror, hesitating in the doorway behind her, blinking in the latticed sunset light.

Lydia's stomach contracted in rage and dread. *Not before a party,* she thought despairingly. *I don't think I can take another scene . . .*

She pushed up her glasses and turned in her chair. Her red hair spilled, an untidy river, down her milky shoulders. She knew she should say something neutral, unargumentative: *Hello, Margaret,* or, *Did you find what you were shopping for this morning?* The governess had been gone when Lydia woke up. But she felt too tired to frame the words. She only looked, and Margaret occupied herself for a few minutes straightening the lace on the edge of her house mitt as if it were the most important task of the day.

Then Margaret looked up. "Mrs. Asher—Lydia—I'm . . . I'm sorry."

From the time she was five years old, Lydia had been trained to smile and say, *It's all right.* Her upper arms were criss-crossed with sticking plaster and dressings. She'd told Dr. Manzetti—and Lady Clapham, who'd recommended the physician and gone to him with her that morning—that she'd been attacked by dogs. Against the sharp points of her collar-bone, the knobs of her wrists, the silver chains that had saved her life felt heavy and cold.

She couldn't even ask, *Why?*

The sonnet she'd found had told her that.

She had lain awake thinking for a good part of the night, and found that the memory of those lines still made her heart beat swift and heavy with an emotion she couldn't define. Nothing at all like she felt for James. All her fear of Ysidro had returned, in strangely transmuted waves. Nothing at all like what she knew, or had ever known.

Grief-stricken, silent, Margaret gazed at her with tears in her blue eyes. Lydia felt the anger within her ease.

"You're afraid for him," she said carefully, "and you want to help him. You're afraid that he will die because of the promises he made to me."

Margaret turned brilliant, blotchy red, and looked down at her gloves again; tears crawled slowly from beneath her heavy eyeglasses. This woman had tried to kill her, thought Lydia wearily. Why was she sparing her?

She knew the answer to that, too. Because Margaret had locked the door behind her, not only for the sake of the sonnet, but because she was Lydia Willoughby, heiress; because of all the sonnets no one ever wrote to the Margaret Pottons of the world.

"I'm so sorry," Margaret whispered. "I'm so sorry. I don't know what came over me . . ." She turned to flee, but stopped and turned back, standing, head down, to take punishment.

For a moment Lydia wondered if the interloper—that animal face, grinning and grinning at her upon those few occasions last night when she *had* shut her eyes—had engineered Margaret's jealousy, as he'd cast upon her the languor that had stifled her own screams.

She didn't think so. But she guessed it was something Ysidro would do in like circumstance.

And she shivered. She didn't want to think about Ysidro: playing picquet in the train, or bare white feet ascending the damp stone of the staircase before her . . .

"It's all right," she said.

Margaret looked away and began to cry.

Lydia thought, Damn; bitterly, wearily, knowing that she must give comfort while she herself was exhausted, aching, wondering if she'd whistled Jamie's life to the wind that afternoon by assuming Karolyi's note to be lies, wondering what she was going to do if Zeittelstein wasn't at the reception, wondering how best to charm him if he was . . . And underlying it all, against her will, aware that she was as drawn to the faded ghost trapped within the vampire immortality—like a mantis in amber—as Don Simon was to her.

"Are you quite sure you're all right, my dear?" Lady Clapham touched Lydia's wrist as they paused in the doorway of Monsieur Demerci's town palace above the darkening Marmara Sea.

Lydia nodded though she felt exhausted. She would have been glad to remain home, as Margaret had done, pleading a headache after the events of last night. Under the opera-length kid gloves and deep festoons of lace on her spinach-green gown, her bandaged arms smarted. The one thing she prayed, blinking at the dazzling electric brightness of the reception room, was that she wouldn't meet Ignace Karolyi amid the moving rainbow of men and women.

"I could do with a little champagne," she confided, as two slim dark servants, incongruous in Western-style livery and powdered wigs, ushered them through the tiled doorway toward the receiving line.

"What you need is brandy," retorted Lady Clapham. "I'll see what I can find."

Their host was a Sorbonne-educated Turk in impeccable evening clothes, though the ferocity of his black mustache sounded an uneasy echo in Lydia's mind of the dark face with glittering fangs that had come so close to hers last night. His wife, a younger daughter of impoverished Silesian nobility, reminded Lydia of a highly bred rabbit in a yellow satin dress. She was probably the one responsible for the ridiculous eighteenth-century livery of the servants, and maybe for the electrical chandeliers, the candy-pink glass of the Venetian mirror frames, the tassled raspberry curtains and white and gold Louis XVI chairs, as well. Herr Hindl greeted her and expressed immediate concern: the beautiful Frau Asher did not look well, he hoped there was no indisposition. It comes of all this dull talk of business and jaunting about the old city; of course, a woman's more delicate constitution would be susceptible . . .

Only concern for her husband, who was to have met her in Constantinople and had not been heard from. Lydia unfurled her spangled Chantilly fan and tried to look interestingly wan without appearing haggard. She had hoped that Herr Zeittelstein might be here tonight. From things her husband had said, she thought that perhaps he and the honored Herr shared a mutual client, and she might glean some news . . .

Certainly! Of course! Absolutely! Jacob had only just returned from Berlin that afternoon, he had been rather out of touch but he would be delighted to help in any fashion he could . . .

And so, indeed, he proved. Jacob Zeittelstein was a young-

ish, strongly built man who in spite of evening dress looked
more like a pipe fitter than his company's representative to the
Ottoman Empire. He listened to Herr Hindl's introduction and
Lydia's explanation with the air of one who never forgets
names, faces, or circumstances and has all information at the
tips of his beefy fingers.

"My husband mentioned that he was in touch with the Dardanelles Land Corporation, you see," Lydia explained, naming
the bank account that had paid out a certified check for eighty
pounds to a Freiherr Feketelo on 26 October. According to
Razumovsky, Ignace Karolyi had left Constantinople abruptly,
mysteriously, and under another name on the twenty-seventh.
She had finally tracked it down, just this afternoon. "He said he
was meeting someone in the company here in Constantinople,
and I was wondering . . . It's absurd," she added, with a slight
duck of her head. "And yet I can't help wondering if they
might have heard anything . . ." She raised her eyes helplessly
to Zeittelstein's. "But I haven't any idea who they are, and I
can't seem to find out."

"Dardanelles Land?" Zeittelstein's eyebrows shot up. "The
mysterious Herr Fiddat?"

"I believe that was the name." Lydia sipped a tiny quantity
of Monsieur Demerci's excellent champagne. "They *are*
clients of yours, aren't they?"

"Ha ha!" Hindl trumpeted. "She's up on everything, this
clever little lady."

"*He,*" Zeittelstein said, with a puzzled expression. "Not
they. As far as I've been able to ascertain, the Dardanelles
Land Corporation exists only on paper. Quite typical, actually.
All those corporations do is pay money to their founders.
Fiddat . . ." He shook his head.

Lydia felt exactly as if she had—not by chance, but by sheer
steadiness of eye and hand—shot an arrow clean into the gold.

She widened her eyes. "What's mysterious about him?"

"Everything. Extraordinary." He shook his head. "It was on
his business that I was in Berlin. Having decided, evidently all
of a clap, to install refrigeration in the Roman crypt under his
palace in the market district, he must needs have it now, at

once. When the valve on the ammonia pump proved to have been cracked in shipping, he would not wait, like a normal person, for an express to Berlin for a new one. No. Five thousand francs he paid—almost two hundred pounds!—for me to return to Berlin, myself, in person, the very day the valve was found to be defective, by the quickest possible route. He even paid for the lost business here in this city that it cost me."

"They are very rich, these Turks," Hindl interpolated sententiously. "Ill-got, I'll wager, some of them. Refrigeration works, you must know, my dear Frau Asher, by compression of ammonia gas, much better than the old sulfur dioxide system. Sulfur dioxide—that's a chemical compound—has the inconvenient habit of becoming corrosive and eating up the machinery which stores it. Ha ha!"

"Truly?" Lydia gave him her most radiant smile and timed precisely the turn of her head back to Zeittelstein, cutting off his further explanations with, "And was he pleased to get his valve?"

Zeittelstein shook his head. "I'm not sure, Frau Asher. This afternoon I find nothing but a heap of hysterical messages from his agent . . . Has your husband ever laid eyes on Herr Fiddat himself, Frau Asher?"

Lydia shook her head. "I thought there might have been some sort of proscription against Mohammedans dealing with Christians face-to-face—not ordinary Mohammedans, I mean, but that he might belong to some . . . some odd sect of dervishes."

"Not any dervish I've ever heard of," put in Hindl, in the act of neatly shagging hors d'oeuvres from a silver plate proffered by a servant. He grinned at Zeittelstein. "Not that you'd know anything about that, ha ha."

Zeittelstein grinned back. "Well, as far as I know, in thirteen hundred years no Mohammedan has ever had a problem dealing with a Jew." His grin faded and the dark, wise eyes grew thoughtful. "I will say this: his agent's terrified of him. I can hear it in his voice. My own suspicion—and I can't exactly say why I feel this—is that Fiddat is a leper."

"How extraordinary!" Lydia said with a wealth of implied *Please go on* in gesture and voice and the tilt of her head.

"Nobody that I know has seen him," Zeittelstein continued, and glanced over at Hindl for corroboration.

Hindl tapped the side of his nose. "Very mysterious chap." He turned to catch the eye of their host. Monsieur Demerci strolled obediently over, pausing now and then to smile and speak to one or another of his guests.

"Ja'far, you've never laid eyes on Herr Fiddat, have you? Or visited his palace?"

"Oh, I've visited the House of Oleanders," Zeittelstein said. "I spent the better part of ten days assembling that wretched compressor—brrr, that vault is cold! But always I am met at the door by servants and conducted down to the crypt by them . . . They stand and watch me while I work."

"According to Hasan Buz—the ice merchant, you understand, madame," Demerci said with a polite bow that made him look considerably less like a Turkish corsair and more like a former soldier made good, "it's the same with his men when they make deliveries. The stuff gets stacked in the corridors—half a ton at a time—and the servants pay them and dismiss them. Hasan has to pay them double. They say the house is cursed."

"Where is the house?" Lydia asked.

A servant, emerging between the heavily carved pillars that lined the reception room, gestured discreetly; Demerci excused himself with another bow and went to speak to the man while Zeittelstein said, "It's in the very old part of the city between the Place d'Armes and the old Sublime Porte, near the Bazaar. If you were walking east along the Tchakmakajitar from the Valide Han, it's the third turning up the hill. The house itself runs into at least three old *hans* and rambles everywhere, but the door I go through is there. You'd have to walk around the walls till you found the main door, if you wish to speak to Herr Fiddat, but personally," he added, "I wouldn't go there without an escort . . . and I don't mean Lady Clapham."

"Oh, no," Lydia agreed, her heart pounding fast.

"Great heavens, no!" Hindl cried indignantly. "A European lady to that part of town?"

Tomorrow, she thought, looking around swiftly for the Russian prince. With Razumovsky and a couple of stout footmen from the Russian Embassy . . . *God, don't let Karolyi's note have been genuine!* It was lies, it had to be lies, and that business of *One close to you is an enemy* was, James had told her, one of the oldest tricks in repertoire. She wondered if perhaps they should wait until dark to include Ysidro in the party, but common sense told her that even were Ysidro at the height of his strength—which he was not—it would be far safer to enter a vampire nest in daylight hours than by night, even if it did mean going in without an expert's assistance. Besides, Ysidro might refuse to take part in an actual assault.

Demerci strolled back, looking worried. "Just a word of warning," he said quietly. "There's more unrest in the Armenian quarter tonight. When you go home tonight, you may want to go through the Mahmoudie and the Bab Ali Djaddessi, rather than through the Bajazid."

Hindl gestured impatiently. "They're not going to call in the army again, are they?"

"I'm not sure. They have not so far. But there have been some rather . . . odd . . . murders, and it wouldn't take much to set off rioting again." He bowed again to Lydia. "It sounds ridiculously feeble of me, madame, to ask you not to hold the actions of the army and the government against my people. We are not barbarians, in spite of what you must think. There are thousands, hundreds of thousands, of us who are horrified at what the army does to the Armenians, and the Greeks, in this city. It is a terrible mistake to put the rifles of tomorrow into the hands of the ignorance of yesterday."

Most of the people at the reception seemed very little worried by the prospect of further rioting, as if such matters couldn't possibly concern them: Herr Hindl essayed a few jokes about what one had to deal with in foreign parts. Lydia wondered if this was because they'd already been through so many riots since July or because they mostly lived in Pera, or because they were as absorbed in selling railway stock or army boots or plumbing fixtures as she was, under normal circumstances, in isolating the effects of pancreatic secretions. One or two of the embassy wives called for their carriages early, but Lady Clapham merely said, "Nonsense. Late's better than early. By the time supper's over they'll all have gone to bed and we'll be able to drive straight onto the bridge and never mind going the long way 'round."

She was probably right, Lydia thought. In any case, Prince Razumovsky—who had a very Russian concept of time—had not yet arrived, and tired though she was, she needed to speak to him tonight. Lydia had the distinct impression that if she went to Sir Burnwell and asked for help in forcing her way into an old palace in Stamboul to find word of Jamie, the result would be a round of polite letters to the Dardanelles Land Corporation rather than the prompt offer of a couple of Cossacks with clubs.

So she waited, too keyed up to do more than peck at the lobster aspic and ptarmigan in green peppercorn sauce, and on either side of her Herren Hindl and Zeittelstein traded head shakings over Mahler's latest symphony and the newest juicy tidbits of the scandal concerning the Kaiser's brother and a Vienna masseur. After supper there was dancing, and Lydia allowed herself to be swept into a waltz by Herr Zeittelstein and a lively schottische by the parson of the American Lutheran Mission on Galata, all the while listening, watching, for sight of His Highness' rich green uniform or the pantherlike grace that even without spectacles she knew as Karolyi.

She had worried a little about leaving Margaret at the Rue Abydos house with only Madame Potoneros and her daughter, though she suspected that unless she herself was there, neither Karolyi nor his vampire companion—*companions?*—would even try to enter the house. In any case, the bolt on the front door had been repaired, the one on the kitchen wing reinforced with another, stronger lock, and every window festooned with garlic and hawthorn.

"I can summon any into whose eyes I have looked," Ysidro had said to her once during a long game of picquet on the train from Adrianople—they had been discussing *Dracula*. "To call one to me who is a stranger—to have them put aside silver, if they are wearing it, or garlic or any of the other flowers and woods which sear and blister our flesh—is a more difficult thing."

Lydia shivered, wondering if the Turkish vampire, the interloper of last night, would have been capable of making her take off her silver necklace had he spoken to her on the street some earlier night or whispered to her in dreams. She had warned Margaret about Karolyi and given orders to the two housekeepers to remain until dawn. It was all that she could do, she felt, in the face of Margaret's blotch-faced, white-lipped refusal to accompany her tonight.

Lydia was standing beside the heavily curtained window that looked out over the Roman walls to the sea, scanning the newest comers to the room for the tall form of Razumovsky—and even at this late hour embassy parties and members of the new government were still arriving—when a cold hand touched her elbow and a voice like wind breath said, "Mistress?" in her ear.

Earlier that day, remembering the sonnet, she hadn't known how she was going to speak to him, hadn't even known how she wanted to speak to him. But in the fierce electrical radiance of the chandeliers, he wore his alien, vampire face. It was the face that must show in the mirror—a skull's face of hollow eyes and staring bones within the long web of hair—and that was easier to deal with than the haunting illusion that somewhere in those sulfur eyes lurked the remnants of a living man.

Under his cloak he wore evening dress. She almost asked him if he'd left his scythe and hourglass at the door, until she saw the look in his eyes.

"They're making for the house of Olumsiz Bey," he said softly. "Rioters—Armenians, hundreds of them, crying for his blood . . ."

"Who . . . ? How do they . . . ?" Then she said, "The ice carriers," realizing it for the truth at once. "Of course they'd know."

"And the storytellers." Ysidro caught her hand, drawing her unseen by others toward the door to the supper room, to the kitchens, to the back stairs. "And the beggars who watch the shadows pass at night. They all know. But they were afraid, until rage and hate at their priest's murder finally drowned their fear. Put this on."

She clutched the folds of the sable cloak, followed him past the unseeing servants cleaning up the plates, past the scullery boys bringing up more ice for champagne . . . past the footmen and drivers keeping warm by the fire in the stable court and looking up worriedly at the rising and falling of voices beyond the roofs, and the occasional snap of gunfire. "What happened?" She paused in the alley and fumbled her eyeglasses from their case in her reticule—all things leaped into clarity, more fearful almost than the comforting dreamlike blur.

"A priest was killed. And then an old man, an inoffensive seller of fig paste who gave to charity and had more grand-children than King David. Vampire kills, careless, deliberate. Meant to be found, and meant to enrage."

In the narrow lanes behind Demerci's mansion, rocky and steep as stairs, the voices sounded frighteningly close. Flame reflected on the wood and stucco, the stained and weed-grown walls. Lydia thought, *If they find me, they'll attack me just for being European . . .*

It was very hard to think past that fact, that fear.

"Karolyi," she said. "Karolyi and the interloper. After I wouldn't cooperate. All they have to do is follow the mob and let it do their work for them."

Through a gap in the houses, she saw by torchlight a man riding the box of a broken-down carriage—black-robed, gray beard streaming, waving a crucifix aloft. Men all around him raised flaming brands, clubs, the edged and pointed tools of marketplace trades. Women's voices keened like harpies.

"And part of that work," said that cool, disinterested voice in her ear, "will be to kill James and anyone else they find at the Bey's palace. If by chance Charles or Anthea are there, they will likely be imprisoned, and in no case to flee. Was your builder of refrigerators among those at the house just now?" He caught her elbow again as she stumbled, guiding her through a space between houses where a river of filth sucked at her shoes.

"Off the Tchakmakajitar Yokoussou near the Valide Han, he says. Third turning up the hill . . ."

"I've seen it," Ysidro said. "It was one of many I suspected, but dared not go close enough to be certain." Thin shards of moonlight blinked on shirtfront, cuffs, face, white on black, increasing her impression that she was being hastened along the insalubrious streets of Hell by a skeleton. "With any luck we shall reach the place before the mob, and—if James is in fact still alive—before the Bey decides to kill him to preserve his silence."

TWENTY-ONE

ASHER knew he must escape or die.

He'd been wakened hours earlier by gunshots in the streets, had lain listening as the sounds of horror-driven fury, the random ululation of violence, ebbed and then flared like the sullen quarreling of a drunkard who returns again and again to the wellsprings of his rage.

It was deep in the night, probably not many hours until dawn, when he heard them coming toward the house. Even in the Tientsin riots, the worst he'd known, this was the hour when such things quieted. Something, someone, was stirring them up, rousing them anew when they flagged.

And for the first time he could hear, among the confused buzzing shouts, words that he knew.

Vlokslak. Hortolak. Ordog.

They were coming to burn the House of Oleanders.

The vampires will flee, he thought.

Olumsiz Bey will kill me, rather than let me tell others what I've seen.

The spotted light of the stairway lamp still outlined the open door.

The thought of getting up appalled him. Just breathing was like being struck in the side with an ax. He rolled carefully off the divan and managed to get on his feet—achingly glad that a Turkish divan wasn't even as high as the average milking stool—the floor icy under bare soles, cold breathing around his ankles and stirring the long cotton shirt that someone had put on him when they brought him upstairs. He found his clothes farther along the divan, and put them on sitting. The boots were the worst. His bandaged arm ached and the stab of his broken ribs left him breathless as he pulled them on, but he knew the streets of Constantinople and knew he'd need them.

To his enormous surprise, he made it to the door on his feet. The house below was soundless. They'd probably break in on the other side, through the crypt where the ice was delivered. If he met them in the crypt, they'd quite possibly kill him out of hand before they realized he wasn't a vampire himself.

Descending the stairs left him dizzy, but he didn't fall. The thing in the crypt hadn't been able to drink much of his blood, though a good deal had been lost. He felt desperately thirsty. Down in the courtyard the sound of the mob didn't penetrate, and it was hard to disregard the voice in the back of his mind that argued that he certainly had time to lie down on the nice, comfortable pavement and rest a little . . .

He took the vigil lamp from its niche and continued. In the Turkish part of the house the mob's fury sounded closer, a heavy sea surge that would stop at nothing.

The tiled room. The overgrown court. The Roman baths. The long stair and the stench of ammonia, of wet brick . . .

Of decay.

The leopard glimmer of the lamp suddenly outlined the dark form standing before him. The light gleamed in the citrine eyes and on the silver blade of the halberd, and Asher, leaning panting on the wall, knew he had lost.

He hadn't even the strength to turn and flee; the Bey would pull him down like a staghound a crippled fawn. Throwing the lamp would buy him seconds, but . . .

"God sent you," the vampire said softly. "Help me. I beg you."

He stepped forward, holding out one hand with its steel talons and winking jewels. "The others have fled. I have to get him someplace where the mob will not find him, have to get enough ice there, that he will live through the night."

In the corridor behind him, when Asher moved the lamp, he could see the wet diamond glint of ice where it showed through the oilskin in which it was wrapped. Masses of it, far more than a living man could carry. But even with a vampire's strength, he could not make it more wieldy. He couldn't carry it, and a body as well, up those twisting stairs.

"Please," the Bey said. "After that you may do as you will. I have the keys to the outer doors, you are free to go. On my honor, by the Prophet I swear it. But help me get him to safety. Please."

Asher set down the lamp. "Is he able to walk at all?"

The Bey stepped forward, some of the terrible tension lifting from the set of his shoulders, the angle of his shaven head. His snake-colored eyes seemed suddenly old, filled with the weariness of uncounted years alone. "With support, I think. We weigh not so heavy as living flesh."

Asher touched his arm, staying him as they edged between the ice blocks and the wall, to the silver bars that guarded the corridor to the crypts. The last time they were eye-to-eye had been here, with the Bey's claws lodged deep in his throat. Those wounds throbbed under a dressing of sticking plaster every time he spoke.

"You know it's not going to do you any good." He spoke, not in triumph, but in a kind of matter-of-fact compassion, for the creature beyond the bars was clearly beyond hope even if, by some miracle, Ernchester or some other vampire could be found to complete his transformation to the vampire state.

He half expected the same rage that, earlier in the night, had almost killed him, but the Bey only shook his head.

"If he can get through the night," he murmured. "If he can last through another day . . . The . . . transformation . . . of the flesh, when it takes place, is little short of miraculous. I have seen sere and aged crones return to the beauty of their girlhood once they have the power of the vampire mind. The flesh returns to the form that is in the mind. And in any case," he added, still more quietly, "though what you say may be true, I cannot leave him. He is . . . dear to me."

The body that the Bey brought forth from the crypt was

wrapped in a sort of shroud of oiled silk, with oilskins on top of that. Still it stank, a limp and filthy thing in the tall vampire's arms, its wet black curls glistening between the bandages, its dangling fingers dripping brownish fluid. Asher flinched back from it, remembering the slimy lips mumbling at his arm, as the Bey set it on its feet beside him; his shoulders cringed from the limp arm the Bey laid over them. Then the bandaged head lolled, like a drunken man's, and the livid eyelids, almost black in the gloom, rose to show dark eyes flooded with agony, horror, and dumb pleading for relief.

The thing lived.

"He was beautiful," whispered Olumsiz Bey. He bent, gathering the corners of the oilcloth around the ice. He had laid down his silver halberd to carry the thing from the crypt, the first time Asher had seen him let it out of his hand. Now he slipped it through the knot of the oilskins, the haft where he could grip it at once. There must have been several hundred pounds of ice, but he lifted it easily, for it was only the awkwardness of it that had prevented him from bearing both it and the boy leaning, weaving drunkenly, on his shoulders. At close range the smell was suffocating, and he tried not to think about the consistency of the arm that held so desperately to his neck. He himself, with his cracked ribs sawing like broken bamboo within him, could barely keep his feet.

"Beautiful," the Bey said, "and more beautiful still in his heart. He was ardent as fire, my Kahlil. A young warrior, and loyal to me to the bottom of his soul."

It was as if he heard Asher's thought, *And you repaid him thus?* But Asher did not speak it, so there was no anger in the vampire's quiet reply.

"He would have been one of my living servants, here in this house. This was what I had planned." The shouting of the mob was very near, the sky above the tall Turkish roof—usually so dark—smoldering with the flare of torches. Smoke and rage burned the air.

"This was hard for me. I wanted to make him as I am, to keep him by me in his glorious youth forever. But I knew this was no longer possible for me. Fifty, sixty years ago, in the days of Abdul Mezid, when my friend Tinnin was killed, I tried to make a fledgling. Though that youth's mind stayed alive, a burning flame in mine through the death of his body, when I returned that flame to the flesh, there was no change, no alteration in the flesh itself. The fledgling rotted as he lay until in mercy I struck off his head. This had happened . . . once, maybe twice before to me, long ago. But afterward all was well. This time—after Tinnin—the power did not return."

He laughed soundlessly, bitterly, a tall figure in robes mottled like a tiger's in the shifting light. The jewels he wore threw back fire from the reddish glare of the sky, echoes of it catching in the ice he carried like some monstrous, Sisyphean gem loaded onto him by hilarious gods.

"I tried three, perhaps four times since that time, and I knew there was little chance of bringing Kahlil across to the vampire state. And I knew this was God's mockery of me: that having found the one I could trust, the one who could help me, I had squandered my gift of dark immortality on such as Zardalu and the Baykus Kadine, and that cobweb witch Zenaida who hides in the old harem, only because I needed those I could command to do my bidding.

"And then the interloper came."

The stairs from the old *han*'s court were the worst. Where it had been silent, now the shouting was clearly audible, and drifts of smoke swirled harsh in the air. Asher abandoned the lamp to its niche again, his own injuries stabbing him as he struggled to help the shrouded form up the long flights, the Bey at his heels with the huge, unwieldy burden of dripping ice.

"Gölge Kurt," said the Bey's soft voice, almost as if it were in his ear, while beneath the bandages Kahlil made soft, broken noises of pain. "The Shadow Wolf. God knows where he came from, or how he came to be vampire. Some Greek witch, no doubt, whom he later escaped . . . But he is a Turk of the new Turks, this upland peasantry that they've given guns and delusions of rule. I saw him first just after the coup, when all the city was in confusion. He had made a fledgling already—as easy as spitting—to challenge my power. I killed the fledgling—but I could not kill him. And after that I had no choice."

They reached the long upper chamber. Asher sank, hand pressed to his side, onto the divan, the wrapped and shrouded living corpse beside him. While the Bey unfurled his oilskin to let the ice clatter down, filling the dry tiles of the fish pool, Kahlil, instead of lying on the divan, remained sitting beside Asher, clinging to him, as if frantic for the comfort of a living touch. Stinking, rotting, horrible within the bandages, but Asher could not thrust him away.

The Bey came back, tenderly lifted the boy's body and carried it to the ice. Watching them in the juddering orange flare of the lamps around the walls, Asher wondered bitterly how many men fell back on that phrase, *I had no choice,* when it came to what they wanted—even when it did that to those they loved.

Ernchester, when he had killed Cramer.

Karolyi, certainly, if he thought at all.

He himself.

Olumsiz Bey knelt on the steps of the basin, holding the putrefying bundle that had been the boy's hand.

"So you tried to make him vampire," Asher said quietly. "Even though you knew."

The Bey nodded, once.

"And when you saw that though his mind survived, his body was beginning to rot, you sent for Ernchester."

"I could rule him," the Bey said simply. "I knew him. I knew he was weak. He could get fledglings but had not the strength to command them. Once away from that woman of his—"

"Who loves him," Asher said. "Who cares for him, as you care for Kahlil."

The Bey did not even look up at that, didn't take his eyes from his friend; only shook his head, a heavy, animal gesture, impatient and puzzled, as if he truly did not understand what Asher said. "Women don't love. Not like men. Not like a man loves one who is the son he would have chosen out of all souls in the Universe. No love is like that."

No, thought Asher. A vampire to the end, even to the nature of his love.

The Bey did not even pause to speculate, to justify. His love was unique, and because it was—and because it was his—that justified all. He went on, "But without the Sultan's power, I had to find what help I could. A savage, Karolyi, for all his civilized manners. A Magyar Hun. I think he had already begun to guess at what I was before I sent for his help. I think he had already wondered what use he—in the name of his country—could make of the Undead."

He leaned over to touch the forehead of the boy who lay now unmoving in his bed of ice. The great uneven blocks were old, dried and cleared and slick; they caught the feeble ember light like monster diamonds, faceting it to a wild rainbow over the walls, as if from a bier of jewels.

"I was able to hold Gölge Kurt at bay for a time—I think all would have been well, had not Karolyi chosen to make what he could of the chance, to try to force Ernchester into the service of his country." His eyes, in their dark hollows, were dying coals of some old rage. "*Country*. We the Undead at least were human once. Our sins are human sin. Magnified a million times, but human. These countries, these nations—they are not human. They care not what they use, so long as it serves them. They care not what they do, and their sins are far beyond ours, literally of a different nature. You have served them. Karolyi told me that, Karolyi who is hollow inside, nothing inside, because this 'country' requires that he be nothing. You know."

"Yes," Asher said, remembering again. "I know."

He shook his head. "And so Karolyi delayed. And Gölge Kurt was able to gain a little more territory, to learn a little more of the city. I fear that when Ernchester tried to come into the city to obey my summons, he was met by Gölge Kurt and made a prisoner, and a slave. I thought that if I could trap the woman through you, I could draw Ernchester to me . . . Or at the worst, use her to make Kahlil whole. But it did not come about. And now it is finished."

Shouts rang in the courtyard, echoing from distant regions of the house. In the windows that ringed each shallow dome, the sky was red, like a cloth used to mop blood. The Bey reached in his robe, threw something to Asher that caught a spangle of the light as it flew. It was a key.

"Go," he said. "First light is not far off. They'll be gone before then, and they will not come here. They will not even realize there is a stairway, though they stand at its foot looking up. Such is still my power." After a moment's thought he took the halberd and slid it across the floor to him, the silver blade flashing.

"You may meet one of them still," he added. "If it is Gölge Kurt, kill him. Not for me. He is a man of the new breed who will try to buy power from whatever country he thinks will give it him. And he will buy it with any terms they ask. He is like your Karolyi. I only wanted one fledgling. They will want hundreds, loyal to their service. And what will come of that I do not wish to think."

He shook his heavy head, turned back to the boy in the ice. His voice was so low as to be almost inaudible, like the murmur of a fading ghost. "And—thank you, Scheherazade. Thank you for your help."

Asher stood in the doorway for a moment, leaning on the silver halberd, shivering, for he had stripped off his death-stinking coat and only the piercing cold prevented him from shedding his shirt as well.

How many had the Bey killed? wondered Asher, looking at the bowed form in its golden robes beside the pathetic, shrouded figure on its jeweled pyre of ice. As many as a war, certainly. Karolyi would justify himself the same way— as he, Asher, had justified himself, time and again. At the time he may even have been right.

Painfully, clinging to the halberd for support, Asher made his way down the long stairs.

In the courtyard the noise was louder, echoing from the archway that led to the Byzantine house. Shouts, and the crash of precious things breaking, the thud of running feet. Smoke rolled in, burning his eyes and catching in the light—too much, too strong, for torches. Some part of the house was in flames.

Legs shaking, Asher leaned on the column at the foot of the stair and wondered if he had enough strength left to make it down the colonnade, across the overgrown court, through the crypts . . .

And home, he thought.

If Gölge Kurt became Master of Constantinople—and Asher knew it lay beyond his strength, now, to stop him—it was only a matter of time before Karolyi, or some Young Turk just as eager for his country's triumph, convinced him to become a weapon of the state.

And then a new age would come indeed.

He would tell Clapham, though he knew Clapham wouldn't believe. Even the redoubtable Lady Clapham would think his ravings delirium. One had to be born to it, raised in it, as Karolyi had been, to believe quickly . . . quickly enough. Razumovsky would believe, and Razumovsky would help him home . . . but Razumovsky would make a deal with Karolyi for what he could get. Bulgaria for you—India for us.

And the infection would spread.

Something dark rushed through the archway into the court, making straight for the stair. It paused before him, dark eyes flaring in the lamplight, and Asher realized, tardily, who it was. Tall for a Turk, with a Turk's black hair and scimitar nose, a feral bristle of mustache . . . the eyes were indeed the eyes of a wolf. All this he saw in less than a second; Asher didn't even have time to raise the halberd from its position as a crutch to that of a weapon when the vampire struck him aside, the impact with the wall like a sword in his side. Breath left him and wouldn't return, and when he opened his eyes again the vampire was partway up the stairs, lithe and silent as a lion in his torn khaki rags.

Asher thought, grimly, *I have to pursue* . . . but knew he was incapable of catching him, of moving more than a step or so without agony . . .

And Gölge Kurt was not alone. Asher had seen vampires run—eerily weightless and without a sound—and knew the second dark form that streamed in like smoke and bones was a vampire as well. Even before he realized it was Ysidro—*Ysidro?*—the vampire of London, gaunt and starved and ghastly, fell upon Gölge Kurt like a silent falcon with a talon-rip at his throat that would have exsanguinated him had he not, impossibly, heard and turned at the last instant to meet the attack.

The two closed, fell, locked together on the steps, ripping at one another with clawlike nails, and seconds later a third vampire emerged from the dark, sprang up the steps. Him Asher knew at once, though in a strange way he seemed to have changed even more than Ysidro. When they last had spoken, by the flame light of the burning sanitarium in the Vienna Woods, Ernchester, if torn by indecision and grief, at least had been his own man. Now his face was empty, faded as the rags of his old black coat and filthy trousers, his blue eyes pieces of dirty glass. He caught Ysidro by the arms, dragging him back from the silent, slashing tangle on the steps, and held him while Gölge Kurt whipped a long soldier's knife from his belt. Ysidro took one cut across the chest before he kicked the blade aside, another across the face as he slid bonelessly free of Ernchester's grip . . .

Then twisted as a pistol roared in the enclosing walls of the court. Ernchester and Gölge Kurt stood frozen, as between them Ysidro sank like a broken thing to the steps.

Ignace Karolyi stepped from the colonnade on the other side of the court. "Go," he said. He had an army pistol in his hand, the barrel smoking. "I'll finish him." He spoke German.

"He's faking." Gölge Kurt looked down at the crumpled tangle of black and white at the foot of the steps. Blood glittered darkly on his face and throat where Ysidro's claws had ripped, but there was no sweat, nor did he pant—in fact, he did not breathe at all. "I never saw a bullet stop one of us yet."

Karolyi grinned. "My dear Kurt, you've never heard of silver bullets? They're a sovereign remedy for Evil. You'll have to look out for them, when you're working for us."

Gölge Kurt's dark eyes glittered warily on the last sentence, but he made a smile, a demon manufacturing one for human consumption. "Even so. Sharl . . ."

Charles Farren, third Earl of Ernchester, had come down the steps to kneel beside Ysidro's body, his hand pressed to his mouth. "Simon," he whispered, half unbelieving, and Asher, still leaning against the wall in the warehouse bay's concealing shadow, knew then that it was true. It was, somehow, Ysidro. *"Simon . . ."*

"Come." Gölge Kurt had mounted a step, half turned back, and Asher remembered how Olumsiz Bey had spoken to Zardalu that night in the garden.

Ernchester looked up, his face struggling to regain an expression, some sign of life. The air was nauseating with the smell of blood. "This man . . ." he said haltingly.

"Come."

He did not touch him, did not make a move, but Ernchester flinched. Vampires do not generally show age, but Ernchester's face, thought Asher, was lined and haggard with the weight of centuries of immortality in which he had never, for one moment, been free.

He rose to his feet and followed. The two vampires passed like shadows up the stairs.

Karolyi crossed the court, cocking the pistol as he moved. From the shadows of the bay where Asher stood it was three long strides to the foot of the stairs, too long to move without taking a bullet in the chest himself. Still, the key was in his hand, ready to throw as a distraction to buy himself time to spring, when a voice called out from the passageway to the house, "Mr. Karolyi!" and Karolyi turned in surprise.

If Asher hadn't spent seventeen years on Her Majesty's Service dealing with the absolutely unexpected, he would have thought, *Lydia???* in sheer, baffled, horrified shock . . . and lost the split second her distraction bought him. He knew it was Lydia's voice even as he was moving, two fast strides, slashing down with the silver halberd blade at Karolyi's neck. The Austrian spun, his bullet cracking the pink plaster of the arch through which Asher came at him, and Asher reversed the halberd and caught Karolyi across the temple with the shaft.

Karolyi fell back, dropping the gun, and grabbed for the halberd shaft. The two men grappled, and someone—absolutely and unmistakably Lydia—plunged out of the salon with a long bronze candlestick in hand whose weighted base she smashed into Karolyi's spine. Karolyi gagged, lurched; Asher kicked him hard in the belly, thrust him away, then stooped and snatched the pistol from the floor—at the same moment Lydia sprang back out of any possible range and stood panting, red hair everywhere, like a disheveled mermaid in a torn green gown and opera gloves, her neck a treasury of silver and pearls.

Karolyi backed, his hands raised, panting. "My dear Dr. Asher." Firelight from the windows of the Byzantine house made everything luridly clear in the court. "You can't shoot me, you know." There was a wryness, almost amusement, in his eyes, his voice; the same glint he'd had in his eye when he saluted Asher as Asher was led away to the Vienna jail.

It was a game. The Great Game.

His clothes were rough, a laborer's clothes, spattered with mud and blood. His dark hair hung in his eyes. But his appearance, thus or in his gorgeous Hussar uniform, had always been only a disguise.

Hollow inside, as the Bey had said.

"Silly niggers broke up the refrigeration coils in the crypt," he said. "I heard them choking behind me. The place is chock-ablock with ammonia gas, and spreading. I know another way out."

"That true?" Asher asked.

Lydia nodded. She was well clear of them both, in the center of the court, firelight a carnival of brass and vermilion on her hair, her spectacles rounds of fire. "We were directly behind them, Ysidro and I. He covered my face with his cloak . . ." She glanced toward the silent, bleeding huddle at the foot of the stairs, but said nothing more.

"You'll never get out of here without me." Karolyi lowered his hands a little. "In fact you look hardly able to get yourself anywhere, if I may say so. They killed two of the Bey's servants already. We nearly fell over them in the alley. They're going to think you're exactly the same."

"And you're not?"

He widened his eyes, amused. "Who, me? You must know me better than that."

"He started the rioting," Lydia said quietly. "He and the interloper."

"Oh, nonsense, madame, the Armenians have been itching

for days to start fighting again." He turned back to Asher with a rueful grin. "So we're stalemated, you see. And you'd better make up your mind soon, because in another few minutes you're going to pass out and that would probably be a bad idea right now. At least I can get you—and more importantly your wife—out of here alive."

He was right, Asher reflected. Every movement of his ribs was a sword cut, and he could feel his hands and feet growing cold. God knew what the mob would do to Lydia . . .

"Come now." Karolyi held out his hand. "A temporary alliance, offensive and defensive. Nations do it all the time. You can't tell me I've done anything you wouldn't have done yourself. You would have done exactly what I did, and for exactly the same reasons."

"Yes," said Asher, seeing again the whore in Paris and the beggar in the alley he hadn't helped. Cramer laughing as he suggested going to Notre Dame for a crucifix. The body of his Czech guide all those years ago in the Dinaric Alps. Fairport dying in the light of the burning sanitarium, and the last, baffled, incomprehending look in Jan van der Platz's eyes. He felt strangely distant from himself, the world narrowing to the handsome face he had seen—what? almost three weeks ago—at Charing Cross. "I would have. That's why I quit."

And he shot Karolyi through the head.

There seemed to be no transition between that and Lydia propping him up, holding him under the arms—it was the stab in his ribs that brought him back from momentary unconsciousness. He clutched her convulsively against him, pressing his face to hers. "Lydia . . ."

"God, Jamie . . ."

It seemed absurd to ask her how she'd tracked him. Ysidro, he thought, turning, even as she broke from him and ran to the vampire lying like a smashed kite on the bloody pavement.

"Simon . . ."

The skeleton hand moved, gripping hers. "Go after them."

"You . . ."

"I shall be well."

She was already tearing his black evening coat aside,

revealing the white shirt nearly as black with blood. "Don't be ridiculous, you can't—"

"It went through . . . I'll be ill for a time . . . the silver . . . burns . . ." He raised his head, long hair falling back bloodied from his face. Surely, Asher thought, horrified, he had not looked like that when they had parted a year ago. "Go." His hand pressed to his side and blood welled between the spidery fingers. "Both must die. The man and the Undead with whom he made his bargain. It is your part of the pact, mistress," he added, still more softly. "For this I came with you."

Asher propped himself on the nearest archway and checked the revolver's chamber. Four bullets left, all silver. He started to say, *Stay with him*, but there was a crashing within the passageway to the house, renewed smoke and voices cursing. Madness fleered in the air. Instead he said, "Stay behind me." But it was Lydia who helped him mount the stairs.

The gallery stank like an abattoir of corruption and blood. The door stood open, and Asher stepped through quickly, gun held ready and his other hand clamped hard on Lydia's shoulder for support.

The long room was still. The few lamps flung huge shadows, glistened stickily on black lakes of gore.

It soaked the pile carpets, ran down the tiled steps to blend with the melting ice; splashed the walls, the columns, the divan. Asher took another step into the room, sickened, heart hammering, and in the heavy blackness made out shapes, the broken ruin of battle.

That thing like a killed dragon, glittering with blood and jewels, was Olumsiz Bey. It was too dark to see well, but he looked as if most of his throat had been torn out and his intestines strewn among the ripped silk of the robes. It might have been a trick of the candle flame, but Asher thought he saw the movement of those orange eyes. Unsheathed and covered with blood, the silver knife lay in his open hand. Beside him was a broken form in a black coat, wounds curling, blistering, blackening with the burning of the silver, short fair hair soaked dark with grue. Asher said softly, "Charles . . ."

And Ernchester moved. Spastic, desperate, unable to rise or

speak, still he flung out his hand in warning. Asher turned, throwing himself against the wall, and fired at the shadow that fell upon him from the denser shadows near the door. The bullet went wild; he fired again, and blackness covered his mind, blinding him, followed by pain in his side, in his shoulder, his neck. He rolled, struck one of the pillars at the end of the hall and someone dragged him back against it—Lydia—and his head cleared in time to see Gölge Kurt walking away toward the broken and bloodied forms of Ernchester and Olumsiz Bey.

He moved unhurried, without the drifting, ghostly swiftness of Ysidro. Asher guessed he had not been vampire long.

Lydia ripped free one of her gloves, fumbled with the tangle of silver and pearls around her throat. "Put this on." She pressed a couple of chains into his hands. He realized Gölge Kurt was between them and the distant door.

Asher obeyed, knowing it would do no good.

Olumsiz Bey was moving. Gölge Kurt pressed the barrel of Karolyi's pistol to the older vampire's head and fired. The report was like a cannon in the long room. In the pit of ice the boy Kahlil cried out, a terrible sound; the Turk turned and fired at him from where he stood. The body jounced and lay still.

Lamplight glittered on Gölge Kurt's smile.

"I should give you to my friend, I think." He touched Ern- chester with his foot. "We are hurt, and the taste of death will make us feel better. But I think with the silver of the knife burning in his wounds, he may be hurt too much. So maybe I'll just have you both myself."

He grinned wider, then threw back his head and laughed, the blood from Ysidro's talons running black down his face.

"I'll hold him," Asher said very softly. "You run for the door."

She had to know it was hopeless, because she nodded. The silk whispered as she gathered handfuls of it to free her legs. "I love you, Jamie."

At the far end of the chamber the door closed, with a sound like the shutting of a tomb. The shadow standing just within it moved, turning the old-fashioned key.

Candlelight flickered on the wicked, curving blade of the silver halberd.

Gölge Kurt turned his head.

She stood there like a witch, like a thing truly risen from a nameless grave, filthy in her rags of luminous blue, blood in the curling raven ocean of her hair. The brown eyes had the weird sanity sometimes found on the far side of madness: calm, but a demon's eyes. There was blood on her mouth, and on her hands to the elbow, but the gold of her wedding band shone through.

Gölge Kurt pointed the gun at her and fired, and she was stepping forward even before the hammer clicked harmlessly on the empty chamber, and with a vicious blow of the silver halberd took the gun hand off at the wrist.

The vampire screamed as blood exploded from the severed arteries, lunged at her only to be driven back with face and chest slashed, clutching, grabbing at the wounds where the silver blistered and burned. *"Orospu!"* he shrieked at her, rage inhuman in his eyes. "Infidel whore!"

She stepped in toward him, slashing with the silver weapon, slicing open his legs, his feet, his thighs. When he tried to climb up the lamp niches, to spring from them to the windows of the dome, she cut the backs of his knees so that, when he fell back screaming with his remaining palm a fingerless charred wreck, he could not stand. And all the while her face did not change, nor did the tears cease to run from the empty demon eyes.

Only when she had driven him into a corner, blood gushing from his wounds to splash her skirts, the walls, the floor, did she stop, looking at him with an inner peace beyond compassion or hate.

"You killed him," she said, quite gently. "You let him take the brunt of the fight, let him destroy the master you hoped to supersede. You cared no more for him than he did, this Bey, this . . . this master. It will be day very soon," she said.

Gölge Kurt made a move to lunge, but with his hamstrings severed he could only flop on elbows and knees, while blood spattered around him like thick and stinking rain. She stood out of his range, looking down at him. Without turning her head she said, "Charles?"

The broken form moved then, lying near Olumsiz Bey on the blood-sodden carpets; moved, and reached for her with one hand. No louder than the scratch of a single leaf blown across a marble floor, Asher thought he heard a voice whisper, "Beloved . . ."

"Beloved," she replied. Her voice shook a little, but she never took her eyes from Gölge Kurt. "You never did want this life, did you?" she asked softly. "Never wanted to continue, Undead but Unalive . . ."

". . . Don't . . . know." Ernchester moved his hand again, tried to raise his head. The guttering candles showed his throat cut almost to the hawse bone. Asher didn't even know whether the dying vampire was actually capable of making a sound. "Don't . . . remember . . . what I wanted. Only that I did not want to leave you."

"Nor I, to leave life," she replied. "Not if your love was part of that life, no matter what the cost to my soul. Nights and nights and nights, killing that I might not die . . . and you killing, that you might stay here with me. Not so?"

"I chose . . ."

She moved back to kneel at his side, though she still watched the Shadow Wolf, bleeding on the floor. One hand still held the master's silver weapon; the other reached down to touch the graying hair. "I understand," she said. "We all choose. And in a very short time it will be time for us both to go."

Black eyes wide with horror now, Gölge Kurt shouted at her, raged at her, cursed her in German and Turkish and broken French, and she listened with a face of stone.

"It is not I who brought him to this place," the vampire shouted. "Not I who did this to him . . ."

"It was you who met him among the tombs," Anthea said. "You who used him, who controlled his mind, because he is what he is, weak . . . Don't you think I was aware of it, hiding among the cisterns and the catacombs of this city, when you two walked its streets to war with Olumsiz Bey? Don't you think I sensed it in my dreams, when you covered and hid his mind that he might not even know I followed and sought? To kill you is nothing."

The yellow light edged her face as it edged the halberd's dripping blade. There was no sound, now, outside, and the windows above showed as squares of ash against the night.

"I have killed every night to stay alive. Brought victims to him to kill when he was so weary of the life he lived that he could not even go to seek his own. All because Grippen wanted him—and Olumsiz Bey wanted him—and you wanted him to keep him from the Bey. And all you wanted was rest, Charles."

Charles shook his head and did not let go of her hand. "No," he whispered. "I wanted you."

It was Gölge Kurt whose flesh ignited first. It puckered, blistered, blackening as he crawled screaming for the door, and Anthea cut at him again and again with the silver halberd until he retreated, screaming, to the corner, where the fire took hold. It swelled up from within him, not great flame, but thick blue-burning sheets. He sank to the floor and ceased to move quite soon, but he continued to scream for some time.

By that time Olumsiz Bey was burning as well, though Asher heard no sound from him. Perhaps he was dead, perhaps only lapsed into the vampire sleep that came at daylight, mercifully unaware of the end of his long unlife.

Anthea, who had begun to nod with the onset of that same sleep, laid down the weapon she carried and knelt beside the man she had loved, gathering him up into her arms. Their mouths were pressed together as the fire took them, and neither moved, except to tighten their grip on one another until the very bones locked within the veils of heat. Lydia watched until the end, but Asher turned his face against her shoulder, the suffocating heat pounding him, nauseated with the stink of burning flesh and blind with tears.

TWENTY-TWO

THE army came soon after. Shock had set in, and as Lydia supported him down the stairs with all the grim expertise of one used to maneuvering dead bodies, Asher felt himself drifting in and out of consciousness, pain coming and going in alternation with eerie, frightening dreams. He half expected to find the charred remains of Ysidro's body at the foot of the steps, but didn't—or the reality in which he did was quite clearly a dream. Only Karolyi's body was there, lying in a pool of blood with a hole in his forehead and an expression of astonishment in his eyes.

"I was terrified he was going to talk you out of shooting him, Jamie," she said, helping him to sit on the bottom-most step and sinking beside him in a rustle of skirts. White-lipped and shaken, she propped her eyeglasses with a forefinger and blinked around her. "I mean, he tried to kidnap me this afternoon—yesterday afternoon—and if we'd gone with him, we'd never have gotten out of here alive."

Trust Lydia, he thought, and wondered who had warned her about Karolyi.

The house around them was utterly silent. The Bey had evidently been right about the rioters leaving before first light. It was almost impossible to reflect that he hadn't seen this woman in three weeks, and that the last time they'd spoken it had been on the railway platform in Oxford. He leaned his back against the wall of the stairwell and asked, in what he considered a reasonable voice, "What are you doing in Constantinople?" and lost consciousness again before she replied.

When he came to, the court was occupied by two squads of the Turkish army, who clustered around Karolyi's body, muttering and whispering. Their captain was an Anatolian highlander who seemed to pride himself on his imperfect command of both French and Greek.

Turkish not being an easy language to speak under the best of circumstances, Asher could only repeat, *"Bilmiyorum ... bilmiyorum,"* and shake his head, while the captain and his men gazed at Lydia's unveiled face, bare shoulders, and uncovered hair with puritan disapproval.

Since Asher was, however, clearly injured, a shutter was brought from the half-burned ruins of the Byzantine house, and two of them carried him on it through the twisting streets to the prefecture of police opposite Aya Sofia as the muezzins began to cry the rising of the sun. Lydia, by holding up her wedding ring and refusing to let go of his hand, managed to convince them that she was his wife and, once at the station, persuaded the sergeant in charge to allow her to telephone the British Embassy. In the wake of the rioting, the telephone exchange was inoperative.

They were relegated, not to a cell, but to a stuffy room on an upper floor, while a messenger was sought who could take a note across to Pera. A Turkish doctor came in around noon, rebandaged Asher's torn right arm and reset his shoulder, strapped up his ribs with sticking plaster, dusted everything in sight with basilicum powder and gave him veronal and novocaine, muttering all the while. On his way out he paused, studied Lydia's face intently, and opened his bag again to mix her a mild sedative as well. She accepted gratefully, knowing that the odd sense of separateness she felt from the events of the night was only the result of shock.

I've done it, she thought, looking down at the face of the man who slept beside her—unshaven, bruised, his neck mottled with sticking plaster and dried blood, his flesh horribly white under the beard stubble.

I saved him. Well, more or less.

I found him. He's not dead.

She realized she hadn't really expected to succeed, to be able to do anything right, especially not that which was most important to her happiness. Not when it involved something as unpredictable as living people.

The happiness filling her had a soap-bubble quality, as if it could be taken from her at an unwary breath, but he was here with her . . . breathing. She checked the gashes on his neck. So deeply asleep was he, on the thin mattress on the floor, that he didn't wake. Like the older, red scars, they seemed like the marks of claws, but lacked the mangled puffiness of a wound from which a vampire would have drawn blood.

Relieved, she touched his hair, the white streaks in his mustache, then leaned back against the wall and, for no reason she could discern, burst into tears. From this she passed very quickly into sleep.

An hour or so later one of the army corporals brought them bread, honey, white goat cheese, and tea. He brought a set of Turkish army fatigues for Asher, who was still deeply asleep—the pile of his clothing in the corner was torn and bloodied and stank even to Lydia's dissecting-room-toughened sensibilities—and a lady's trousers, tunic, vest, yashmak, veils, and slippers.

"Wife's," he explained, with a shy grin. "Wife she say—" He gestured to Lydia's torn and blood-crusted gown. "—not good. Better." He held up the veils, grinned quickly again—he didn't look old enough to *have* a wife, thought Lydia—and took a hasty departure.

She hung one of the veils over the judas in the door and another over the window, and changed clothes, glad to be out of the gown with its dried blood and the smell of charred flesh caught in its folds. The horror she had experienced made her want never to see the green gown again, but she knew that feeling would pass and she'd be glad of the copious samples of vampire blood. She wondered, as she settled back in the corner by Asher's head—the room was innocent of furniture other than one chair and the mattress on the floor—whether there was any way she could talk the authorities into letting her see the remains of the burned bodies.

Probably not, she thought. She felt better for having slept and eaten, and despite the nightmare of her memories—blue fire, charred flesh, screams like nothing human—she found herself wishing she'd had a notebook with her, and a watch.

Ysidro . . .

Cold tightened in her chest. Had he gotten to safety? The rioters had been gone by dawn, but he'd been unable to stand. And where in the city could he go?

Gölge Kurt's words returned to her, about the taste of death bringing healing. In the riot-torn streets a victim wouldn't have been far to seek. She closed her eyes, not wanting to admit to herself how close she stood to condoning an innocent person's murder.

Looking back—remembering how Ysidro had torn like a mad wolf into Gölge Kurt on the stairway—she felt a vast astonishment that he had refrained from hunting at all, upon her bare word.

Their compact was done.

Ernchester was dead. Karolyi had taken the secret of the vampires with him to the Constantinople morgue.

Jamie was alive.

Like an echo, she heard the whisper of a voice in her mind: *There's a brightness dwells not in the veins* . . .

Had he really been drawn to her, as to a flame of warmth? Or had that only been a literary conceit to compare the red warmth of fire and blood to the auburn of her hair?

She didn't know. She didn't know if she wanted to know. There was a strange hurt inside when she thought of him, a dark wanting that she didn't know what to do with. It felt nothing like the love, the need, that had made it impossible for her to contemplate a life that did not include James' arms around her when she woke up in the night.

When Ysidro had carried her inside after Gölge Kurt's attack on her . . .

She did not finish the thought. She curled up close to her

husband, and taking his hand as for protection, let herself drift into sleep.

At sunset Asher woke to the cries of the muezzins of Aya Sofia, calling the Faithful to prayer. His startle of panic woke Lydia; for a moment his grip closed hard enough around her fingers to bruise the bones.

"I never thought I'd find you."

"Find me?" Asher said. His voice was raw and hoarse. "If I'd known you were looking, I'd have white hair by now!"

Lydia laughed a little shakily, and touched the silver glints in the brown. "I'm sorry." She pushed aside her own heavy red coils, groped for her spectacles as if to satisfy herself that they lay on the floor beside her, but did not put them on. "I was afraid I wasn't doing it right, but I was as careful as I could be. I always wore silver and carried a gun and made sure someone knew where I was—well, mostly. Not that that would have done me much good some of the time. But I did try."

"You did well." He cupped the side of her face in his good hand. "But then I never thought it would be otherwise, in anything you set out to do."

Lydia started to protest, and he covered her mouth with his own.

Someone knocked at the door, and a man called out in bad French, "Monsieur Ash? Madame? Here we have of the British Embassy Sir Burnwell Clapham, and a lady, for to fetch you away."

The house on Rue Abydos was absolutely dark when the embassy carriage left Asher and Lydia at its door. "I expect poor Miss Potton's still out looking for you," Lady Clapham said as Lydia unlocked the gate. "We didn't get back ourselves until nearly dawn, what with looking for you and making a detour and our carriage being attacked by rioters. We sent a man over at about nine, and he said the house was locked up and silent, so we knew she must be doing what we proceeded to do: check all the hospitals in the city. It was only toward evening we started checking police stations."

"Then you didn't get the message?" Lydia asked. In her all-encompassing black garments, with her red hair piled on her head again and the mud washed from her face, she felt like a schoolgirl playing dress-up; Asher, beside her in his khaki uniform, with his arm in a sling, appeared some casualty of a war.

"Heavens, did you send one?" The attaché's wife shook her head. "We haven't been back to the villa all day, child. We'll probably find it under the door—if those villains at the prefecture bothered to send one at all."

The carriage rattled off into the dark. Lydia shivered. The house had a cold, unused feeling. She thought at first that Madame Potoneros and her daughter had departed that morning as soon as Margaret would let them, but found the kitchen fires unlit. They must have left sometime the night before. Lydia wondered uneasily, as she fished a match from the drawer in the hall to kindle the lamp on the little table, whether the housekeeper lived in Pera or across the Horn in Stamboul. The riot had spread to Galata, where the army had killed almost a dozen Armenians. Soldiers had been posted on the street corners as they'd come up the hill.

The back entry to the kitchen was unlatched. They could have fled that way as soon as the sounds of strife were heard at the foot of the hill.

"I hope Margaret hasn't come to grief herself." Lydia raised the lamp as she returned to the front hall. "She's really not very bright, and completely out of her depth here. I shouldn't like to think of her trying to negotiate with a Turkish cabdriver, or . . ."

Asher straightened up from examining something heaped on the hall table—a wreath of garlic bulbs and hawthorn. "There are four or five of them here," he said. "And none on the windows."

"Madame Potoneros may have taken them down," said Lydia, though she felt a qualm of cold within.

"Maybe." They looked at each other, then turned as one to hasten up the stairs.

Lydia froze in the doorway of the bedroom, lamp lifted so that the light fell through to show the unshuttered windows, the protective wreaths heaped in the corner, the still figure lying on the bed.

Asher disengaged his arm from her shoulder at once, crossed to the bed. Lydia set down the lamp, a little numbly, on the vanity, and with a taper kindled the two smaller lights there. The added glow warmed the colors of the room but did little to dispel the dark in the corners.

The woman on the bed was Margaret. But then, she hadn't really had any doubts.

Asher touched the woman's neck. There was a little dried blood around the mangled puncture marks, but of that, also, Lydia had never really had any doubts.

The waxiness of the skin, the blue color of the lips, the fingers, the bare toes visible under the white flannel nightgown, were very clear. Lydia set the lamp down again on the bedside table next to Margaret's eyeglasses, reached down—as Asher had already done—to touch the mangled neck, the short, unpretty jaw.

They were still rock-hard. If Margaret had died at the beginning of last night's darkness, rather than at the extreme end, almost at dawn, the rigor would be wearing off now.

"She took the herbs from the windows herself," she said softly. "Ysidro said . . . a vampire could get a mortal to do that, if once he met her eyes."

Something made Lydia look around. A noise from the doorway, she thought later, though she could not have said what it was.

Gold-stained by the lamplight against the dark of the hall, Ysidro had returned to something of his old appearance, the death-head mask filled out a little, the black rings of pain and fatigue around the eyes less staring, though a great bloodless cut ran from his scalp down forehead, cheekbone, chin, from Gölge Kurt's claws, and two others crossed the fine-grained flesh of his neck. They were like the slashes a sculptor might make in a wax that he had suddenly come to hate: horrible, clean, without puckering. Ysidro seemed collected into himself again, perfect as an ivory angel, as if he had never dropped anything in his life or held strengthless to a doorpost, or written a poem admitting to dreams of warmth that did not come from stolen lives. As if he had never been anything but perfect, and the master of himself.

Lydia thought, *He has fed.* All her body seemed to be one giant pain. *He had no further need of her, save for that.*

Rage exploded in her, all the stored horror at Anthea's death, all her sickened bitterness at Ysidro's arrogance, at those pathetic, melodramatic dreams he had sent to Margaret, kindling love in her like the flames kindling from the vampire flesh, and she fell on him, striking with her open hands at his face, with her fists at his chest and shoulders, hating him with a rending hatred that seemed to rip something deep in her soul.

After a moment he took her wrists and held her from him. Under the bloodless cut his yellow eyes were aloof, looking without expression into hers.

"You cannot expect us to be other than we are, mistress," he said, in a voice she knew was pitched for her alone. "Neither the living nor the dead."

Then he was gone, and James was beside her, holding her in the circle of his good arm. Lydia clung to him, weeping, from exhaustion and shock and blinding, bitter grief at what she had lost.

I will find you, Ysidro had said to him once. *For those of us who hunt the nights, that will be no great task.*

Above the looped chains, the cobwebbed mazes of counterweights, the hanging lamps of silver, gold, and ostrich eggs, darkness soared like the exultation of ancient spirits, nearly two hundred feet upward to the shabby painted plaster of Aya Sofia's dome. Below, Asher's footsteps ran whispering to all corners of the mosque, as if they had some mouse-sized secret to tell. Only a few of the lamps burned. By them he could see his breath.

He had walked here from Pera, down the steep steps of the Yusek Kalderim, across the New Bridge. Through narrow streets under the eyes of the Sultana's Mosque and the raw gray granite buildings of the new administration, up the gentle hill to this most ancient place.

A Roman emperor had built it, or a man who thought of himself as a Roman emperor—he and his beautiful, scandalous, red-haired wife. After everything that had passed around it, Asher still heard their names in the silent music of the columns, the unheard bass rhythm of the domes. As he had walked in the cemeteries and the cisterns under the eyes of Olumsiz Bey's fledglings, bait for the trap, so he walked now.

If Ysidro would find him, he thought, he would find him here.

Charles Farren, Earl of Ernchester, would have walked here. A living man, two and a half centuries ago—periwigged, ruffled, and court-suited—dreaming of the woman who waited for him in England. *All I ever wanted . . . and all I ever had.*

I wish you could have known us as we were.

He closed his eyes, knowing that he should not feel about her what he did.

When he opened them again, it was to see the ghost-flicker of movement in the darkness among the line of columns in the apse, the touch of pallid lamplight on a colorless web of hair.

Asher remained where he was. The vampire's footfalls made no sound on the dusty carpeted acres of the floor.

"I wasn't sure this was an appropriate place to find you." The echoes of Asher's voice were solitary drips of water in the immensity of an underground cave. "But in the streets I felt unsafe, and there was a chance that the others—the fledglings—wouldn't enter a place considered holy to them."

"There is no reason why they should not." He moved carefully, in obvious pain, though his face showed no expression; Asher knew that Ysidro was a little tougher than younger vampires with regard to silver but guessed Karolyi's bullet had left an agonizing track of burns and blisters within.

He wondered who had dressed Ysidro's wounds.

"Unless one has put up garlic or silver, or some other thing inimical to us around the entrances, there is no limitation upon what building we may go in. Neither crosses, nor crescents, nor horseshoes nailed with cold iron above the door forbid us any more than they forbid a living man, nor must we wait to be invited to cross a threshold we have not crossed before."

Ysidro gestured, the black kid of his glove spiderlike against the white shirtsleeve.

"Though we do tend to avoid holy places. Not because God is there—for presumably God is everywhere, something men seem to forget in their battlefields, bedchambers, and boardrooms—but because man is there, and woman, without the defenses they erect to protect their minds from one another. The yielding up of their innermost dreams—love, and hatred for those different than they—charity and violence all mingled—makes a music which remains in such places even in their emptiness. Dreams lie thick here, like the smoke of incense; the smell of the blood that has been shed here seeps still from its stones. Many of us barely notice, but I find it— unpleasant."

The silence returned, like the cloak of vampire powers: the turning aside of attention, the blinding of living eyes. All the things that someone like Ignace Karolyi—someone like Gölge Kurt—would have sold to living men preparing to fight a war.

And might still, thought Asher wearily. And might still.

But that was something about which he could do no more. He should have known that, he reflected bitterly, before he got on the Paris train. He had known about it *this time*, stopped it *this time* ... Plucked up a single weed, knowing already that the seeds were everywhere in the air, looking only for fertile soil.

"Thank you for looking after her."

Ysidro turned his face away. "You have married a very foolish woman, James," he said softly. "I would have looked after her better had I broken both her legs, to teach her to stay out of vampire nests, and sent her back to Oxford under care of a nurse. I did ill and stupidly, for we all go back home nursing our hurts, hers maybe the worst of all. And nothing here will change."

"Which is as well," Asher said, "considering what changes

might have come had Gölge Kurt become Master of Constantinople. We did win this time, you know."

The colorless eyes touched him, rested on him, giving away nothing of their thoughts, then moved away. "This is not my affair. The dead are the dead."

"You will miss her," Asher said, "won't you? Anthea."

Ysidro looked aside without replying.

"I don't think," Asher said, "that she was sorry."

He did not think the vampire would answer him, and for a long time he did not. Then he said, "She was. But I do not think she would have lasted long after he was gone."

He had known her, thought Asher, for all of that two hundred and fifty years. Worlds were hidden in the stillness of the alabaster face, the pale, champagne-colored eyes. Questions forever unanswered.

"You didn't kill the Potton girl, did you?"

Ysidro said nothing.

"It's not something I'll speak of to Lydia. There were other vampires in the city, maybe others besides those I saw in the House of Oleanders. I don't know. If the laborers and mechanics and beggars put together Lydia's inquiries with the house of Olumsiz Bey, there must have been vampires who became aware of you. Who waited for the servants to flee the sound of the riot. Who had, perhaps, met her eyes somewhere, sometime, and could command her in dreams to open the windows for them."

"The girl was a fool," Ysidro said. He glanced sidelong at Asher. "You may tell Mistress Asher I said that."

"Many years ago," Asher said, "when I was in Vienna, I loved a woman there, and she me. She was clever and had great integrity. I was a fool to speak to her after the second time, because I should have known where it would lead. But after the second time I met her, it was too late. When she began to guess that I was a spy sent to find military secrets that would hurt her country, probably kill her friends and family who were in the army, I . . . betrayed her. I stole her money and left town in ostentatious stealth with the most brainless and beautiful member of the demimonde I could convince to accompany me—knowing that Françoise would take her own rage, her own hurt, into account, and more than into account, and not look further into anything else that had to do with me. She was that kind of person. I did this not only to protect myself and my contacts, but so that she would cut from me cleanly, never regretting or thinking that what had been between us could ever be repaired."

Ysidro was silent for a long time, cold crystal eyes fixed on some middle distance, as if, through the walls, he could see out into the night, back to the London that had been his haunt and his home from his twenty-fifth—and last—year of human life.

"There was nothing ever between us, you know."

"I know." She hadn't told him about the sonnets, but he had found them—including the torn one—in Miss Potton's crochet basket. Asher's own passion returned to him, yearning and illogical, for Anthea, and for the moonlight girl in the Vienna Woods who had later helped to empty Fairport's veins. He remembered Lydia's voice when she said, *Simon . . .* and recalled, too, the disillusioned agony of her tears.

She would recover, he knew. But the hurt ran deep.

The vampire shook his head. "Life is for the living, James. Death is for the dead. As for her attraction to me, it is our lure to be attractive. It is how we hunt. It means nothing."

Asher thought about Anthea again, and knew that Ysidro lied.

Ysidro considered the matter in silence for a moment more, then went on, "As for Miss Potton, I cannot say that I wouldn't have killed her, in the end, as Lydia expected me to. In truth I don't think she would have minded. But I think it was a woman named Zenaida, a concubine who haunts the deserted areas of the old seraglio, abandoned now even by the palace servants. Zenaida saw her there—I think she may even have summoned her, using the illusion that I might wish her to follow me. Afterward I thought I saw her once or twice around the house on Rue Abydos, but by then my perceptions were not acute enough to be sure. Another reason I would keep Mistress Asher in ignorance of how this came about. She would take it as her own doing. I trust you have not left her alone."

Asher shook his head. "She's with Lady Clapham and Prince Razumovsky. I asked them to stay with her till I returned. I told them she has nightmares—not that Lydia has ever had a nightmare in her life."

The defaced ivory mask relaxed, momentarily, into a smile. "Will you be all right, returning home?"

"The Dead always find ways," Ysidro said, "to get the living to serve them. Some, like the Deathless Lord, buy that service, or use hate, like Gölge Kurt, or love. Sometimes the living don't even know why they serve."

Asher studied the narrow, enigmatic features, the rucked ruin of fresh and bloodless scars. Like Anthea, like Ernchester, Ysidro was a killer and would have been as deserving as they had the sunlight trapped and consumed him in that upper room. The fact that Ysidro had risked his curiously friable immortality to help him—to save Lydia—should have no bearing on that deserving. The fact that Ysidro had not killed Margaret Potton did not change the fact that he had killed someone else—possibly several others, if he had been as long fasting as Lydia had said—that same night.

"Sometimes they do." He held out his hand to the vampire. "They know . . . but damned if they understand."

Ysidro regarded his hand for a moment with an air of slightly startled offense, as if at a familiarity; then smiled, like a man remembering his own follies, and very quickly, with two cold fingers, returned the touch.

"In that they are not unique," he said.

And he was gone, in a slight, quick blanking of attention that covered a soundless retreat. Asher found himself alone in the immense darkness of the ancient holy place, without so much as a flicker of motion among the dark pillars to show that any soul, living or dead, had passed that way.

Weary of dark, I asked to see the day,
And Jesus, jesting, to a mountain's height
Upbore me, and spread before my sight
The Kingdoms of earth in morning's bright array.
I saw a man betray two dames who wept;

Saw a mother cripple her child with love;
Saw priests flay Jews, their piety to prove,
And brother sell his brother while he slept.
    A man gave up his dreams, a child to save.
    A woman bound a beggar's bleeding sores.
    A youth pursued war's summons to his grave
    While th'king for whom he died gave gold to whores.
    And all died frightened, weeping and in pain.
    I left the mount, and sought the dark again.

TURN THE PAGE FOR
AN EXCERPT OF BARBARA HAMBLY'S
UPCOMING NOVEL:

MOTHER OF WINTER

A NEW ADVENTURE IN THE WORLD OF
THE DARWATH TRILOGY!

1

"Do you see it?" Gil Patterson's voice was no louder than the scratch of withered vines on the stained sandstone wall. Melding with the shadows was second nature to her by now. The courtyard before them was empty and still, marble pavement obscured by lichen and mud, and a small forest of sycamore suckers half concealed the fire-black ruins of the hall, but she could have sworn that something had moved. "Feel it?"

She edged forward a fraction of an inch, the better to see, taking care to remain still within the ruined peristyle's gloom. "What is it?"

The possibility of ghosts crossed her mind.

The five years that had passed since eight thousand people died in this place in a single night had been hard ones, but some of their spirits might linger.

"I haven't the smallest idea, my dear."

She hadn't heard him return to her from his investigation of the building's outer court: he was a silent-moving man. Pitched for her hearing alone, his voice was of a curious velvety roughness, like dark bronze broken by time. In the shadows of the crumbling wall, and the deeper concealment of his hood, his blue eyes seemed very bright.

"But there is something."

"Oh, yes." Ingold Inglorion, Archmage of the wizards of the

West, had a way of listening that seemed to touch everything in the charred and sodden waste of the city around them, living and dead. "I suspect," he added, in a murmur that seemed more within her mind than outside of it, "that it has stalked us since we passed the city walls."

He made a sign with his hand—small, but five years' travel with him in quest of books and objects of magic among the ruins of cities populated only by bones and ghouls had taught her to see those signs. Gil was as oblivious to magic as she was to ghosts—or fairies or UFOs for that matter, she would have added—but she could read the summons of a cloaking spell, and she knew that Ingold's cloaking spells were more substantial than most people's houses.

Thus what happened took her completely by surprise.

The court was a large one. Thousands had taken refuge in the house to which it belonged, in the fond hope that stout walls and plenty of torchlight would prevent the incursion of those things called only Dark Ones. Their skulls peered lugubriously from beneath dangling curtains of colorless vines, white blurs in shadow. It was close to noon, and the silver vapors from the city's slime-filled canals were beginning to burn off, color struggling back to the red of fallen porphyry pillars, the brave blues and gilts of tile. More than half the court lay under a leprous blanket of the fat white juiceless fungus that surviving humans called slunch, and it was the slunch that drew Gil's attention now.

Ingold was still motionless, listening intently in the zebra shadows of the blown-out colonnade as Gil crossed to the edge of the stuff. "It isn't just me, is it?" Her soft voice fell harsh as a blacksmith's hammer in the unnatural hush. "It's getting worse as we get farther south." As Gil knelt to study the tracks that quilted the clay soil all along the edges of the slunch, Ingold's instruction—and that of her friend the Icefalcon—rang half-conscious warning bells in her mind. What the hell had that wolverine been trying to do? Run sideways? Eat its own tail? And that rabbit—if those were rabbit tracks . . . ? That had to be the mark of something caught in its fur, but . . .

"It couldn't have anything to do with what we're looking

for, could it?" A stray breath lifted the long tendrils of her hair, escaping like dark smoke from the braid jammed under her close-fitting fur cap. "You said Maia didn't know what it was or what it did. Was there anything weird about the animals around Penambra before the Dark came?"

"Not that I ever heard." Ingold was turning his head as he spoke, listening as much as watching. He'd put back the hood of his heavy brown mantle, and his white hair, long and tatty from weeks of journeying, flickered in the gray air. He'd trimmed his beard with his knife a couple of nights ago, and resembled St. Anthony after ten rounds with demons in the wilderness.

Not, thought Gil, that anyone in this universe but herself— and Ingold, because she'd told him—knew who St. Anthony was. Maia of Thran, Bishop of Renweth, erstwhile Bishop of Penambra and owner of the palace they sought, had told her tales of analogous holy hermits who'd had similar problems.

Unprepossessing, she thought, to anyone who hadn't seen him in action. Almost invisible, unless he wished to be seen.

"And in any case we might as easily be dealing with a factor of time rather than distance." Ingold held up his six-foot walking staff in his blue-mittened left hand, but his right never strayed far from the hilt of the sword at his side. "It's been . . . Behind you!"

He was turning as he yelled, and his cry was the only reason the thing didn't take Gil full in the back like a bobcat fastening on a deer. She was drawing her own sword, still on her knees but cutting as she whirled, and aware at the same moment of Ingold drawing, stepping in, slashing. Ripping weight collided with Gil's upper arm and she had a terrible impression of a short-snouted animal face, of teeth thrusting out of a lifted mass of wrinkles, of something very wrong with the eyes . . .

Pain and cold sliced her right cheek low on the jawbone. She'd already dropped the sword, pulled her dagger; she slit and ripped and felt blood and intestines gush hotly over her hand. The thing didn't flinch. Long arms like an ape's wrapped around her shoulders, claws cutting through her sheepskin coat. It bit again at her face, going for her eyes, its own back and spine wide open. Gil cut hard and straight across them with seven-inch steel that could shave the hair off a man's arm. The teeth spasmed and snapped, the smell of blood clogging her nostrils. Buzzing dizziness filled her. She thought she'd been submerged miles deep in dry, living gray sand.

"Gil!" The voice was familiar but far-off, a fly on a ceiling miles above her head. She'd heard it in dreams, maybe . . .

Her face hurt. The lips of the wound in her cheek were freezing now against the heat of her blood. For some reason she had the impression she was waking up in her own bed in the fortress Keep of Dare, far away in the Vale of Renweth.

"What time is it?" she asked. The pain redoubled and she remembered. Her head ached.

"Lie still." He bent over her, lined face pallid with shock. There was blood on the sleeves of his mantle, on the blackish bison fur of the surcoat he wore over that. She felt his fingers probe gently at her cheek and jaw. He'd taken off his mittens, and his flesh was startlingly warm. The smell of the blood almost made her faint again. "Are you all right?"

"Yeah." Her lips felt puffy, the side of her face a balloon of air. She put up her hand and remembered, tore off her sodden glove, brushed her lips, then the corner of her right eye with her fingertips. The wounds were along her cheekbone and jaw, sticky with blood and slobber. "What was that thing?"

"Lie still a little more." Ingold unslung the pack from his shoulders and dug in it with swift hands. "Then you can have a look."

All the while he was daubing a dressing of herb and willow bark on the wounds, stitching them and applying linen and plaster—braiding in the spells of healing, of resistance to infection and shock—Gil was conscious of him listening, watching, casting again the unseen net of his awareness over the landscape that lay beyond the courtyard wall. Once he stood up, quickly, catching up the sword that lay drawn on the muddy marble at his side, but whatever it was that had stirred the slunch was still then and made no further move.

He knelt again. "Do you think you can sit up?"

"Depends on what kind of reward you offer me."

His grin was quick and shy as he put a hand under her arm. Dizziness came and went in a long hot gray wave. She didn't want him to think her weak, so she didn't cling to him as she wanted to, seeking the familiar comfort of his warmth.

She breathed a couple of times, hard, then said, "I'm fine. What the hell is it?"

"I was hoping you might be able to tell me."

"You're joking!"

The wizard glanced at the carcass—the short bulldog muzzle, the projecting chisel teeth, the body a lumpy ball of fat from which four thick-scaled, ropy legs projected—and made a small shrug. "You've identified many creatures in our world—the mammoths, the bison, the horrible-birds, and even the dooic—as analogous to those things that lived in your own universe long ago. I hoped you would have some lore concerning this."

Gil looked down at it again. Something in the shape of the flat ears, of the fat, naked cone of the tail—something about the smell of it—repelled her, not with alienness, but with a vile sense of the half familiar. She touched the spidery hands at the ends of the stalky brown limbs. It had claws like razors.

What the hell did it remind her of?

Ingold pried open the bloody jaws. "There," he said softly. "Look." On the outsides of the gums, upper and lower, were dark, purplish, collapsed sacs of skin; Gil shook her head, uncomprehending. "How do you feel?"

"Okay. A little light-headed."

He felt her hands again and her wrists, shifting his fingers a little to read the different depths of pulse. For all his unobvious strength, he had the gentlest touch of anyone she had ever known. Then he looked back down at the creature. "It's a thing of the cold," he said at last. "Down from the north, perhaps? Look at the fur and the way the body fat is distributed. I've never encountered an arctic animal with poison sacs—never a mammal with them at all, in fact."

He shook his head, turning the hook-taloned fingers this way and that, touching the flat, fleshy ears. "I've put a general spell against poisons on you, which should neutralize the

351

effects, but let me know at once if you feel in the least bit dizzy or short of breath."

Gil nodded, feeling both slightly dizzy and short of breath, but nothing she hadn't felt after bad training sessions with the Guards of Gae, especially toward the end of winter when rations were slim. That was something else, in the five years since the fall of Darwath, that she'd gotten used to.

Leaving her on the marble bench, with its carvings of pheasants and peafowl and flowers that had not blossomed here in ten summers, Ingold bundled the horrible kill into one of the hempen sacks he habitually carried, and hung the thing from the branch of a sycamore dying at the edge of the slunch, wreathed in such spells as would keep rats and carrion feeders at bay until they could collect it on their outward journey. Coming back to her, he sat on the bench at her side and folded her in his arms. She rested her head on his shoulder for a time, breathing in the rough pungence of his robes and the scent of the flesh beneath, wanting only to stay there in his arms, unhurried, forever.

It seemed to her sometimes, despite the forty years' difference in their ages, that this was all she had ever wanted.

"Can you go on?" he asked at length. Carefully, he kissed the unswollen side of her mouth. "We can wait a little."

"Let's go." She sat up, putting aside the comfort of his strength with regret. There was time for that later. She wanted nothing more now than to find what they had come to Penambra to find and get the hell out of town.

"Maia only saw the Cylinder once." Ingold scrambled nimbly ahead of her through the gotch-eyed doorway of the colonnade and up over a vast rubble heap of charred beams, shattered roof tiles, pulped woodwork, and broken stone welded together by a hardened soak of ruined plaster. Mustard-colored lichen crusted it, and a black tangle of all-devouring vines in which patches of slunch grew like dirty mattresses dropped from the sky. The broken statue of a female saint regarded them sadly from the mess: Gil automatically identified her by the boat, the rose, and the empty cradle as St. Thyella of Ilfers.

"Maia was always a scholar, and he knew that people were using fire as a weapon against the Dark Ones. Whole neighborhoods gathered wherever they felt the walls would hold—though they were usually wrong about that—and burn whatever they could find, hoping a bulwark of light would serve should bulwarks of stone fail. They were frequently wrong about that as well."

Gil said nothing. She remembered her first sight of the Dark. Remembered the fleeing, uncomprehending mobs, naked and jolted from sleep, men and women falling and dying as the blackness rolled over them. Remembered the thin, directionless wind, the acid-blood smell of the predators, and the way fluid and matter would rain over her when she slashed the amorphous, floating things in half with her sword.

They picked their way off the corpse of the building into a smaller court, its wooden structures only a black frieze of ruin buried in weeds. On a fallen keystone the circled cross of the Straight Faith was incised. "Asimov wrote a story like that," she said.

" 'Nightfall.' " Ingold paused to smile back at her. "Yes."

In addition to her historical studies in the archives of the Keep of Dare, Gil had gained quite a reputation among the Guards as a spinner of tales, passing along to them recycled Kipling and Dickens, Austen and Heinlein, Doyle and Heyer and Coles, to ease the long Erebus of winter nights.

"And it's true," the old man went on. "People burned whatever they could find and spent the hours of day hunting for more." His voice was grim and sad—those had been, Gil understood, people he knew. Unlike many wizards, who tended to be recluses at heart, Ingold was genuinely gregarious. He'd had dozens of friends in Gae, the northern capital of the Realm of Darwath, and here in Penambra: families, scholars, a world of drinking buddies whom Gil had never met. By the time she came to this universe, most were dead.

Three years ago she had gone with Ingold to Gae, searching for old books and objects of magic in the ruins. Among the shambling, pitiful ghouls who still haunted the broken cities, he recognized a man he had known. Ingold had tried to tell him that the Dark Ones whose destruction had broken his mind were gone and would come no more, and had narrowly missed being carved up with rusty knives and clamshells for his pains.

"I can't say I blame them for that."

"No," he murmured. "One can't." He stopped on the edge of a great bed of slunch that, starting within the ruins of the episcopal palace, had spread out through its windows and across most of the terrace that fronted the sunken, scummy chain of puddles that had been Penambra's Grand Canal. "But the fact remains that a great deal was lost." Motion in the slunch made him poke at it with the end of his staff, and a hard-shelled thing like a great yellow cockroach lumbered from between the pasty folds and scurried toward the palace doors. Ingold had a pottery jar out of his bag in seconds and dove for the insect, swift and neat. The roach turned, hissing and flaring misshapen wings; Ingold caught it midair in the jar and slapped the vessel mouth down upon the pavement with the thing clattering and scraping inside. It had flown straight at his eyes.

"Most curious." He slipped a square of card—and then the jar's broad wax stopper—underneath, and wrapped a cloth on over the top to seal it. "Are you well, my dear?" For Gil had knelt beside the slunch, overwhelmed with sudden weariness and stabbed by a hunger such as she had not known for months. She broke off a piece of the slunch, like the cold detached cartilege of a severed ear, and turned it over in her fingers, wondering if there were any way it could be cooked and eaten.

Then she shook her head, for there was a strange, metallic smell behind the stuff's vague sweetness—not to mention the roach. She threw the bit back into the main mass. "Fine," she said.

As he helped her to stand, there was a sound, a quick, furtive scuffling in the slate-hued night of the empty palace. The dizziness returned nauseatingly as Gil slewed to listen. She gritted her teeth, fighting the darkness from her eyes.

"Rats, you think?" They were everywhere in the city, and huge.

Ingold's blue eyes narrowed, the small scars on the eyelids and on the soft flesh beneath pulling in a wrinkle of knife-fine lines. "It smells like them, yes. But just before you were attacked, there were five separate disturbances of that kind in all directions around me, drawing my attention from you. The vaults are this way, if I remember aright."

Since her coming to this world in the wake of the rising of the Dark, Gil had guarded Ingold's back. The stable crypt opening into the vaults had been half torn apart by the Dark Ones, and Gil's hair prickled with the memory of those bodiless haunters as she picked her way after him through a vestibule whose mud floor was broken by a sea-wrack of looted chests, candlesticks, and vermin-scattered bones. An inner door gave onto a stairway. There was a smell of water below, a cold exhalation like a grave.

"When the vigilantes started hunting the city for books—for archives, records, anything that would burn—Maia let them have what he could spare as a sop and hid the rest." Ingold's voice echoed wetly under the downward-sloping ceiling, and something below, fleeing the blue-white light that burned from the end of his staff, plopped in water.

"He bricked up some of the archives in old cells of the episcopal dungeon and sounded walls in the vaults to find other rooms that had been sealed long ago, where he might cache the oldest volumes, of which no other known copy existed. It was in one of these vaults that he found the Cylinder."

Water lay five or six inches deep in the maze of cells and tunnels that constituted the palace vaults. The light from Ingold's raised staff glittered sharply on it as Gil and the old mage waded between decaying walls plastered thick with slunch, mold, and dim-glowing niter. The masonry was ancient, of a heavy pattern far older than the more finished stones of Gae. Penambra predated the northern capital at Gae; predated the first rising of the Dark thousands of years ago—long predated any memory of humankind's. Maia himself came to Gil's mind, a hollow-cheeked skeleton with arthritis-crippled hands, laughing with Ingold over his own former self, a foppish dilettante whose aristocratic protector had bought the bishopric for him long before he was of sufficient years to have earned it.

Perhaps he hadn't really earned it until the night he hid the books—the night he led his people out of the haunted ruins of their city to the only safe place they knew: Renweth Vale and the black-walled Keep of Dare.

Before a bricked-up doorway, Ingold halted. Gil remained a few paces behind him, calf-deep in freezing water, analyzing every sound, every rustle, every drip and dull moan of the wind, fighting not to shiver and not to think of the poison that might be in her veins. Still, she thought, if the thing's bite was poisoned, it didn't seem to be too serious. God knew she'd gone through sufficient exertion for it to have killed her twice if it was going to.

Ingold passed his hand across the dripping masonry and murmured a word. Gil saw no change in the mortar, but Ingold set his staff against the wall—the light still glowing steadily from its tip, as from a lantern—and pulled a knife from his belt, with which he dug the mortar as if it were putty desiccated by time. As he tugged loose the bricks, she made no move to help him, nor did he expect her to. She only watched and listened for the first signs of danger. That was what it was to wear the black uniform, the white quatrefoil emblem, of the Guards of Gae.

Ingold left the staff leaning in the corridor, to light the young woman's watch. As a mage, he saw clearly in the dark.

Light of a sort burned through the ragged hole left in the bricks, a sickly owl-glow shed by slunch that grew all over the walls of the tiny chamber beyond, illuminating nothing. The stuff stretched a little as Ingold pulled it from the trestle tables it had almost covered; it snapped with powdery little sighs, like rotted rubber, to reveal leather wrappings protecting the books. "Archives," the wizard murmured. "Maia did well."

The Cylinder was in a wooden box in a niche on the back wall. As long as Gil's hand from wrist bones to farthest fingertip, and just too thick to be circled by her fingers, it appeared to be made of glass clear as water. Those who had lived in the Times Before—before the first rising of the Dark Ones—seemed to have favored plain geometrical shapes. Ingold brushed the thing with his lips, then set it on a corner of the table and studied it, peering inside for reflections, Gil thought. By the way he handled it, it was heavier than glass would have been.

In the end he slipped it into his rucksack. "Obviously one of Maia's predecessors considered it either dangerous or sacrilegious." He stepped carefully back through the hole in the bricks, took up his staff again. "Goodness knows there were centuries—and not too distant ones—during which magic was anathema and people thought nothing of bricking up wizards along with their toys. That room was spelled with the Rune of the Chain, which inhibits the use of magic . . . Heaven only knows what they destroyed over the course of the years. But this . . ." He touched the rucksack.

"Someone thought this worth the guarding, the preserving, down through the centuries. And that alone makes it worth whatever it may have cost us."

He touched the dressings on the side of her swollen face. At the contact, she felt stronger, warmer inside. "It is not unappreciated, my dear."

Gil looked away. She had never known what to say in the presence of love, even after she'd stopped consciously thinking, *When he finds out what kind of person I am, he'll leave.* Ingold, to her ever-renewed surprise, evidently really did love her, exactly as she was. She still didn't know why. "It's my job," she said.

Scarred and warm, his palm touched her unhurt cheek, turning her face back to his, and he gathered her again into his arms. For a time they stood pressed together, the old man and the warrior, taking comfort among the desolation of world's end.

They spent two days moving books. Chill days, though it was May and in times past the city of Penambra had been the center of semitropical bottomlands lush with cotton and sugar-cane; wet days of waxing their boots every night while the spares dried by the fire; nerve-racking days of shifting the heavy volumes up the crypt stairs to where Yoshabel the mule waited in the courtyard, wreathed in spells of "there-isn't-a-mule-here" and "this-creature-is-both-dangerous-and-inedible." The second spell wasn't far wrong, in Gil's opinion. On the journey down to Penambra she had grown to thoroughly hate Yoshabel, but knew they could not afford to lose her to vermin or ghouls.

Sometimes, against the code of the Guards, Gil worked. Mostly Ingold would send her to the foot of the stairs from the stable crypt, where she listened for sounds in the court as well as watching the corridor outside the cell where the books were. He left his staff with her, the light of it glistening on the vile water underfoot and on the wrinkled, cranial masses of the slunch. What they couldn't load onto Yoshabel, Ingold rehid, higher and drier and surrounded by more spells, to keep fate and rats and insects at bay until someone could be sent again on the long, exhausting journey from Renweth Vale to retrieve them.

In addition to books—of healing, of literature, of histories and law—they found treasure, room after room of Church vessels of gold and pearl and carven gems, chairs crusted with garnets, ceremonial candleholders taller than a man and hung with chains of diamond fruit; images of saints with jeweled eyes, holding out the gem-encrusted instruments of their martyrdom; sacks of gold and silver coin. These they left, though Ingold took as much silver as he could carry and a few of the jewels flawless enough to hold spells in their crystalline hearts. The rest he surrounded with War-signs and spells. One never knew when such things would come in handy.

They took turns at watch that night. Even in lovemaking, which they did by the glow of the courtyard fire, neither fully relaxed—it would have been more sensible not to do it, but the strange edge of danger drew at them both. Now and then a shift in the wind brought them the smells of wood smoke and raw human waste, and they knew there were ghouls—or perhaps

358

bandits—dwelling somewhere in the weedy desolation along the canals. Gil, her face discolored and aching in spite of all Ingold's spells of healing, fell asleep almost at once and slept heavily; wrapped in his fur surcoat, Ingold sat awake by the bead of their fire, listening to the dark.

This was how Gil saw him in her dream the second night, when she realized that he had to die.

They had made love, and she dreamed of making love to him again, in the cubicle they shared, a small inner cell in the maze of cells that were the territory of the Guards on the first level of the windowless Keep. She dreamed of falling asleep in the gentle aftermath, her smoky dark wilderness of hair strewed like kelp on the white-furred muscle of his chest, the smell of his flesh and of the Guards' cooking, of leather oil from her weaponry and coat, filling her nostrils, smells for which she had traded the car exhaust and synthetic aromatics of a former home.

She dreamed that while still she slept he sat up and drew the blankets around him. His white hair hung down on his shoulders, and under the scarred lids his eyes were hard and thoughtful as he looked down at her. There was no gentleness in them now, no love—barely even recognition.

Then he began, while she slept, to work magic upon her, to lay words on her that made her foolish with love, willing to leave her friends and family, her studies at the University of California, as she had in fact left all the familiar things of the world of her birth. He lay on her words that made her, from the moment of their meeting, his willing slave.

All the peril she had faced against the Dark Ones, all the horror and fire, the wounds she had taken, the men she had killed, the tears she had shed . . . all were calculated, part of his ploy. Taken from her with his magic, rather than freely given for love of him.

Her anger was like a frozen volcano, outraged, betrayed, surging to the surface and destroying everything in its path. Rape, her mind said. Betrayal, greed, lust, hypocrisy . . . rape.

But he had laid spells on her that kept her asleep.

She would not be free of him, she thought, until he was dead.

She woke and found that she had her knife in her hand. She lay in the corner of the bishop's courtyard, fire between her and the night. Yoshabel, tethered nearby, had raised her head, long ears turning toward the source of some sound. Ingold, his back to the embers, listened likewise, the shoulders of his robe and the mule's shaggy coat dyed rose with the embers' reflection. Gold threads laced the wet edges of the slunch bed, the leather wrappings of the books. Somewhere a voice that might have been human, half a mile or more away, was blubbering and shrieking in agony as something made leisurely prey of its owner.

Good, she thought, calm and strangely clear. *He's distracted.* Why did she feel that the matter had been arranged?

The blanket slid from her as she rose to hands and knees, knife tucked against her side. In her bones, in her heart, with the same awareness by which she knew the hapless ghoul was being killed for her benefit, she also knew herself to be invisible to the stretched-out fibers of Ingold's senses, invisible to his magic. If she kept low, practiced those rites of silence the Guards had taught, she could sever his spine as easily as she'd severed that of the thing that had torn open her face.

His fault, too, she thought bitterly, surveying the thin fringe of white hair beneath the close-fit lambskin cap. *His doing. His summoning, if the truth were known.*

I was beautiful before . . .

She knew that wasn't true. Thin-faced, sharp-featured, with a great witchy cloud of black hair that never would do what she wanted of it, she had never been more than passably pretty, a foil for the glamour of a mother and a sister whose goals had been as alien to her scholarly pursuits as a politician's or a religious fanatic's might have been.

The awareness of the lie pulled her back—pulled her fully awake—and she looked down at the knife in her hand.

Jesus, she thought. *Oh, Jesus . . .*

"Ingold . . ."

He moved his head a little, but did not take his eyes from the dark of the court. "Yes, child?"

"I've had a dream," she said. "I want to kill you."

MOTHER OF WINTER
by Barbara Hambly

Published by Del Rey® Books
Coming this fall!

DEL REY® ONLINE!

The Del Rey Internet Newsletter...

A monthly electronic publication, posted on the Internet, GEnie, CompuServe, BIX, various BBSs, and the Panix gopher (gopher.panix.com). It features hype-free descriptions of books that are new in the stores, a list of our upcoming books, special announcements, a signing/reading/convention-attendance schedule for Del Rey authors, "In Depth" essays in which professionals in the field (authors, artists, designers, sales people, etc.) talk about their jobs in science fiction, a question-and-answer section, behind-the-scenes looks at sf publishing, and more!

Internet information source!

A lot of Del Rey material is available to the Internet on our Web site and on a gopher server: all back issues and the current issue of the Del Rey Internet Newsletter, sample chapters of upcoming or current books (readable or downloadable for free), submission requirements, mail-order information, and much more. We will be adding more items of all sorts (mostly new DRINs and sample chapters) regularly. The Web site is http://www.randomhouse.com/delrey/ and the address of the gopher is gopher.panix.com

Why? We at Del Rey realize that the networks are the medium of the future. That's where you'll find us promoting our books, socializing with others in the sf field, and—most importantly—making contact and sharing information with sf readers.

Online editorial presence: Many of the Del Rey editors are online, on the Internet, GEnie, CompuServe, America Online, and Delphi. There is a Del Rey topic on GEnie and a Del Rey folder on America Online.

The official e-mail address for Del Rey Books is delrey@randomhouse.com (though it sometimes takes us a while to answer).